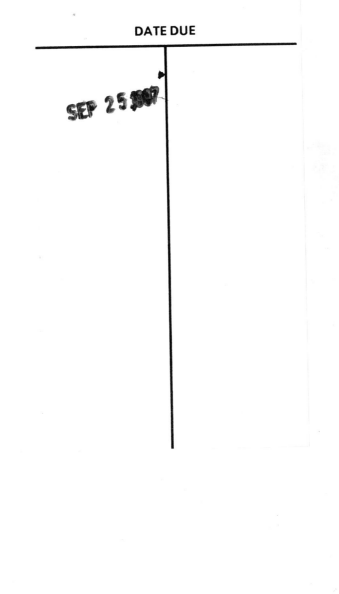

PALAZZO

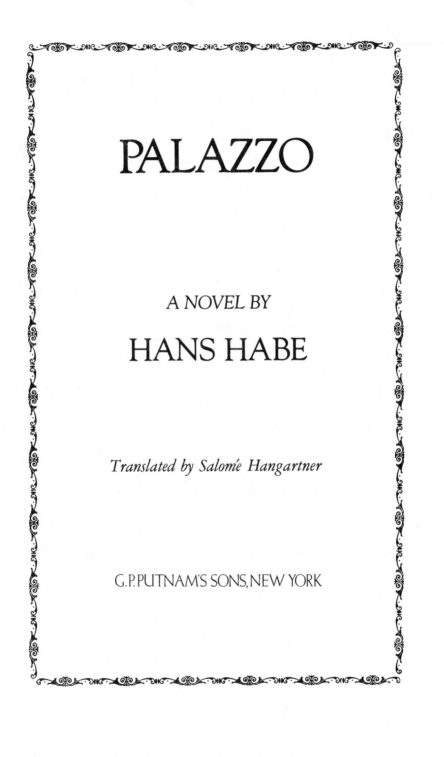

PALAZZO

A NOVEL BY

HANS HABE

Translated by Salomé Hangartner

G. P. PUTNAM'S SONS, NEW YORK

First American Edition 1977
First published in Great Britain 1977
© 1975, Hans Habe
This translation © W. H. Allen & Co. Ltd., 1977
SBN: 399-11983-3
Library of Congress Cataloging in Publication Data

Habe, Hans, 1911-
  Palazzo.

  I. Title.
PZ3.H114Pal   [PT2615.A18]   833'.9'12   77-2261

PRINTED IN THE UNITED STATES OF AMERICA

Dedication

To the fighters for the salvation of Venice, and
the guardians of the beautiful and enduring—
even if they are fighting in a lost cause

In Venice Tasso's echoes are no more,
And silent the songless Gondolier;
Her palaces are crumbling to the shore;
And Music meets not always now the ear:
Those days are gone—but Beauty still is here.
States fall—Arts fade—but Nature doth not die,
Nor yet forget how Venice once was dear,
The pleasant place of all festivity,
The Revel of the earth—the Masque of Italy.

BYRON, *Childe Harold's Pilgrimage,*
Canto IV

Determined to shore up the foundations
of both her decaying palazzo and her
discordant family, Signora Santarato
becomes the symbol of those who fight
corruption and uncaring opportunists
to preserve and restore the glories of
Venice.

The Bible speaks of the flood and of Noah and his ark. One hundred and fifty days did Noah dwell in his ark, with his sons and his wife and his sons' wives, "and of every living thing of all flesh, two of every sort . . . male and female. . . ." But the Bible passes over in silence the fact that there must have been a chronicler aboard the ark.

I am the chronicler of the ark, and of the flood drowning my city, the city in the flood. I am a Venetian.

I sing no hymn to my city. Others have done that for many centuries. They have called her the most beautiful city in the world, Queen of the Seas, Serenissima, crowned island, jewel bathed by the Silvery Sea, Nymph of the Lagoons, Beauty's Password, Tasso's Song, La Dominante, White Swan among cities.

Now my city lies in an agony of humiliation, like the beautiful Lady Hamilton, who ended her days in the gutters of the heartless port of Calais. My city's features are marked by leprosy, there are adders nesting in her hair, her belly is bloated, her breathing heavy. The sea wreaks its vengeance on its queen. Its waves storm her palaces, roll over her squares, devour her streets. They grind down her beautiful flights of steps, scatter her statues, spit on her saints, mock her bridges, break over dams already breached.

From the mainland, another army is closing in. The factory chimneys are gun barrels aimed at the sky, firing poison over Canaletto's visions. A rainbow of flames spans the harbor; Lombardo's angels cross their arms over black breasts; the gazing beauty on the facade of the Palazzo Miani resembles a sinner; San Marco's tetrarchs cling to each other like children forced to watch their mother being ravished; the angels of the Salute are fallen angels, *angeli caduti;* from the depths of the sea frogmen emerge, bearing slime and moss and muck.

But God has sent the Flood; that is, men have called it down on themselves. They hate the dethroned queen, as they hate beauty and abundance and splendor and the exquisite. They reach for her, not to conquer her but to destroy her. They undress her, not to admire her nakedness but to expose her private parts. They greedily suck at her breasts, not like children but like vipers. They play the hypocrite, bandaging wounds they themselves have inflicted, putting out fires they themselves have lit, garlanding tombs they themselves have dug.

My city's inhabitants have given themselves up to the flood. They have made my city the harlot of their greed. The money with which they could have ransomed her in her captivity, they have gambled away at the gaming table of their vanities. They sell the birthright of their past for the mess of pottage that is their future. And they flee in their thousands as in the days of the plague.

The flood takes its time flooding. Everything else is happening so fast, only the flood happens slowly. It knows its way and its work. But there is no flood without an ark, and no ark without a Noah.

But that is another matter, the matter of this story.

2

The Palazzo Santarato is not a vessel like Noah's ark, "the length of the ark three hundred cubits, the breadth of it fifty cubits and the height of it thirty cubits." Neither is it one of the famous palazzi, the Foscari or Grimani or Pesaro. Wagner produced no music here, Byron no poetry, Guardi no paintings, Eleanora Duse no love scenes. It is a small palazzo squeezed between the big ones, as if nervously drawing in its shoulders, narrow but four stories high—like the ark. The second floor boasts a large balcony with Moorish shadows, on the third there are two small crow's-nest balconies. The fourth is a mere attic with tiny square windows.

The main entrance on the Canal Grande has long been blocked up. On the steps, which are semicircular like a shell, moss grows as thickly as if it were deep in the forest. The wooden beams in the latticed windows may serve as protection from burglars but they do not keep out the waves. The lining of the walls hangs in shreds from a red brick skeleton. There is broken glass in the lamps. The oak piles, in their white and violet stripes, stand out like banners in the gray of the hostile waters. *Come si chiama questo palazzo?* The gondolieri row past, ignoring the question. It is only in the evenings that you can see someone lives there.

The city that has lost so much has lost even her sense of shame. She exposes her wounds and hides her hope. At the back, on the landward side, is the garden, behind a high wall. A cat sits next to the stone lion. There are some trees, a small patch of green in a city without green, a fountain with no water gushing forth. One window is open.

The ground floor is empty. Spices and bales of cloth, sacks full of flour and crates with crystal, were once stored here. Some time later gondolieri would wait here for orders, dozing, gambling, swearing. Now it is a cave, wet stones to slip on, walls sweating with cold, the shadows inert. There are unused marble stairs, like a house painter's ladder left behind; and right beside them a wooden staircase leading up to a rather ugly letter box.

On the second floor everything, or nearly everything, remains as it was. The drawing room is suspended above the Canal Grande like a free balloon, with its columns, paintings, statues, showcases, stuccowork, damask, ascending angels, falling curtains, cool marble, glowing glass. But in the small dining room next door, only every third lamp is lit, the engravings are pockmarked, the loose frames have turned the paintings into reliefs. The corridors are dark, and poverty creeps through the cracks of the locked kitchen door. The bedrooms on the third floor are the stage sets of a forgotten theater. The two guest rooms are bleakly superfluous. Only the bedroom with the canopy, fashioned after a gondola, with the gold-lacquered tables and dolls' chairs and frills, presents a lace curtain dropped over the dusty stage.

Those who do not want to be misled will enter the palazzo from the side canal. There the sun is locked out, and the sky is a faded silk ribbon. Beneath it lies stagnant water, coagulated oil, luxuriant rubbish.

3

Dario Ortelli fastened his motorboat, a shabby vessel he had been using for twelve years, at the pile of the side door. Then, having stepped ashore, he jumped quickly back into the boat. He seldom wore a tie, but always kept a bottle-green one in the glove compartment. He fastened this around his neck now, realizing as he did so that he had never yet appeared before the Signora in anything but the most formal attire.

Dario was fifty-two. The son of a glassblower, he had wanted to become a painter, but since his self-knowledge was greater than his talent, he soon turned to dealing in antiques. He did not grow rich on this, however, for he understood more about works of art than about the business of selling them. His marriage to Francesca Faravelli had remained childless, but this had not affected their happy harmony. Childless couples can be particularly happy or particularly unhappy, depending on whether they are able to live with their reflected image. Dario was still as lean as in his youth, and even his bony face with the deep-set eyes, ascetic and crafty, had scarcely changed. By meeting the years, he had avoided them. At twenty-five he was proud of his wrinkles, at thirty he stopped counting them. Throughout his life he had never coveted anything he did not have, or done anything he really objected to doing. He found pleasure in his work but felt no guilt in his leisure. He never cheated anyone and let no one cheat him. He was that rarest of creatures, a contented person.

His relationship with Anna-Maria Santarato, known locally as the Signora, was also most unusual. Over twenty years ago, the architect Vincente Santarato had summoned Dario to his palazzo because, being hard up and plagued by presentiments of death, he wanted to sell a set of silver. On that occasion, a graceful lady had entered the room. Vincente Santarato fell silent at once. When she had left, the master of the house said: "You should know, my dear Ortelli, that my wife cannot tell the difference between a bank account and a bird cage. When I die, there will be no one around to look after her. In this, she is like the chatelaines of medieval times. She takes it for granted there will always be a knight to defend her castle." He proved a good judge of potential knights. After his death, scarcely a year later, the indigent antique dealer was looking after the widow. Whenever the Signora called Dario up, Francesca would say, "Your daughter wants to speak to you." Had the Signora not been his senior by twenty-two years, Dario himself would have mistrusted his motives. And such a suspicion would not have been entirely unfounded, for he was never quite sure how he would have answered the horrible hypothetical question, "In case of fire, which would you save first, your wife or your daughter?"– and if a man asks himself such a question, his love is never as pure as he might prefer to think.

Like someone doing something disagreeable to avoid having to do something even more disagreeable, Dario remained among the wet ruins of the entrance hall longer than necessary.

His mission was not a happy one. The French art dealer René Naville, a well-known charlatan who would readily mistake old for antique, had hinted that the Signora was thinking of selling her Titian, *Girl with Flower Basket,* and indeed had discussed it with him quite seriously. "Her" Titian, Naville had called it, but Dario knew that at best one quarter of the Titian was hers. It is not exactly customary, however, to divide a Titian into four parts.

Vincente Santarato was a descendant of the famous Florentine builder who had come to Venice in the sixteenth century, and in addition to other more important buildings had designed the palazzo on the Canal Grande. Vincente had not really loved anyone or anything, not even money, of which he left little, for money needs to be loved as much as men do. If it is not loved, it will react coyly and reluctantly. So he had nothing left at the end except objects and mistrust. Anna-Maria had seen a new side of her husband for the first time twenty years before, almost to the day, when his will was disclosed. She was of an old Venetian family; the branches of her family tree did not reach beyond Venice. She was eighteen when she got married to Vincente Santarato, many years her senior, because her father wanted her to and because Vincente resembled him. In those days you did not look for something you could not find. Consequently she was not disappointed until she heard of Vincente's provisions. Testaments have a sincerity rarely found among the living, as if a person's real will emerged for the first time in his last will.

For this palazzo, whose destiny brought Dario to the Signora on this June day in 1972, had been left by Vincente to his widow as sole user, with everything it contained of movables and immovables to use, not to own. He had bequeathed three quarters of it to his children, Paolo, Laura and Claudia, but he had shown no more sense with them than with his widow. Just as she could not sell even one item without the consent of them all, neither could any one of them get rid of even an engraving without consent from the others and the Signora. There is no surer way of tearing people apart than to chain them together.

As Dario approached the stairs, he realized that it was the glacial relationship of the Signora with her children which made his mission so difficult. Paolo, a man of many trades and none, was married to an heiress in Milan. Laura, widowed after an up-and-down marriage to an American colonel, was vegetating in New York. Claudia was single, a painter with squandered talents; she lived in a crumbling palazzo on the Venetian island of Giudecca.

Was the Signora to blame for the eccentricity which had led her to make the secret pact with Naville? Dario remembered a story from the Talmud, which was very familiar to him; although a Catholic, he had grown up in the old ghetto, and since childhood had been attracted by the teachings of the Talmud, that anecdotal Bible. It relates how Danna, the son of Netriah, renounced a profit of sixty or even eighty myriads because the money he needed for his deal was lying under his sleeping father's pillow. He was considerate for his father, who had always been considerate for him. Should reciprocity in love apply only to husband and wife? There are bad parents, but there are also bad children. Dario did not regard the Signora as a good mother. Noah's relationship with his sons, at least with Ham, had been extremely uncertain. It must have been the ark; Noah was much too busy with it. But life in the ark cannot have been as peaceful as the Bible would have us believe. Much is known about Noah, but little about his children.

Dario stepped onto the stairs he called the hen roost. He adjusted his tie and rang the bell.

"Oh, it's you, Dario," said the Signora, as if she had not been waiting for him, and as if she had a continuous stream of visitors, each on departure opening the door for a new arrival.

She noticed at once that his glance went to the Titian. "Yes, it is still here, my dear Dario," she said, "even though a French art dealer, a certain Naville, has promised me mountains of gold–do you know him?"

She knew that he did know Naville. There was no lapse of memory about it. People sometimes pretend to be drunk, so as to reveal in assumed drunkenness what otherwise nobody would credit them with. This was the sort of way the Signora was behaving.

The huge dimensions of the drawing room did not diminish the graceful figure of the seventy-four-year-old Signora. On the contrary, she seemed to rise in stature. She reminded Dario for a moment of Venetian glass, but glass which in the twentieth century had taken on the bluntness of the age. Clad in black, spreading her wide skirt over the armchair like the dying swan on the stage floor, she looked like a dark ballerina. But she was not always a dying swan; when she moved, she was more of a marching dragoon, the quiet house loud with her steps. The restless beauty of her youth had faded but not died. When she first met Dario, she had had one face, now she had many faces. At times it seemed to Dario as if she had laid aside her beauty, like someone who no longer has to please in order to win what he wants. She was not sure that her smile would disarm anyone now, so she sometimes smiled like an old clown, a plucky, wry smile, sad and funny, kindly and sly. In reality she had never given up the weapons of her femininity, she was simply using different ones from those of her youth.

Dario wondered whether to tell her to her face that he had seen through her little game. But which Anna-Maria Santarato was he to tell that to? There was one Signora who would knowledgeably advise him on purchases and sales, and there was that other Signora who was incapable of paying a simple electricity bill. During Vincente Santarato's lifetime there had been rumors of her love affairs; after his death she wore an invisible veil. She was as agile as a girl. Dario had sometimes found her on the top step of a ladder; but at other times she would say she was too tired and could not accept a tempting invitation. Once, when he had gone to fetch her and was leading her to the boat, she had said: "Take hold of me, Dario!" It was only as he was lifting her into the boat that he realized she hadn't needed his help at all.

As always, his tenderness prevailed. "You know perfectly well that I know Naville," he said. "Naville hasn't suddenly materialized. For months, people have been saying that the *Girl with Flower Basket* was on the market. You must understand, once and for all, that you will never obtain your children's consent. You can't sell what you don't own; that's a criminal act. If the Titian leaves here, you will land in jail!"

The Signora at once gave up her plan to make Dario an accomplice. Dario had two characteristics, neither of which was much use in present circumstances: he was poor and honest. But even if he were not an accomplice, he might be useful as an ally. So she brushed aside Naville, the Titian and the crooked plan, as if she had never intended to speak of them. How was she supposed to save the palazzo without selling any of her valuables? "With my ridiculous annuity I can barely keep myself above water, let alone the palazzo—literally in its case." Forget about the Titian, but how were the wooden piles to be repaired, the pillars supported, the cracks cemented, the tiles replaced, the plaster cleaned? She went to a glass showcase empty as a jeweler's display window on a Sunday. "Now you probably think I've sold the china. It is stored in the attic, wrapped in silk and cotton, you can see for yourself if you like. Even the pieces that were broken in the flood. I should have sold them and repaired a pile."

There was nothing for Dario but to report on his unsuccessful errand to the Honorable Mayor, the *Onorevole*. A hard errand and a difficult report. Dario resorted to his parrot act. He was excellent at imitating his fellow men, and hoped he might entice a smile from the Signora. It was true, of course, that the worthy *sindaco* was extremely easy to imitate, like most people who have mannerisms in place of a personality. "He would have liked to throw an inkstand at me, but being a good civil servant he merely bombarded me with figures. 'Imagine, *caro amico*'—*caro amico,* of course, I'm one of his constituents, aren't I?—'what the opposition would say, if we tossed a building subsidy to an old lady, while half of the forty thousand apartments urgently need repairs, three thousand apartments are too dilapidated to be rented, four thousand eight hundred apartments are constantly exposed to flooding, and there is an urgent need to find four thousand new apartments.' Urgent, more urgent, most urgent, his favorite adjective, you know, and what you're talking to him about at the time is lest urgent. And how could I be sure, he asked, that Signora Santarato—'please convey to her my sincerest greetings' "—this imitation did entice a smile from the Signora—" 'is not intending to use her palazzo for speculation purposes? Such things are happening every day; first it's restoration, with municipal assistance, then exorbitant rents. Yes, indeed, if I were free to do as I please!'—looking up to heaven, every inch the Honorable Mayor—'but one cannot shut one's eyes to logical argument, even though it is put forward by the socialists.' "

The Mayor, who was remarkably well informed, had also mentioned Paolo. "The Signora's son is married to the heiress of the Andreoli Breweries, isn't he? A rich man, nothing against private initiative, you know where I stand, sincerest greetings." But Dario didn't mean to bring up this painful point.

The Signora's hands were lying in her lap. They were beautiful hands, a little too large for the rest of her figure. Dario had often admired them. She held them loosely interlaced, as if one finger were afraid of hurting another, and he turned aside, because he did not want to see that these hands, spotted with pale brown freckles, were older than the woman.

Was she a fool, hanging her heart on dead stone? Over eight hundred buildings abandoned, of the four hundred palazzi every second one doomed to ruin, one palazzo more or less, who would notice it? Nobody was planning to pull it down, not a palazzo on the Canal Grande! What did it matter if others lived in it, workmen, clerks, bankers, tourists? All you had to do, so the Mayor had hinted carefully, was to "make it available," hotels and offices and housing for workers. These bring in rent, elevators bring in rent, and so do bathrooms and kitchens. If repair meant salvation, who said you had to patch the cloth instead of making a new dress? Wasn't the only obstacle to salvation the monstrous self-centeredness of this old woman who believed the palazzo would not be a palazzo without Anna-Maria Santarato—that she would have to be saved with it to keep everything as it was? But perhaps she was right. Perhaps somebody had to stand back critically to decide what was going to collapse anyway and what could still be saved. Perhaps somebody had to stand guard to make lasting values last, because otherwise nothing would remain, only devastation in transformation, first nothing but elevators, and then no palazzi.

A feeling of envy crept over Dario. It was a feeling unfamiliar to him. He loved the Signora, how could he envy her? There were many motives for envying others; you envy most of all those who have dared to do what you yourself have recognized as the right thing to do, but haven't done. Two lunatics with the same obsession, but perhaps that lessened the lunacy. He thought of the thousands of madhouses in the world, of the mental hospitals on the islands of San Clemente and San Servolo—the lunatics of Venice need more than one island. They alone have hundreds of patients to look after, but one of them thinks he's God, another has decided he's a writhing worm, a third believes the Furies are pursuing him. No two of them are possessed or obsessed by the same idea; at least lunatics are individualists.

"We shall see," he said.

Evening was falling. Through the open door to the balcony the clatter of the boat engines could be heard, the *vaporetti* beating the waves, the gondolieri calling *Sia premi!*

Dario had stopped at the *Girl with Flower Basket*. Francesca had said to him: "It's possible, after all, that the children have agreed. One can't imagine the Signora being capable of a swindle." But to which of the Signoras had he been speaking: the helpless one who had to be lifted into boats, or the agile one who climbed ladders?

4

An American by the name of Wilcox, Mr. Richard R. Wilcox, had asked if he might call on the Signora. Like it or not, she had to receive him, for he had said his friend Paolo was sending him, "my dear friend Paolo."

Why had Paolo not telephoned himself? She had heard nothing from him for ages. Could anything good come from Paolo? In the past she had often blamed herself for loving him more than the other two children. She did not love him in the way parents sometimes feel special love for a difficult child—because he was not difficult, just a boy who stands looking helplessly at the toy he has broken. She used to be proud of his good looks, his winning manners, his success with women, too; but she had wanted him to find a different fulfillment from security in beds and drawing rooms. He had always refused to give help for the palazzo or his consent to the sale of any heirlooms. Not that he was attached to them. She presumed that after her death he would auction them off at once, a magnificent auction—the Palazzo Santarato, going, going, gone—which would make him a rich man at one sweep and free him from the fetters of his marriage.

She was closing one of the rear windows when she saw a couple approaching through the garden. Mr. Wilcox had not said anything about a wife: bad manners put the Signora out of humor.

Mr. Wilcox, a slender, undistinguished man in his sixties, did not apologize. He left the talking, at first, to his very pretty wife whose snow-white hair made her look even younger than she was. She bathed in a foam of platitudes: Venice was *wonderful,* meals at the Fenice were *wonderful,* but the gondolieri were asking exorbitant prices, and you couldn't see St. Mark's Church for all the tourists—still she loved the Venetians, they were *wonderful.*

Mr. Wilcox expressed admiration for his wife's artistic sense—"Regina hangs about the churches all day long"—he himself unfortunately did not have time for such things. Nor did he want to take up the Signora's time. Encouraged by his friend Paolo, "my dear friend Paolo," he would like to know if she was willing to sell the palazzo, "fully furnished," of course, since the walls were "not worth much." When he observed the Signora's amazement, the sudden blankness in her eyes, he said that he was well aware of the difficulties, but Paolo had assured him that they were not insurmountable since the other heirs also wanted to save the palazzo from certain ruin by selling it. Last but not least, Paolo was thinking of her old age, her loneliness, the wretched servant problem. Here Mrs. Wilcox made her contribution: in America the servant problem was *impossible.*

The Signora might have declined immediately, but she had learned to measure treason by its price.

"What sort of amount were you thinking of?" she asked.

"We didn't discuss a specific amount."

"Do you intend to live here?"

"Oh, no," Mrs. Wilcox said. "We are living on the yacht. It's anchored opposite the Bauer-Grünwald. If you would like to give us the pleasure . . ."

"Thank you. I have never been on a yacht."

"I have interests in Venice," Mr. Wilcox said. "Paolo would like to get in on them."

The Signora began to take a kinder view of her late husband's will. She scarcely remembered him and she felt no guilt about it. Maybe he had loved her after all. Without the will Paolo could now turn her out and "get in on" somebody's interests. That phrase was not very good manners either. If Vincente had not loved her, he had loved Venice. Maybe he had foreseen it all, the darkened sky and the dying fish, and the insolent islands of swamp and sand and rubble called *bareni* by the Venetians. Had he meant to protect her from exile or the city from extermination? Was he a prophetic accomplice?

"What is your business, Mr. Wilcox?" she asked.

"Oil."

Up to that moment she had only had a vague idea of the enemy. In the dusk guns are positioned, the wind carries the rattling noise of the tanks, autumnal leaves crackle like fire, a patrol sneaks closer. Morning, at last, brings distant things into focus. The enemy takes shape. Marghera, Mestre, Malamocco, Murano, Malcontenta: the hostile M's with legs like the letter M, while Venice was open to the sky like the letter V. But Venice was tired. All day long oil tankers trail past the Church of Our Saviour, the Redentore, ten thousand tons, thirty thousand, tomorrow sixty thousand, the lagoon with a border of oil storage tanks, all around, a glaze of pus floating on the water, iron scaffolding like giant candles in flame, the skyscrapers staring with dull eyes, "malocchio," the evil eye.

"Oil?" she said.

"Refineries. Progress Oil."

"I did not know Paolo was interested in oil."

"A great opportunity. We plan to install the administrative offices in this palazzo."

"It is only four and a half miles to the lagoon, of course," said the Signora.

Her idea of an oil magnate had been different; he should be fat and oily. Mr. Wilcox was an amiable gentleman who had no time and left the churches to his wife. What could he know of Venice? The Venetians were a mistrustful lot. They had even mistrusted their doges. Every year, the doges were forced to renew their marital vows to the sea. They threw a ring into the sea, and if they broke their faith with Venice, they were blinded over a burning furnace. Nineteen of them were chased away, exiled, burned to death. Anyone who drove an oak pile into the lagoon without permission was thrown into jail; anyone who threw a rotten apple into the lagoon was banished. For a whole century no one might utter the word lagoon, it was taboo.

"You are not intending to tear the palazzo down, are you?" she asked.

"One's not allowed to. That's what makes the whole thing so expensive."

Mrs. Wilcox had risen to admire the Titian and then moved over to the empty showcase.

"The china is in the attic," said the Signora.

"Your personal belongings ... of course ..." said Mr. Wilcox.

A feeling of weariness came over the Signora; her heart had given her some trouble during the past few weeks. Why was Paolo so impatient? Seventy-two was normal "life expectancy," she had read somewhere recently, so for two years now she had disappointed the expectancies.

"Come this way," she said, and stepped onto the balcony.

It was a late June afternoon, the air was balmy, and a light breeze was ruffling the waves. Far out to the northeast the sky was red. The setting sun was red too, behind the chimneys, a red target. Above the Canal Grande a shy blue, but somewhere, above the Fondamenta Santa Lucia—she knew the city so well she even knew the sky above it—the blue was turning into black: the besieging army which, sure of its victory, takes a last rest before the gates of the city.

The Signora coughed slightly, though she felt no irritation in her throat. "That is the plague," she said.

Then she told them what most Venetians think but don't say, for truth tires quickly. That the oil refineries could have been built sixty miles farther inland, but then profits would have been smaller, so it was preferable to paint over some rather worn pictures. That during the past ten years the water had risen above its confines three hundred times. That in spite of this the drillings for fresh water continue and the high waters are rising even higher. That the *murazzi* are falling to bits because walls are old and waves are renewed. That the speculators are buying up the palazzi by the dozen, buying up the Renaissance in square feet. That money cannot save Venice, money is destroying Venice. That man is a thirsty animal, but the sea is thirsty too, and that while some people want to make money, others want to breathe, and those others will fight for what they want. "Paolo will no doubt have told you that you can get the palazzo cheap," she said. Now she really needed to cough. "Why not? Oh, be careful, the balcony might collapse." She enjoyed the young woman's frightened movement. She pointed to the left, over the canal. "Why don't you buy the Palazzo Dario? It is much more famous and already quite dilapidated. It's tottering—it has drunk too much. Perhaps you would be allowed to tear that one down. Why don't you wait a while? Before long you might get the Titian at a bargain price; the girl is already quite leprous around the nose."

"Paolo . . ." Mr. Wilcox said.

"Paolo does not know me," said the Signora.

When they returned to the drawing room, she apologized for her vehemence. Mr. Wilcox did not want to burn his boats either. One must look at things in the larger context, he said. Fifty thousand people, who would otherwise not earn their daily bread, had found work in Marghera alone. The distance from the Suez Canal to Hamburg was close on fourteen thousand nautical miles, but to Venice it was only fourteen hundred. "Why should Venice lag behind Genoa, Augusta and Trieste? You can also look at it that way."

The Signora accompanied her guests to the door. Mrs. Wilcox said that it would be *wonderful* to see the Signora on the yacht.

"Look out, the stairs are rotting," said the Signora.

She remained standing in the doorway and watched Mr. Wilcox give Mrs. Wilcox his hand. She heard Mr. Wilcox saying to his wife at the bottom of the stairs: "What a crazy old woman."

5

Every June, for the past ten years, she had met Romolo at the station. Even though she did not feel too well, she was not going to let it stop her this time either.

Ten years ago, when he was not quite five years old, the boy had traveled alone for the first time. His parents had put him on the train in Milan. Later he had often told her that his vacation began only the moment he saw her on the platform.

For days the Signora had been preparing his reception. She loved him as she had not loved any of her children. Everyone makes some economies in love, some consciously, others from natural meanness, some with more of it to give, others with less. It does not follow that those who have most will be most lavish with it. At the marriage at Cana in Galilee the mother of Jesus complained because the wine gave out, but Jesus said to her: "O Woman, what have you to do with me?" Jesus was not a family man. His love was inexhaustible–he just did not have time for his mother. The Signora often wondered why she loved this grandchild more than her children, with his black locks, wide-set eyes and high forehead, and as tall as Italians appear only in their compatriots' paintings. Romolo at an earlier age resembled a Botticelli boy. But after puberty, when human beings slip out of their tiresome larvae, his nose had grown bigger, his chin firmer. She found him attractive, but the attraction did not really lie in externals. He was intelligent but not obtrusively clever, cheerful without being too noisy about it, kept himself clean without fussing too much. Why should you love everyone equally? Don't they say that love has to be earned? Only why make it difficult to love?

As soon as she heard when he was to arrive she contacted the gondoliere Carlo Paglia. The journey home from Santa Lucia was part of the solemn prologue to the vacation. She had known Carlo for more than thirty years, but now the old man refused to accept payment. The gondolieri were asking five thousand lire for an hour, not a lire cheaper. Sometimes, when the Signora watched the gondolas in front of the Ducal Palace, rocking to and fro between the stays while waiting for customers, almost like wintertime—there was no call for four hundred and fifty gondolas even in summer—the gondolieri seemed to her like a strange kind of beggar. As beggars do, they held out their hands, crying "gondola, gondola," yet they would not accept a single lire less than their pride demanded. The law of supply and demand did not apply to them, they rowed across time. This thought made the Signora smile, because she was also gliding across time and would not give in more cheaply.

When Carlo obstinately insisted on pressing his services on her—"we have always fetched Signor Romolo together"—she decided on a compromise. She pretended to have some business near Santa Lucia—and he was to wait for her at the station. She took the vaporetto from Santa Maria del Giglio to the station.

The railway station was a little over twenty years old, which for her was practically new; but it looked like a night ward in a concrete bunker: flapping posters, rotting fruit, broken windows, sleeping bags on the flagstones, human shapes stiff with grime, wearing long hair and mended spectacles, wrapped in sheets like Indian beggars, drug addicts dozing in sad ecstasy, young men in discarded uniforms, deserters without an army, amateur mercenaries, demonstrators searching for an injustice, boys and girls fondling unlovingly, unpaid whores, foreign workers squatting on their bundled belongings, on their way to Sicily, as alien here as abroad, emigrants all; people who had been kicked out and kicked around, not traveling but fleeing.

Romolo saw the Signora from some distance. When he got up to her, he embraced her and kissed her on both cheeks. "You look marvelous, you're getting younger all the time." After greeting the gondoliere almost as effusively, he helped her into the gondola.

Despite all her questions about his father and his mother and his brother Remus, even though he appeared as cheerful as usual, he spoke little. While the gondola glided through a side canal toward the Canal Grande, stopping once at a grotesque traffic light, his glance wandered over old walls and new houses, over garbage cans, cafés, wooden crates, lions, up to the balconies and laundry flying like flags, eager to rediscover what he had known for ages. At the open door of the fire station, where the red motorboats were lined up, he made one of his first remarks. "I do like those! Do you remember, I wanted to be a fireman in Venice."

Before, it used to bother her that he rarely spoke about his home in Milan. Since then she had come to accept it. Young people too want to leave everything behind at times, and who was to say how much or how little this "everything" might be? It was not until they were sitting down to dinner–the Signora had left the dinner to Emilia, the charwoman who otherwise took care of cleanliness and confusion for a few hours twice a week–that he answered her questions.

His father was now selling cars, he said, or rather, he was now representing a German firm. He said "now," the Signora noticed. Today it was German cars, yesterday English insurance, tomorrow some American product, hopeful games of chance, hopelessly doomed to fail. "Mamma was surprised by my good marks," he said, "four A's, five B's, just one C, and that was only stupid math." He said "surprised," but what else should she be, since she had probably never asked throughout the term? Her days were filled with fittings and parties and shopping, with peace missions between Paolo and her father, and with chasing Paolo's mistresses.

When the conversation turned to Remus, he became more ready to talk. He let the *ossobucco,* his favorite dish, grow cold, leaned back, and played with his napkin. The Signora could tell, as he spoke of his brother, ten years his senior, that he veered between feelings of admiration and anxiety. Remus had abandoned his education altogether, and for two years had been busy with a film he wanted to direct–"Well, you know, be responsible for the whole thing. He meets all sorts of famous people" (admiration), "people you read about in the papers. Only most of them" (anxiety) "are really horrible creatures, and nothing ever seems to come of it, they haven't got a single foot of film so far. Remus has fabulous ideas," (admiration) "but last winter" (anxiety) "he completely disappeared for three weeks. They were just going to call in Interpol, the international police, you know, when he came home. Then he set fire to the furniture in his room. It was crackling away merrily by the time the firemen got there. Anyway I get along fine with him," Romolo concluded, and returned to his *ossobucco.*

When they went back to the drawing room, the cool evening air was blowing in. He wanted to fetch her a shawl, but she wouldn't let him, for her chest of drawers was not at all presentable: scarves and tissue paper and twine and photographs and stockings and small change were all messed up together. She turned to him and asked:

"Do you know a Mr. Wilcox?"

"The American with the fabulous yacht?"

"Yes. It's anchored in front of the Giudecca."

"Do you think I might visit it? He's been to see us several times. Papa's now thinking of the oil business."

"Your father sent him to me. He wants to sell him the palazzo."

Perhaps her heart was full, perhaps she wanted to denounce Paolo, perhaps it was her curiosity, a bit of spying. Had they discussed the plan in Milan? Or else she just wanted to know what Romolo thought about the "attempted murder." She had a single ally, Dario Ortelli, and his view was the same as hers. Romolo was fourteen years old, the palazzo was four hundred.

She regretted at once having said what she did, having said it on his first evening. Romolo's blood rushed to his face, and there was a quiver at his mouth, as with children who think they may be going to cry. Anger and shame and fear came bubbling out from deep inside him. At first he merely observed that the American had certainly been "conning" her. But then he immediately forgot all respect for his parents, spoke of "low-down tricks," and said they'd be quite capable of all that. "And those horrible people, of course, it's just like my father, and my mother's always saying the palazzo costs too much—as if she'd *give* you anything." He stopped abruptly. "Or ... do you *have* to sell the palazzo?"

"I don't have to do anything. And I shan't do anything. You didn't let me finish." She chuckled. "I threw Mr. Wilcox out." He jumped up and ran over to her as he used to do when she would hide a present for him behind her back.

Now the Signora was no longer sorry she had let him into the secret. She embraced him, and he gave her a hug.

Later they went out on the balcony, and she told him how she had scared Mrs. Wilcox: "She really believed the balcony was going to give way and plunge straight into the canal." He chortled delightedly.

A vaporetto passed across the dark waters, like a house all lit up. In its wake rolled a barge rowed by two men. It was trimmed with garlands of dull green and red and yellow lightbulbs, and three men sat at a table with a guitar and a mandolin on it. They were returning from a serenade. It looked like a floating bar without its customers. In the house diagonally across the canal, a freestone block overgrown with ivy, all the windows were lit, and you could hear the engines starting up in the waiting boats.

"Dorothy Ginsburg, too, would probably like to have the palazzo," said the Signora. "She doesn't have enough room for her awful paintings."

"Tough!" said Romolo.

An hour later the Signora lay awake in her bed. The door to Romolo's room was ajar; she always opened it secretly after he had gone to sleep. For two months every year she could listen to someone breathing in the room next door.

In recent years she had not been too fussy about telling the truth to others. But these lies could be a vaccine which kept you from lying to yourself. Was the palazzo just a home, a property, a habit, a memory to her? It could not be any of those for Romolo, she thought; he is still living in houses as yet unbuilt. She could not get off to sleep, for since her youth she had always found it harder to go to sleep in hours of happiness than in hours of trouble.

6

Writing history is an attempt to fathom why man destroys what he has built.

Historians look for the beginning of Venice's decline in the sixteenth century, because they believe that loss of power means loss of happiness as well.

I prefer to think of Napoleon. The ape of Roman emperors, the epitome of the common man, the revolutionary reactionary persecuted Venice with a hatred that might be inexplicable if it were not well known that Venice has always invited the hatred of the *nouveaux messieurs*. The *parvenu* hates the old establishment because now he is himself the establishment. He tears at the past by which he is still bound. Venice is unchangeable. That is why, even in weakness and humiliation, it has challenged change. Anything that survived yesterday may also survive in the future. Nothing arouses more hatred than survival.

"Non voglio piu," said Napoleon, and took pride in being the Attila of Venice. So much hatred for a thing of innocent beauty? Like all conquerors he proclaimed a new ethic. Once or twice every century a new morality is proclaimed. It is seductive, this new morality, for though it may not promise anything good, no one can deny that the tired old morals stand in need of renewal. The new morality does not want to forgo beauty, and yet it cannot help seeing beauty as its enemy. Beauty is proven, morality still in doubt. Beauty is too old for turning somersaults in the playroom of adolescent ethics. Because its eternal quality resists revolution, it has to be destroyed. Unchanging aesthetics grimly defy rampaging ethics. Ethics are for revolution, aesthetics for tradition: they cannot reach an understanding.

Napoleon's plundering hordes carried off Venice's most magnificent paintings to the Louvre. The eight-eyed lion was stolen for the Dôme des Invalides, the gently trotting bronze horses in St. Mark's Square were to parade at the Arc de Triomphe: laurels from the stripped city made into a triumphal wreath for the conqueror. Napoleon had no wish to destroy Venice's treasures; they were dangerous only in Venice. He failed. The paintings and lions and horses returned: Waterloo and Ararat.

What Napoleon could not do, two Venetian counts and a Venetian senator achieved. It began in the middle of the First World War, when a belt of factories was constructed around Venice. Soon, however, greed was no longer satisfied by the land itself; the lagoon had to be filled in, turned into solid land. The shallowness of the water favored the plan. Only eight inches down, and the cry came from the masts of the conquerors: "Land!" In those days twenty thousand souls lived outside the city gates in Mestre and Marghera. Today there are seven times as many, close to a hundred and fifty thousand.

But the water did not seep away, it rose. The tides, determined by the moon and the sun, will not be cheated. The alternating ebb and flow, the rising and falling, are the most natural things both in a man's life and in the life of the elements.

As long as man had made common cause with the flood, it had been mildly disposed, and prepared to withdraw after its time. Flood and ebb shared the possession of the hours. When it realized that man wanted to outmaneuver it, the flood grew violent. Even in my youth it sometimes broke angrily against the ramparts, the *murazzi*—rising every fifteen to twenty years to the high-water level. But those had been mere warnings: *si vis pacem, para bellum*. Now in the face of an overwhelming army, it decided to embark on guerrilla warfare. Like the shrewd strategist who has chosen secret paths to avoid meeting superior forces, the sea has now reached a position where it can surge over the streets of Venice—which are called *Campi* and *Calli* and *Campielli* and *Salizzade* and *Fondamente,* for nothing in Venice is called the same as anywhere else in Italy.

The ice of the Arctic and Antarctic regions is melting faster than before. The seven seas are rising by a millimeter and a half every year. To the layman this seems slight, but it is not. The ground is sinking everywhere; on the coasts of the Adriatic it is sinking more than in other areas. The con men I know, a host of speculators and statisticians and city planners, as well as the *nouveaux messieurs,* say that the *sussidenza,* the sinking of the ground, amounts to two millimeters here, but in fact it is as much as five, even seven or eight millimeters.

The accomplice of the flood is the ebb. As long as not too much was asked of it, it sucked up the filth of the city and carried it away into the open sea. But when it was expected to drag out in daily drudgery everything Venice's neighbors were spewing into the lagoons—the oil, the excrement, the glass and wood and ships' refuse—then it chose the modern form of conflict—the strike. The flood's guerrilla warfare, the ebb's strike weapon: my poor city has never gone short of symbols.

The statistician calculates what he cannot change. The geologist calls it high water if the waters rise seventy centimeters above their normal level. Now they are rising, on and on, without intermission. Three or four times a year the geologists report high water. The Venetians, who do not carry a centimeter gauge, face it ten or twenty times. During the last ten years the flood crossed the threshold of the Piazza four hundred and eighty-two times, and thirteen times it rose to over a hundred and twenty centimeters.

At the beginning of the century several spots in Venice were almost thirty centimeters higher than today, while the Campanile has "shrunk" fourteen centimeters. The horror becomes really horrible when it knows its place. Calamity seems bearable if it stops short of being a catastrophe, and there's no catastrophe if it comes in installments. Barbarity which leaves a trace of human life is considered humane. We have added the word "total" to the word "annihilation" to show we can accept annihilation if it is not complete.

Centimeter figures are for others; for us it is tragic reality. In winter the city is sunk in melancholy. Then the colorful man-woven quilt is lifted, and its affliction is exposed. The squares and streets are fringed by boards and planks and hundreds of laths, small A-shaped frames for putting boards on. You might think a building project was being prepared, but it is the wood Venice's coffin is made of. The boards, indeed, are projected into the streets in anticipation of the flood, almost as if railway officials placed coffins along the line before the train is derailed. The scaffolding of resignation: the flood is sure to come, *sauve qui peut*! No other city has so many regulations and instructions pasted on the walls, ordinances—*Il sindaco ordina*. . . . It is like during the war when people were told how to behave in case of air raids, with sirens wailing and the blackout. Fear of the deluge, not even *après moi*, produces new delusions of fear.

True, Venice might have been turned into the Rotterdam of the south. In her port area seven railway lines, six motorways, seven national highways and all Italy's inland waterways converge, glory be. Rotterdam? No one had dared yet. Now they built canals, ten miles long, fifty feet deep, two hundred yards wide, so that ships can moor in Venice, can park in front of the oil cylinders like cars outside suburban houses, so that goods the concrete monsters need can be unloaded at their feet. Today there are already twenty-six miles of piers, thirty-eight miles of harbor roads, a hundred and thirty-one miles of harbor rails. Fifty years ago the flood washing the Lido beach took two and a half hours to reach Marghera. Now it rolls past Venice in forty minutes.

The besieging armies have to be provided for. Men and machines want to drink, that is the logic of logistics. The factories and refineries and workmen's dwellings and office buildings need fresh water. So nearly a hundred artesian wells were opened up, and the thirsty drills bored deeper and deeper, a thousand feet deep into the sea. The shafts collapse like emptied sacks, the ground-water level sinks even lower, the pillow has been pulled out from under the sleepers' heads.

That, it is said, was not the Venetian counts' intention. Such is the common lot of inventors and pioneers: they are sorcerer's apprentices who find the magic easy to start and impossible to stop. They merely planned, we are told, to set up some metalworks, similar to Murano's glassblowing plants, and they were trying to put bread in Venetians' mouths. When the rich want to get richer, they say they want to help the poor; and before the poor devour the rich, they help them to fatten up. In the end the rich cannot contain their greed nor the poor their envy. Since nobody cared what was to become of Venice, small factories were torn down after the Second World War, individualists were chased away, the sea was dried up, the metalworks had to give way and let chemicals take over their usurping position.

The phrase "pollution of the environment" was coined later on for the lethal outrages committed then. The word "environment" surely belongs to the same family as the words "brotherhood" and "mercy," "neighborhood" and "nature." Who would now use it in any but a derogatory sense? Beautiful world, ugly environment, as if they were two different things! Victim of the environment, as if it were an ensnarement or a jungle! In Venice the "environment" claims more victims than in any other Italian city. The authorities decided that the highest tolerable level for pollution of the atmosphere was 0.3 per million parts of air. In Venice it is 0.9 parts sulfur oxide per cubic meter—a full milligram would be the end. Owing to the capillary effect, the water rises up the walls, the salt attracts humidity from the air, sulfonamides and azides; and when the water rolls back, it has had its devastating effect. Venice is like a Polish village after an attack by the Cossacks. The algae disappear, the water carries the bodies of dead fish, the birds fall dead from the trees, and the tourists are happy to discover that the gnat invasion has stopped. Not even gnats can survive.

Lootings, as in the days of Napoleon's armies, might almost be a rescue operation. Vicenza's stones, Verona's red, the *bianco d'Istria,* cannot withstand the bane of stone. It is breaking, brick by brick, from *cuci-scuci,* caries of the walls. Every year the poison called environment destroys six per cent of the marble facades and marble walls and marble floors, five per cent of the frescoes and furniture, three per cent of the paintings on canvas, two per cent of the paintings on wood. One third of all works of art suffers fatal damage.

What else? The destruction offers a humane alternative. In a museum there is ample room for beauty, but only rats can live in a museum. If you don't want to live in a museum, you have to leave. If you want to, you will starve. Leave Venice and it will be preserved; stay in Venice and you will be poisoned. Do you intend to resist progress? Why does Venice need a hospital when it is so expensive to be taken by motorboat from Marghera to Venice, and it is only a stone's throw by taxi to Mestre? Close the hotels—you can stay at Mestre and "do" Venice in half a day. It is unhumanitarian to protect Tintoretto and let the workers go unemployed. What is your objection to the decay of the walls, since it is so very picturesque, and indeed a lesson to those who resist progress? If everything that has been destroyed were rebuilt, this would mean work for hundreds of thousands, but it would also mean you could put together again what has been smashed to pieces, that fatal injuries are not necessarily fatal, that the new can rise from the ashes of the old, that a new belief may mean something different from unbelief, and in the last resort, indeed, that San Francesco della Vigna will survive Esso. *Non voglio piu*! In the year two thousand Venice will no longer exist.

7

Laura Santarato Hill found her mother's letter under the slot in the door on the morning of the eighth of June. The janitor, not averse to a tip and contrary to New York custom, had brought up her mail.

It was half past ten. The letter must have been lying there at least an hour, but she liked to shorten the day by prolonging the morning.

During his fourteen-year marriage Colonel Edward E. Hill used often to sneak off in the evenings, and sometimes during the night as well. When he absconded from life in the same sort of way, Laura had accepted his death with suppressed relief.

She had met him in Venice, shortly before the Second World War. In those days many Italians were pinning their hopes on the Americans, and the fact that Major Hill was in Venice on a secret mission made him a romantic figure, not only in the eyes of young

Laura Santarato. On the very day of her wedding Laura followed her handsome, if considerably older, major to the States.

For several years they led a vagrant life: army camps in Oregon and Kentucky and Nebraska. They had also been in Washington, in Tennessee, and in a goddamned hell-hole called Paris. As steadily as Ed climbed the military echelons, so did the level of alcohol in his blood. He died twice.

One morning when they had been living for some time on Long Island, New York, Laura was called to the morgue, where she would have duly identified him had he not done so himself. There he lay, on a huge slab of ice alongside the other corpses admitted during the night. But among those reliably dead bodies, Ed proved as unreliable as he had always been. The shivering Laura had scarcely approached him, when he opened his eyes and sat up. His heart, well-preserved in alcohol after a twelve-hour drinking bout, had only appeared to have deserted.

Another year passed by before Ed took death as seriously as others do when they meet it for the first time. This time he fell over at a party, martini glass in hand. Here everybody knew him. Laura did not have to identify him.

During that last year, between the two deaths, she had not slept with him because his touch invariably gave her the shivers, probably in recall among all those bodies.

After his death that pretty brunette, as tall as her father had been, slim but with shapely breasts, had had so many cursory affairs that in her dreams she no longer recognized her lovers by their faces, but only by their genitals.

She dreamed often. Her expectations, relatively modest in her youth, had grown more and more pretentious—if modesty doesn't pay, you grow immodest. Laura had become more and more lonely. She had rejected the thought of returning to her hometown, Venice, soon after Ed's deaths, even though her widow's pension, paid in dollars, would have permitted a life of luxury. The thought of Venice was linked to her defeat; she remembered her city with pride but without nostalgia, like a ruined castle where her forebears had lived.

After burying Ed at Arlington National Cemetery, a favorite home of rest for dead heroes because they are there for free, and a long way from their relatives, Laura moved to a tastefully furnished two-room apartment on East 70th Street. In a country where widows are a minority almost as feared as blacks, she contrived to live as a widow among widows. The longer her existence as a widow lasted, however, the more tender were her recollections of her deceased husband. He had never given her time to feel bored, but now boredom had come to stay.

That is why she started her day at such a late hour. A robe around her shoulders, powder-blue curlers in her hair, she looked for her mail, which generally consisted of gaudy promotion circulars and did not disappoint her today either.

She did not open her mother's letter at once, but followed her daily routine. She put the coffee on the stove, took the orange juice from the refrigerator, adjusted the elaborate electric cooker for a three-and-a-half-minute egg, turned over the cup she had put upside down on the table the night before, and let the water run in the bathtub. At breakfast she leafed absently through the *Daily News* which she had brought home the night before. Only then did she go, letter in hand, to the pink-tiled bathroom richly garnished with bottles, flasks, combs, brushes, jars, salves, bathtub tray and mirrors.

Standing naked in front of the big mirror, she once more went through her daily exercise in semi-masochism. She checked the number of wrinkles in her face and on her throat, raised her arms to discover whether the skin between arm and body had gone slacker overnight, examined the upper part of her thighs, and turned round to measure the sag of her buttocks. Her breasts, which were spared the annual rings, satisfied her as usual. In the bath her ill humor dissipated. As always she decided that her body looked best in a reclining position, and reflected that she might still have considerable appeal in bed; it was just that her way there with a man had become more difficult. Now, finally, she turned to her reading.

Her mother did not write often, and it was not one of those boring letters reporting merely on her state of health, an imminent visit from Romolo, the absence of Paolo and Claudia, occasionally an artistic event and, inevitably, the disastrous condition of the palazzo. To be sure, this letter was devoted to the palazzo as well. The building's disrepair had now reached a "critical state," and since Paolo "as you know" would not, or could not help, a "decisive rescue operation" had to be determined on. This operation might be called "Girl with Flower Basket." "I do not want a single centesimo more than belongs to me," wrote the Signora. Her quarter from the sale of the Titian would be used "to the last lira" for saving the palazzo. "Before you make up your mind, I beg you to consider your own interests. Your quarter from the sale would make you quite a wealthy woman. It would certainly more than suffice for the trip around the world you have, I know, been longing to go on for many years. At the same time, however, and you may not have thought of this, the value of the palazzo would increase considerably. After my death—Doctor Einaudi is not at all pleased with my heart—this would bring substantial advantages to you all." The Signora closed with the assurance that although the offer was urgent and favorable, Laura was the first of her children she had contacted. "If we two agree, Paolo and Claudia would find it pretty difficult to say no once again."

The letter was on Laura's mind all day long. She had nothing to do. Not even the nearby supermarket tempted her; her freezer was full. The icy larder where nothing spoils was spoiling her common pastime.

The longer she was on her own, the more difficult any independent decision was becoming for her, either because she was not made for solitude, or because she was playing at decisions the way you play a game of patience. She could not talk about the Titian to the shapely black girl who did her daily cleaning. Cleopatra had her hands full managing her thirteen-year-old son with an exorbitant need for marijuana—as usual she had brought him along with her today. Laura's women friends, treated by her anyway with a certain amount of condescension, were busy with their households or their jobs during the day and little inclined to offer their advice before evening. There was nothing to do but wait for the session at night when the telephone always came alive. There was Geraldine, and Louella, and Patricia, to discuss her viewing with between midnight and two o'clock in the morning—whether that film from the fifties had still been worth watching, whether *Upstairs, Downstairs* was good this week, or the Johnny Carson show had come up to expectations.

Geraldine in particular was thrilled by the idea of even the prospect of a journey around the world where Laura would easily find a husband—"and I'll come along as chaperone." Louella warned her not to listen to the schemes of the "tricky old woman," which would mean quarreling with the whole family and selling the Titian in a panic, probably below its value. Patricia, who had never been to Venice, needed to have it explained that Titian had been a fairly well-known painter. She had no opinion. As usual after opinion polls, Laura was no wiser than before. She decided to sleep on it.

Her decision was an amalgam of emotions and reasoned reflections, in which the reflections tried hard to catch up with the emotions.

Her psychoanalyst, whom she had been visiting for five years every Tuesday and Friday, had revealed to her the traumatic effect which the palazzo had had on her. Her parents had lavished less love on her than on the palazzo. Once, when she did not get the big doll for Christmas, her father had immediately quoted the expense for some nebulous repairs. The grave consequences of her disappointment had become clear to Laura since her analysis. Also, for years she had had to share her room with her younger sister because in the spacious house there was more room for entertaining than for beds. Laura recalled the antiquated castle with its shadows which touched you, and its objects you were not allowed to touch. The prisons which regularly recurred in her dreams had Gothic towers and Moorish balconies, and were ravaged by the Flood, which she used to watch as a child behind tearstained windows.

Should she of all people save the palazzo instead of chasing it from her dreams? The longer she lay awake, the angrier she grew with the old woman who wanted to tear the chain at its weakest link. Oh yes, she could well believe her mother would ask her first, making the Titian the apple of discord. Her mother couldn't persuade Paolo to chuck away the property piece by piece. So now she was bringing up her weak heart—she would bury the whole family yet! Paolo was the only adult male in the family, and even though Laura neither loved nor respected him, there was no other man to cling to. Let the stupid females in the women's lib movement say what they liked, the weakest man was still worth more than the strongest woman. She remembered Ed. After all, he had not been drunk all the time, at least not during the first few years; surely he would have advised her to say no.

In the morning she wrote to her mother. She said no.

8

The palazzi of Venice are built on thirty million oak piles. There were three oak piles which specially worried the Signora.

"You know it's urgent, Luigi," she said to the young architect she had sent for.

She had known Luigi Primavesi since his childhood: his father had been a colleague of Vincente's. Gifted and successful, he had several times given her disinterested advice. Even though Primavesi was in his middle thirties, a short, smart man with thick, unframed spectacles and slicked-down hair, cut in a straight line above his forehead, choirboy fashion, he still reminded her of the quiet boy to whom she had given his first rocking horse. Consequently she called him by his Christian name, while he, in a mixture of affection and respect, called her aunt. Zia Anna-Maria.

"The danger is from the north," she said. "The piles are eaten away as if they'd got leprosy. I had a terrible dream. I saw a clown, like in my childhood, one of those clowns, you know, that you keep on picking up and they keep on falling down. But my clown was a leper, and his face was full of pus."

"Replacing the piles would be exceedingly expensive," Primavesi said. "I cannot advise you to do it."

"Expensive? I don't have any money at all."

"Even if you did have! Think of the clown!"

He spread out his drawings. "I have investigated the whole structure. We can bandage the foot but we can't get rid of the paralysis. Or at least not without investing millions."

She did not want to talk about the leprosy, only about her patient.

"Couldn't anybody be found . . . ?" she said.

"Nobody has any interest in it."

"Does nobody want to save Venice?"

Primavesi decided to tell the old lady the plain truth. He considered himself a good Venetian, but his world did not end at the Ponte della Libertà which joins Venice with the mainland. He had studied at progressive universities; while gaining his qualification there, he had lost his sentimentality. When the stones of the Venetian houses broke, the Venetians turned to stone; they did not yet realize that cities, the same as men, are born equal; it all depends what you make of them and what they make of themselves.

Venice, he said, in his usual mild tones, was still living on foreigners. "We've got three hundred hotels, boarding houses and hostels, all doing pretty well, thank you. The foreigners still want to have their photograph taken feeding the pigeons in St. Mark's Square, eating ice cream at Quadri's, sighing in front of the Bridge of Sighs, and rocking along in gondolas."

The Signora wondered what the tourists had to do with the palazzo. She decided that Luigi was wanting to distract her, so he had fallen off the rocking horse. "The gondolas are making trips through a tunnel of ghosts," she said.

"A Dutchman recently asked me," said Luigi, " 'Is a Venetian druggist like any other druggist?' And I answered, 'No, he has his mind constantly on Venice as well as his medicines.' With us, every druggist is also a museum keeper. But there's no scope for the two thousand-odd museum keepers who lived here when I was born. And if there are even half as many today, that's still excessive, even for the largest and most beautiful museum in the world. Forgive me, but do you know how many Venetians are over sixty-five? Seventy-eight per cent. Twenty years ago we had twelve thousand schoolchildren, today there are less than five thousand. Twelve babies are born, and eighteen adults die," he added quickly. "Being a museum keeper isn't a job for young people."

The Signora might have come out with, "You've barely climbed off your rocking horse and you can't wait for us to die." Instead she said: "So the museum has to be left to decay?"

"Nobody wants that, we socialists least of all. Museums are kept alive by living cities ..." He had no desire to give Zia Anna-Maria a political lecture. He would have had to tell her that you cannot ask people to live in picturesque ruins. But she would not understand that; also, it was not his way to shock those he was working with. You achieved more by a friendly gesture, taking them along with you. "There are supposed to be three hundred thousand million lire available for saving Venice," he said. "That money is rotting in the banks because nobody wants to admit that it's really a question of preserving a museum. What we lack is the sincerity of the socialist states. There's no country which loves and cherishes its past like the Soviet Union. All the Czar's palaces are perfectly kept, I saw them myself last year. Only the Czars were chased away."

"Ending with Czarina Anna-Maria," said the Signora.

"You know that I don't mean it that way, Aunt. There are some very nice new houses on the Lido and in Venice. We've built several ourselves. Why don't you move into a sunny three-room apartment? I can obtain one for you."

"So I am the only obstacle to the salvation of the palazzo?"

"You must see things in the wider context."

She knew that line. If you are at a loss for an answer, if you wanted to dodge a problem, put a solution on the shelf, and rest your head on it for a good sleep, then you speak of wider contexts. But when she did in fact see things in their wider context, it stopped being a wider context.

"Individually, Venice cannot be saved," Primavesi said. "Three hundred thousand million lire, or even a billion, is a mere drop in the ocean. Every third house is privately owned. One person asks for a loan he can never pay back, another feels that his Tiepolo is more important than the Botticelli in the Accademia; another asks for tax exemption on the sale of his furniture so as to recondition his palazzo, for which he will then ask shamefully high rents, and all join forces to attack Marghera."

"Marghera is the plague."

"And Venice is a sacred cow. Naples has more industries than Marghera. What harm has it done to Pompeii?"

"Pompeii was destroyed by earthquakes and by Vesuvius, not by men. The more Pompeii falls into decay, the more valuable it is."

"Nobody is going to let Venice fall into decay. Once all the palazzi and all the art treasures are state-owned . . ."

"You'd expropriate the palazzi?"

"The communists would do that. We would pay."

She fixed her eyes on Primavesi so piercingly that he winced, but she did so only because for an instant she thought she had Mr. Wilcox facing her. Oh no, they didn't want to pull down the palazzi, they simply wanted to get them cheap, either as museums or as hotels. With the Botticellis and Veroneses and Carpaccios and the lacquered chests and pagoda chandeliers and Marco Polo's coffers all thrown in; people can move to Mestre, others are offered a three-room apartment. The sum works out neatly for Mr. Wilcox or for Luigi. "Do you know why the foreigners come to Venice?" she said. "In Pompeii they stop and drive on and don't come back. You visit a cemetery only once."

A Venice, she thought, in which you can't look up at the chandeliers in the drawing room, where you can't ask "Who lives here?" is no Venice at all. The light had retreated into the houses. When those lights went out, the museum would be in darkness. So Luigi was a socialist. He wanted to put out the lights of the past. His demagogy crept up the walls of the palazzi like the salt water, an architect who tore down what was standing in his way.

He saw that she was exhausted and felt sorry for her. He wanted to help her. But could you help individuals without jeopardizing the principle? It is hard to love one's fellow men, but it is easy to feel sympathy for them. Almost as soon as an idea is conceived for a particular form of society, people break away from the conception and resist the idea. The rich man who gives to a beggar is damaging his society, which is built on achievement and should not shed any tears over the beggar; while the revolutionary who gives to a beggar is damaging the revolution, which needs beggars so that they may rise against society. And anyone who ignores the beggar, whether rich man or revolutionary, is doing damage to himself. Primavesi was convinced that capitalism was evil, but not all capitalists were evil, not all of them were even rich. He did not want to help the beggars or to ignore them.

The Signora dropped her hands. She was talking to a boy on his rocking horse, but a boy who no longer existed. But she had called Luigi on account of the three wooden piles, and if she had to humble herself, then the humiliation must be put in the service of her plans.

"It may well be that you are right," she said. "I am too old to understand it. You can only start a new life if you're confident of having some life ahead of you. I shall die in this house, and it would be a pity if it happened because the walls caved in on me. Some day Paolo will realize it and contribute at least toward renovating a few piles. Till then, I might save a small amount from my pension every month . . ."

He pushed his thick spectacles onto his forehead and brought the papers closer to his face. Paolo would never pay, and her idea of installments would not even be enough for a television set. He was touched by the allusion to her meager pension. Everyone had a weak spot; that, after all, was a luxury everyone could afford.

"No, no," he said, "that's out of the question. The piles could possibly be supported without putting up new ones. For the moment we shall try with cement. I have some workmen I can spare next week, leave it to me."

She thanked him so effusively that he hurried to leave the drawing room. At the door he said: "You will be here next week, won't you . . . ?"

"I am always here," she said.

9

Dario Ortelli had wanted to be a painter, he became an art and antique dealer, but in fact he was a poet. That is why he collected netsukes.

Netsukes are small Japanese figures made of wood or metal or porcelain or mother-of-pearl or ivory, but Dario's netsukes were exclusively of ivory. In the past, when the Japanese wore kimonos and had no trouser pockets, they had been useful objects; a thin twine was pulled through the two holes hidden somewhere in the figures. They served as toggles for the *inros*–tobacco or tea pouches–which were fastened on the belt. Poets are great netsuke collectors, because there is a legend attached to each netsuke, just as the netsukes are attached to the belt. Each figure tells a Japanese fairy tale. There is Tennin, the fairy, who danced in front of the fisherman Hakurjo so that he would return her the robe she had taken off to bathe. There is Uma, the horse of the painter Kanaoka, whose paintings were destroyed by his neighbors because the paintings were so true to life that the farmers believed Kanaoka's horse would step down from the frames at night to trample on their fields. There is Shojo, the drunken demigod, who gave the kind innkeeper Kofu a barrel full of *sake* which refilled by itself;

and there is the mermaid whose flesh, if eaten, bestows eternal youth. Dario did not believe in that business with the mermaids; he did, however, have a special relationship with Oshidori, the mandarin duck from the Akanuma river (or it could just as well have been a drake), for the legend has it that Oshidori ducks, once they have mated, will never part.

Dario and Francesca were like the mandarin ducks from the Akanuma river. Their marriage had no history. He was a glassblower's son, she was a glassblower's daughter, and they were both born in the same district, near the Campo Ghetto Nuovo. He was two years her senior, so they were in effect the same age. They had been brought up strictly in the Catholic faith, and they had never rebelled, nor did they ever visit a church unless there was no service held there. When they met people, they went home and were of the same opinion about them. Since they were of the same opinion they could converse until the small hours. What they had earned, they had earned together; so much and so little that they never thought of it. Francesca, nearly as tall as Dario, had been a much sought-after girl in her youth. Now her figure was fuller, but to Dario this meant reliable health. Since she still found him desirable, she freed him of the compulsion to think about his virility; she satisfied his little vanities, so that he did not have to get them accepted by other women. His small band of friends chaffed him over his fidelity, and he chaffed them over their infidelity. She did not feel particularly moral because he had remained the only man in her life, and sometimes complained that no other man pleased her. She compared him with other men without deeming him better than the rest, and when he jokingly said that he was incomparable, she would answer, "You're just simpler, I've grown used to your faults."

Dario's small shop, with some choice antiques and a good many pseudo antiques marked NUOVO in large letters (a curiosity in Venice), was on the ground floor in the Piscina di Frezzeria, and they also lived there. It was next to the Cinema Centrale and opposite the famous restaurant alla Colomba. Dario and Francesca had a choice of noises to keep them awake—the tourists dining on the terrace of the Colomba, or the youngsters thronging to Westerns dubbed into Italian. But in fact, despite all the Westerns, they slept soundly. Dario did not keep strict business hours. He opened and closed his shop when he felt like it. Since the roomy apartment was directly above the shop, he could always be summoned with a gentle ring. He never let an ungentle ring disturb his siesta.

He was accustomed to long lunch hours, but to Francesca's surprise he did not make any preparations to take a nap on this afternoon in June. René Naville would be calling, he said. Francesca frowned, for one thing because of the lost siesta, for another because she could not stand the French art dealer, and lastly because she thought he was coming for the netsukes. Naville, in the manner of most art dealers, would always pretend at first that anything he wanted to sell at a high price was his private property and not for sale, so he could not accept the fact that Dario would not part at any price with a single one of his collection of netsukes, which in the meantime had grown to about three hundred.

"No," Dario assured her, "this time Naville's visit has nothing to do with the netsukes. I'm pretty sure he's after the Titian."

Naville did, in fact, broach the subject of the Titian after only a brief introduction. He spread himself at the dining room table, which Francesca was just clearing, and now made an appeal to Dario's old friendship, which, he emphasized, was perfectly mutual, for he was prepared to assign one tenth of his ten per cent to Dario—"one per cent of the total price, not bad with such a sum, *n'est-ce pas?* And practically without any work on your part. All you have to do is advise your friend to sell, which is good advice for her and is going to be quite expensive for me."

Dario did not refuse the offer indignantly. All his life he had found that the only people who cry "get thee behind me" are those who find Satan pretty tempting. You had to find out where you stood, gather information, not really about the broker's intentions—he would tell you nothing but lies anyway—but about the Signora's intentions.

It soon turned out, though, that Naville was not lying. Apparently, he did Dario the honor of regarding him as a reliable accomplice. "I am acting," he said, "on behalf of a Titian collector whose name I am not allowed to mention, but he is a most respectable man. Whether and how the painting will travel abroad is, after all, not our concern."

When Francesca, who was just removing the fruit bowl, turned at the door and remarked that Dario would never lend himself to such a deal, Naville claimed that he was very well aware of it, that Dario would have nothing to do with the future of the painting, he had known his friend long enough, "*un honnête homme, un homme pauvre.*" But as a matter of fact illegality was a question of scale, and the larger the scale the smaller the illegality.

"If I am to do anything," Dario said, "I need to know how far your negotiations with Signora Santarato have progressed."

"*Elle est drôle, très drôle,*" said Naville. "I am paying her direct the full amount in cash. Most satisfactory, you must admit, because of tax. But just imagine it, this very detail may stop the deal coming off. She wants me to pay one quarter into her account, and three quarters in three equal installments into three accounts she intends to open for her children for this special purpose. Have you ever heard anything crazier?"

Dario exchanged a glance with Francesca, who had had second thoughts and remained in the room. Should he tell Naville that the Signora owned only a quarter of the painting, that she could at most sell half a head, or the breasts, or the hips, or the flowers? That could easily have meant the end of the deal, even with a man like Naville. But Dario did not have the heart to expose the Signora. If he prevented the sale, it would be enough; where there is no seller, the buyer is left high and dry.

"These are all details," he said. "You have not answered my question whether Signora Santarato is willing to sell."

"We are in agreement," Naville said.

"And what do you need me for?"

"Do you think I'm a fool, Ortelli? I'm not likely to give up a tenth of my commission for nothing. Your job is to bring Signora Santarato around so that she will accept the money in cash, a trunkful, and in one lump sum. Otherwise the deal is off. She's crazy, I'm not. I'm not bringing in any banks, let alone some unknown children."

Dario avoided Francesca's glance. Whenever a painter tried to sell Dario a fake painting, Francesca would impulsively demand that he tell the seller to his face what a swindler he was. Women who don't bend the rules will say they don't bend the rules; men are satisfied with not bending them.

"I will talk to the Signora," Dario said. "Without commitment, of course. I have to find out why she is proposing such terms."

Naville rose with difficulty. "*Bon,*" he said. "But remember that my client will not wait. I am meeting him in Paris next week, and shall have to give him an answer by then." He passed one of the glass showcases with the netsukes. "How about this stuff here?"

"This stuff is not for sale," said Dario.

10

It only struck Claudia at her third Rogers that she had forgotten to visit her mother, and had not even phoned to say she wasn't coming. She had meant to do so, but that too had gone straight out of her head again.

I forget things easily nowadays, she thought, a little less fuzzily than usual. It can't be my age, I'm only forty-five after all, nor the amount of alcohol I've been drinking for twenty years, sometimes less, generally more. Perhaps I want to forget something, but if so, I don't know what it is, nothing in particular anyhow. Anything I'm thinking just gets lost on the way.

She was sitting at the counter of Harry's Bar, at the long counter near the door which was carved in imitation of the swinging doors of American saloons. Outside, the rain was splashing on the Calle Vallaresso. If she turned around, she could see the wet boots of the pedestrians through the lower half of the door. When the door moved—it was moving constantly and opened the place to the damp breath of the street—you could see the crowd: late shoppers, tourists, gondolieri, bellboys who had met their guests at the vaporetto station and were pushing their carts before them. Above the doors umbrellas were floating.

Harry's Bar was Claudia's second home, her real home. Twenty years ago, after her father's death, when Claudia left the palazzo, she had temporarily settled on the Guidecca in a ducal palace which its owner had found uninhabitable, so he had divided it into eight apartments and let them mainly to artists. That Claudia happened to be assigned the huge dining room did not bother her in the least. Here she could spread herself—dining room, bedroom, living room, guest room—all in a single room; and if the light was not exactly favorable, she could set up her easel in the attic, which wasn't used by anyone and which not even the clever Count would have dared to ask a rent for. This temporary state had lasted twenty years, and sometimes it made Claudia laugh that she was the mistress of a larger palazzo than her mother. For with the crumbling walls the occupants had crumbled away: one after the other they had fled from the dirt and damp and dark. Only it was libelous to say there were mice; the vagrant cats which populated the empty rooms, elevators and stairs would never have permitted it.

No one who met Claudia at Harry's Bar between half past six and half past eight would have guessed how strange an abode she had left an hour earlier. The beautiful woman, slim with blue-black hair, blue eyes and an ivory complexion, looked extremely well groomed. With the painter's art she skillfully conjured away the bags below her eyes which had been growing heavier during the past years, and only the men who undressed her were sometimes surprised by the lingerie under the fashionable dresses, blouses, trousers—emerald green, her favorite color—which was dotted with a variety of large and small safety pins, as on the draped mannequins of the silk merchants. She belonged to Harry's Bar, just like the low tables, the cashier who reminded you of a croupier, the constantly jammed corridor with the stairs to the restaurant on the second floor, the painting of the Hotel Cipriani on the long wall and the huge jugs used to haul in the prepared Rogers and Bellinis in summer, the Mimosas in winter—their recipes a secret of the house. In Harry's Bar she knew everybody, everybody knew her, and the tourists, largely Americans, wondered who she was, or said on return visits to Venice, "The dark one in green is sitting at the counter again, right next to the desk."

Now that summer had come and the artists flocked to the *Esposizione internazionale d'arte,* she was even more at home on her regular seat. She was sitting between the German painter Breitbart, a fair-haired giant with a brutal child's face, a discovery of Dorothy Ginsburg's whose collages were considered the latest craze, and the Italian sculptor Bistesi, called "Alexander the Great"—an allusion not to his small stature, but to his gigantic bronze wheels, which were brought to the Biennial on a freighter because no lighter vessel could have carried them.

While the fourth Rogers was being poured for her, Claudia pondered whom she would go to bed with tonight. At one time, before her abstract period, she had painted a woman whose hair was made up of the triangular shapes of pubic hair, and she had called the painting "self-portrait," even though the woman did not resemble her at all, because she felt that the soul was in the head and the head had the sexual organs on top of it. Not that Claudia didn't, like most people, have a soul, perhaps even a heart which beat for beggers, the downcast, the downtrodden, misguided and misplaced; for children, dogs and cats. But the hungry womb couldn't care less; it rumbled like her stomach, only somewhat more impatiently.

Breitbart had already slept with her. But this charming, big-mouthed giant had a member of child-like dimensions, so a repetition was out of the question. And Bistesi was married, a point that wouldn't have bothered her except that he had brought his young wife to Venice for their honeymoon.

She took in the company and nodded to Dario Ortelli, who had just entered the bar and was craning his neck, obviously looking for one of his customers. Now she remembered her mother again, whom she really must telephone. It was getting on eight, and the old lady had been waiting for two hours. On the way to dinner, she decided.

The customers who had not found any room at the bar were now standing in two solid rows behind her; over the heads of those perched on stools, drinks and hot hors d'oeuvres, daintily prepared in paper napkins, were being passed. Even the tables, with their tablecloths, flowers, candles and napkins—all pink—were occupied. She had rarely sat at one of those tables. The tourists, treated with impatient condescension by the waiters, were spectators. They were mainly American men with women whose hairdos were the only fresh-looking thing about them. They were busy watching the counter menagerie with the local clubby society of young aristocrats in tight tuxedos, Venetian women dressed for a party or a concert, artists in open shirts with hairy chests, long-haired camp followers of the Biennial, solitary elderly drunkards who tried to make confessions to the waiters behind the bar, and which the latter did not want to hear.

The conversation was about the demonstrations planned for the opening of the exhibition. The artists themselves would be partly responsible for them. Some art-loving students were also said to be marching on Venice, but it was felt that the Venetian students, even though art-loving, were not going to be properly involved; it would make a bad impression when the arrests were made, if there were too many foreigners and non-resident Italians among the victims of police brutality.

A young Dutch painter declared that the whole to-do achieved very little. Instead of paintings, empty canvases ought to be exhibited so as to point out the emptiness of society. "Have them framed," a Belgian colleague agreed, "as a symbol of the establishment, which is also a burned-out frame." "Some with words from Che Guevara," a Polish painter proposed. Breitbart, however, felt that such demonstrations would not attract the citizens. An Austrian painter, Wolfgang Pollack, a pretty boy with girlish features who had made a name for himself last winter—he had exhibited himself naked with his easel outside the History of Art Museum in Vienna, at 16 degrees Fahrenheit—had been speaking of a secret plan all evening; now he revealed it. Ronaldo De Gindice, the man from Verona who some years ago had been awarded a prize but had stoutly refused the award, had hired a deaf-mute, mongoloid idiot as an exhibit, acquired from the exhibit's father for five thousand lire. A realization of the problem "work or behavior," *opera o comportamento*.

Claudia was silent. She had nothing against the artists of the *comportamento*, and why shouldn't they exhibit an idiot?—but did it have to be Venice? However hard she tried not to paint in the Venetian manner, some of the light of Giorgione, Veronese, even Tintoretto, that terrible Stakhanovite of the Scuola di San Rocco, had fallen on her paintings. Even in her abstracts she had not managed to hide completely the "incredible realism" spoken of by Henry James. Even a cocktail was called Bellini here. She was the only Venetian in her circle, and it seemed to her that the long-haired artists at the bar and the gray-haired Americans at the tables, who felt a mutual contempt—like that felt by the visitors to the zoo and the animals in their cages—had something in common: they did not know anything about Venice. For the first time she found some respect for the steak guzzlers, since at least they admired what they did not understand. Again she remembered her mother.

As usual, at this late hour, everyone decided to move. Pollack had several times touched Claudia's bare arm; now he offered her the protection of his umbrella. He had borrowed it from his hotel; it was enormous and brightly colored, the kind doormen use, but for Pollack it was the umbrella of a tightrope walker. On the way to the Ristorante al Teatro he cautiously put down one foot in front of the other, balancing the umbrella to and fro above his and Claudia's heads. From time to time the rain would trickle over her right arm.

With the acrobat leading the way, the rowdy gang passed the Frezzeria, where elderly prostitutes pressed themselves against the wall to avoid the rain, reliefs with protruding breasts. Pollack bowed to them, and to one of them he jokingly offered his umbrella. He talked in a steady flow of Viennese English; but outside the San Moisè church he stopped, because a sculpture of a Biennial artist was exhibited here, a huge square-hewn stone with a smaller stone cube suspended above it like a ballerina on the tip of her toes. His pink baby face, almost hidden by his wet, silky hair, turned serious, and forgetting his circus act, he pressed Claudia to him.

"We have won," he said, "we have won, we have broken free of the Biennial. Don't you see, San Moisè looks like nothing more than the wings of a provincial stage–have you seen Grasel's *Porta a doppio angolo* in front of the Ducal Palace, and Jarnuszkiewicz' *Grano?* St. Mark's dome has finally disappeared, in chromium." He pointed at the church. "My compatriot Meyring piled up a horrible Mount Sinai in there– gone!–so the bourgeoisie can get stuffed ... I saw an American stumble over Robert Müller's *Refugio* before the Palazzo Ducale, he almost broke his neck. Where the Guardi kitsch is hanging now, our paintings will be hanging in twenty years' time!"

"I'm soaked," said Claudia.

Pollack did not speak until they reached the piazza with the Teatro La Fenice; he was holding the umbrella in one hand and clasping her hips with the other. She recalled the picture in the newspapers of his naked body outside the museum in the snow, viewed from the rear only. More and more she was attracted by very young men, a sign of age, and the more girlish their looks the more she liked them, but it was not what you would call the lesbian in her. It was the contrast which attracted her, the fascination of a girl who revealed all her masculine elements in bed.

It was just about intermission time at the Teatro La Fenice, and because Claudia's thoughts were taking strangely sharp contours today, she realized that her friends had not chosen this bistro as their regular meeting place by chance. Everybody was sitting on the terrace, waiting for the intermission. Ladies in evening dresses and gentlemen in dinner jackets, the carabinieri, promenading up and down with their long sabers like clockwork puppets, ridiculous tin soldiers. Tonight the square was empty, the picture all the more symbolic, the theatergoers sticking to the pillars of the pseudo-rococo building, under one roof with the carabinieri—culture and police—you just had to sit there to scare them stiff.

"Where do you live?" Pollack was asking.

"In a haunted castle."

"Alone?"

"Yes."

"Couldn't we go there?"

"Ride there, at best. The haunted castle is on the Giudecca."

"In an hour I'll take you home."

"I have to dry myself," she said, already inside the café. Her way to the toilet led past the telephone booth, and the glass booth appeared like an obstacle she could not dodge. As always when she was excessively late, she did not dare to look at her watch. She entered the booth and dialed the number of the palazzo.

Evidently the Signora had her hand on the receiver, like someone who is expecting a phone call day or night.

"I'm sorry I couldn't call sooner . . ." Claudia started her apology.

"Never mind, but I must talk to you urgently."

"Is anything the matter with you?"

"No, no. It is about a letter I have written to Paolo. About the Titian. I thought you should read it and perhaps sign it with me. You have not been here since Christmas. The situation is desperate."

"I know. But I am very busy. The Biennial, you know. . . ."

Pollack had followed her; he was standing in front of the booth and making funny faces.

"Do what you want," she said. "Tell him I agree."

"But you don't even know yet . . ."

"It doesn't matter," she said. "I agree. It's not that important."

11

Venice, Monday, June 12, Night

At eleven o'clock Angelina Mossi, thirty-two, wife of Giustino Mossi, forty, foreman in an oil refinery, decides to call the doctor. She has no telephone. She wakes her eldest son, ten-year-old Angelo, and tells him to look after his brother, eight-year-old Italo. Pia, ten months old, is sleeping peacefully.

Dr. Pontiggia lives just a few blocks away. On the way there she looks into the Café Garibaldi. They tell her they haven't seen her husband. Union meeting, strike.

In the windows of the reddish barracks few lights are burning. A beam of light falls on the balcony. The railings are like prison bars.

Angelina has to pass the car dump. At the top of the scrapheap a white car is charging into the void.

Il dottore is a man of forty, prematurely aged by sobriety. He had been Angelina's witness at her wedding. She was married at San Giovanni Elemosinario, the church behind the Rialto, where she was living at that time. A record of the ceremony was preserved in the family album. The doctor also lives in Venice. They call it Venice even though Marghera is a suburb.

The doctor's wife calls her husband. His pajamas hang loosely around the gaunt frame.

"You must come," says Angelina. "Italo is retching blood. He can't speak. He has the shivers."

"You go home," says Dr. Pontiggia. "I'll be right there." He calls the ambulance. While he gets dressed, he says to his wife: "They should not have let the boy go home from the hospital. Mossi insisted."

"Will he die?"

"Probably. Croupous pneumonia. Perhaps an embolism."

"Last week there were six."

"The poison gases," says the doctor. He ties his laces.

There is no point in taking his little Fiat. He hurries past the car dump. The white car is shining like a lantern. He thinks of his Fiat, which he will bury soon. The instrument bag in his hand is getting heavy; it is as useless as a car. The diagnosis he made the day before yesterday is an unalterable fact. Why did he order the ambulance? Mossi has come in the meantime. The doctor wishes the man were still at the meeting. Mossi shouts incessantly: "Must Italo die?" He accuses his wife of being the one who wanted to take the child out of hospital. "If only we had stayed in Venice!"

The air knows no boundaries, the doctor thinks.

The child's face is blue. Dr. Pontiggia is reminded of the posters with the skeleton children in the developing countries. Mossi is earning a lot, and he spoiled Italo. In Venice too there are skeleton children. The doctor takes the child's pulse: two hundred and twenty. His temperature is 106 degrees. He tries to put cold dressings on Italo's chest, but fails because the child is tossed to and fro by the shivers. The rust-brown sputum is typical. Sheets, pillows, blankets—all carry a rust-brown stain.

Mossi flings himself to the ground and invokes the Madonna.

"Shut up!" says his wife.

She piles quilts on top of the child, until only a black tuft of hair remains visible. The doctor lets it happen, even though heat is harmful.

He orders Mossi out of the room, sits down at the bed and holds the child's pulse. He feels very angry. Oh to be a politician! But which party? One lot protects profits, the other lot jobs. No one protects children. And then they invoke the Madonna.

The doctor takes the child into his arms. His suit becomes bloodstained.

Now the woman is also asking: "Will he die?"

In the distance Dr. Pontiggia hears the ambulance siren. Should he end Italo away? Before the sun rises, Italo will be dead.

The rain favors his enterprise. The Campo Santi Giovanni e Paolo is deserted. You can't tell whether the wind is driving the rainwater into the putrid canal, or whether it is whipping the water of the canal across the square.

Tonino Villorini, sixty, a burglar by profession, is standing in the shelter of the archway. Above, it says: Sotoporteggio e Corte Bressana. The gate leads to a tiny yard which does not deserve such a sonorous name. The houses, crumbling like moldy cake, are dark. Two dripping cats have settled beside Villorini.

The houses may sleep peacefully. Villorini's intentions are not evil. He wants to return stolen property. The stolen property is a painting, *The Bread of St. Anthony*. Until a year ago it had adorned the church of Santi Giovanni e Paolo, called San Zanipolo by the Venetians.

Not long before this short, skinny man with the crumpled face had celebrated the fortieth year of his professional career. The thieves and burglars of Venice brought him their gifts. Gangsters were excluded. Stolen goods as well. In replying to his toast, Villorini announced that he would return St. Anthony to his place. But this had nothing to do with his anniversary, nor with his decision to retire.

Villorini had brought the painting here during the day when it was inconspicuous because of the crowds. The painted side toward the wall, he had leaned it against the foundation under the archway.

Technically there is no difference between theft and replacement. Psychologically, the latter is more difficult.

His sons, Tonino junior, thirty, and Aldo, twenty, protested against the return, even though no fence had so far been found. They are his heirs. Particularly energetic protests were voiced by Aldo, nicknamed Kitcat—because of the "gap" between the births of the two boys.

Tonino does not admit to himself that he fears the two will not keep their appointment. That would destroy the image he has of his own authority.

But there is nothing amiss with his world yet. As he steps forward from the archway, two shapes detach themselves from the shadow of the equestrian statue of Colleoni.

Tonino looks up at the statue.

Colleoni was a colleague, a thief like himself, even if burglars were called *condottieri* during the Renaissance. He stole half of Milan. In return he left half a million ducats to Venice, his hometown, on condition that the city should erect a monument to him in the Piazza San Marco. Venice cheated him. They found a second, less well-known, square named after the same saint. His body, on the other hand, was stolen by two Venetian merchants in Alexandria, just as the pile workers stole their material from the quarries of Istria, and the shipbuilders stole the wood from the forest of the Cadore. The number of thieves is legion.

Tonino greets Colleoni and his sons. They are big and strong. Without effort they carry St. Anthony to the green side entrance.

Because the sons are still cross, and because one's heirs aren't real professionals, Tonino tackles the lock. His sons watch him with surreptitious admiration, especially Tonino junior, who specializes in safes. The lock has been replaced, rather poorly, after the theft. Locksmiths are the sleeping partners of burglars.

Tonino moistens two fingers with holy water and crosses himself. To see his sons are following suit makes him smile. Their disbelief cannot be quite as strong as they pretend it is.

Tonino is a believer. He had always refrained from stealing holy objects, even though it is practically unavoidable in Venice. Directly after the theft, Amalia, his wife and the mother of his children, fell ill. Some weeks ago the doctor said that only a miracle could save her. Ever since Tonino decided to return the saint to his church, she has been improving. Anthony of Padua is the patron saint of horses, of marriage, and of the recovery of lost objects. The horses are irrelevant. But Amalia is the best wife a man could wish. For thirty-seven years she has been faithful to Tonino. For eleven years, when he was out of action, she ran the business by herself. And if tomorrow the lost object is found in the church, everything may yet be all right.

The church is sparsely lit. The three men have to use their flashlights. The beams glide over the sarcophagi of the twenty-five doges. They were grudged their place in St. Mark's Church, just as Colleoni was grudged his in St. Mark's Square. One of them is Jacopo Tiepolo, who bequeathed the church to the beggars. No churches are bequeathed to burglars.

Tonino is annoyed to see the beam of Aldo's flashlight glide over Lorenzo Lotto's *Distribution of Alms by St. Anthony,* because the light strays to the blue church windows. Kitcat still has a lot to learn.

The sons want to place the picture against a pillar. Tonino has brought nails with him and wants to have the painting fitted as best they can into the empty frame. They quarrel. The chair brought up for the purpose turns out to be too low. Tonino climbs onto his elder son's shoulders. Kitcat stands by to catch him if necessary, just like a younger acrobat in a circus turn. He is swearing to himself, but when Tonino says, "Mamma wants it this way," he falls silent.

Tonino steps back a few paces, views his work and nods.

Then he adjusts the frame. Pictures not hanging straight have always bothered him.

While the sons are walking to the door, he kneels before the altar. Since he cannot think of anything else, he mumbles the shortened version of the pater noster.

Outside, the two sons walk on either side of the little man and slowly saunter across the square.

Tonino senior looks up at the armored thief who is riding through the rain into the lagoon.

Count Fornara is searching for Enrico. He has been to half a dozen places and it is nearly midnight. He has peered into the expensive Martini nightclub and into cheap bars on the other side of the Rialto bridge. Enrico is not choosy.

At midnight he runs into Enrico where he least expected him: under the colonnades in St. Mark's Square. Enrico is standing in front of the latticed window of Nardi, the jeweler.

"What are you doing out here?" Enrico asks.

"I am going for a walk," says Fornara.

He puts up his umbrella. They start walking. The Calle Larga XXII Marzo is practically deserted; only a fool of a photographer, the collar of his raincoat turned up, stops in front of the antique shop on the left side of the street. "I want this vase," Enrico says.

"What do you need a vase for?"

"Just because."

Fornara knows that Enrico does not need a thing, least of all a vase. His father made a fortune in the Second World War.

"You're just a fairy," says Fornara.

"No, I'm a high-class prostitute," says Enrico.

In the Campo Santa Maria Zobenigo the cats are running away from the echo of their steps. They freeze in the corners and look like the small St. Mark's stone lions in the souvenir shops.

"This is where the student Naumov assassinated his rival," says Fornara.

"I am not your rival," says Enrico.

Their steps die away. Dying steps are the music of Venice.

Fornara thinks: this boy, twenty-three, ten years my junior, is not my rival. All the hatred bottled up in his hours of search falls off him. The

Neapolitan fisherman's son, the Persian salesman, the Spanish painter: they were not his rivals either.

At the church of San Vitale they turn into a narrow street leading toward the Canal Grande. They pass latticed windows, crooked wooden doors, mortar on the street, a forgotten wheelbarrow. Above are covered birdcages. The calle is so narrow that the houses almost touch. There is no room for Fornara's open umbrella. The water is dripping down his neck. There is a smell of mortar and cat excrement.

Enrico leads the way. He stops in front of a stone entrance, waits for Fornara and opens it. From the rear of the palazzo, the light falls on stone dwarfs and rococo hedges.

The servants have gone to sleep hours before. Maria opens the door. She is taller than either of them—half striptease girl, half Renaissance Madonna. She is naked under her dressing gown. All the lights are on in the large drawing room, but the room has a yellowish-green tinge as if lit by gas. The Gobelin tapestry covering the whole side wall depicts the battle of Lepanto. In marble on a high pedestal stands Ludovico Manin, the last doge, who proclaimed *finis Venetiae.* One of Fornara's ancestors transmitted his surrender to Bonaparte. Under the messenger's portrait the latest issue of *Vogue* lies open. Maria has been leafing through it.

Fornara pours the cognac.

"More!" says Enrico, and once again: "More!"

"Do you need that much to sleep with me?" says Maria.

Enrico warms the glass between his hands; he puts his feet on a Gobelin armchair, and says: "I'm leaving tomorrow!"

"Where are you going?" asks Fornara.

"Sweden. This place is too hot for me."

"For how long?"

"I don't know: Maybe forever."

"You can't do that!"

"Why not? You will find someone else."

"You can have the vase," says Fornara.

Maria is scanning *Vogue.* She has crossed her legs. Below the belt her dressing gown splits open. Enrico has emptied his glass and now pours himself another.

Fornara does not drink. He paces to and fro, sits down behind his desk, opens a drawer. He caresses the revolver. He could easily shoot

Enrico like a dumb jackrabbit. Enrico would look very comical in the photographs of the homicide squad, with his trousers halfway down. After that, he would shoot himself, but that would make a rather more conventional picture.

Maria is sitting naked in the armchair, below the battle of Lepanto, with Enrico kneeling in front of her.

She drops to the floor.

If Enrico failed now, Fornara thinks, he would be almost human. But no one had failed—neither the Neapolitan fisherman, nor the Persian merchant, nor the Spanish painter.

He bends across the table.

His excitement subsides as suddenly as it gripped him.

He gets up and leans over the copulating pair. Maria stares into his eyes. It is lucky for her she didn't have her eyes closed. The day she closes her eyes for the first time, he will kill her.

He kicks Enrico. "Come on!" Enrico obeys.

Maria goes into the next room. Enrico gets dressed.

"The vase is too good for you," says Fornara. "I will give you money."

Even though it is a visiting day, the sign on the main door says: CHIUSO.

Dorothy Ginsburg has had a cold for days. The butler gave her a worried look when she told him to put up the sign. "Are you ill, Signora?" She is not ill. When she is ill, she withdraws to her bedroom, but the palazzo always remains open. Visiting hours Monday, Wednesday, Friday, from nine to twelve, from fourteen to seventeen hours.

Shivering, a thick red shawl around her shoulders, she walks through the brightly lit rooms.

The cold rises from the bare flagstone floor.

The Lhasa terrier, with his gray hair looking more and more like her own, rubs against her legs.

Why no soft, subdued lighting, why no warm rugs, why these eggshell-white leather sofas? Because all this belongs to the Picassos and Duchamps and Tanguys and Mondrians, to the sculptures by Moore and Lipchitz and Boccioni and Giacometti.

Some of these painters and sculptors had been her lovers. She had supported them and they had given her their works. With one painter she had slept during his blue period, with another in his yellow period. Her memories are blue and yellow periods.

She longs for New York, where she was born over seven decades ago. You cannot defy New York, the city itself is defiant. You can defy Venice. Her palazzo was like no other palazzo. Now it is beginning to be more and more like the others. The young artists still visit her—there were five or six yesterday. They wanted to be told about Tanguy as she used to be told about Velázquez. But those who told her about Velázquez had not known him. It is the difference between Paestum and a city you yourself have seen going up in flames.

It is hard to live among ruins that are not old.

She stops in front of Mondrian's *Scaffolding*. Scaffolding, or the barbed wire of a concentration camp? Can you learn to understand something you understood yesterday?

She reaches to switch off the white light so conveniently placed above the Picasso in the anteroom. There is a draft through the door. Alexander Calder's *Mobile* is moving, autumn leaves, but made of sheet metal. They are hanging from wires, not branches, and they will not fall. These branches will not be rejuvenated.

Lama, the terrier, starts barking.

"You want to go out?" she says, and wonders at the tenderness in her voice.

She fetches her long cape, which looks so like a cardinal's cloak.

It has stopped raining.

She walks down the seven steps and stops at Marini's *Angel of the Citadel*. From the very beginning Lama preferred to relieve himself at the foot of the bronze statue. The light from the entrance hall falls on the huge stiff penis of the angel.

Some steps further on she stops again at the wrought-iron grille. The rising waters of the canal have almost reached it. She is attracted by the canal just as she was attracted by the rails of the New York subway in her childhood.

The palazzi on the other side are cloaked in the night's haze. Only in one of them is a light still burning. The old lady living there never wanted to receive her.

Lama shivers and barks.

12

This time the Signora could not refuse to receive Dorothy Ginsburg. Dario had asked her to–it was important for Venice.

She decided to look her best for this visit. For a moment she was sorry all her dresses were black, her wardrobe a black safe. Even though in the past she had enjoyed wearing bright dresses, it had nothing to do with mourning–rather with pride. Vincente had not protected her from men, but from being ridiculous. Besides, the black dresses were not at all alike. Dario, for instance, would notice at once when she was wearing a new one. This time she chose her best, a *pazzia*, a folly, from the most expensive shop in the Merceria, discreet, but richly trimmed with Venetian lace. The scanty jewelry she had received from Vincente had long since gone to the pawnshop and not returned. Only the long string of pearls was genuine. She did not feel it was frivolous of her to have exchanged a few rings for clothes.

Only after applying more lipstick than was customary for her did she turn her mind to the visitor. Mrs. Ginsburg was as old as she, perhaps older. Prodigious tales were told of her vitality. She commuted by plane between Venice and New York, opened exhibitions, appeared at the film festival. The Signora didn't care a bit whether young people thought her old, but before a person of her own age she did not like to look it. Not old, but herself. She wanted to serve tea herself, but Romolo and Emilia had helped her with the preparations–silver on the trolley, doilies, china.

"I cannot offer you a cocktail," said the Signora. "Will you have tea?"

"Please," said Mrs. Ginsburg. "Some milk, thank you. I hate cocktails."

Mrs. Ginsburg's appearance disconcerted the Signora, but also reassured her. The American lady was wearing a red sports dress with a high-collared green pullover showing, and she had white boots reaching to her knees. Above the turtleneck there was a small bulldog's head, the purplish white hair was cut short in masculine fashion, in deliberate disorder. The dark glasses, shaped like a butterfly and set with glittering little stones, its wings separated by the tiny yet fleshy nose, practically covered half her face. You don't conquer age by refusing to bow to it.

"It is strange that we have never met," Mrs. Ginsburg said in Italian, with only a trace of an accent. "I have been admiring your house for a long time. So this is it, the famous Titian."

"Yes."

"Obviously a late work."

"He was ninety when he painted it."

"Painters never grow old. It must be the happy combination of mental and physical exercise. By the way, it is not certain that Titian really reached his century. At eighty-two in a letter to the king he passed himself off as ninety-five. We would not do such a thing."

"I didn't know that," said the Signora. Mrs. Ginsburg's familiarity was embarrassing her, and she would have also liked to divert the conversation from the Titian.

"*Girl with Flower Basket*," said Mrs. Ginsburg.

She said it admiringly, even though she found the painting lifeless and conventional, mere window dressing. Dorothy had the impression that the old lady did not want to talk about the Titian. The old lady! Seventy-four, she had been told, but it seemed to Dorothy that the Signora was much, much older than she—a forgotten person from a time she herself could scarcely remember.

"Are you living alone in this big house?" she asked.

"One of my grandsons is staying with me at the moment. Otherwise yes, all the year round."

"Are you not afraid?"

"Of what?"

"I am often afraid. Although the house is usually full of people," said Dorothy.

"You have art treasures."

"So do you."

"Mine are not coveted."

"The Titian!"

The Titian, again! Did Mrs. Ginsburg want to buy the *Girl with Flower Basket*? She would have told Dario. And what would Mrs.

Ginsburg, who thought the world began the day she was born, have done with a Titian?

Dorothy turned away from the Titian. She started to talk about the rain, which had caused considerable damage last week. What else could you talk about with this old woman, who had taken the widow's veil twenty years ago? She judged beds by their mattresses, all her life she had met only people like herself. And now she probably thought of herself as an aristocrat, because the miserable portrait of a Santarato from the eighteenth century was hanging on the opposite wall to the Titian.

Dorothy was nineteen when she had first come to Venice. She had hated the city immediately, just as, consciously or unconsciously, Montesquieu, Henry James and Emerson had hated it. It offered everything to the eye but nothing to the mind, one immense outburst of emotion, unrestrained by any reason, a permanent temptation to sentimentality, thronged with admirers who admired what they were told to admire—this country fair, this slum of beauty, this mixture of primitive and baroque, this carnival of dishonesty, this unflawed mirror of a crooked world, this flirtatious corpse, this authentic fraud. But Dorothy was never a person to run from what she could not conquer. One had to make a clean sweep of this "theater store" as her friend Mary McCarthy had so aptly called Venice; and when the new art came into fashion, she resolved to fly its flags from the pinnacles of the gilded illusions.

The longer their small talk babbled along, the more insecure Dorothy felt. The Signora could not lose in any competition because she evidently never competed. These curtains would never fall apart, they had defied old age much too long. If this wallpaper faded any further, it would be admired even more. If every third light bulb were burning in the crystal chandelier, instead of every second one, then it would look like candlelight and be a blessing for the porous curtains and the faded wallpaper.

Abruptly Dorothy said: "There's an exhibition we are planning following the Biennial: Venetian Art Through the Centuries. For this we need"—she did not mention who "we" was—"your Titian."

"Compared to the Titians in the Accademia and the Palazzo Ducale my Titian is a mere daub."

"Don't say that! Besides, there will be only privately owned paintings. From Giorgione to Max Ernst, we do not want to go any further. This is an act of social welfare. The young people who come to Venice," Dorothy continued hoarsely, "only get to see museums and churches. The palazzi they pass hungrily. We cannot open up every palazzo to them, but we can assemble some treasures. For four weeks only, in September. . . ."

The Signora waved away the cigarette smoke with an impolite gesture and regretted it immediately. Why did she let Dario talk her into receiving Mrs. Ginsburg? Dario was unaware of her resolve: either Paolo and Laura would now agree, after Claudia had said the Titian was not that important; or she would sell the Titian without their consent. If you were living with decay, you would barely notice it, like the wrinkles in a friend's face. But Romolo had thrown up his hands aghast at the idea of selling anything. "Perhaps we should carry some of the things up from the drawing room to the floor above"—exile to the higher regions, in fact. So Mrs. Ginsburg was talking of social welfare. Surely it was social welfare to sell the Titian so that the young people would not stumble over an archaeological corpse.

Dorothy Ginsburg, who understood people, knew that the Signora's answer would be no. Something strange, proud, stormy, she felt, was going on in her antagonist's soul.

"I could lie to you," said the Signora. "An excuse is easily found. Or I could simply refuse—I am a Venetian, and therefore unfairly immune to the reproach of not giving my very best to Venice. I shall tell you the truth."

As so often happened, her words had outrun her resolve.

She was glad of it. The old woman with the butterfly spectacles and white boots was lonelier than she. The Palazzo Santarato was to be made a museum. The Palazzo Ginsburg was one already. The catalogue of ailing palazzi was not offered for sale at street corners, visiting them was not recommended by hotel porters. Mrs. Ginsburg had slept with the painters, and now she was standing at their neon graves. Or her lovers had turned into her children; it was a bad thing to live with your children.

Was it pity or wickedness that made her expose her plans to Mrs. Ginsburg, or was she trying to prove to the conqueror what her palazzo means to a native?

"In September," she said, "the Titian will no longer be here. My friend Ortelli must not know this. I have to sell the Titian if I am to save the palazzo."

"Is the Titian to be lost to Venice?"

"I hope not. But I have no choice." She smiled. "The young people do not notice when a frame is empty in a museum. But a gap in a row of houses on the Canal Grande they *would* notice. Or a new house."

"New houses grow old," Mrs. Ginsburg said. "I might offer to buy your Titian. But it would be bad taste. Worse, it would be a deceit. For I find this Titian horrible." She smiled too. "Like most of my own paintings, by the way. It's getting late."

She rose. The Titian was mediocre, but its owner liked it, her own paintings were not mediocre, but she did not like them.

"Rest assured, Signora Santarato," she said, "that I shall not abuse your confidence. I shall say that the *Girl with Flower Basket* is unsuitable for the exhibition."

"Thank you," said the Signora.

After Mrs. Ginsburg had left, she went to the window. The motorboat left the side canal and crossed the Canal Grande. The red cape had disappeared inside the cabin.

She heard Romolo's steps and turned.

"Did she also offer to buy the palazzo?" Romolo asked.

13

The reputation of Anselmo Mozetti had come to the Signora's notice long ago; she now decided to visit him.

The ride in the vaporetto had always been an adventure to her. Since gondolas and motorboats had become expensive, many foreigners used the floating trams, but the vaporetto had remained Venetian all the same: workers with sailors' caps, housewives with shopping bags, officials engrossed in *Il Gazzettino*, lovers, students, monks; and nobody looked up, nobody admired the agile captain avoiding the gondolas, the skillful sailors throwing ropes. The palazzi passing by were houses, not museums.

She left the vaporetto where the Canale di Cannaregio turns off from the Canal Grande, and took the well-known way to the ghetto.

Although the Jews no longer lived in the ghetto and it was no Jew she was about to call on, she felt the uneasiness most Venetians experience in this place.

The Venetians have been inventors of so many things, easels and income tax, the violin and hair-dying, the gaming table and book censorship, statistics and beauty spots, the theory of the rainbow and the construction of the skyscraper. And they also invented the ghetto, which in Venetian means foundry: cannons were cast here, and the Jews shut in. Jews had been in Venice when the city was founded, refugees; the name of the island quarter Giudecca comes from *Giudei,* but that has never meant much, for resident and native are not the same. At the beginning of the sixteenth century the Franciscans demanded that the Hebrews should be burned, but the Venetians never had much time for the brutality of their authorities. They isolated the Jews, like bacilli. They forbade them to build new houses, and since Jews are a resourceful people they invented the skyscraper. Even the Jews whose fathers and grandfathers and great-grandfathers had been born in Venice needed a residence permit. That, to be sure, was *not* a Venetian invention, but to this day it has remained a well-tried method of legitimizing second-rate citizens. For the renewal of this permit every few years, the Jews had to pay. That they were able to pay had deservedly given them the reputation of being smart businessmen. They paid to be allowed to live, behind boarded-up windows, cut off at night from their neighbors, and strictly guarded—for their own safety, mind you; and they paid so heavily for this that in 1735 the inquisitors had to report that the Jews had been fleeced, now they could be burned like withered leaves. Again the Venetians refrained, for secretly they felt a kinship with the Jews, as an ejected and selected and surviving people. Gradually Venice accepted the Jews. But since the pride of descending from a long line of ancestors is independent of whether the forebears were prisoners or jailers, persecuted or persecutors, chucked-out or chuckers-out, who knows, there may be deer fathers proudly telling their deer children that their grandfathers were shot by the grandfathers of the hunters.

Of Venice's eight hundred Jews, thirty are still living in the ghetto; rather few, admittedly, for five synagogues and many memories.

The memories would have weighed less heavily on the Signora if the most northerly part of the city had not still been the poorest. Even now it consisted of bare facades, shabby washing, stinking fountains, dark corners, trees dying of thirst, scurrying skeletons of cats, children so wretched they might be Jewish children. And in a narrow *calle* a young rabbi was walking toward her, without the red hat his forebears had been forced to wear, but his sandy hair fell in ringlets over his ears, a man forgotten by the centuries.

She stopped for a rest on the bridge over the Rio di Ghetto Nuovo, and viewed the windows nailed up with boards and the warped doors and exposed tiles. All this made the houses seem little different from the Palazzo Santarato, as if a Jewish curse had been fulfilled and Venice had become a ghetto.

A cloudless sky spread itself over the rooftops. Suddenly the heat was almost like midsummer. The Signora dried her forehead with her lace handkerchief. The wind from the sea had driven the clouds up-country. But one could still see what damage the heavy rains early in the year had done. The water almost reached the steps of the bridge; it washed against the lower windows of the houses. Below an archway, a woman stood with a bucket, bailing out the water from the room into the canal.

During the rainy days the Signora's idea of visiting Anselmo Mozetti had ripened into a decision. Luigi Primavesi had phoned her—yes, they were going to fix the oak piles, but she would have to be patient. The weather had upset his plans, his workmen had been requisitioned, an emergency. And she had talked to Dario—yes, upon her insistence he had applied to the Mayor's office once again, and the Mayor was willing to receive her, but owing to the terrible storm he was swamped with work, urgent, more urgent, perhaps next week, or the week after next. Finally Paolo's telephone call. "Good to hear your voice"—for six weeks he had deprived himself of the pleasure. "That letter you wrote me, on Claudia's behalf too—what does Claudia know about it! I understand your feelings perfectly well, but they are only emotions, the palazzo has survived four hundred years, it will survive the twentieth century too. . . . Why on earth did you show Mr. Wilcox the door? Anyhow all these matters are not so urgent. Besides, we shall certainly visit you this summer, then we can discuss it—how's the weather?"

"It is raining," she had answered.

Nobody was in a hurry, tomorrow was another day, neither Primavesi nor the Mayor nor Paolo. Dario! She had not told Dario either about her intentions. She did not want to incriminate him, she lied to herself, but actually it was from fear of his strict honesty.

She reached the Campo Ghetto Nuovo, and stopped.

The "Mozetti case" had kept the newspapers busy for weeks some years before. When Mozetti was released from prison a year ago, it had flared up again. The young Venetian painter, a genius (that much was admitted), had put on the market canvases of van Dyck, Gainsborough, Tiepolo, Goya, and also some by Manet, Degas and Cézanne. All were fakes, but the experts had been fooled and authenticated them as unknown works by the masters in question, until the accumulation of these "finds" aroused suspicion and the comedy ended in tragedy. In spite of that, the sentence of the Venetian judges was milder than expected. It was true that the forger had passed off as a van Dyck, Cézanne or Degas what was in fact just a simple Mozetti, but he had not copied the masters. The portraits and landscapes and still lifes were his own, and merely in the style of the great masters—though also, unfortunately, carrying their signatures.

A baker's boy in dirty white showed the Signora to the Mozetti studio, which was not, as she had expected, on the top floor of a house, but on the ground floor of the building in the Campo Ghetto Nuovo, set back in the dark of the arcades.

She looked incredulously through the dimmed window, a shop window really—in a former glassblower's shop, as revealed by the washed-out lettering. She was appalled. In the low room, which was practically empty, stood a tall, gaunt, bald man with a goatee beard, with an easel in front of him. He looked young, but prematurely aged, a carnival figure, if not a ghost, for he wore a flowing black robe of shabby velvet, that must have been unbearably hot for the time of the year, trimmed with a red fox collar, supplemented by a white ruff, silk stockings and buckle shoes: every inch a grandee of the seventeenth century. Had the man dressed up in so strange a way in order to be his own model? But there was no mirror to be seen in the whole room, and on the easel, turned toward the window, there was no likeness of him to be seen. Instead there was a pale-blue Christ beginning to take shape.

Should she turn back? Every step in the ghetto had made her more unsure of herself, and now a cowardly sense of the impossibility of her venture was creeping over her.

René Naville had visited her again. The amount he had offered for the Titian was incredible. Nothing but a few cut corners separated her from the salvation of the palazzo. Absolute discretion, *parole d'honneur,* Naville had assured her. "The client is a private collector, a 'Titian fiend,' and an eccentric. In his private house, with no one there to notice, he'll be all on his own talking to the *Girl with Flower Basket.* A unique stroke of luck, Signora, this opportunity will not occur again."

Will not occur again, thought the Signora. Certainly not in my lifetime. What about the consequences? During sleepless nights she had seen the headlines: A SECOND MOZETTI CASE; SENILE DELINQUENCY AT WORK; OUTRAGEOUS FRAUD. But those were nightmares, how could the fraud be discovered? And, after all, was it fraud? Naville and his fiend were to have their genuine Titian; it was only in her own drawing room that the fake would hang, a kindly Mozetti she might learn to love. Where did the money come from? she would be asked. A loan from the city, or UNESCO, or an American connoisseur. Dario was the only person who might discover the forgery, but even that was improbable without close scrutiny, particularly with a work by Mozetti—and Dario would not give her away. There were many who willed the right end, you simply had to make your allies your accomplices. The real trouble was not enemies but faint-hearted accomplices. They looked and nodded and deplored and looked and lamented and swore, and they did not really *see* or *do* anything. They were good-natured in the face of evil and helpless in the face of guns and patient in the face of impatience and mute in the face of speeches and honest in the face of fraud. Until the flood swallowed them. But she, the Signora Anna-Maria Santarato, would not be good-natured or helpless or patient or mute. And she would not be honest either.

Some urchins had gathered around her, attracted more by the sight of the well-dressed lady than by the painting ghost; they had got used to him. She entered the room.

"I am Signora Santarato," she said. "Did you receive my letter?"

"Yes, yes," the man said, his mind elsewhere, and examined his work.

"May I have a glass of water?" asked the Signora.

"Beer," he said, and because he had seen her disapproving glance, he rinsed a glass with beer.

There was nothing for it but to swallow the nitroglycerine tablets, which she carried in a small pill box, with a sip of warm beer. Since she consistently refused to admit that the weakness of her heart was brought on by emotional excitement, she blamed the long vaporetto journey, the walk and the sudden heat for the symptoms that threatened an attack.

"What do you want from me?" the Spanish grandee was asking.

"I own a Titian. *Girl with Flower Basket.* I should like you to copy it."

"I do not copy anything."

She had rehearsed every word of her speech. Would he do a kind service for an old woman? Her son had this one desire—he wanted the Titian, but she could not part with the painting she had grown so fond of. "One lives with a picture, as you well know." The reproduction would have to be ready for her son's birthday—a surprise—nobody was to know about it.

She had presented this implausible story without conviction on purpose. Mozetti's eyes narrowed, either because he doubted her, or because he was measuring the picture he had continued to work on.

"Nonsense," he finally said.

She had sat down on a low stool. "No," she said contritely, "it's not nonsense, but there *is* something else. My daughters are jealous and don't want me to give this present. I don't mind if they take the copy for the original."

Her gamble that the swindler might be attracted by a swindle involving so little risk proved correct. At least Mozetti seemed no longer completely against the whole idea. "Your daughters will discover," he said, "that there are two identical Titians."

"My son lives in Milan. He is not on speaking terms with his sisters."

"It is difficult to become Titian when you are El Greco," he said.

"I don't understand ..."

Impeded by his wide sleeves, he tried to wash his brushes. He

stroked his long chin, further lengthened by the goatee. "I explained it
to the judges and they did not understand either. I am Velázquez and
Tintoretto and Rembrandt. All I do is this"—he snapped his thumb
and middle finger—"and their souls slip into mine. Right now, I am
Domenikos Theotokopoulos, called El Greco. I am living in the early
seventeenth century, in 1602 to be exact. In what year did your Titian
flourish?"

"They say around 1570."

"I would have to develop backward. El Greco is supposed to have
learned from Titian, but luckily he forgot everything . . ."

"All you have to do is this," said the Signora. She was pleased and
amused to have brought off her snap of thumb and middle finger so
well.

"Perhaps. Perhaps not. I have never copied any painter. I am greater
than all of them. My forgeries! I do not paint the way they painted, but
the way they should have painted."

"Indeed you are very good at your trade!"

"When I feel like it." He looked down at her. "I think I like you.
But it might happen that the copy is better than the original. How big
is your flower girl?"

She indicated the size of the picture.

"How much are you going to pay me?"

"How much do you ask?"

He named a sum which, though not exorbitant, would still use up
her savings.

She agreed hurriedly.

He went into the next room. Through the open door she saw a
room in semi-darkness which looked like a theatrical wardrobe:
costumes of bygone centuries, Italian and Spanish and Flemish ones,
silk and velvet robes with puffed sleeves, knee breeches, frock coats, top
hats, turbans, straw hats.

"There is no Titian among them," he said on returning. "The
costume will be at your expense."

"Of course. How long will it take you?"

"Don't know. Three weeks, perhaps four."

Some urchins had gathered outside and pressed their noses against
the windowpane. You could hear their laughter.

"Of course, you will have to work at my place," said the Signora.

"The painting must not leave the house for a single hour. And we shall have to agree on your working hours. My daughters often come to see me, and at present I have my grandson staying with me."

"That is too inconvenient."

"You can change at my place. I have a room with good light, in the attic. This must be a real conspiracy between the two of us. Don't forget: if you do this painting in my house, it will be my sole responsibility."

He went over to the window, bent forward and stuck out his tongue. The boys ran away.

"You had better phone me tomorrow," she said quickly. "Meanwhile I have brought a down payment."

She took some paper money from her purse, and since the painter did not hold out his hand for it, she placed it on the easel.

"The greatest El Greco," he said, pointing to the picture. "But for the sake of those idiots I shall sign it Mozetti this time."

She handed him her card.

He grinned, revealing two rows of unusually large, unusually yellow teeth. "I don't believe a word you've said. You are an extremely devious old person."

With quick steps she crossed the Campo Ghetto Nuovo. She would probably have to wait a long time for the vaporetto. But the constriction was gone, and she no longer found the heat oppressive. Mozetti was a madman. Everything depended on finding madmen.

The houses on either side of the bridge did not bear any resemblance to the palazzo.

14

The electric clock on the Excelsior beach on the Lido said half past eleven. Not a breeze was stirring. It would not be worth taking out one of the small sailing boats. But it was too early to have lunch.

Romolo always brought sandwiches and kept them in the lobby behind the porter's lodge. Between him and one of the porters there was a tacit agreement, arranged by the Signora, that he could change in the lobby and keep his sandwiches there. The Signora did not want him to bathe on the public beach or to sneak on to the Excelsior beach from there, as so many trespassers did, wading through the shallow waters.

For some time he had been collecting shells, had left them to dry out on the seat of a boat, and forgotten about them. But now he remembered them, and felt miserable. It was no fun anymore looking for shells. He had done it automatically, repeating the gestures of childhood, from habit, from memory, to hold on to something that doesn't after all offer any support.

In Milan, too, he was often alone, but it was only last year, quite suddenly, that he began to mind this. He had schoolmates, but no real friends. He took part in everything they did, but wouldn't have cared if he hadn't. His pals listened to records for hours, but he didn't understand how you could be satisfied because the ear was satisfied. Most of them were at war with their parents. Some said the parents' world had to be overturned. Romolo despised his parents, his father with some affection, his mother at times rather fiercely, but he did not think all parents were like his. If his pals said society was unjust, he wanted to know what they meant by that. Remus was ten years his senior, but to Romolo his brother seemed to be still looking for shells at the age of twenty-five. Romolo wrote poems, which he at once destroyed. He read court records and always put himself in the position of the counsel for the defense. He did not know what he wanted to be, which profession to choose, but he kept worrying over it as if he had to decide almost at once. When he read of bygone times, he felt a stranger in his own time; he slipped into the souls of knights and lovers and scholars and priests, and found his way back to the present only with difficulty, as if a bridge led from today to yesterday, but none from yesterday to today.

He sat down in the sand outside one of the empty cabins and closed his eyes.

The heat and the sight of the all-naked girls had aroused his senses. About half his class had slept with girls, and he had made up his mind to emulate his schoolmates next year, perhaps even this summer. When he resorted to self-gratification, he did not have a bad conscience. There were many women and girls he slept with, young and old, blondes, brunettes, redheads; he slept with Anna Karenina and with a dancer he had seen on a poster. But although he could imagine any situation, his imagination failed when it concerned a female he had seen in person an hour before. The strangers of his fantasies came to him indirectly—an accidental encounter in a railway compartment, a woman with an unloved husband running to him, kisses after a walk in the woods, a girl crying in front of a discotheque—and then he stretched out his arm and stroked the girl's hair and watched her in her sleep. "When did you meet her?" he once asked Remus, who was talking about one of his love affairs. "Two hours before our first go," Remus had said, and Romolo decided to wait for an encounter in a railway compartment, or to elope with a married woman, as Count Vronsky had done.

The sand was still wet, a brownish-loamy color. Romolo, who had not made any acquaintances so far this year, got up to take a look at the hotel.

The Hotel Excelsior, easily reached in ten minutes by motorboat from Venice, rises immediately behind the beach, a pseudo-Moorish monstrosity, half harem, half factory. At street level there is a marble hall with jet fountains, a hairdresser, showcases, lounges and dining rooms, all pomp and gilt. But the furniture is new, and the wicker chairs are of avant-garde design. Turn-of-the-century bad taste and the bad taste of the 1970s are on amiable nodding terms.

The hall was practically empty, and in the bar, leather cushions on the floor, fully contemporary, the waiters appeared to be bored. Romolo turned around and stepped back onto the terraced staircase—a relic of the era when people walked with dignity—which led from the hotel and the nineteenth century to the beach.

On one of the top steps he stopped and looked out at the beach. Why did other boys of his age make such a show of their boredom? He felt at home on the Excelsior beach. Yesterday and tomorrow kept a friendly date here. The sandy beach, miles long and over half a mile wide, looked every morning as if it had been swept with a vacuum cleaner. It was dotted with people strolling, playing with balls, children building castles, but nobody lay in the sand. That had not been done in the era of parasols; the parasols were still skipping invisibly across the Lido. Right and left of the terraced stairs were the endless rows of *cabine* with their awnings, striped in different colors, apparently of the same kind, and yet not quite, for those in the first row were exclusive, and the cabins in the very middle were the *crème de la crème*. In front of them were couches covered with towels by the bath attendants, striped like the tents; the couches of the patrons at once recognizable by their own linen, in the family colors, as it were. A remnant of the past were the lifeguards with their straw hats. They sat in red boats on dry land, and since nobody was in danger of drowning they were selling bits of coral and shells and starfish and sea horses. The wandering fruit sellers— "*Frutti! Frutti!*"—were also from the past, and so were the old American women who were there at the very beginning of the season, as if they had been mummified on the beach and hibernated in their wicker chairs. Romolo knew all this; he also knew that it would soon change, at the latest in the first few days of the film festival. Then directors, cameramen and reporters would swamp the beach, well-rounded and naked starlets would slink their curves into the cameras' range and offer a wealth of natural phenomena artificially produced.

He wandered around again for a bit, and then decided to go across the jetty, which reached far out into the sea, to a round platform where the younger bathers usually gathered. Today there were only a few youngsters lying on their backs or admiring a yacht which had just anchored.

Romolo was attracted by the rock music rolling out of transistors. Crossing his legs, he sat down next to a girl resting on her long, honey-blond hair. The music from her transistor soon got scrambled into a jumble of sounds. Without looking, the girl groped for the set. Romolo, surprised by his own audacity, turned the dial and freed the music from its background noise. The girl said thank you, but did not budge. Without betraying the slightest curiosity in him, she asked if he understood English. He said he was Italian but spoke English fairly well, and was she English or American? She was English. In Venice for the first time? Yes, and "a terrible bore," sunbathing in the mornings, churches in the afternoons, and in the evenings music for old people. Didn't she want to swim? No. He was going in for a dip. "Go ahead!" At the age of seven he had already been an excellent swimmer, and now, taking a deep breath and filling his chest, he dived in headfirst. He stayed underwater a long time and swam back to the ladder in a fast crawl. In the meantime, the girl had turned on her belly, opening her bikini, but she had still not looked up. He asked what her name was.

"Barbara." He introduced himself. The fact that he mentioned his surname seemed to surprise the girl. At last she lifted her head, but he was not sure she was looking at him.

She took her radio and they went toward the beach. The seashells had spread a silver carpet across the sand. He called her attention to it.

"How old are you?" she asked.

"I'm nearly fifteen."

"Are you? I'm nearly sixteen." She looked down at the beach. "The water's filthy."

"Oil from the ships."

"Look at this," she said, raising one foot to show him that her sole was sticky with tar.

"Leave it to me."

She realized what he meant and sat down on the edge of the jetty. He took a stone, washed clean by the water, kneeled and quickly removed the tar from her foot.

"Now the other one," he said.

She found that unnecessary, and got up without thanking him. "I need a drink."

The open bar between the cabins and the beach restaurant belonged to the young. They sat at the counter with their legs dangling. The girls seemed to be fully occupied with their hair and their bras. Some of the boys and girls sat skin to skin, while loud jokes flew from table to table. This was the lunch hour; the hotel guests strolled through the bar or past it, most of them covering their nakedness in gaudy colors, either too fat or too skinny, but certainly too old for so much unmerciful sun. They were ashamed of their fat or their wrinkles or their colors, or the shamelessness of the young. Romolo fidgeted with his too short swimming trunks.

"What is it to be today, Miss Barbara?" the young barman asked.

"Prairie Oyster," she said, and looked the waiter deep in the eyes.

"Coca-Cola," said Romolo, and was sure he had done something wrong.

He apologized, remembering that his money was in the trousers he had left in the porter's lobby. She nodded as if she had barely heard him.

When he returned almost at a run, Barbara was surrounded by young people. One of them, with long curly hair and gold-rimmed spectacles, sat at the bar observing the others as though staggered by their silliness. Another boy was balancing a Coke on his elbow; a girl was leaning over the counter so skillfully that either the right or the left strap of her bra was bound to slip over her arm. Romolo suddenly longed for his brother, who was as superior to these boys as they seemed superior to him.

A headwaiter in an egg-colored jacket came from the dining room and said that Mr. and Mrs. Donovan were expecting Miss Barbara. Romolo was glad to know she had parents.

She said: "This evening we'll all be going to Venice. Want to come along?"

She told him that they would meet at Quadri's at nine. It was only then he realized how carelessly he had accepted the suggestion.

He returned to Venice earlier than usual. On the way from the station he thought over several ways of obtaining the consent of his grandmother. From time to time the Signora allowed him to go to a theater, a concert or a cinema, and in the cinema in the Salizzada San Moisè he had discovered that an American picture was playing which he had seen in Milan–he could easily give an account of it. The lie was not easy for him, but nor was it as hard as he had feared. He wanted to find out at all costs who the girl was, and maybe she would ask him who he was.

The "group"–consisting of two American boys and one German boy, one French girl and two American girls, evidently in their late teens–certainly knew all the cafés and the only discotheque worth mentioning, but he was the only Italian who knew Venice like the back of his hand. He always led the way with Barbara, and when he explained to her–they were just crossing St. Mark's Square and heading toward the Bridge of Sighs–that there used to be markets and fairs here in the old days, where witches and quacks cured any ailment, even lovesickness, stopped nosebleeds and offered remedies against the evil eye, where a rhinoceros was displayed and bullfights were held, she said he was a "great guide" and gave him her hand. In the discotheque shortly after, she rocked back and forth to the music in blasé rapture, not noticing that he was a better tourist guide than dancing partner. Did she notice his presence at all, would she recognize him tomorrow? To his relief they drank Coca-Cola, to his alarm she alone was drinking gin and tonic, "a lot of gin, please, not much tonic." To his relief she did not smoke, to his alarm she asked him if he had ever tried marijuana.

Added to the fear that she might slip away from him tomorrow, he now felt fear for her, and it increased further when she spoke of her "group" in London. "I never get to bed." "And your parents?" "Good lord, they don't have the slightest idea!" She was talking only to him, now it was the others she did not see. He felt like the roving caricaturist at the restaurant he had been to with his parents, who was asked to portray him. After drawing several quick lines, he would tear off the sheet from his block, crumple it, and throw it away. Probably none of the drawings looked like any of the others—or like the model. With the girl just now in the Piazza San Marco, he would have walked on and on, hand in hand, through all the narrow streets, over every bridge, and then he would have lifted her into a gondola, and outside the palazzo they would have disembarked, and they would have pressed close together and gone up to his room. But the girl who was dancing so absentmindedly and talked about the group and marijuana was not the girl in the gondola. You could do nothing but crumple up the drawing and start afresh. When he timidly put his arm around her hips, she pressed herself so tightly to him that her hair curled around his ear, and when he smoothed back her hair, she laughingly blew her breath into his ear. But later, when he told her about the palazzo, she listened with her eyes wide open and said that Venice was no longer a terrible bore, and she asked if his grandmother would be terribly shocked if one day she called at her door.

The others said to hurry if they were not to miss the last motorboat from the Danieli to the Excelsior. She said she wanted one more gin and tonic, there was a boat to the casino on the Lido and from there they could walk. But when the group finally rose to go, she managed to have herself and Romolo escape from the others.

She walked close to his side along the deserted Riva degli Schiavoni. "Petrarch lived here," he said, and she asked, "Who was Petrarch?," and he said, "A great poet," and she said, "I'm terribly stupid, you will have to read me something by him someday," and he said, "In the winter there is a fair here," and she said, "I shall come in winter and we'll ride in the big wheel," and he said, "In winter I'm in Milan," and she said, "Then we'll both run away and meet at the fair."

At the boat station they met up with the others. When he gave her his hand to help her get in, she kissed him, and he felt her tongue in his mouth.

15

The afternoon was pleasantly cool. After the Signora had delivered the letter to Laura at the post office, she took the route to the Campo Manin, where Signora Bigarello, her dressmaker, lived. The dressmaker had warned her that a protest march of the workers of Mestre and Marghera was planned for the afternoon, and when she remembered this, she was too busy with her thoughts to feel like changing her plan. Besides, she was not afraid of protest marches—she read about them in the *Gazzettino* every day.

Luigi Primavesi might be right: she could not walk in the streets of Venice without being concerned about the city.

She recalled many other cities. In her childhood she had traveled with her parents—her father was an archaeologist, often away, and her mother was descended from an impoverished line of Venetian aristo-crats—to Rome, Paris, Brussels, London, Amsterdam. Vincente too, in the first few years, had wanted to please his young wife with trips to Biarritz and Ostend. She remembered many pictures vividly, but the contrast had begun to fade like old postcards. When as a girl she had sat in strange railway stations on a mountain of trunks—for her mother believed that traveling light was "rather common"—Anna-Maria had always felt strangely uneasy, as if the trunks contained something quite different from what had been packed at home. Hidden among the clothes and the linen lay the conflict with her beautiful, sickly, touchy mother, the anxiety about disappointing her domineering father, who demanded perfection as a matter of course, the fear of her own inadequacy. She could remember how all this disappeared, as if by magic, the moment the luggage was lifted off the gondola on the steps of the small palazzo at the corner of the Calle Mandola. Over the years, this and many other memories had reappeared, but not much more alarmingly than the foggy reality you wake into between two dreams.

There was a big crowd. The Signora did not mind. In other cities, the crowds all rush off in different directions, hysterical particles, whereas here they converge on the calm center of Venice. Other cities were crushed in the embrace of the masses. Venice embraced the masses. Yes, Luigi Primavesi was right: this poor city was stronger than its poor citizens. Was this why the oppression she had felt as a girl while away from Venice vanished when she came home? Had she been born into an illusion? Reality was the open eye, illusion the closed one, but you spent half your life with closed eyes, and Venice helped you to close them.

The foreigners marveled. Were they really so beautiful, these sad houses? Most of them were not beautiful, but with the water at their gates they conjured up that infinite element, illusion. If the foreigners looked up, they were like the blind who walk and walk and don't see where their feet are carrying them. Luigi seriously believed that the palaces of Venice were something akin to the Czar's palaces in Moscow or Petrograd's Hermitage. But the foreigners who unpacked their suitcases here and did not find what they expected knew that Venice was not a museum, not even a city, only an idea. Therefore the stones were allowed to break, but you could not remove one of the stones without breaking the idea. She had written something of this sort to Laura, and even though she did not expect much from this new appeal, she was glad she had done so.

Suddenly the Signora stopped short. For a moment she thought she was meeting a ghost, or one of those youngsters who play macabre tricks. The man coming toward her was wearing a gas mask. Now there were thirty or forty crowding from all directions, gas masks over their faces or under their arms, men and women; and the Signora remembered that today the workers from over two hundred factories were protesting against the pollution of the air. Men and women helpless before the dirt invading their homes, the children racked by bronchitis, the hospitals crammed with heart cases. Fifty thousand workers had been prescribed gas masks by the official doctor, like a prescription you take to the druggist. Ten thousand lire a mask, an expensive remedy.

The Campo Manin was not far now. The Signora hurried on.

"You shouldn't have come," said the dressmaker, a plump, rosy, resolute woman with five children, three of whom would crawl between the customer's feet during the fitting. Signora Bigarello held the youngest in her arm.

"I should like to see what is going on below."

The workers had marched up in rows of eight, and in the front row all of them were wearing gas masks. They looked like creatures with snouts, disguised men or disguised snout creatures. In overalls, working clothes, checked shirts, men with bare chests, women in summer dresses, animal heads, round glasses for eyes, cheeks made of rubber, food tins in front of their mouths.

"Here of all places," said the dressmaker, but the Signora knew why. The lawyer Daniele Manin had rallied the opposition to the Austrians here in 1848. Now the workers were protesting against a new invader, one that seeped from the air.

On the banners which had reached the monument, the Signora read: ANDREOTTI IL BUFFONE D'ITALIA!—CAPITALISTS CAN BREATHE, WHILE WE CHOKE!—GAS MASKS FOR THE NEWBORN!—WE DEMAND AIR! A woman held her baby above her head, she had put a gas mask on his face. The square was now strewn with red flags set in rows along the facades of the palaces, outside the monstrously modern glass palace of the closed Casa di Risparmio, below smiling baroque angels—and one of them on a door had a hammer and sickle painted on it. The policemen were standing helplessly in the crowd, abused by the men, jostled by the women.

"The police ought to shoot into the crowd," Signora Bigarello was saying. "If they had tried that under Mussolini, he would have shown them."

The Signora was not listening.

In the square below, the noises subsided. The speaker was not wearing a gas mask, but the Signora was unable to understand him. Sometimes the snout creatures raised their fists, sometimes they shouted, "Air! Air!" It sounded like the desperate cry from a collapsed coal mine.

"It's air they want, and yet it was the building of the Third Zone they went on strike for," said the dressmaker. "At that time they scrawled all over the walls. It all has to happen in the Campo Manin."

The dressmaker's rooms were the same as so many years before, when the Signora had come for the first time: turn-of-the-century furniture, humming shells, fair-haired dolls, the beveled standing mirror. In the dimly lit room the children were leaning out one of the windows. "Just like my picture book," little Iacopo shouted, referring to its pictures of the assembly of animals going into the ark.

The snout creatures shouted "Bravo!" and "Abasso!" Through the gas masks it sounded like the howling of sirens. Some of the demonstrators took off their gas masks. The square was overlaid with heat; you choked in the gas masks and you choked without them. Some had sat down on the head of the lion at Manin's and the speaker's feet, and the pigeons took wing. The child in the dressmaker's arm began to cry, and because silence had fallen again the speaker heard the crying; he looked up at the window.

"Don't you want to try it on?" asked the dressmaker. "The dress is ready."

Standing before the mirror, the Signora saw only the upper facades of the aristocratic houses; all the windows were closed. The shouts of the demonstrators resounded from the walls. The dressmaker was grumbling and pulling at the dress, sticking pins into the silk, grumbling some more. She had given the baby to one of the girls. Iacopo reported jubilantly from the window. The Signora ignored the dressmaker's questions and assented to the alterations without attending to them. They were her allies, those who were demonstrating below, but the simple woman who was assessing her work in the mirror was also right: her allies were the same who painted the hammer and sickle on the nose of the baroque angel and called for more and more factories, and a larger and ever larger port. All this, they thought, would belong to them one day, but the chimneys do not know whom they are smoking for.

The Signora was too tired to walk home; the vaporetto station in the Rialto was close by. The demonstration had dissolved, but in the streets you could still meet a few groups. On the Rialto bridge, some workers in gas masks were staring into the canal. A pair of lovers in a gondola looked up at them. Others tried to scare the foreigners on the terraces of the cafés near the vaporetto station, by bending over them and uttering animal noises. Still others had planted themselves in front of the main post office in the Fondaco dei Tedeschi and were chanting the *Internationale*. Through air tins they were hard to understand. The tie hawkers were haggling. A few gondolieri had borrowed gas masks—gas masks and straw hats.

In the vaporetto the Signora wondered if she had done right in writing once more to Laura. She had considered Mr. Wilcox her enemy, now the snout creatures of Marghera were also her enemies. And after her children had made common cause with the enemies of Venice, was there any sense in resisting . . . ?

16

She had wanted to go alone to the Mayor, but Dario insisted on accompanying her.

As he stood steering his motorboat, he admonished the Signora to act diplomatically. She should put the idea of asking for a loan out of her head, first, because the Mayor had already rejected it, and second, and more important, because without the consent of the other heirs to take a loan was as unlawful as the sale of the Titian. "By the way, Naville is still hanging about Venice," he said.

"I know. He came to see me again."

"And what did you tell him?"

"I put him off."

"Why only put him off?"

"I have written to Paolo. Claudia has agreed."

"Naville told me you had made promises."

"That is what I call putting off. Would I go to the Mayor if I were trying to sell the Titian?"

Who was lying, Naville or the Signora? Dario decided to keep careful eye on things. He said: "Certain funds have been reserved for the restoration of artistic monuments, and the Palazzo Santarato, for its situation alone, will have to be considered as such."

She was glad he had mentioned Naville only in passing. Mozetti had agreed to start on his work the following week, after finishing the El

Greco. The short delay was most opportune, for she had to go about her preparations so that Romolo would not notice. Also, she secretly hoped she could at the last minute dispense with the forger's services.

She took her reception in the palatial Mayory on the Canal Grande as a good omen. After she had presented herself at the door, an usher appeared instantly to take her upstairs, not a common usher but a black-and-white-liveried footman who could have played a dignified walk-on part in the *The Tales of Hoffmann*. The waiting room, completely decorated with red damask, also seemed auspicious. Dario, who was pacing the room while she sat in an uncomfortable high chair, called her attention to a memorial tablet which extolled the visit of his Royal Highness, the Duke Emanuele Filiberto di Savoia on May 4, 1918. "Great importance is attached to the continuity of history," Dario said, "except that they'd rather forget Mussolini's visit in 1937. The day before yesterday is never as dangerous as yesterday."

Her good mood vanished as the time passed. She had been summoned for half past ten, and although nobody else was waiting, the Mayor's door had still not opened at ten past eleven. Finally, at a quarter past eleven, a secretary appeared and showed her to the Mayor's office. To the Signora's indignation, the secretary did not leave after the introductions; instead, like a sort of mute assessor, he sat down next to his superior.

She guarded herself against the tendency of old people to consider all those under retirement age as young, but the Mayor did seem surprisingly young. He was probably in his forties, but looked younger. Of average height, and with an average face, in his black suit with the striped trousers, he could have been the director of a first-class undertaking establishment. Her immediate aversion increased when he returned to his desk instead of offering her a seat at the round table. As she sat down in front of him she felt like a delinquent. The Mayor was her judge, the secretary a juror, she and Dario the defendants.

"At the request of Signor Ortelli," the Mayor began, "I have examined all the documents; the council will shortly deal with the question of a building subsidy, but honesty will not permit me to raise your hopes, Signora. The saving of Venice, our most passionate desire, can, as I often say, be divided into three stages: urgent, more urgent and most urgent."

"Is it not most urgent to repair houses which are collapsing on the heads of their inhabitants?" Dario said.

"Of course, of course. But how many people are living in a block of apartments—and how many in a palazzo? Scarcely have we restored a palazzo to a proper condition, before the owners are asking a hundred thousand a month or more for a small apartment in it. In Mestre, they charge fifty thousand at most."

"Signora Santarato is not intending to take in tenants," said Dario.

"We must not tell the council that." The Mayor gave a smile of collusion. "One has to see things in the wider context. The press is reporting that there're three billion lire available, and a newspaperman of the *Corriere della Sera* has even alleged that part of this money has actually been stolen. I am taking him to court, because, I pointed out"—a complacent smile—"even a skilled thief such as I can only steal what is there, and the billions exist only on paper."

"And what about the three billion lire credit from UNESCO?"

"All I hear is three billion. The state alone will take ninety-three thousand million. You must know, *caro amico,* that out of the twenty-six articles contained in the *Lex Venetia,* only three have been approved unaltered by Parliament up to now, and not the essential ones, needless to say."

The Signora wondered why she had come. How long did she have to listen to the Mayor's laments? He was receiving a constituent, that was all.

"Distributing money is a rewarding task," said the Mayor. "That is why the state wants to take over. Anyway, I have to deal with seventeen communist city councillors."

"You have a majority," Dario said.

"In a democracy, I always say, the majority can only *sub*scribe to what the minority *pre*scribe for them. Did you know that there are five ministries concerned with saving Venice? There are also investigating commissions, research centers, laboratories, observatories, syndicates, international organizations and institutions. Over a hundred people are employed by the international *Commissione* for the Defense of Venice alone. In Voltobarazzo, a scale model of Venice is being built on an area of twelve thousand square meters to study the water fluctuations; the model is costing eight hundred million lire."

The Signora was silent. Models: how often had she read this word lately! Model—it seemed to be a synonym for castles in the air, and uncaring indolence, for evasion and procrastination, for self-satisfaction and ineffectiveness. The Mayor talked of millions, thousands of millions, even billions, and she had to give her savings to a forger! The Mayor was speaking to Dario only; he probably thought she would nod and thank him and return to her palazzo and die.

"After all," he said, "it is not as if we were watching the decay with folded hands. We support new building projects with mortgages for periods of twenty-five years."

"And historic Venice is decaying," said Dario.

"During the past four years we have spent hundreds of millions on restoration. We have restored ten thousand square feet of paintings, and thirty buildings. International solidarity is absolutely overwhelming. The British have restored the church of Madonna dell' Orto, the Germans Santa Maria dei Miracoli, the Americans the Palazzo Ca' d'Oro, and the French are working on the Salute."

"Restoring the Palazzo Santarato will cost only a trifle," said Dario.

"You cannot possibly compare it to the Santa Maria della Salute."

"The Palazzo Santarato is inhabited."

The Mayor turned to the juror, who was nodding all the time; sometimes he had nodded even before his superior began to speak.

"Yes, indeed, living people," said the Mayor. "I feel a responsibility for living people. I was not elected by Tintoretto, I always say." He leaned forward, the neutral eyes turned partisan. "Venice cannot live by tourism alone. Mestre and Marghera are to blame for everything, they say, but what would it be like without Mestre and Marghera? Venice would starve. Twelve thousand people commute between Venice and Marghera every day. Are they to go unemployed?"

"What do you call Venice?" Dario asked. "The number of commuters is barely one tenth of the population—twelve hundred. The others come from the mainland. Venice lived without Mestre and Marghera before."

"All of us were more modest. Something has to be done for the younger generation; of the seventy thousand Venetians who have left Venice during the past twenty years over seventy per cent have been under fifty-four. And is this nothing—the sports grounds in Marghera and Mestre and Cavallino, and the swimming pool in Luna Park, the gymnasiums in the Castello district and in the Guidecca? Not to mention the new prison at Santa Maria Maggiore." He smiled, and the juror smiled too.

"But of course," Dario said. "In the hall of frescoes at the Scuola

Grande della Misericordia I hear they're already playing basketball."

The Mayor preferred not to hear this. "You can't alter the fact that investors, mainly the foreign ones, see Venice as a port. And if you think about it, what are the objections to this? True, out of a turnover of twenty-four million tons, about thirteen are destined for oil in Marghera, but it doesn't have to go on like that. Crude oil can be unloaded at Trieste and pumped to Venice through a pipeline. But such projects call for economy, and if you want to save the whole city, you can't dissipate your energies over details. If we only meet foreign investors halfway, there's nothing to stop the building of a Munich-Venice motorway. An underground railway is being planned, a hundred-and-eighty-million-dollar agreement has just been signed with the Soviet Union, the Yugoslavs are quite well disposed to building a seventy-mile dam right across the Adriatic, from Umag to Chioggia. The idea of the Fondaco dei Tedeschi can be revived, there are two hundred thousand square yards available. If only we are sensible, *caro amico*"–he consistently ignored the old woman sitting in front of him, who had grown smaller and smaller–"Venice will experience unprecedented prosperity. But the absurd resistance to the Third Zone has to stop, it has been planned for over a decade, more than sixteen square miles have been drained, the wheel of history cannot be turned back. Venice has to become a new city–with the old heart, of course, but we cannot resist progress."

The Signora clapped her hands.

The obviously ironical applause came so unexpectedly, it was so clearly heard in the quiet room, that the Mayor and Dario both looked up aghast; the juror half rose from his chair.

The panic she had caused amused the Signora. She clapped her hands some more, perfectly aware of the fact that she invited comparison to the animated stuffed toy animals her friend Gianfranco peddled in the restaurants–the ones which struck their cymbals together when wound up.

"Bravo!" she said, after the clapping had died away, as if the mechanism had run down. "Bravo, Mayor, that was a splendid election speech. But the elections are still a long way off, and now you will listen to me."

She did not look at Dario, because she knew he would try to stop her having her say. He, the Mayor of Venice, she said, had been talking like one of those foreign speculators who are invading Venice like a swarm of locusts and are causing the ruin of the city. She ignored his interjection—"London is sinking faster"—and continued: "They are poisoners, that's all. You wail because you are short of a few billion, but instead of using the money there is for Venice, you make deals with the assassins of Venice. What do we need the Third Zone for? Or do you also intend to direct the giant tankers through pipelines to Venice? You are not fighting the plague, you are bringing it to Venice."

The Mayor was trying to contain himself. He leaned back, and the juror leaned back too.

"I fear, Signora," he said, "that you have been the victim of propaganda. We are told that industry discharges fifteen thousand tons of sulfuric oxide a year over Venice. Perhaps. But you know as well as I do that the winds are practically always from the sea, not from the land. 'Who cares about Padua?' my colleague from Padua recently asked, and I could not argue. Believe me, nobody takes a greater interest than I do in the matter of pollution of the environment." He turned to Dario, hoping for more appreciation there. "In the Grand Council pollution of the environment was first mentioned in 1889, exactly five years after the so-called sanitary facilities were introduced." Then, to the Signora: "If you will excuse my asking, do you want to punish everyone who flushes his toilet? Come to that, only sixty per cent of our houses have sanitary installations, seventeen thousand apartments are without a bath, fifteen hundred without a lavatory, in sixty per cent the kitchen stove is the only source of heating, thirty per cent of the apartments are uninhabitable. It's a disgrace to civilization, but nobody ever mentions it. I admit it may be in better taste to speak of the horses on St. Mark's Church. I always say, people think that civilization is something which consists exclusively of stone and marble and canvas and bronze. We have to realize that Venice is a city like any other city."

The Signora had only paused for breath. She went on now: "If you believe that Venice is a city like any other, you are not a Venetian and ought to be mayor of Padua. How often during the past few years did you take a ride through Venice? Or a walk? My eyes are too tired to read your statistics, but they are still better than yours: you don't even see the houses. You listen to your industrialists, and I listen to my charwoman. Do you know what people call the houses? Gorgonzola they call them, green cheese. Your motorway! Will the foreigners come to Venice to see oil storage tanks and chimneys? Your younger generation! Who is to blame for the fact that Venice aged by a hundred years one single day in November six years ago? Your optimism! I have seen a lot of misery in my life, and most of it was caused by optimists. Don't take me for a bigger fool than I am! One more canal and one more special area and another skyscraper, and yet another zone! What do you care if Venice dies out? The most it will mean for you is people moving to Marghera and Mestre—and they'll still be your voters. Marghera and Mestre and Favoro and Veneto and Chirignano and Zelerino are the masters of Venice. The corpse does not elect a mayor. When are you going to sell the Canal Grande to the highest bidder?"

"Signora!" said Dario.

The Signora rose.

Dario wanted to support her, but she would not have it. She felt neither old nor frail. She had forgotten why she had come. She had forgotten the Titian and Mozetti and the palazzo. Through the tall windows she could see the Canal Grande.

"If the Venetians were like you," she said, a little less vehemently, "you would be right. But we survived our doges as well."

The Mayor, who had risen simultaneously with his juror, tried to say something. She did not listen. She crossed the anteroom, where the waiting people eyed her with curiosity.

"Now I have spoiled everything," she said sheepishly when the motorboat started.

Dario tried to steer his boat very carefully between two gondolas so that it would not touch either of them.

"In my youth," he said, "I read a Danish or a Norwegian detective story, I don't remember which, but I know it was called *The Iron Carriage*. In that book the police chief is after a murderer. And the reader does not realize until the very end that he is the murderer himself. *The Iron Carriage* ought to be compulsory reading for our Venetians."

"Then you are not angry with me?" said the Signora.

"We are going to Martini's for lunch," said Dario.

17

All this is not new. It has been going on for nearly four hundred years.

In the sixteenth century there was a man called Alvise Cornaro. He was no relative of the Caterina Cornaro, the Queen of Cyprus, who is worshipped in Venice to this day because in 1489 she bequeathed the whole of Cyprus to her city and established a Muses' Court in Venice. On these premises, by the way, there now stands a pawnshop.

Alvise Cornaro, though not of royal blood, was a powerful man, immensely rich and lord of lands reaching far into the plains. Like most rich people, he was not satisfied with the property he could proudly enough call his own. Since Venice was his home, he wanted to change it.

In the area where Marghera is spreading now, and in Mestre with its rows of oil storage tanks and blocks of buildings staring out in cowardly similarity, there were green gardens and lush cornfields and fragrant fruit trees as far as the eye could see. But on the seashore Alvise Cornaro's realm ended, or rather his possessions did not reach the sea, for between them and the sea was the city, the *Serenissima,* imposing a check on the greedy waters, but also on the lustful land.

Cornaro did not like this. The lagoons had grown into the reeds, the salty water was seeping bit by bit into the thirsty city; and the *bareni,* mounds of swamp and sand, were sticking out their dirty noses more and more brazenly from the deep. When Cornaro rode through the Canal Grande in his sumptuous gondola and looked out of the *felza,* its protective cage, he realized how superfluous his city was. So much unused land, beautiful only for the tired eye, a monument of the past! If it were possible, he thought, to drain the lagoon, which was drying up anyway, the land would spread all the way to Rovigo, full of waving stalks down to the waves of the sea, a granary for the whole of Venetia.

Who could deny that this Croesus of Venice thought not merely of profit, but also in humanitarian or social terms, as it is called today? For many Venetians were living in poverty, out of work, the miserable servants of beauty; so Cornaro, the philanthropist, would offer them work: they would plant and sow and plow and reap and milk their cows on the Canal Grande and offer the products of their labor for sale in the Piazza San Marco. "Let us resign ourselves to the inevitable," was his motto; that is, to Venice being inevitably lost.

Men like to find something they can be resigned to. The poor, in particular, are accustomed to this, and among the poor Cornaro gained a good hearing. Many had found work with him and were not sorry, but the daily journey to the fields and back was tiring. Now, it was said, the fields would come to those who tilled them. The authorities were also tempted by Cornaro's promises, for it is a thankless task to stand watch over beauty. There had also been difficulties with the collection of taxes, and many inhabitants of the city had even fled. Authorities, too, love to accept the inevitable.

Who knows, perhaps everything might have come to pass as Cornaro had planned, had it not been for a man by the name of Cristoforo Sabbadino who lived in Chioggia, at the southern tip of the lagoon, a sailor and a fisherman and a poet by trade.

This Sabbadino had nothing but his conviction and his love for Venice. He did not even have sound arguments; love seldom does. It is no good just saying you want to preserve something. This sounds narrow-minded and anti-progressive: tried and trusty suggests old and rusty, whereas untried suggests unboundedly promising. Besides, nobody believes that in conquering new land he will lose the land he has.

Just as Cornaro repeated over and over again that you had to live with the inevitable, Sabbadino repeated with equal persistence that things are only inevitable if faint-hearts think they are. He went about and preached outside the palaces, churches, convents and hospitals. The rich did not listen to him, for they were already surveying their land; they would ensure that Cornaro could not cheat them. The poor listened to him, but they did not understand, for he talked only in praise of stones, and did not promise them bread.

Sabbadino revered Petrarch, and like him believed in the *miraculosissima civitas Venetia*. But Sabbadino's sonnets were not so melodious that the city presented him with a palazzo on the Riva degli Schiavoni, as they had done for Petrarch. At any rate he distributed his sonnets on the bridges, and one of them contained these lines:

Great were thy walls, O Venice, as thou knowest.
Behold, alas, their parlous present state.
Unless a check be put on danger soon,
Without walls wilt thou stand and desolate. . . .
Then chase the rivers, curb the evil greed
Of men. And let the sea alone remain.
Yet thou wert always by the sea obeyed.
So do not close thine ears to thine own good
When I this message to thee loud proclaim:
In water Heaven gave thee immortal life.

People read the sonnets, but they said that poems had never avoided the *sussidenza* nor built *murazzi*. Sabbadino saw this, for he was not only a poet, he was also a sailor and a fisherman, and he did not like to use big words for the words' sake. So he joined forces with experts, with engineers and master builders and architects, but in an eccentric way: he expressed his plans in sonnets. The engineers and master builders and architects translated them into figures and drawings.

In the meantime Sabbadino continued to stir up the people. How many cows, he asked, could go to pasture on the Canal Grande, and would they belong to the people? The water, he said, would certainly make the fields fertile, but it would also flood them, and, without the *Serenissima* standing between them and the sea, would flood them far inland, so they were cutting off their noses to spite their faces. But even the rich were listening now; they gradually realized that they would not gain anything if Venice was turned into a village, like all other villages, no queen, merely a maid.

And so the Honorable Senate had no choice but to oppose the inevitable. To the north and to the south large dams were built; the threatening rivers retreated, the Piave and the Sila and the Brenta; ebb and flood asserted their rights, flushed into the city the breathing water, and out of the city the suffocating mire. Defeated, Cornaro withdrew to his estates.

History frequently offers us a play on words. For instance, in the very church of Campo Sant' Alvise—Cornaro's Christian name, you remember—a Dominican said in his Sunday sermon that it was no accident the sailor and fisherman and poet Sabbadino had been given his name Cristoforo; it was after the saint, a giant, who had carried Christ as a child through the torrent.

Agriculture and cattle breeding had been Cornaro's desire, just as oil towers and factory chimneys are the desire of his sons today, and the farmers and cattle breeders had acclaimed him, just as today's workers and craftsmen are making common cause with his sons.

And then Sabbadino came and distributed his sonnets on the bridges.

Looking out over Marghera and Mestre, those who have their eyes open may see the colossal shape of Alvise Cornaro in the poisonous fog. Where is Cristoforo Sabbadino who carries the drowning city across the torrent . . . ?

18

Paolo had not been serious when he told his mother that he and Teresa would be visiting her this summer. For thirty years, since the time he had met Teresa Andreoli on the Excelsior beach, he had done all he could to prevent encounters between the two women.

Anybody can lightly be called superficial. A person's way of life determines the opinion we hold of him, although many will share that way of life, and the reasons for their living like this and in no other way may be quite different. Also, some wear their way of life like camouflage or a carnival costume: for their own protection, for fun or to deceive others. Paolo *was* superficial, but primarily for comfort's sake. To be perceptive is uncomfortable, to be receptive is easy. It was easy and comfortable to accept that the two women had been mutually jealous from the beginning. The Venetian aristocrat and the daughter of a self-made man from Milan could never have understood each other. Paolo had been duly receptive of these and similar explanations.

In reality Teresa Andreoli-Santarato had never ceased to hold the Signora responsible for Paolo's every adventure. That was Teresa's own comfort. She could not understand that somebody should be wholly without ambition, should not want to prove or achieve or hold on to anything. But the Signora had brought up Paolo completely as an heir—and without an inheritance at that, as Teresa sometimes added bitterly—so there was nothing left for him but to prove himself in bed. Not in the marital bed, of course, since that is least suitable for proving unusual ability. To the Signora, on the other hand, Teresa was like the swimming teachers who believe you can teach children to swim by throwing them into the water: sink or swim. The Signora felt that nonswimmers might be loved too.

Paolo was almost indifferent to the enmity between his wife and his mother, for since his youth the only women he had known had been at war over him. He had not married Teresa Andreoli because of her money; that would have been a successful speculation, and speculation was as alien to his nature as success. In the early days he had loved her, though admittedly in the same way as he loved many others; she wanted to marry him, so he got married to her. The marriage happened to him, as everything happened to him, without his wanting or resisting it. That went for his love affairs too. He neither wanted nor resisted them—all his life he had been floating peacefully between two women, between his mother and Teresa, or Teresa and his current mistress.

Tonight as well, at one of those parties where people who see each other regularly greet each other rapturously at first, but have nothing to say to each other for the rest of the evening, it was the same. For a year he had been having relations with a young widow, which had begun most comfortably before Eleanora's husband was killed in a car crash. That this attractive woman should move in the same circles as he and Teresa did was nothing unusual for Paolo: if you can pick the fruit in your garden, you don't need to go and look for it in the wood. It was inconvenient, however, that Eleanora believed his lies and half-truths, that he had long been indifferent to his wife, and had not slept with her for years. That was one of the lies, since not to sleep with Teresa would have been most inconvenient for him. It is annoying that mistresses should take such courtesies at their face value. Why should Eleanora walk out of a party offended, just because he had spent more time with his wife than is proper for an adulterer?

The inconvenience, familiar enough, would not have bothered Paolo, but he was upset to find he had started to worry about it. And this had happened at the very time that Richard R. Wilcox, whom he had to learn to call Dick, had started to root up his comfortable existence.

He did not feel guilty of having defrauded the buyer. Teresa had married a "Venetian David"—occasionally she still called him that after the Michelangelo figure—a David pre-eminent in the suits, silk scarves, and shoes he wore, a Santarato of a Venetian aristocratic family, a man without interests, a lover who, regardless of his moods, did know how to make love. It was unfortunate that she was so unlike the child in Andersen's fairy tale who in his innocence pointed out the nakedness of the emperor; that she, on the contrary, saw him in the purple no one else detected. It was true enough that he never succeeded in anything, but then, would he ever have tried at all without her? In society, which mattered so very much to Teresa, fashionable cravats were sufficient, nobody bothered about purple. Old Andreoli, too, had always taken him as he was, had even shown the winking comprehension of a man who never has time for such things himself. Was it Paolo's fault that the lonely tycoon had no sympathy with business losses? Teresa had often told him that her father used to remark to her even when she was a girl: "You lose on horses, not business deals." Paolo used to feel sorry for people with ambition rather than envying them, but since his temples had started to turn gray, he felt sorry for himself, since it is bad enough to be driven by your own ambition, but far worse to be driven by someone else's.

And now this American, the first person to see him in purple as Teresa did! The wretched man seemed determined to entrust him with the management of the Venetian branch office, even making him a partner in Progress Oil. Andreoli would not contribute a penny; his money went on horses, not oil. Teresa certainly wouldn't want to ask her father for it. She'd rather sell the palazzo, her investments, millions of profit, and all that merely so that she could someday go to the old man and say: I told you so!

On the way home from the party—it was nearly midnight—Paolo realized that Teresa's tolerant silence was also related to the "project," as she kept on calling it. Remus was to drive to Venice in the next few days, and Teresa had certain plans in connection with his trip. She wanted to talk to her son about them tonight; this was the only reason Paolo could think of why she was not making the usual scene.

"We'll wait for Remus," Teresa said, as she sat down in the drawing room.

She did not make herself comfortable; she was not that sort of

person. There she sat, as she had at the party, playing with her long
pearl necklace, fifty-two years old, and still a beautiful woman, more
beautiful than a decade ago. At that time she had stopped looking slim
and suddenly looked merely thin. Now she had caught up with time
and was looking more and more like the *contessa* and *principessa* of her
aspirations.

Remus had some influence on the Signora, Teresa continued; he
would have to make it clear to her that she had no alternative to
consenting to the sale of the palazzo.

"Nobody has any influence on my mother," Paolo said, "least of all
where the palazzo is concerned. And what makes you think you can
persuade Remus?"

"First, because I want to," Teresa said, "second, because he hates the
palazzo, and finally, because I'm going to bribe him. One has to exploit
his strange ambivalence over money. On the one hand he despises it;
but he doesn't despise the help my father can offer him for his film."
Paolo objected that her father had refused a dozen times, but she
dismissed this with an impatient gesture. "Anyhow, if she refuses, she
will simply have to be declared incapable of managing her affairs. Then
the court will of course appoint an official to make all decisions for
her."

He did not protest, although the thought was abhorrent to him.
Teresa had often told him what a bad mother the Signora had been. He
wondered whether she thought herself a good mother. Remus
resembles me, he thought, as a caricature does the original. He wants to
change the world all right, but he's not willing to change himself. He
never finishes anything and blames others, but he rebels against failure.
At times he does what I'd have liked to do, but it ends as if he'd never
started on it. His features are sharper than mine, or perhaps they aren't
really, it's a matter of the caricaturist's pencil. Teresa hasn't thought of
using Romolo, though he would be in a much better position to talk
to Mother in spite of his age. He doesn't resemble me or Teresa, he's
grown up beside us like an adopted child who has had his real parents'
identity kept from him and behaves as if he didn't know, but both he
and the parents do know. Teresa sometimes says she's proud of him,
but she might be just as proud of her father's thoroughbreds. Is my
mother a bad mother? Everyone has his own palazzo, Paolo decided,
and Teresa has several of them: clothes and jewelry and high society.
Perhaps I myself am one of her palazzi.

But he did not say anything of this, for he also had his palazzo. He was as little inclined to give up his comforts as his mother was to give up the house on the Canal Grande.

The night was unusually warm for the middle of June. The door stood open, and Paolo went out onto the terrace. The villa lay outside the city, but the smog, which covers Milan all day like a plastic bag, had not lifted. Even the small forest which started right at the fence seemed soaked by the sweat of the factories, the scent of pinewood and the stink of gasoline.

Paolo had not seen his mother for a year; now he was longing for her. Perhaps I ought to drive to Venice myself, he thought. She'll say no to my proposals and not demand anything of me. I'll tell her: keep the palazzo, and I won't go into the oil business.

"Remus is here," he said. A cone of light had shown above the garage.

He came back into the drawing room, and since they had been talking about the palazzo, he realized what a long way he had come from the house where he had grown up. The drawing room was decorated completely in white, white walls, white wall-to-wall carpeting, white covers on the furniture. Only the abstracts with their gaudy color compositions—mostly paintings he had bought from Claudia—differentiated it from a giant bottle of iced milk.

"Are you still up?" Remus asked.

"I have to talk to you," Teresa said. "Let's hope you haven't drunk too much."

Remus slumped into a low easy chair and stretched his long legs in their blue jeans.

"I don't drink any more. It doesn't agree with pot."

"Are you taking pot?" Paolo asked.

"No," said Remus, without giving any explanation for the inconsistency.

"Are you going to Venice?" Paolo asked, hoping Remus would say he wasn't.

"Yes, but not till the end of next week. We're looking for test shot sites. Location shots."

"Will you stay at your grandmother's?" Teresa asked.

"It's cheaper."

Teresa came out with what she wanted. Mr. Wilcox wished to buy the palazzo, with furniture, carpets, paintings and china. He was offering Paolo an executive position, but it was more than that. "It's a unique chance for your father to go into partnership in the oil business with his own capital."

"Where do I come in?" Remus said.

"You need money for your film."

"So what?"

"When the palazzo is sold, we can talk about it. You must try to make it clear to your grandmother that it's impossible to live in that ruin, which is what you really think anyway. Say repairs must be a bottomless pit. And that she won't get a penny from us. It's a matter of appealing to her conscience, too. She can't stand in the way of your father's success forever."

She honestly meant it. The fascination young Santarato had exercised over her was still the same as in that summer on the Lido. She had not given any other man even an encouraging glance. For thirty years she had believed that Paolo was suffering terribly from being merely the husband of the Andreoli heiress. He had never had the chance of starting on his own, and that was the crime of the old lady who kept his inheritance from him, stubborn, wicked, selfish. If Dario Ortelli, the Signora's counselor, suspected Teresa of opposing the sale of particular pieces, then the crafty broker was right and yet wrong—with his share of the Titian Paolo would at most buy some new girlfriends. With the huge fortune itself he could buy the freedom to be himself.

"How much longer is she likely to live?" Remus asked, pouring himself a glass of whisky.

"Until we're as old as she is today," said Teresa. "Also, on behalf of your father and myself, you can promise her a peaceful old age—the sale will make her a rich woman. She'd have to be mad not to understand that. If she refuses to see sense, we have no choice but to get her declared feebleminded by a court, who will appoint someone to manage her affairs. We've just been talking about it, as a matter of fact."

Remus looked at his father. Paolo got up and went out on to the terrace.

"Am I supposed to tell her that?"

"You should simply imply it," Teresa said.

"A charming commission. Don't you dare do it yourselves?"

"It's to your advantage."

Remus felt sickened by the woman in the ruby evening gown playing with her pearls all the time. He felt sickened by his father, who had taken refuge on the terrace. He felt sickened by the old lady in whose moldering house he was going to live. His father deceived his mother, his mother wanted to deceive his grandmother, who deceived both of them. His parents wanted to sell a palazzo, to purchase a position for selling oil. Purchase, sale, purchase, sale. That was their whole life, and if you did not understand that, you were declared feebleminded. But the old woman was feebleminded, of course, and if her affairs were put under some court official—which merely meant that she couldn't buy or sell anything—then that was all right, within the rules of the game. The only thing more sickening than the haggling about the palazzo was the palazzo itself, that decayed theater in which ghosts played various parts so that the spectators in the gondolas, which in turn were coffins rowed by galley slaves, had something to admire. Now his mother was promising him money for the film she had never asked about, and she wouldn't care if she and his father and his grandmother and their whole sickening society game were going to be unmasked in his film. The point was that the film could be sold, for anything that could be sold was valuable, the film or the palazzo. They would try to cheat him in the process; why not after all, they were mutually cheating each other. All that mattered was to cheat them before they cheated you.

"I shall be busy on location," he said, determined to push up the price, since that was the law, you had to push up the price, for the film, for the oil, for the palazzo, or if you had nothing else to sell, for yourself.

Paolo did not hear the rest of the conversation, since he had moved away from the door. He stood at the balustrade of the terrace and filled his lungs with the scent of pinewood, and the stink of gasoline.

It was not till they had gone upstairs and he was cleaning his teeth in the bathroom that he heard Teresa's voice from the bedroom. "I think everything is all right, we're on the right road." He gargled noisily and pretended he had not heard.

19

The rain fell for two days.

Professor Ceribelli had gone the night before to the house where the marigraph was installed which indicates the imminence of a flood. Now the earth "was corrupt; for all flesh had corrupted his way upon the earth." But God no longer speaks to Noah, saying, "I have determined to make an end of all flesh." He leaves such announcements to the instruments which indicate the Flood.

Professor Ceribelli was a volunteer. This is what you call people who do what everyone ought to be doing. Whenever the *acqua alta* threatens to rise, a haggard old man, looking like a cab horse in the era of motorcars, can be seen hurrying across St. Mark's Square, a shabby fiber suitcase in his hand, like the cases carried by immigrant workers. He will spend the following nights–he cannot tell how many–at the marigraph. He will never sleep more than an hour without interruption, hardly closing his eyes, so to speak; he will read Tacitus and make coffee; the stove is in this case, along with underwear, blankets, rubber boots and books. Venetian, geologist and historian, retired academic, former deep-sea diver, Professor Ceribelli is something like Venice's last lighthouse keeper, an eccentric, of course, and–come to think of it–a descendant of the philosopher Paolo Sarpi who considered all air detrimental, slept on his bookshelves and taught Galileo how to build a telescope. When the professor puts his hand on a push button, the sirens wail.

The Signora had been waiting for the sirens' alert throughout the first night. For the second time this week Romolo had asked her to let him visit some friends at the Excelsior. With some hesitation she had agreed; but when the rain had started, he stayed. "Go to bed, don't worry," he told her. "I'll go downstairs and check every hour."

The sirens did not sound the alert, because Professor Ceribelli had instructions not to sound it unless extreme danger was imminent, and the extreme danger depended on the tourist season: who was to chase the visiting population from their beds and out of the city in the months of the tourist season? In earlier days his "ancestor" Sarpi had written: "I never lie, but I don't tell everybody the truth"; and even in the times of the Great Plague, in the sixteenth and seventeenth centuries, the habit of not telling everybody the truth had persisted until on one occasion seventy thousand and on another nearly a hundred thousand Venetians had been cut down by the Black Death.

The next morning Venice was flooded.

The doges used to be wedded to the sea, now the sea was wedded to their palace. Wedding means a joining together, and the sea was joined with the land. Slowly it ascended the stairs, as you ascend the steps to the altar. But this was not the only wedding, this marriage of land and water, there was an incestuous relationship too, like the one Lord Byron, the melancholy bard of Venice, had maintained with his half-sister Augusta: the waters of the earth and the waters of the heavens were joined together, the flood and the rain.

From the direction of the Lido the brown waves surged, in soiled armor they stormed the city. The seagulls sitting on the poles—which mark the way for the ships—fled across the sea. They flew high. The waves ground up the sandbanks, the *bareni*, and carried off toward the city what had accumulated on them during sunny days: boards, refuse, crates, broken prams, discarded dolls, torn dresses, snapped oars. Briefly they broke on the island of San Giorgio Maggiore; the dark training vessel lying in the ducal *bacino* was attacked from the sea side; white sails were lowered to the water, like the flag of the vanquished before the enemy.

Then the floods swept over the pier and hurled themselves against the pillars of the Palazzo Ducale. They locked their teeth in the heels of the columns, jumped up at them, tore at their clothing. All the shops in the Piazza San Marco were closed; within an hour the iron sliding shutters had come rattling down in front of the shop windows, one big rumble, a brief close-range action under the arcades. Courageous helpers had erected the narrow bridges of boards on their platforms, but the gangplanks had already sunk beneath the surface, and their timbers floated away. If the frightened tourists behind the windows of their hotel rooms had known more about Venice, they would have realized that the golden clouds of Venetian baroque are like the raging foam which was dashing up the pillars and shop windows of the colonnades. The more hard-pressed the sea, the greater its wrath.

The gondolieri had not waited for the howl of sirens, the whisper of instinct was enough. The poles where they tied their boats had become unsafe, a forest of defoliated trees shaken by the wind. Across the Piazzetta, past the Ducal Palace and toward St. Mark's Church, the gondolieri were rowing, still careful not to obstruct each other. They fastened the gondolas to the four-armed lanterns with their roots in stone, like cowboys tethering their horses outside the saloons; only *they* could not walk inside for a drink, the gondolas would have gone wild and torn loose.

The Signora had experienced this so often that she saw the city before her, and what her eyes could not see was blown to her by the wind. Initially, she heard the rumbling sea only from afar, but the wind had preceded the waves, it whistled through the canal, the windowpanes rattled, the beams were creaking. The winged Fortuna on the golden globe of the Maritime Customs office, which looks more like Mercury, god of the merchants and the thieves, than the goddess of fortune, was rotating frantically. Police boats with policemen in summery white were driving back and forth; once in a while a red fireboat appeared, called up by the rage of one element, failing before the other.

Without warning, not content with their conquest of the Ducal Palace, the Piazzetta, the Riva degli Schiavoni, and St. Mark's Square, the waves invaded the side canals. The lions of the Palazzo dei Leoni had quenched their thirst at the feet of the columns; now their nostrils, their eyes disappeared; at last their manes were engulfed. Red-white, blue-white, violet-white poles fell, like drunken sailors going overboard. On the Fondamenta dell'Osmarin the water whisked away a street painter's easel; red, blue and green dissolved into brown. Some fruit vendors and fishmongers had not saved their wares in the market early enough. Eggs toppled into the water, oranges sank, only the dead fish felt back in their element. The Church of San Lorenzo echoed the waves' maniacal laughter at catching a painting here just as it was being saved, and tearing it from its hiding place. In the court of the Palazzo degli Orfei they met with unexpected resistance: after the last flood the garden was wildly overgrown, bushes and thistle hedges and fallen trees blocked their path.

Onward to the Canal Grande! Here they stood, the proud palaces, the Palazzo Balbi and the Palazzo Contarini del Zaffo and the Palazzo Loredan, all mere pretense, for they were built on the tops of a subterranean forest, and now the forest started to move, Macbeth's marching Birnam wood. The water hammered against the iron gates, it tore the boards from the joints of the windows, it shook the gratings, a prison riot from outside.

The sky aided the riot. The floods had not yet reached the Merceria, but the rain had submerged it; water dripped over the tiara and the mutilated nose of St. Alvise di Agostino, it poured from the flower-decked balcony of the house where Goldoni was born, it turned the smiling chapiters of the Ducal Palace into weeping grimaces and Noah's beard into the limp clusters of a forgotten vineyard.

As the second evening approached, only black shadows slipped across St. Mark's Square. The street lamps no longer spread their pink light; the water was standing so high that the circles of light, pushed up from the ground toward the lamps, formed large yellow blots, and were soon swept out to merge with the others, like spreading leprosy.

The Signora did not leave the window. One solitary gondola—where did it come from, where was it going?—struggled against waves and wind. The Signora pricked up her ears because she had heard a woman singing. Was it an illusion? Who would want to sing now? Now and then she went to the kitchen where the water dripped from the walls. The grocer with a shop around the corner had fought his way through the narrow alleys and brought a basket full of groceries.

Romolo came down every hour by the hen roost—as Dario called it— to the entrance hall. He had put on the boots the Signora had bought him two years ago; they were too small now, but he didn't tell her.

The water had forced its way in from two sides; through the door of the side canal it had washed in bottles and boards. "We have a complete wine cellar," said Romolo. "We can collect the bottles and sell them." First the lowest step of the stairs disappeared, then the second and the third. "We stop at number four," Romolo reported. The Signora listened for the sound of the sirens wailing as they had done that time six years ago; but that was in November, of course. The Venetians had been among themselves.

Then Romolo returned breathless. "Carlo is here," he said. "He couldn't fasten his gondola, but he shouted to me that you should not get upset, he'll help us to bail out the water, and the rain will stop by this evening if not before. He said something about Dario. Dario will come too. You'll see, everything's all right."

In the evening of the second day the rain ceased. The Signora still heard the roar of the waves all night long, but her trained ear could clearly distinguish the attack from the withdrawal. This was the rumbling of an army about to withdraw.

Next morning the clouds fell apart, as if the second sky showing above them had been wearing rags just for fun. A pale blue tinged the Guidecca, a sun ray was caught in the mosaic of the Palazzo Dario, the goddess of fortune stood quiet and firm.

Romolo rushed out, but returned after an hour and a half to report to the Signora. People were wading over St. Mark's Square up to their knees, the boys barefoot, gaily swinging their shoes in their hands. Chairs had been put up outside the cafés Quadri and Florian and Levana, some foreigners were sitting there taking foot baths, the band was getting ready for the evening. The photographers were doing a roaring trade—"greetings from the flood"—The souvenir shops were open, across the planks the tourists were hurrying from one shop to the next. The umbrella peddlers—"*Ombrelli! Ombrelli!*"—packed up their wares. Only the wet pigeons still sat under the sheltering roofs, and soon they too would flutter over the Piazza once more, Noah's dirty messengers. "Imagine," Romolo said, "a German who had hired a gondola to have his picture taken in a gondola in St. Mark's Square had to be towed away"—what fun it all was!

Toward noon Dario and Carlo arrived. They went out onto the balcony. Above Marghera the sky was the color of a rusty blue church dome.

"Has anything happened in Marghera?" asked the Signora.

"Marghera is invulnerable," said Dario.

20

Every time Mozetti came, the Signora had to ask him to take the Titian to the upper floor. She had furnished one of the three small rooms up there so that the counterfeiter could feel he was in a studio.

On his first visit, Mozetti had turned up with a heavy suitcase which contained, in addition to his implements, numerous garments. It took him a good half hour to complete his disguise. For his work he wore a dark brown gown reaching to the floor, with a white collar and a thin, two-strand gold chain–he had also charged her for that–plus a black cap which left the forehead free and covered the neck, like Titian in his famous self-portrait of 1565 admired by visitors to the Prado.

The Signora could offer nothing but appreciation to her accomplice. Once he had finally started to paint, he called every morning to inquire if "the coast was clear"–it amused the Signora that a man of obvious breeding should like using expressions he must have picked up in prison. "We've pulled off a good job again," he used to say after work, or, alluding to the swindle: "Take care nobody gets a line on us" or, alluding to the buyer of whose existence he was convinced: "If that sucker notices anything, my name's Titian." Yet he was constantly complaining of "psychological inhibitions"–"Why on earth should you have a Titian of all things? I can't stand the man, he was a time-server, look at the clerical ass-kissing in his unfinished portrait of Paul the Third, and anyhow it's perfectly clear that the Venus of Urbino is masturbating. I'm wearing this old man's costume. Titian only became a real artist in his old age, probably because he had enough money at last. Except for the *Crowning with Thorns* I don't approve of anything."

It was obvious that Mozetti's liking for the Signora increased progressively each time. When Romolo was on the Lido, she had little to do; she asked the painter if she might watch him at work, promising to be "quiet as a mouse." The first time he gruffly refused her suggestion, the second time he shrugged his shoulders, the third time he invited her to have a glass of beer with him; he invariably carried a whole briefcase full of beer bottles with him. From then on she sat behind him most of the time or came and went on tiptoe. More and more she admired the copy and its resemblance to the original; which was all the more astounding because Mozetti hardly ever seemed to glance at the flower girl. He painted with amazing speed, but could spend several hours mixing a single color. "I'm not a painter at all, you know, I am a chemist," he said, and by this he meant Titian. But since she did indeed keep as quiet as she had promised, he soon called her "Mousie," and this too the Signora found delightful.

"Mousie," he said one day, while placing a rose with such perfect assurance into the flower basket that she feared the Mozetti might actually surpass the Titian—"Mousie, you are a terrible little cheat. You will sell the painting as genuine, and we shall both land in jail, which wouldn't be all that bad if we could continue our conversations there, but you will be put into the women's prison in the Fondamenta delle Convertite, and then you'll have to deal with those toffee-nosed nuns. Still, I don't care about that. What bothers me is the fact that you're cheating *me* too. You're paying me a pittance and getting rich on my art. You've probably never heard of honor among thieves."

Why did she not tell Mozetti the truth? Whenever she saw Dario she was tempted to initiate *him*, and but for the fact that she wanted to spare Romolo she would have confided in her grandson long ago. Truth was a heavy burden. If you carried it all alone, you were in danger of breaking down under its load; but lies were even harder to carry all by yourself. She had never felt lonely in her long widowhood, and when Laura or Claudia complained about their loneliness, as they had sometimes done in the past, she had pitied without understanding them. Now that she could not tell anyone the truth, could not let anyone in on her lies, she understood loneliness. What did she have to hide? Selling the palazzo would have made her a rich woman, the palazzo meant trouble and worry and daily toil. The kitchen could only be used sporadically, Emilia's hourly rate had increased by leaps and bounds, whereas her own pension was losing its purchasing power day after day, and in most shops she was several months in arrears with her bills. She had no love of possessions, perhaps not even the possession of these wet walls. Carlo, the old gondoliere, had once said to her: "If men do not save Venice, what will they ever save?" She didn't know much about the history of mankind; there must have been destructions in a good cause, for a good end. But this was not a good end. Everything was turned upside down; what had been on top was now at the bottom. Some pretended to be helping the poor, and grew richer on the help they gave them. The State was the name of the new lord walking in rags and yet looking like yesterday's lord clad in brocade; the brittle past was being sacrificed, but the future had no foundations; the sleeping watchman was chased away, but the new one destroyed what he was supposed to watch over; the palazzi fell and the huts remained, and they were no better huts in spite of being piled up twenty stories high and although hundreds lived in them. Shouldn't she be proud of her swindle?

Mozetti was talking more and more about himself. Before he slipped into the velvet gown or after having neatly stored it—"I take the key for safety's sake"—he talked like Mozetti, not like Titian. He told her about his father, who had been a carpenter and painter—"there were nine of us children; one day he sawed off two fingers from his hand, probably he'd been thinking of his paintings." He spoke of his eldest brother who had become a priest—"now he's preaching the Kingdom of Heaven on earth to the poor in South America because the business above the clouds has gone broke." He mentioned the only woman he had loved and who had left him when he was in prison—"she couldn't wait." Another time he said: "You know, Mousie, that I am greater than Titian, and the judge asked me why in that case I had gone in for faking. I did not answer him, but I will tell you: faking is what I want to do, that's the whole purpose. You have to fake yourself out of the present, for the whole present is a fake." He was always speaking of his art. "It is not true that there is always something new, someday there simply can't be anything new, and that is where we stand now. The new just pretends to be new, that's why it's a fake. El Greco was new, but he didn't intend to be, and if I paint an El Greco, I paint something new. But Miró is a fake, he's faking Miró—but you won't understand that, of course. They want to tear down the ghetto now and build new houses, and in a few centuries, so they say, the Campo Novissimo Ghetto will be admired as the Campo Nuovo Ghetto is admired today. But that's a fake too, for what is being built now has decayed before the roof is on. The imitators are the world's boon. Rembrandt was an imitator of Lastman and Caravaggio, Tiepolo copied Veronese, and Botticelli returned from Florentine realism to Gothic. All originality is a return, but nobody says so. Not even God can recreate the world, although it is high time he did."

On the sixth day, when he reproached her once more with cheating him over his fake, she said: "I have had enough of your silly remarks," and she told him the truth.

At first he stroked his beard pensively, then he scratched his bald head with relish, and finally he slapped his thighs, laughed in a deep bass, showed his yellow teeth, grabbed the Signora around the hips and whirled her around the room. Then, putting her in a chair like a doll, quite breathless, he said: "If you were a few years younger, Mousie, I would marry you, and you would not refuse me, for we are cast in the same mold, and that is a rare thing. So you want to deceive your

children, those social butterflies, to save the palazzo! I am with you."
He stopped. "I cannot pay you back the advance, because of my
expenses, and the rest I've squandered away in drink. Nor can I pay for
the togs, but otherwise you are not going to pay me a single
centesimo"—he bowed low—"always at your service, it is my pleasure,
accept the gift of your devoted admirer!"

And when she objected, he said he would feel like a cheat if he
accepted even a lira from her: "I am not running any risk. What do
you want to pay me for . . . ?

21

Claudia got off at the Church of Our Saviour. With one hand the
driver helped her onto the firm ground, with the other he stroked her
buttocks.

She was drunk, yet not so drunk that she did not notice. A new
despair had come over her during the past weeks: no longer agonizing
doubts on the meaning of her existence, but the conviction of its
meaninglessness. She was drinking more all the time, like a bather
wading further and further out, to find out when he will get out of his
depth. She did not get out of her depth, but her lips were full of salt.
Her misery emerged from the alcohol like the ugly tops of the
sandbanks from the sea.

Some time ago, on a sudden impulse, she had bought roses at a
florist's in the Frezzeria and had them sent to Signora Claudia Santarato
in the Giudecca. That evening the flowers were lying outside her door;
she stepped over them, and next morning they were withered.

More and more often she came home alone. If she crossed the canal
in the vaporetto she did not care, but when she had to pay the driver
she remembered the flowers she had sent herself. The man was quite
right to run his hand over her bottom.

She staggered through the nocturnal Calle San Giacomo. She

observed herself staggering. She despised herself for her drunkenness, just as she despised her talent and her indecision and her wrong decisions and her hopelessness, which did not teach her to give up hope. The houses, with their walls like torn maps, no light showing, were hiding from the glassy light of the street lamps. They seemed like couples who had died in their sleep. They must have been dead for a long time, they were found in close embrace.

Claudia was afraid she might be going to be sick and stopped at a door. There were two or three bronze plates on it. She muttered the unknown names as if trying to remember them: Berrenini, Sassi, Molteni. But she knew that when the postman went past the plates it was only once in a while he would hesitate and stop, for only he knew who was left. There were many bells and few plates. She looked up at the closed shutters. It was as if she were living alone in the Giudecca, not an island, but a piece of land which had broken loose and was floating into nothingness.

One night she had crossed St. Mark's Square alone. On the stone floor, leaning against the wall of the Campanile, a young man was sitting, with long fair hair, in dirty blue jeans, torn shirt open, guitar at his side. When she stopped, she saw the noble profile of his slim head, a white angel fallen from the white chapter of the Ducal Palace. She accosted him, and he looked up at her. "*No denaro*," he said. He was a German, and "no money" was all the Italian he knew. She laughed. She didn't want any money, she said. He got up slowly, took his guitar and his square rucksack. At the Palazzo Ducale he hired a motorboat, and on the whole journey she did not speak a word. Nor did they talk on the way through the dark streets, though once he strummed his guitar. She took some time looking for her key, the fallen angel eyed her suspiciously, but the door was open, she had forgotten to lock it in the morning. Upstairs, in her room, he sat down on the floor and started to play. She lay down on the couch which served as her bed; the bed was not made. Then she undressed, and the boy stripped off his trousers but he kept his shirt on. He smelled of sweat. He rushed upon her so hungrily that she screamed with pain when he penetrated her, but he did not touch her breast or kiss her mouth. He dried himself with his shirt and sat down on the floor and grabbed his guitar. When she called him, he came to her again. She stroked his thighs and buried her mouth in the fair hair between his legs, and when she aroused him, she sat on him, because he would not kiss her anyway. Directly afterward he got dressed. She lay there with closed eyes. When she opened them, he was standing over her and rubbing his thumb on his index finger, indicating that he wanted money—he didn't even say "*denaro.*" Did he need money for the vaporetto, she asked—day was breaking—but he shook his head and said: "*Molto denaro.*" She gave him everything she had at home; she did not have the strength to throw him out, and he took the money and the guitar and the rucksack.

Although that might have been about a week ago, she was not sure, she had the impression that the room still smelled of sweat. The charwoman had been here in the morning, the room was as neatly cleared up as it always was just once a week—so today must be Thursday. On the table was the charwoman's bill with all sorts of instructions; Claudia used to throw away these commandments without reading them. Now she tore the paper into bits, but her anger did not subside, the tidiness made her angry, and the fresh bedclothes and the shiny tables and the paintings, placed in a row against the wall, increased her anger. Nothing was right. She threw herself on the bed without taking off her shoes, and stared up at the stuccowork, at the frescoes with the enthroned Madonna and the obsequious saints and the flute-playing angels.

She had enough poison, somewhere, but every time she had thought of destroying herself she had searched for a reason, and since she was searching for a reason, she had doubted her intentions, because there were reasons practically lying in the streets. Small and big reasons, clean and dirty ones, reasons belonging only to her, and reasons belonging to everybody, you simply had to pick them up. She had paid the fallen angel, and on the vaporetto she had lost her ticket and had to buy a second one, and the cats had not touched their milk, and in her childhood, in the Palazzo Santarato, the beds had been damp, and when the picture she was painting was finished, she did not know what she had meant to paint, and the flowers outside her door had withered, and Paolo had written asking if she had gone mad, and the guards on the Biennial premises were like lion tamers at the circus, and in Vietnam the children were dying, and in Harry's Bar she had knocked over a glass, and on Laura's wedding day she had had flu, and in the middle of a picture she had run out of a color, and she had forgotten to visit her mother, and if you wanted to eat, you had to shop, and in Greece they were deporting the prisoners to a rocky island, and the intarsia on the dining-room table were shining, and above the bed, where she had meant to place a mirror long ago, the Mother of God was smiling.

She dragged herself to the bathroom because she thought she could at last be sick, but only a dry cough came out; she returned to the room to look for a spoon. She found a knife instead. Her glance fell on the paintings on the wall; she should have chosen long ago what the gentlemen of the Biennial might like. She had painted monsters, thinking of the gentlemen on the committee, but they would not recognize themselves, it was simply a black canvas with white spots, the eyes of the committee; the painting was as meaningless as the curdled milk and the lost ticket and the blue Madonna.

She set the knife to the painting, the paints were still soft, the canvas resisted. Eventually it tore in the middle, the fibers crackled, they hung from the black halves like the wires from a destroyed switchboard.

Slowly she walked along the sides of the room. She mimicked someone going around a gallery, inclined her head like an art expert about to buy a picture. She looked for the picture she liked best—it had been standing there for years—a horse copulating with a woman. She sat down on the floor, knife in hand, and operated like a surgeon. First she cut one of the woman's breasts from the canvas, then her shoes, then the horse's head, then the genitals, then she beheaded the woman, and each time she put the cut-out parts on top of each other with strict precision. She picked them up and went to the window. On the way she slashed her paintings, and if they did not yield, she kicked them.

She opened the window. The dome of the Redentore was rising from the gray dawn. She threw the woman and the horse out, piece by piece, in a wide curve, as if she were holding bread crumbs in her hand and feeding the.seagulls.

22

Venice, Tuesday, July 4, Afternoon

As a rule, only lighters pass through the canal alongside the house of
the widow Fasulo, on the island of Burano. A single gondola is moored
at the narrow street. A soft breeze moves the washing on the ropes
hanging between the single-story houses painted crimson or pale blue.
On the right lives the retired vaporetto captain, on the left there are
two old spinsters who sit at their window and weave bobbin lace all
day long.

Ermania Fasulo, fifty-nine, does not dare look out. Tomorrow they
will come for the gondola. For forty years she has seen the gondola
every day. She was nineteen when she married the gondoliere Pasquale
Fasulo. Six years ago he died. He inherited the gondola from his father,
who had inherited it from *his* father. The gondola and the name
Pasquale were left to her eldest son by his father, but he married a
young widow and a baker's shop and moved to Verona. Her two
daughters are married. For the past four years her youngest, Edoardo,
has been rowing the gondola. Today he is moving to Mestre.

Edoardo, twenty-three, pokes through his spaghetti, long gone cold.

It all started with a ball made of rags. Outside the Scuola Merletti
they had played soccer; the little bobbin-lace weavers leaned out of the
windows and watched them. Later the boys played with a real football,
in the Burano Club. When Edoardo scored a goal, he jumped in the
air, his arms stretched high over his head. Like the stars of Lazio and
Juventus. Then the talent scouts came from FC Mestre. Edoardo scored
from thirty yards, he was unstoppable. They called him the Bomber of
Burano. Once a week, then twice, Edoardo neglected his gondola. But
the week has seven days, and if a man does not train assiduously for six
of them, he can't jump in the air on the seventh. In the end FC Mestre
offered him a fee he could not earn by rowing. And a job at the post
office. Where Edoardo did not have to work hard, quite the contrary.

"I'll visit you every week," he says.

He had promised his mother a washing machine long ago. The dishwasher is going to be a surprise.

"Why don't you eat?" asks his mother.

"You're not eating either," says Edoardo.

She turns the fork with the spaghetti on the edge of the plate, but puts it down again at once. A carpenter's son may become a lawyer, a glassblower's son may become a millionaire. But a count's son is a count, and the son of a gondoliere is a gondoliere. You can get rid of an inheritance by gambling or drink or extravagance. And if you get rid of it by selling it, it doesn't bring you any luck. All the washing machines in the world can't replace a gondola.

Edoardo is sitting with his face toward the window, but he is glad he cannot see the gondola. The six spikes of the *prova,* the prow, in the shape of the ducal hat, signify the city districts of San Marco, Castello, Cannaregio, San Polo, Santa Croce and Dorsoduro; the spikes at the back are the Giudecca. The gondola weighs over half a ton, the right side is ten inches narrower than the left. So the gondolieri, who hold their oars like the neck of violins, are said to have learned how to play their instruments. Edoardo knows better. You don't learn the art, you inherit it. And you don't row, it has its own name, *vogu alla veneziana.* And yet—one gondola looks like another. The days of the gondolieri are like their gondolas. And no one gets applause. At the oar, you don't jump in the air.

"If only we had not sold," says the widow.

Edoardo tries to eat, he does not want to hurt his mother's feelings.

"We should have waited for a gondoliere," says the widow.

"Who needs two gondolas?" says Edoardo.

In the past there were two gondolieri for each gondola. Four hundred years ago ten thousand gondolas and twenty thousand gondolieri. Now there are four hundred and fifty gondolas, as well as the *sandoli,* so flat and unaristocratic; and even that is too many. A gondola costs one and a half million lire. An American has bought the gondola. Once every five or six years he wants to ride in his own vessel. He paid six hundred thousand lire for it; a Fiat costs five hundred thousand. "He could surely have left it here," says the widow. "I would have looked after it."

"He doesn't realize that gondolas hibernate in the water," says Edoardo.

The widow goes to the kitchen. From there she can see the gondola. When her husband was carried to his grave, two hundred gondolas followed behind the coffin.

Edoardo pushes the plate aside. The money belongs to his mother, but he will buy a car. Right from his childhood he has already dreamed of a car. He'll have a car to take his mother to Rome, to an international match. He will pull off a "hat trick," perhaps against Brazil. He will jump in the air three times, thousands will shout "Fasulo," and Mamma will be proud of him.

The widow brings a basket from the kitchen. Bread, cold chicken, cheese, the bottle of red wine peeps out of the wickerwork. "But I'm only going to Mestre," says Edoardo.

"Do you have to go already?" asks the widow.

He steps over to the window. It is a good thing that you can't see any gondolas in Mestre.

"Battista is here," he says.

"Is he rowing you to Mestre?"

"No, the vaporetto is faster."

Now she too looks out. The gondola's prow is sparkling in the sun. For one more night the gondola will be there outside her window.

The flag of Panama—a red and blue rectangle, a blue and red star—flies from the stern of *The Poseidon*. However T. Tibbett has never seen Panama. He is an American, from Oklahoma. But he is not sailing under false colors. He has rented the yacht at Algiers. It is anchored in front of the entrance to the Giudecca, right next to the goddess of fortune. Howard T. Tibbett, fifty-two, president of Okla-Oil, is expecting a business friend, Amadeo Ronchetti, forty-nine, a Milanese, member of the Venetian industrial *consorzio*. Ronchetti has been negotiating with the party leaders all day.

Tibbett's traveling companions are friends, not business friends—you shouldn't let business stop you having some fun. They are assembled on the open stern terrace. Greta, with her legs pulled up, could be a figurehead, except that she is on the stern. She is Swedish, aged twenty-two, and the gentlemen picked her up on one of the Greek islands. She calls herself a photographer's model. None of the three travelers has made passes at her. Tibbett's two friends are wearing white suits, the elder with a black shirt, the younger with a purple shirt. Twice a year they come to Venice, to their tailor. "The best tailor in the world." They are beautiful men. Howard T. Tibbett is a beautiful man, too.

After Ronchetti's arrival the steward, an Arab, serves drinks. Ronchetti sits down near the Swedish girl and puts his hand on her knee. Tibbett waits for the steward to leave. He has no secrets from his friends. Greta does not know what they are talking about. The "Secret Plan" is under discussion. It has been worked out by the city fathers. Loans, state funds, foreign aid, international assistance: all into one pot. Then Venice will be divided into three zones. Zone A is to cover the center—what foreigners think of as Venice. St. Mark's Square, the Ducal Palace, the Bridge of Sighs, the Canal Grande, the palazzi. These are to remain. Zone B: the belt around Venice. The outlying parts, the ghetto, most of the Giudecca. Ready for demolition. New buildings, housing developments, commercial centers. Finally Zone C: Mestre, Marghera, the port. Expansion of the Third Industrial Zone: canals, drainage drillings, refineries, new workmen's districts.

"The opposition comes from the center," says Ronchetti.

"Don't they want to save Venice?" says Tibbett.

"They want to know how the money is being divided up."

"In other words, they want the whole amount for the old palaces!"

"Just about. There is a man called Terraneo. He's always shouting 'Mafia' like a slogan."

"Does he accuse us . . . ?"

"Of course not. He talks in symbols. He says the Mafia is clearing out of Sicily because there's nobody left to be blackmailed. The Mafia, he says, have killed the goose that laid the golden eggs. The capitalists are killing Venice."

"Did you tell him that we have the agreement of the unions?"

"He says they are as short-sighted as we are. They're killing the goose, too. First Venice, then the capitalist."

"He can leave that worry to us," says Tibbett.

"He has an answer for everything. He appeals to nationalism, says there isn't a single Italian company in Marghera. I replied: All the workers are Italians. But he knows, of course, that out of every ten workers only one comes from Venice."

"Venice, Venice!"

"Shall I get dressed?" says Greta. "It's Harry's Bar time."

Ronchetti has worked his way up from the knee to the thigh. He says: "I pointed out that of the three hundred million tons of commercial traffic in the Italian ports, Venice handles a mere twenty-one million tons."

"Can't this Terraneo be bribed?"

"He doesn't look as if he could."

"A party contribution?"

"I don't think so."

"Do we really need him?" says Tibbett.

The two beautiful Americans have turned toward the shore. They have a quiet talk. The crowd outside the Ducal Palace looks like an impressionist painting.

"I made it clear to the gentlemen," Ronchetti says, "that saving Zone A is a net loss proposition. If over ten per cent of the capital is assigned to it, we'll withdraw."

"I hope you were not too clear."

"Just clear enough."

"The plan makes sense only if the allocation of funds is not decided beforehand."

"The Center Party has only four deputies. But it's strong in Rome."

"Rome doesn't bother about Venice. I have enough people in Rome. How sure are we of the *sindicato?*"

"The union is not interested in churches."

"Shall I get dressed?" asks Greta.

"The center is talking about pollution of the environment," says Ronchetti. "I have taken the wind out of their sails. We have nothing against the changeover to meta-gas."

"Quite right," says Tibbett. "Okla-Oil will be ready to include the *Consorzio* in the meta-gas deal."

"The majority are enthusiastic about the meta-gas deal. It is part of the salvation of Venice."

The two men in white have risen and are waving to some friends on a yacht dropping anchor outside the Maritime Customs building. It is very still. The goddess of fortune is not stirring.

"You may get dressed now," Tibbett tells Greta.

Eric van Dongen, twenty-six, arrived in Venice on the morning train from Amsterdam. He missed his connection to Naples. The next train to Naples leaves at six, and it is now four o'clock. He has stayed at the Santa Lucia Station.

In the sleeping car Eric van Dongen made the acquaintance of a reporter on an American film magazine, and when they parted the man gave him his card. "If ever you come to Hollywood ..." About his own age, a nice fellow, although he snored terribly. "*Arrivederci,*" the reporter said, "this is Italy, you know."

Before Eric van Dongen's eyes pictures of Venice unfold like a filmstrip of postcards.

He has never been in Venice. His firm has sent him to Milan and Florence, and several times to Naples. He has twice been on vacation in Italy. He was in Rimini with a girl. Three years ago he wanted to get married. He had already planned his honeymoon, to Venice. His bride went to England, to her parents. She wrote him a goodbye letter from Manchester.

Every hour the temptation to leave the station increases. What does the woman at the newsstand think of the young man with the sleek fair hair and rimless spectacles? Eric van Dongen looks at the magazines stacked side by side, each girl has only one breast visible, the left breast: a hundred left breasts. He buys six or seven postcards. St. Mark's Square and the Ducal Palace and the Canal Grande and *The Night Procession* by Francesco Guardi, 1712–1793. He can't think whom to write to.

In Amsterdam he lives with his mother. He wanted to be an electronics engineer and has become a traveling salesman. You bury a lot of dreams, and when they are dead, new ones are born. His mother is worried that he doesn't find "the right girl." And glad too. He writes a postcard to his mother. Marieschi's *Veduta di Venezia a Riva degli Schiavoni.* "Passing through," he writes.

The sign USCITA attracts him. He counts the exits, but it would be treason to leave the station. Treason to the right girl.

He has been in the station restaurant twice already. He sits for an hour with an espresso.

In the waiting room, an old man tells Eric the story of his life. "I am dead, you know," the old man says. When he returned from the war, his wife was married to another man. For the authorities had declared the soldier dead. Dead is dead, his wife told him. "She should know."

Eric reads the *Telegraaf* and the *Haagsche Courant.* Including ads and

suicides. He knows the timetables—ARRIVO, PARTENZA—by heart.
A Greek offers him hashish.

A pickpocket is marched off. The policemen inspect the young
Dutchman. He doesn't look like a thief, but only thieves hang around
a station all day long.

Eric counts the railway tracks. He watches the signals at their green
and red semaphore play.

He sits down on a bench and looks out through the exit. Someday . . .

In St. Mark's Square you buy small paper bags with corn, and your
wife feeds the pigeons. You sit under the arcades of a small restaurant
in the Campo San Filippo, a blind singer sings in a falsetto voice, his
wife collects the money. You wait for the Torre dell'Orologio to strike
the hour. Names are scratched into the bell, Karin and Ilona and
Angelica—how did they get there? The nuns smile at you, full of
understanding. You buy a necklace for the wife, with blue and yellow
and green glass pigeons. Not a cloud in the sky, but in the shade of the
palazzi you stop, and you know you are alive. The street vendor is
selling dancing dolls. "I want you to have one, dearie." So many
people, and all in apparent agreement. The smell of fried fish and the
rotting lagoon fail to spoil things. In the evening, three bands play in
the piazza. Women pass with black silk scarves around their shoulders.
People stop and listen, with their arms crossed, as if there were no radio
and no records. The gondolas rock patiently on the water, there's an
invisible couple in the next gondola, the gondola with the musicians
emerges from the dark, they play a serenade, then "Santa Lucia." One
more glance from the balcony, then you close the shutters. All this is
waiting for Eric van Dongen.

The signals have changed ninety-one times. The porter has brought
beer three times. Four trains have arrived in an hour. All of them have
disgorged the same people. Eric has counted eleven honeymooning
couples, but he may have missed a few. The police sentry is relieved.
The policeman going off duty points his thumb over his shoulder at
the strange Dutchman.

Platform four, you might go there, but the tracks are empty. The
signal is red.

Eric buys two more postcards. The Rialto bridge and the *Piazza S.
Marco* by Antonio Canal, detto il Canaletto, 1697–1768. A new girl has

just started at the stall, she doesn't pay him any attention.

Someone next to him says: "Has the *Herald Tribune* arrived? You can't get it in the city."

It's the film reporter from California. "You still here?" he asks.

"I missed my connection," says Eric.

"Have you had a nice day?" says the film reporter.

Eric thinks of a woman he does not know in a city he does not know. Till the great moment he will keep Venice. Like the postcards in his breast pocket.

"A very nice day," he says.

Since early morning there has been a lot of coming and going at the Mayor's office.

First farmers from the mainland. Somebody told them that a hatching tent had been erected overnight in St. Mark's Square. Hundreds of thousands of cabbage white butterflies were to be incubated and set free. Danger, for the vegetable fields. Police report: Yes, some young people, probably Belgian students, have erected a wooden shack, right outside the Quadri, it might be a hatching place. Hundreds of thousands of larvae? The breeding tent is too small for that. Cabbage whites? Perhaps just harmless butterflies. The next person to appear is the representative of the Society for the Prevention of Cruelty to Animals. A cruelty of gigantic proportions is planned. The butterflies cannot survive, the pigeons will eat them.

Police report: One of the Belgians was ready to talk. The butterflies in question *are* cabbage whites. Possibly about ten thousand.

The coffee shop owners are making calls. The hatching box obstructs the view.

Police report: Leaflets are being distributed at various places in the city. The movement calls itself Mass Moving Group. Invitations to the "butterfly happening." With hammer and sickle.

Further inquiry: What's it in aid of? The Belgian has stated: "This is to show that a shabby cocoon turns into an iridescent butterfly. A call to world revolution." Is the hatching tent to be removed? The larvae would perish, cruelty to animals. Instruction from the city council: Watch out, don't let the demonstration get out of hand! No fuss! That's what the demonstrators want.

One of the city fathers drives to St. Mark's Square. The hatchery looks like a huge old-fashioned desk, with a slanted top and drawers. The drawers are locked.

Police report: Small gathering, no crowd. The Belgians are spread across the Piazza. They behave inconspicuously; they're probably watching to see the drawers aren't opened ahead of time. No need to intervene.

It's hot. The sun is blazing down on St. Mark's Square. The foreigners have taken refuge in the restaurants or the shade of their hotel rooms. But between noon and two o'clock new shapes have turned up. They sell butterfly nets. No objection from the council. Antonio in *The Merchant of Venice* speaks of "the trade and profit of the city." Tradition. One authoress has called Venice "a miser's sparkling treasure." Yesterday, dolls and sparkling yo-yos and gondolas with ballerinas. Now the vendors are swinging transparent green nets over their heads—"*Rete! Rete!*" Police report the first incident. Belgian students have beaten up a vendor. One student is taken into temporary custody. "We won't let them sell the revolution," he announces. The net sellers are unperturbed.

Small gatherings outside the hatching tent. Mainly children. Heaps of tourists on the gallery of St. Mark's Church and the Campanile. They want to see the "butterfly happening" from a private box. One says: "It's like an airport terrace."

Four o'clock. The students appear from all sides. They have been sitting outside the coffee shops, crouching below the arcades. They push aside the intrigued spectators in front of the hatching tent. Two of them carry keys. Inquiry to the police: How many are there? Answer: Not more than twenty.

The drawers are opened.

The ugly hatch box turns into a fountain. The butterflies are like rising and falling foam. They are cabbage whites, *Pieris brassicae,* transparent white with tiny black specks, the lower side is gleaming yellow, flying glass.

Inquiry to the police: How many cabbage whites are there?

"We can't count them, can we, not more than two thousand anyhow." Many larvae didn't hatch, they are dying off in the drawers. Some of the students are pouring out the larvae. The pigeons' beaks peck into the larvae.

The fountain foams up once more. The bright life comes to a quick end. The drawers were too narrow. Butterfly wings got broken. With folded wings the cabbage whites fall to the ground. The pigeons take them for grains of corn. A glassy mush. Two waiters fetch brooms.

Clashes? None. A gondoliere slapped a student. At twenty past four the students under the arcades outside Missiglia, the jewelers, chant "Arise, ye starvelings from your slumber." Probably alluding to the butterflies. They can't mean the tourists, for to *them* the gentle swarm is merely a diversion. Children hunt for the butterflies. "Buy me a net, Papa, please!" The children run across St. Mark's Square as if it were a field. A dozen carabinieri have assembled across the square, outside the Café Florian. A student is shaking the hatching box in a fury, as if it were a vending machine which had embezzled his coin without producing a bar of chocolate.

Hardly any child has caught a butterfly. Some cabbage whites were weary. Pigeons kill them in flight. The waiters serve *Cassata con panna.*

The city father treats himself to an ice cream.

"What do those bastards want?" asks the waiter.

"Headlines," says the city father. "With us everything is headlines."

"The poor creatures," says the waiter.

The pigeons appreciate the butterflies. Cabbage whites taste better than grains of corn. "They clean up everything," says the waiter. "At least that's something the pigeons are good for."

"That's how it is," says the city father.

Over his walkie-talkie the sergeant directing the police operation reports:

"The nets are sold out. The Belgians are withdrawing in the direction of the Merceria."

Only in the distance now: "Arise, ye starvelings from your slumber!" The defiant song dissolves in the sunny afternoon.

"All clear," reports the police sergeant. "No damage worth mentioning. A few thousand dead butterflies." A cabbage white circles the column of St. Mark and disappears between the seagulls. The gulls will eat it.

"That's how it is," says the man on the line in the Mayor's office.

23

Love and unease are one. Love, the longing for the partner's presence, is the only feeling that will not yield to any other feeling, the only thought contained in every thought; it accompanies all other feelings and thoughts, fainter or stronger, louder or quieter, always present. The longing for the partner's presence *is* his presence. You take leave of him, but his shadow breaks loose from his body and turns into your own. There was a legendary figure called Peter Schlemihl who on turning around discovered he had no shadow. With a lover it is even worse: he casts the shadow of someone else. The shadow is limned on the wall, falls on your writing paper, flies through the wood, envelopes your pillow. Only when you meet again does the shadow slip back into the body it belongs to. It reunites with its owner, but the unease does not stop, for now you miss the shadow that was accompanying you. Was it his shadow, and will he break loose from it again?

Romolo was full of unease. If he could not leave the palazzo under some pretext in the evening, he went out on the balcony over and over again, to consult the weather angle. Would it be nice enough tomorrow to go to the Lido? He would look at the sky, a gray streak in the west; only a cloudless sky could calm him. Despite his sky watching he got dressed every time so late that he almost missed the boat at the Hotel Danieli; his nerves would not have been up to lengthy preparations. Almost as soon as he was back from the Lido he had to interrupt everything he did. He would close his book, pause in his decorating—he had decided to paint the kitchen—get away from the Signora for a minute or two. He had to be alone with his shadow.

But did the shadow find its body? For two successive days Barbara was standing at the jetty behind the Excelsior, where the boats from Venice touch, and although she might call it a coincidence, he knew she had been waiting for him. But the day after, and several days after that he looked for her in vain, nor was she to be found on the beach.

She appeared an hour later—"I slept late"—and he wondered whether she was anything like the girl he knew. Out on the pier she put her head on his arm and kissed him under his armpit. But an hour later she barely seemed to notice him, and when he asked: "What are you doing tonight?" she said: "I don't know," and let him go. He was on the lookout for someone he might have been jealous of, but she did not give her attention to anyone else, and he had no choice but to be jealous of everyone: of the waiter at the bar, the film actor who had his picture taken doing a handstand, or the ancient owner of a yacht. On the way home he held conversations with her shadow; he knew every word he would tell her. They used to walk along the *cabine,* their feet in the shallow water, to the beach of the Grand Hotel des Bains. But when they were alone, she would speak of indifferent things; it was only when they were with the "group" that she would whisper into his ear: "I love you." He made plans. "I really ought to improve my English," he told the Signora. "I wonder if my father would send me to an English school?" Barbara said her parents were only waiting for the opening of the film festival and she said it as if this summer were like any other summer. She mentioned the family lawyer, twenty-eight years old, and Romolo was sure she had slept with him; he wanted to invent a woman *he* had slept with. She said that Italian girls had "a hundred experiences" by the age of fifteen, and having first feared that she might take him to be innocent, he now feared she might expect him to be as experienced as Bob, the lawyer.

One day, at the end of an afternoon, in which she had not touched his hand even once, she said. "There's a film on in Venice with Liz Taylor, I absolutely must see it. Shall we go, the two of us?"

He told the Signora that the parents of "a very nice girl" had invited him to dinner, English people, very respectable, "they have their *cabina* in the first row."

For almost an hour he hung about the cinema. During the hour he pondered whether to put his tie in his pocket, but in the end he kept it on; and he combed his hair four or five times in front of shop windows. He reckoned that by making two more rounds of St. Mark's Square he would be right on time, but he made a detour and approached the cinema from the Piazza San Moisè, for he wanted to say: "I just made it . . ."

She came four minutes after the crowd outside the cinema had ebbed and the film had started. He had decided to wait exactly twenty-six minutes more.

"I hope you haven't bought tickets," she said, "I wouldn't dream of seeing silly old Liz Taylor. Besides, the film's two years old."

He wanted to ask: Why didn't you say so right away? But he acted as if this were exactly what he had expected.

For a while they walked along the Merceria. The business street was deserted. Then they wandered at random in the side streets, and stopped on the bridges. At one of the bridges there was a house with a flower-decked oriel, and he said: "This is the place to live." She said: "It's summer, we're in Venice, what more do you want?" Few windows were lit, the street lamps were humming. "I should like to have lived when there were only gas lamps," she said. He said: "I always wanted to be Marco Polo." While they were again looking down from a bridge, a gondola appeared around the corner of a narrow canal, as if drifting without any guiding hand or oar; and then they saw a couple, kissing. Romolo held Barbara around the hips and felt her small budding breasts. "I could go on like this forever," she said. In a deserted square she stopped and asked: "Did you play here?" and he said yes, although he had never played in the street. They knew only the "group" and the barman and some people they had watched on the Lido, so their conversation always returned to their narrow common ground; he was content that she considered the old director with his young mistress and the headwaiter and the "group" "silly." The drying washing spread white sheets over the glassy canal. The barges lay as if forgotten along the sick walls: bleeding entrails protruding from white walls. Suddenly she began to talk and she talked so much that he couldn't follow her; her tales were of London, and they hurt him, because they were like tracks in the sand, coming from nowhere, leading nowhere. The rotten timber of the Rialto bridge creaked under their steps. At the top of the bridge, the crest of a wave over the Canal Grande, they stopped. "Where is your palace?" she said. At one of the boarded-up shops on the bridge he said: "This is said to have been Skylock's shop." "I don't want to know anything about Shylock, I want to hear about you," she said. Music could be heard from a bar in the street of the goldsmiths. "Shall we go in?" he asked. "The man decides," she said. But as he was walking toward the door, she said: "I'd like to ride in a gondola with you."

He was afraid he might run into Carlo, but luckily Carlo did not row at night. At the Riva del Ferro they got into a gondola. "Where to?" asked the young gondoliere. "Through the side canals," said Romolo, "and then past the Palazzo Santarato."

The gondoliere chose the darkest canals. Barbara leaned her head back, and he kissed her. Then she took his head into her hands and kissed him the way a child kisses, more and more kisses there were, and less and less those of a child. First she kissed only his lower lip, then only his upper lip, then her tongue touched the right corner of his mouth, then the left corner. He didn't let her kiss him any more, he took her into his arms, but when his hands clasped her breasts, she withdrew and held his hands fast to her knees. She looked up at the balconies. "With you by me I could get well," she said. "Are you ill?" he asked. She shook her head. In the silence there was only the gondoliere's shout of "Oi." He did not dare to kiss her again, and he said: "I knew it straight away when I turned your radio on"—a memory of the beginning.

Near the Accademia, the gondola reached the Canal Grande. Was it imprudent to ride past the palazzo? In the big drawing room the yellow lights were still burning; Romolo remembered that the Signora had expected Dario. You could see the crystal chandeliers and the stuccowork on the ceiling and the top half of the gold frames. The balcony door was open. Romolo was afraid his grandmother might find out, though the canal was in the dark; yet at the same time he felt like sharing his secret with the whole world. For a long time she looked up at the balcony and the windows and the chandeliers and the yellow wallpaper and the golden frames. "You are a fairy prince," she said.

They got out at the moorings of San Marco and went past the Giardinetti Reali. Here some souvenir stalls were still lit, old people were dozing on the benches, and some sailors were accosting a group of young Venetian girls. Barbara's face was serious, and her cheeks were so pale that he asked if she wouldn't like him to escort her back to the Lido. "No, no," she said, "it will pass."

24

The Signora was expecting Dario and the Contessa Crivelli.

For three evenings, and also several hours during the day, the Signora had been working on a short speech she was to deliver at an assembly; the Committee of Citizens and the Italia Nostra had organized a rally.

Why had she accepted? She had never spoken in public, had not attended any meetings for years, had never belonged to any society. "Nor have I," Dario said, "but Italia Nostra is standing up for Venice, it has great influence in Rome. The Committee of Citizens alone has fifteen thousand members. There will be at least a thousand people present. All you need do is speak for five or six minutes. We live in a collective era, nobody is anything by himself."

She was sitting in the drawing room, dressed smartly, with spectacles on her nose, trying to learn by heart what she had written. It might be too short or too long, she didn't know.

The name Santarato carried great weight, the Countess had said, appealing to her vanity, but the nearer the time came the uneasier the Signora became. She had not told Dr. Einaudi that she had accepted; perhaps she ought to phone him, he would forbid her to expose herself to the strain. A collective era—what did that mean? It was said as if it had to be accepted. Was it not an era of surrender, with the individual's own will acknowledging defeat? Didn't that era resemble the alpine climber who ventures on a daring ascent all by himself, and then calls for the rescue party? The sum of collective intentions looked like an addition, but didn't it turn into a subtraction sum, giving the answer "zero" for the individual's intentions? True, the people striving toward the same goal were going hand in hand, but once the hands were united, could you still tell whose fingers they were? A drop in the ocean is not happy. Venice must be in an evil plight if an old lady was scared out of her decaying palazzo to testify for the ruins!

The Signora had no talent for cowardice. She took her pen to correct the last sentence once more; she would scarcely be able to read her writing.

She was only casually acquainted with the Contessa Crivelli; she admitted she was curious to get to know her better. Angela Crivelli was considerably younger, in her middle fifties, of stately beauty; nobody would have taken the blond woman with the strong cheekbones for a Venetian. For years her life had been dedicated to the salvation of Venice. Her father was one of the two Venetian aristocrats who had opened up Mestre and Marghera for industry at the end of the First World War and had started the development of the port. Did the Contessa, as richly married as her father had been immensely rich, wish to atone for something she considered a crime? She was not like the children who are content with predictably doing the opposite of what their parents did. Her father, she said, had wanted to save Venice, and indeed the Signora, who in those pioneer days had been still in her teens, remembered the enthusiasm which had greeted his plans. At that time the city had been going through one of its worst crises since A.D. 600, when only the citizens' desperation had saved the lagoon from the tyranny of the sea. The last year of the First World War: even in midsummer St. Mark's Square was empty, the young gondolieri were in the army, the old ones were looking for any odd job, every second shop was closed, the shop windows were empty, the young had fled the city, the timber needed for repairing the posts could be acquired only with difficulty on the black market. Her father, said the Contessa, had envisaged a new Venice, rooted in tradition and well disposed to progress. But wasn't this hypocrisy, this marriage of tradition and progress, did not one have to yield to the other? The daughter thinks you can make things good without admitting that they have been made badly, that you can justify a misjudgment (to put it at its most charitable). "I'm very much his daughter," the Contessa used to say. "His concern was the salvation of Venice, and mine is too. But what you've got to save and how you do it, that's different in each age."

"You look fabulous," said Romolo, coming into the room; he wanted to accompany the Signora. "You'll sweep them off their feet like Cato."

"I'll have to read the stuff. Don't you think I look terrible with spectacles?"

"You look even younger in spectacles."

The next moment the Contessa appeared, and with her a wind of activity whirled into the room. She thanked the Signora effusively, but with obvious sincerity. She declined a glass of port; "We shall have to hurry, I'm sure the audience must be impatient, you can't keep the Mayor waiting."

"Don't you want to read my little speech?" The Signora turned to Dario.

"It'll be excellent, I'm sure," said the Contessa.

"You're behaving like a public orator," said Dario, "you've got stage fright. That's a sign of the professional. Only dilettantes aren't nervous."

In her motorboat the Contessa also showed agitation. "Dealing with the authorities," she said, "is like trying to get a grip on some mush. Some say there's no money; others talk of exactly five hundred and ten million dollars, all allocated—a hundred and fifty-eight to absorb the excess water, a hundred and fifty-two million to restore the houses, palaces and monuments, and with the remaining two hundred million they could build an aqueduct to bring drinking water to Venice. Then there are others again who rave about some vast new plan, but one which they can't yet reveal. Everyone has his own interests, senators, deputies, representatives of UNESCO, industrialists, museum directors, geophysicists, biologists, bacteriologists, oceanographers, town planners, sociologists—I'm at the end of my tether."

The Signora was only half listening. She was trying to recite to herself the words of her speech, while at the same time observing the blond woman in her summer suit who sat in the boat with her back toward Marghera—not by chance, it seemed to the Signora, for the evening sky above the greedy cities which Angela Crivelli's father had established on Venice's border had the flaming rainbow there. The Contessa had asked her to speak on the salvation of the palazzo, but surely the passengers of this crested motorboat were a bit like the quacks who paint over the leprous patches and neglect the actual disease. A collective era, and each had his own interests—how could this be reconciled?

The assembly hall was on the Bocca di Piazza, on the upper floor of the post office, directly on the west side of St. Mark's Square. Dario, whose arm the Signora had taken, frowned. "No crowd," he said, "or else they've already closed the gates."

The Signora did her best to go up the stairs with quick steps, as she always did when she was in company. At the same time she clutched her small silk bag; it contained the nitroglycerine capsules.

They entered the hall from the back and had to go down the central aisle through the audience. The Signora could read the disappointment in the Contessa's face. A thousand people, Dario had said, but there were hardly two hundred—sparse rows, you had to look around for your neighbors. A rustling movement had started: the people in the back made themselves comfortable up front; everybody drew closer. The Signora did not know anyone at the long table set up on the platform, which had behind it the flag of Venice with St. Mark's lion. There were three men and one woman; the Mayor was not there. While the Signora was asked to sit on the right of the man who was taking the chair, she heard him apologize to the Contessa, a monstrously fat man in a suit that was too tight, an official from the city council. He would try, he said, to be a worthy replacement for the Mayor, who unfortunately was unable to attend.

The Signora could not read without her glasses, but at a distance she recognized each individual face in sharp contours. To the right of Dario in the first row, there was a white-haired man with black horn-rimmed spectacles; next to Romolo there was an old lady with a veil over her tiny straw hat. People of rank? The Signora was not surprised that Romolo should be the youngest person present, but even the people in their forties or fifties had to crane their necks if they wanted to see someone their own age. The meeting seemed to have snow lying on it. Did you have to be old to want to save the past? Did old age alone care for the future? Had you written your will for yourself, since the survivors did not even open it?

The council official's speech aroused the Signora from her sadness; irritation is a cure for melancholy. He was enumerating everything that had been done to save Venice, though certainly there was more still to be done. Venice would have to prove worthy of the world's love—his voice quivered with touristic patriotism. He quoted Sannazzaro: *"Quis rursus Venatae miracula proferat urbis?"* The Signora watched his left ear lobe, hanging over his cheek like a plum. Someone spoke on behalf of Italia Nostra, someone else on behalf of the Committee of Citizens, the audience nodded, and those who clapped did it for all those who had not come. The Signora's glance returned again and again to Romolo. She felt ashamed before youth: it was hard to find passengers for

Noah's ark. The lifeboats picked up women and children and the old first, so why should anyone be surprised there were only women and children and the old in the lifeboats? But they could not row against the storm. Where were the sailors?

Now Contessa Angela Crivelli had risen, greeted by deafening applause, as it would be reported in the *Gazzettino* tomorrow. The Contessa was an experienced speaker. Clearly and passionately she championed the project she and her friends had been advocating for years: movable sluice gates would have to be built at the end of the petroleum duct, to be opened thirty times a year; that alone required five hundred million dollars, but where there's a will, there's money. No new canals were needed, an anchored oil duct could be fastened on a floating platform near Malamocco.

The Signora turned to look at Dario—perhaps he would understand all this. All she heard was: petroleum canal, oil duct, port, sluice gate, platform, zone, storage tanks. Everyone seemed to be in agreement. When the council official nodded, the plums on his ears shook. The old gentleman in the second row was nodding incessantly, as if everything he heard were what he had long thought himself. Somewhere in the back there was an old lady who regularly started the applause. The caretaker was leaning against one of the columns, yawning. Agreement paralyzed the assembly, and tomorrow the *Gazzettino* would report that the Committee of Citizens had agreed on the salvation of the city. But what did they intend to save, these ladies and gentlemen? Venice, of course, but also the greedy port and the smoking chimneys and the bubbling wells and the gushing oil. The victim and the murderer. Could she pretend she was unwell? Dario and Romolo would quickly see through that. The Mayor's representative had already introduced Signora Anna-Maria Santarato, the widow of the great architect, a true-blue Venetian lady, here present for the first time, and more in this vein. When the Signora rose, she realized that she had crumpled her script in her fist.

She began to speak, and spoke freely. Perhaps it was only because she was afraid of looking ridiculous up there, behind the table covered with red, in front of the flag with St. Mark's lion, if she started flattening out her crumpled sheets. At any rate she had no evil design in her head as Dario later alleged. She could prove it, for her first sentence corresponded to the script; she knew it by heart. Then she paused, folded her spectacles—her vanity preferred it that way—and said:

"I had prepared a little speech, but you will forgive me if I do not deliver it." She saw Dario's horrified face. "My friends told me a thousand people would be coming here tonight, for this concerns the future of our city, but I believe I can still count correctly: there are probably about two hundred of us." The laughter in the hall was kind, and the Signora knew that it was on account of her tininess: when she had mentioned the absentees, she had risen on tiptoe to peer around the hall. "I don't mind," she said. "I am not used to speaking in public, but I do think we are too few, don't you? Also, I have just heard how well the salvation of Venice is being taken care of, and I don't know what more I should say." Dario covered his face, Romolo looked up at her with laughing eyes. "What amazes me are the grandiose plans which, if I am not mistaken, amount to enabling Mestre and Marghera to live at peace with Venice, and Venice at peace with Mestre and Marghera. I may be too old to understand this. Italy needs ports, and Italy needs oil. But there are many ports, and the oil we need does not have to flow from Venice or to Venice. If fresh-water wells are bored, the sea water will be drained. If canals are excavated, the Canal Grande will only be a small canal. I once read that the sky does not recognize any frontiers. If Mestre and Marghera do not yield, the sky above Venice will always be black. And when heaven and hell merge, hell does not turn into heaven, but heaven becomes hell. I believe we shall have to decide between the two." She hesitated, but she had heard that speakers usually end their speeches with "Thank you very much," so she said "Thank you very much," and sat down.

The council official tried to wipe out the impact of her words with his thanks, but his speech was drowned in the applause. The Contessa seemed to reflect for a moment, then she hurried past the fat man with the plum ears and stretched out both hands to the Signora. The Signora was still sitting, astonished at herself and astonished at the people who no longer seemed to her quite so old—the snow had melted. The Mayor's representative announced that the meeting was closed, but nobody was listening.

"You were great," said Romolo, as they were going down the steps.

The Signora looked at Dario. He said: "What am I to do with you? You're hopeless. I must have been raving mad when I let you out into society!"

She said to Romolo: "I left my purse on the table."

25

Now both guest rooms in the Palazzo Santarato were occupied. Remus had arrived from Milan in the evening.

The following morning he rode to the Lido with Romolo. They were standing in the open, near the boatman in his white shirt and the skipper's cap, enjoying the mild breeze blowing through their hair.

"The palazzo is in terrible shape," said Remus. "What does the old lady think about selling?"

"Nonna wouldn't dream of it," said Romolo, stressing "Nonna."

"The oldies"– Remus was speaking of his parents now–"have instructed me to bring her to her senses."

"Don't waste your time."

"I'll try at any rate. There's something in it for me. If you help me, you'll get your share. Although the oldies tell me your lily-white soul would never be party to such a dirty trick."

"If I puke all over you," Romolo said, "you can pretend I got seasick."

"You're really screwed," said Remus, and put his arm around Romolo's shoulders in a friendly gesture. "By the way, are you learning to paint?"

"What gave you that idea?"

"I found some paintbrushes in the kitchen. The old girl blushed when she caught me."

Romolo had also found some paintbrushes a few days before. He said quickly: "Yes, they belong to me. I'm painting the kitchen."

"With those brushes? You might as well cut the lawn with nail scissors."

The boat engine stopped. Along the hospital island, the motorboats had to run silently.

"What a society!" said Remus. "They stop the engines for two minutes, but forty-thousand-ton vessels can cross the lagoon undisturbed."

"Grandmother's also wise to that."

"You ought to realize where we're at, junior. Two minutes of respect for the sick when it's motorboats; but forty-thousand-ton vessels are acceptable. When there's bread involved."

The boat took a sharp right turn behind the Lido.

"How are we set for dolls?" said Remus.

"O.K.," said Romolo.

He would not be able to avoid introducing Barbara to his brother. The day he had met her, he had longed for Remus. Barbara would surely be just a "doll" to Remus, but the two had certain similarities, and the things he couldn't understand in both, they might understand in each other.

As soon as they had put on their swimming trunks, Remus left his brother. His friends had arrived that morning. There were three of them: Bruno Cesarini, a young writer who up to then had published mainly poems; Pietro Masina, who worked as a sound engineer at the Italian broadcasting company, and André Gaillard, a Frenchman, a cameraman-to-be who had been hanging about Milan for a year, unemployed.

They sat down on the sand at the water's edge and began to talk about the film.

It would be set in Burano. Burano had excited Remus ever since his childhood. There, on the second floor of the town hall, small bobbin lace makers in their teens were working, pale girls in worn apron uniforms. For eight hours a day they sat bent over their work in the half-dark room, and they only looked up when tourists came and— "how lovely"—admired their skill. Remus had also investigated the secret of the Scuola dei Marletti. Nuns looking like men in drag— Remus recalled one of them very clearly, a huge woman with a thick moustache—supervised the work; they patrolled between the tables like warders in a women's prison. It was said the Society of the Jesurum sold the lace for charitable purposes. And if this had been true—charity would have been the silver wrapper for the Society's brutality. But it was not true: out of the enormous prices paid by the foreigners in the Society shop of the Bridge of Sighs for shirts and mats and tablecloths and pillowcases, the nuns got only a few lire, and the pale girls got nothing: their wages were the same as half a century ago. Who owned the sad factory? The nuns had mentioned a Contessa Margherita, but that was a bitter joke, for there was no Contessa Margherita. All there *had* been was a Queen Margherita, the patroness of the pale bobbin lace makers.

"The more anonymous the enemy, the better," said Gaillard—in his late twenties, with short hair and burning eyes—who was considered the ideologist of the enterprise. "With a Contessa Margherita we might assume it was an isolated case. A joint-stock company is called a *société anonyme*. This whole fucking society is a *société anonyme*."

"It would make quite a good title," said Masina. He was the youngest, twenty-one, a Neapolitan with extravagant gestures.

"Not international enough," said Remus.

"Let's hope the hammer and sickle are still on the wall of the town hall," said Gaillard. "I picture that wall as the final shot."

"If necessary we could daub it on," said Remus.

"We must have a look at the location this afternoon," said Gaillard.

"Burano is no problem," said Masina. "The expensive thing, though, will be the contrast."

They all nodded. Each of them knew what "contrast" meant. Cesarini had not written a script. "Outdated rubbish. The main outline is enough, we'll shoot spontaneously whatever occurs to us." But at least half the film would take place in Venice. On one side, the factory in the dark—"hospital, orphanage, workhouse, asylum, the poor in spirit ... nothing tragic, but full of helpless impotence," Mauriel had written in *Quinze jours à Venise* over half a century ago. The nuns, sprinkling holy water on the stench of society, the cruel crucifix in the hall of the pale lace makers, the Renaissance facade of the town hall with misery crouching behind it. On the other side, the halls of the luxury hotels, the private boats on the Canal Grande, the evening gowns paraded at the film festival, the whitewashed splendor of St. Mark's Square, the corrupt artists in Harry's Bar, the phony magic of the palazzi. Contrast.

They spent a bit of time casting the film. No stars, of course, but beginners or amateurs? Opinions were divided, and only the down-to-earth Masina mentioned that amateurs will ask for more than beginners. A million lire had been raised so far, barely enough for one day's shooting, and even this capital had lain idle for the past year; it had not increased.

"Can we shoot at your grandmother's?" Gaillard tried to get away from a tiresome subject.

"We're not going to ask her," said Remus.

"That's not even half a reel," said Masina. "Venice is expensive." He turned toward the beach. The vanguard of the film festival had arrived. A young man, tall and fat, with shoulder-long hair and side whiskers, was trying to attract attention. He had wrapped himself in a fishnet and was rolling across the sand. An old man, easily recognizable as a millionaire even in his bathing trunks, panted along dragging water skis after his young mistress. Only a few bathers moistened their bellies with seawater; everybody made for the new swimming pool. In front of a cabin, the famous French director of the twenties held court; his films would be de-mothballed as a special attraction.

"*They* will have to give the money," said Gaillard. "First of all because we don't have it ..."

"Reason enough," said Masina.

"Second, because suicide proves more than murder," said Gaillard.

"I can wangle something from my old man," Remus said. "Provided I talk my grandmother into selling her old crate. But that's no problem."

"We ought to get the money from the Society of the Jesurum," Gaillard said. "I'll go to the Mother Superior and say: 'Dear lady, we are selling Jesus Christ. And lace.' "

Everybody laughed.

"Here, look," said Remus. Romolo was approaching with Barbara. "My brother," Romolo introduced. His friends—"Pietro, André, Bruno."

Remus, Masina, and Gaillard stood up, Bruno Cesarini remained seated.

"Barbara is English," said Romolo.

"How do you do?" said Remus, and eyed her bosom.

"They're shooting a film in Venice," said Romolo.

"You never told me that," said Barbara.

"I don't think it's important," said Remus.

"What do you mean?" said Romolo. A brother shooting a film in Venice was quite something, although Remus was probably speaking the truth: he really didn't feel you could make too much fuss about a film which for two years had existed only in its creator's head. To Romolo's relief Barbara said: "We're going swimming. Coming with us?"

"She could be in the film," said Masina, also inspecting her bosom; and to her he said: "I've got a super part for you."

"We'll follow you," said Gaillard. "We're having a script conference."

They watched Romolo and Barbara go off; only Cesarini, the poet, did not move. He was twenty-six, pale, with a muddy complexion and tiny dark eyes which were barely discernible, for he was wearing a pince-nez, framed in tortoiseshell, the kind that teachers and book-keepers favored at the turn of the century. The pince-nez dangled from a broad black silk ribbon over his hairless chest. He enjoyed a high reputation among his comrades, on account of his poems which were occasionally published in avant-garde periodicals, but also because among all the sons of wealthy families he was the only worker's son.

"Have you read the *Unità?*" he said. "On page four—in the bourgeois rags you can read it on the front page. An oil magnate's son has been kidnapped."

"Palestinians?" asked Masina.

"No. The Last Judgment has accepted responsibility. They're asking for a three-million-dollar ransom."

Gaillard was first to guess what Cesarini was planning. He propped himself on his elbow.

Cesarini looked at Remus. "We could kidnap *you,*" he said.

"You're out of your mind," said Remus.

"But since you're not worth much, we'll only ask for one tenth. A hundred and fifty thousand dollars will pay for the film, and we'll give a hundred and fifty thousand to the little lace makers."

"Two hundred thousand and a hundred thousand," said Masina, who was in charge of finances.

"Venice is just the right place for it," said Gaillard. "In Venice everything turns into a public relations hit."

"I'm not the right person to be kidnapped," Remus said. "If any kidnapping is to be done, I'll do it."

"You are a megalomaniac, Mr. Director," said Gaillard. "Pietro's father is not rich enough, and my father would pay to be rid of me."

"Nothing would happen to you, Remus," said Cesarini. "I know a gondoliere in Murano. A comrade. He will feed you spaghetti for a few days. You'll have to do without caviar just for a time."

"My father is happy when he gets enough pocket money for himself," said Remus.

"Exactly," said Cesarini. "Your grandfather will have to pay. The most he need do is jack up the price of beer."

"I'm here to look for shooting locations," said Remus.

"Without money, you'll be shooting with blanks," said the poet.

"Anyhow, I didn't come to Venice to be locked up by you lot," said Remus. "Besides, in your youthful enthusiasm, not to say childish lunacy, you don't seem to have thought about the risk."

"Before we release you, we'll demand immunity," said Cesarini, playing with the ribbon of his pince-nez. "The sympathy of the working class all over the world will be with us."

"Society doesn't keep its agreements," Remus said.

"It has to!" said Cesarini. "Otherwise the next kidnappers will be angry."

"I'm not sure you'll release me," said Remus. "And if you do, the entire press will know it was a put-up job."

"So what?" said Cesarini. "Unity is always a put-up job. The revolution will be successful only if the victim cooperates. And the worst we can be accused of is blackmail; because you'll have done it of your own accord."

"After your release, the trial will coincide with the release of the film," said Gaillard.

Cesarini nodded. "Violence meets with approval if it shows that the use of violence has become a necessity. Any revolution is an act of despair; if the despair is justified, so is the revolution. For two years we have been trying with peaceful means: All we wanted to do was to shoot a film critical of contemporary society, but society could not bear that. They"–he pointed to the beach with his pince-nez–"have thwarted it. We shall prove the inability of the authorities to counter our violence by theirs. Our violence is new, theirs is threadbare. In any case, the one who pays is the loser; people stick to winners. This society is so rotten that it prefers the rapist to the raped. This time we'll even have the laugh on our side. We'll prove how much money a man such as Andreoli can spare, if he's forced to fork it out. If he pushes up the price of beer, we win over the beer drinkers. The revolution needs fellow travelers, from the bars as well."

Remus let the sand run through his fingers. Had Bruno concocted this crazy plan of his because he, Remus, happened to be the grandson of Andreoli, the multi-millionaire? Weren't they simply counting on his weakness? Ever since his childhood he had been afraid of the similarities with his father. But what did weakness mean? Was it weakness to go along, or was it weakness not to go along? If he let himself be kidnapped, he would be doing it because the others wanted him to. Their unanimity was striking, possibly they had discussed it all beforehand in Milan, with the other members of the syndicate, which, after all, he and nobody else had set up. If he did not let himself be kidnapped, that meant he was still attached to the umbilical cord of this rotten society, because there was no return from the refuge at the gondoliere's, no return to the villa, to having his bills paid, to the Alfa Romeo.

"Venice is the ideal stage setting," said Gaillard. "Kidnapped—in the middle of the civilized world! The veneer is off!"

Romolo and Barbara were swimming from the pier toward the beach. They waved their hands.

"I'm going for a swim," said Remus.

26

Sometimes my way takes me to Marghera. It is only ten minutes or less by motorboat. The canals spreading from the Canal Grande are like long, dirty fingers. Ten minutes from Santa Maria della Salute, and you come to coal heaps, mountain-high, light yellow, phosphorescent piles of nitrate. Monte Catini Phosphati, the oil storage tanks striped red like monsters in the bathing costumes of the turn of the century, colonies of the Montedison Company—Esso, Irom, Total; russet mounds of earth burning, the chimneys coughing up their breath, noises like a constant yawn, corrugated iron hangars large enough for jumbo jets; national flags fluttering from the freighters, the *Mary II* from Anvers, the *Giambattista Venturi* from Genoa, the *Medina* from Malta, the *Le Shui* from Canton, ships lying alongside the factories; bridges leading from one terrain to the next, but not called bridges of sighs, they're drawbridges, across the canals, above the heads; ships drinking fresh water from fresh wells, under an arched oil pump, forming a rainbow; the tankers passing, fire gushing from steel skeletons, the sky dark by day and bright by night, the smoke askew, zebra stripes on the horizon; twenty-four columns, a mockery of classicism, supporting the building of the Olio San Marco corporation; the sandbanks sticking their noses out of the water, construction taking place on some of them, an illegal Third Zone secretly completed, workmen's dwellings, wrapped in dust; the cranes like tired horses, drooping their heads; broken windows, factory buildings, already decayed, some stray seagulls on the buoys. The motorboat drives slowly through searing stench, avoiding mud and wood, impudent islands of dirt. The black sea stands still, no wave ventures here.

Then I return to Venice. And all at once the *Serenissima* seems like a jewel disappearing in the clutch of a giant fist. Small and poor and gray are the Accademia, St. Mark's Church, Santa Maria Gloriosa dei Frari; for the eye has grown accustomed to the industrial palaces and the oil storage tanks and the coal heaps. The angels on the cathedrals, the chimneys of the palazzi, the very towers and domes are helpless doves.

Murder is a mortal sin. But for most of my life I have been in doubt about the law of the church which condemns suicide. For the same reason it forbids the murder of the unborn child: we should not take away from God's hand what has grown there, for better or for worse. I am learning to recognize the wisdom of the law. The man who is unable to wait for his death mistrusts life, its changes and chances, its boons and bends. If hope is a cardinal virtue, then hopelessness must be a mortal sin, and despair is godless. The Talmud tells of the martyr Cahnnina of Terjadon who was burned alive by the Romans. They had wrapped his body in a Torah scroll and soaked him with water, so as to prolong his suffering. His disciples shouted to him: "Open your mouth and swallow the fire!" But he said: "It is better he should take your soul than that you should do violence to yourself." Venice swallows the fire.

I once read of a man who went to murder his enemy. When he broke into the splendid bedroom, he believed that his victim was asleep. He stabbed at the sleeper, who did not move or try to fight back, for he was dead already, he had poisoned himself. The jury deliberated for a long time. Was the murderer still a murderer if the victim had forestalled him? Finally they found him guilty of desecration of the dead, but they acquitted him of the charge of murder, since you cannot kill a dead body.

In my city the murderers and the suicides conspire, indeed they are one and the same.

Shall I, on my return from Marghera, accuse the greedy for gain who, intoxicated by their thoughtless profits, are strangling the city built by Tritons in the sea, the "dream come true"? They are killing *themselves*. Elsewhere their greed would have passed unnoticed, here they are challenging their enemies—and their friends. They pretend to be servants of the future, but only those who have nothing left to experience want to experience everything. The suicide's impatience has made him an accomplice of the murderer. Why should the giants of the ocean moor in front of the submerged city? And if the colossal factories and the oil storage tanks do not sink with it—will they be anything but monuments to greed, welcome proof for those who have been preaching all along that progress is nothing but the accumulation of compound interest? Once the leprosy spreading from Marghera over Venice has completely disfigured the body of my city, Venice will still be on display; but each guided tour will turn into an accusation, and then the retreat of the profiteers will be too late, for it will be said: behold, they have destroyed Venice, what else will they destroy? They appeal to their glorious past, to the preservation of past achievements, and to tradition, but they make common cause with those who destroy everything. Should it only be a criminal offense to aid and abet murder? Why not aiding and abetting suicide? Quick victories are slow defeats.

Or should I accuse the tens of thousands who profit from the profiteers, the masses in working clothes? Venice means nothing to them, or only the hated past: churches remind them of the Inquisition, palaces of exploitation, saints' portraits of fraud. At the pyramids of Giza they cannot think of anything else but slave labor. Oh yes, they do see a bit further than the anonymous lords of Marghera. Like many figures in the Venetian carnival, they carry a dagger under red velvet. Someday, they think, they will themselves be the anonymous lords. It does not occur to them that Venice, if there was a will to save it, could offer work for tens of thousands. They choke in poison gas to prove that they are being poisoned. Culture for all, they demand, and they trample culture to death. Will the realm they rule in their day be worth ruling over? They will bequeath Marghera to their children, but will their children live to see it? And surely the children who do live to see it will look out of the windows of the skyscrapers across the lagoons and the submerged city, and they will say: behold, this is what our parents have squandered!

I am a Venetian, and to me Venice is the world.

My world does not resist her murderer, she goes to meet him. She has her bed covered in silk before she dies in it. The murderer thinks she is sleeping and she is: the sleep which is a prologue to her death. She does not need to despair, but she does despair. She sacrifices freedom on the altar of profit. She enjoys the life of which she is weary. She gives in to blackmail and cannot bear her own acceptance. She yields to the extortioner and dupes her allies. Although she has no other weapon but her morality, she becomes as amoral as her murderer. She underestimates her strength. For fear of the dagger she resorts to poison.

The Talmud tells of a father to whom money destined for the orphans was entrusted. When his distrustful son asked him where the money was, he said: "The money lying above belongs to us. And the money lying below belongs to us. But the orphans' money lies in the middle." The son did not understand, and the father said: "If thieves should come, they will take the money above. And if the earth trembles, it will take the money below. But the orphans' money will remain."

Some destroy the world from above, others from below. Sinners all of them: murderers and suicides. Venice is the money of the orphans.

27

The telephone near Laura's bed rang at an unusually early hour of the morning. In Milan, however, it was noon.

Laura did not recognize Teresa's voice at once. Teresa had never called her before. Twice Teresa had come to America with Paolo, and Laura had twice visited her in Milan, but the relationship of the two sisters-in-law had remained studiously polite.

Laura had always felt that her brother's marriage to "that Andreoli girl" was a *mésalliance.* Her own marriage to Ed might have been a *mésalliance,* but she was too haughty to let her own laws apply to others. She called herself Hill-Santarato. Among the Signora's children she was the proudest of her ancestry. She had traveled farthest from Venice, but in her own eyes she remained a Venetian aristocrat. To her friends who visited Venice she described the site of the Palazzo Santarato in perfect detail. The wealth of the Andreolis made her brother's marriage seem even more unseemly. One might marry—she was fond of using the word "one"—a ballet dancer, but not a *nouveau-riche.* Though she read little—visits to exhibitions and a subscription to the Met were enough for her—she sneered at Teresa's lack of education. She considered her sister-in-law's taste absurd, and once she had remarked to the Signora: "Teresa could mis-seat a table with two guests." Teresa was aware of her sister-in-law's opinion. Since the two women did not want to contradict each other, they spoke little; since they could not attack one another openly, they walked side by side in the no-man's-land of harsh indifference.

And now this call! Remus was in Venice, Teresa said, and this was a last attempt he was making to persuade the Signora into selling the palazzo; Paolo's future depended on it. Should the attempt fail, they would have no alternative but to get a court to declare the obstinate old woman mentally incapable and appoint an official to manage her affairs. "I'm sorry, Laura, but she just is feebleminded. Paolo and I have been in touch with a Venetian psychiatrist, and there's an excellent lawyer available. Paolo can file a petition to the court on his own, but the tacit agreement of all the heirs is required."

"I'll think about it," Laura said.

Then Paolo came to the phone, probably to show that Teresa had not made the call behind his back. But he didn't say a word about the mental incapacity petition, he only asked how Laura was doing and what the weather was like in New York.

In her white Volkswagen, on the way to Geraldine, Laura turned the conversation over in her mind. Had this proposal roused her opposition simply because it came from Teresa? Selling the palazzo was different from selling the Titian. The whole family would be rich. She was not bothered about Paolo's career—why didn't Teresa go to her father, that self-important *parvenu?*—but after all, she had hated the palazzo all her life. The palazzo was a trauma, her psychoanalyst had explained to her. "Your difficulties with orgasm, my dear," he had said, "date back to the palazzo—at least where your love life among us vulgar Americans is concerned. Throughout your childhood you suffered in the palazzo, but you always felt like the lady of the castle, and because the masochistic element is poorly developed in you, you don't like sleeping with the servants."

Perhaps. The masochistic element poorly developed but the snobbish element all the more pronounced. Snobbery? The Palazzo Santarato would remain the Palazzo Santarato, even if others lived in it. The Ducal Palace without doges is still the Ducal Palace. So that was not the reason. It was the word "feebleminded." She had never loved the old woman. A clear case of an Oedipus complex—clear, not curable. Her mother might be feebleminded, a Santarato never! The mental incapacity proceedings could not be kept secret; such matters were displayed on the blackboard at the town hall. One could chisel the name Santarato into bronze plaques, one did not nail it on the door of the town hall, between births and banns and death notices. She decided to talk to Geraldine.

However, this did not prove possible; the party at Geraldine's was too large. They were seven women. Once a month they would meet in the nice home on Long Island which had been assigned to Geraldine after her divorce in Reno. Geraldine was a small, elfin woman who looked less than her more than fifty years. She had taken the house from the shallow adulterer, her husband, only out of anger and revenge, for she came from a rich Kansas family and could live very comfortably off her trust fund. She did, however, maintain a friendly relationship with Andy, the said ex-husband, who had meanwhile spent his last dollar on dumb blondes. Once or twice a month she would sleep with him in a most enjoyable manner, though only in the afternoon, since Andy would have misinterpreted a made-up bed as a sign of reconciliation and a claim to the villa.

At these ladies' cocktail parties there was much talk of handsome Andy; indeed most of the conversation was likely to be about absent men, some of them alive but far away, some dead and departed. The ladies exchanged disappointments. These were hard to understand, Laura felt, both for herself and for the others, since each and all of the ladies were of attractive appearance, so well groomed as to be almost sterilized; only the back zippers of their dresses were at times slightly open. It occurred to Laura that they were grooming their loneliness like their immaculate complexions. Their disappointments must have been the uniting element between them. When at long last they met a man they wanted to keep overnight, they appeared only rarely and eventually stayed away altogether. Laura drove to Long Island every first Sunday in the month, but she participated very little in the conversations. Loneliness was an infectious disease, a society without men was like butter without bread. And although she felt at home in New York, she had to admit that she always remained a Santarato, even in this circle; she found it difficult not to look condescending. For the present problem she would have to decide by herself.

Laura's taciturnity was not noticed. Everyone else talked incessantly; people who are alone a lot need to communicate. They admired the others' clothes and accessories, quite sincerely, rather as if to say: the men who do not see all this grace must be blind. Besides, Geraldine had prepared a surprise this time, something special, she insinuated; the surprise upon leaving was as much part of the monthly meetings as the bittersweet report on disappointments. The friends' financial circumstances were very different. Patricia sold costume jewelry at Saks Fifth Avenue, Marie-Jane owned a prospering antique shop on Madison Avenue, Regina traveled from one golf course to the next. But despite these differences they all appreciated small attentions. They were on intimate terms with objects: books, flowers, a necklace or a make-up jar were their conversational partners.

As the hour of parting drew nearer, the talk began to center on the dangers of the streets at night. Each of the women had had unpleasant experiences at one time or another; one of them had come upon an exhibitionist, a second had been mugged, a third had been knocked down by a black. Even in a car you were reportedly no longer safe.

"Your worries are over," said Geraldine. "I've got a sensational novelty!"

The things she brought from her bedroom looked at first sight like three of the folded jackets carried on airplanes which are called Mae Wests after the full-bosomed film star of the thirties. Soon enough, however, it transpired that this had nothing to do with life jackets, nor were full-bosomed shapes in question.

While the women gathered around, Geraldine positioned herself in

the center of the drawing room, filled her lungs with grotesque
exaggeration, put her lips to the nozzle of one of the gray shapes, and
lo and behold, what ballooned from her mouth turned out to be the
head, neck and chest of a man, the sort of man with swelling chest and
bull neck, as realistic as the painted-on coat pockets, the buttons and
the tie between the white collar. Ugly and brutal the rubber man
looked, despite his pink cheeks, a real FBI gorilla. The only disappointment was that he didn't have a lower part to his body. He was a half-
man, a cripple, his bloated trunk contained in a curve below his belly.
Still, the women understood without Geraldine's explanation what the
novelty meant: the solitary woman's escort, a rubber homunculus, you
simply had to seat him next to the driver in the car to deter street
robbers, muggers and drug addicts.

Laura felt revolted by the sight of the pink cripple with the stupid
face sitting in an easy chair. These women were satisfied with rubber
virility. Was it this that made her shudder? Or was it that the scene
reminded her of Teresa's telephone call? The old woman described by
Teresa as feeble-minded was enthroned in her palazzo, while she, Laura,
sat in a country house on Long Island where everybody gathered
around an air-fed protector.

Geraldine quickly returned to her bedroom to introduce her own
rubber knight, already blown up, looking like the others, but even
more animated through the man's hat she had put on him, one of
Andy's battered hats. "I call him Andy, you've got to give names to
your boys."

Laura did not want to spoil the fun. She breathed life into her future
companion, but she found the ceremony even more monstrous than
the air-birth. Regina christened her Woman's Best Friend, the firm's
name for its product, by the name of Donald. Marie-Jane called hers
Little Joe. Only Laura could not think of a name. She was appalled by
Regina's remarks that she was going to seat Donald at the table too:
"He looks as if he might fancy spaghetti." Laura was also distressed by
Marie-Jane's tasteless comment: "I'm not going to take Little Joe to
bed. That's one place he won't be any use."

Their Best Friends under their arms, the women exchanged cursory
kisses and left their hostess, who had taken the hat from Andy's head
and was waving to them with it.

Since the women without cars had been brought by Regina and

Marie-Jane, Laura was left alone to make conversation with her bloated partner.

A violent downpour flooded the expressway.

Feebleminded? The women she had just taken leave of were twenty or thirty years younger than her mother, but even in twenty or thirty years' time they would not have the slightest inkling of the dignity natural to the woman in the decaying palazzo. The Signora did not wave with a worn man's hat. The Signora was resigned, like herself, but wasn't there a cheerful resignation as well? She cast a look of hatred at the roly-poly beside her. Should she throw him out onto the wet road? A driver might be frightened and believe he had severed a man's lower limbs from his body. For the Signora, a Woman's Best Friend was not made of rubber but of stone. Laura's haughtiness was crumbling: she began to feel like a little girl who has lost her mother in the crowd.

In the diffuse light of the oncoming cars Laura saw the palazzo. There it lay, in the afternoon sun, with its grated windows and its bolted gates and the chimney which rarely produced a thin stream of smoke. Prisons did not let anyone out, nor did they let anyone in: if defense was something more than mere existence, what had she, Laura, ever defended? She recalled the many houses she had lived in, but the windshield wiper seemed to sweep them away. She remembered every corner of the palazzo very clearly. Why had she not given a name to the rubber ghost? What made her feel so superior when she looked down on the Geraldines and Reginas and Marie-Janes? Could her analyst have been wrong? Did she hate the palazzo because her childhood in it had been so unhappy, or was she more like Eve hating her paradise lost?

At the entrance to the Midtown Tunnel she paid her quarter fast so that the policeman would not see the brother of Andy, Donald and Little Joe. She dovetailed into the stream of cars as it moved through the tile-lined tunnel.

In Manhattan the rain was falling through thick fog. The gondolas are now rocking gently past the palazzo. Tourists are sitting on the black benches, or honeymooning couples. But no Andy, no Donald and no Little Joe are sitting near you, no Woman's Best Friend. A thin curtain veils Venice, thin but impenetrable. The church bells chime. The domes shine in opalescent green.

Would the doorman still be up? She would have to be careful

getting out—even East 70th Street was no longer safe—the legless idiot
would not get out with her. "You'll get your share, of course," Teresa
had said. And what would she buy with that money? A larger
apartment, for Cleopatra to wipe more dust? Some more rags, for her
friends to wonder why no man gets caught in them? A companion, not
made of rubber? The airport on the Lido. "Palazzo Santarato!" she
would tell the motorboat driver. He would know immediately what she
meant—that was different from East 70th Street. Teresa expected a
written reply. I shall see for myself, she would write. I am going to
Venice. Through the glass door she saw the uniformed night man. As
usual, she looked for her key with her engine running; she used to hold
it in her hand when she left the car. She touched the flat silver
matchbox, a Christmas present from Geraldine. Slowly, almost sen-
suously, she tore off a match, cupped the other hand over the flame,
then said "Arrivederci!" and set the burning match to her best friend's
belly.

The noise made the night man rush out in a hurry.

28

The Signora had not been to a cinema for years, but the name of
Fausto Massarotti was known even to her. The fake Titian was almost
completed, but Mozetti had had to interrupt his work for two or three
days because of a cold. When Massarotti came to call, she was quite
ready to receive the famous man.

Prince Massarotti was descended from one of Italy's oldest families.
In the fifteenth century the Massarottis had been condottieri—Carlo
Massarotti was the first of them to be mentioned by historians; but
already by the beginning of the sixteenth century they had not only
won high respectability, in addition to large estates in the north and in
the south, but also royal princesses, so that they could boast of blood
relationships with the royal families of Naples and France. One of the
Massarottis who had ruled during the early Renaissance had been a

patron of Leonardo da Vinci. This Ludovico Massarotti was the only one of his lineage Fausto Massarotti liked to remember; in any case he called himself Massarotti, without the prince, wanting no association with the condottieri or their descendants. But since it is easier to forbid a prince to use his title than to stop his valet from addressing him as Your Highness, Massarotti was generally called the Red Prince, and the director had well merited this designation on account of his films.

The Signora, an avid reader of newspapers, was well aware of all this when Massarotti entered her drawing room one late afternoon, punctual to the minute.

He looked the picture of a Prince Massarotti; he did not strike one as at all red. In his late sixties, with a bony face, unusually deep-set eyes, marked by a grave illness—he had recently suffered a stroke and tried in vain to hide the paralysis of his left hand—a knight's armor would have suited him well. In fact he wore a light-colored flannel suit with a striped shirt and a navy-blue tie.

He noticed the Titian at once and made a polite, complimentary remark about it. He also commended the port, although remarking that the secret of this excellent beverage evidently could not be torn from the Portuguese.

The Signora might have heard, he began, that he was making a film in Venice. She said she had; one of her two grandsons, a budding director, had spoken about it. All the better, Massarotti said with a slight smile, for he intended to shoot some scenes—"important scenes, but only two or three days' work"—in the Palazzo Santarato, and he would need her permission to do so.

"Why particularly the Palazzo Santarato?"

Massarotti was embarrassed in his answer; he put his lame left hand on his knee with his right hand. He used tortuous phrases, changed the subject, tactfully mentioned a not inconsiderable fee, and was glad when the Signora interrupted him.

"So you have not found any palazzo in a worse state of disrepair," said the Signora, smiling in her turn. "Are you intending to show the decline of Venice?"

"Venice is not my subject. Only the photogenic symbol of the decadence of our society."

"So you think Venice is bound to go under?"

"Venice *is* going under. The question is whether, and for how long, and by what means, we try to oppose the future. Fascism is nothing but violent opposition to the inevitable."

He had not meant to say that. He loved developing theories; but all he wanted to do was to convince the Signora that her palazzo would make a perfect setting for *Decadenza.*

"Wouldn't it be a shame for Venice?" she asked.

"Beauty is proof neither of vitality nor of morality, quite the reverse. Venice is living on borrowed time."

"Most of us do that."

"But the dying person does not stand in the way of the living. It is different with society. The coffins are standing in the way of the cradles."

"Do you want to burn the coffins?"

"The corpses," said Massarotti. He realized that he was wasting his time, but the surprise the old lady had given him made him feel he had to go on. "In the days of the Great Plague Venice was the place where scores of corpses were secretly burned, although it was against Christian law—a most sensible thing to do. Titian was given burial rites, but they said he hadn't died from the plague, which he had."

"Venice survived the plague."

"Men die all the time, but civilization takes a little longer."

She had imagined Massarotti differently. She felt sorry for the aging director. Because youth is impatient, he hoped that impatience would rejuvenate him. He had sold his castles and now he felt he understood the poor.

"And who is to be blamed for the new plague, Prince Massarotti?" she said.

"We are, for not burning our dead."

"Then Venice must burn, so that Marghera may live?"

A slight irritation crept over Massarotti. He had been told the Signora was obsessed with the idea of saving Venice; he should have deceived her.

"I am not making a film about Venice," he repeated.

"I hear you have been ill," said the Signora, averting her eyes from Massarotti.

"As you see."

"But you did not die. Nor did you know if you were going to die. Where would we be if we mistook illness for death? I assume that you planned a new film on your sickbed—on the inevitable demise of society, for instance."

"On its fatal illness," said Massarotti.

"I am ill too. Cardiac weakness, which is normal at my age, say the doctors, but those idiots take me for a bigger fool than I am. They are giving me nitroglycerine, which helps with angina pectoris."

There was no other palazzo better suited for his shots—and now this old lady, after having lured him onto the ideological ice, was embroiling him in a medical debate as well.

"My case is more intricate," he said. "From a relatively early age I have suffered from arteriosclerosis."

"This will make you laugh, but I am a firm believer in the old household remedy of a garlic cure."

Massarotti did laugh, less over the garlic cure than over the strange paths onto which he had let himself be enticed.

"You played a trick on death," said the Signora, "and I am doing my best. Why do you expect Venice to lie down and die of arteriosclerosis without resisting?"

"Resisting death is the same as resisting life."

"Surely we cannot be such cowards as to fight only when we are certain of success. Do you consider the past a torn-off sheet of a calendar? I was in Marghera recently. There are factories decaying there which were built only a few years ago. The future did not even last ten years. It is sick. But not so sick as you and I. Although you are sick, you fight society, and although I am sick, I have a few piles renovated."

Massarotti started to get up. It was not new to him that a strange power could emanate from a possession, but he had never felt it more strongly than in this dilapidated palazzo. He said: "I turned my back on this society long ago."

"You cannot turn your back on yourself. Admit that you feel at home within these walls. You don't know the walls of Marghera from the inside. What you call the future does not have any use for you, it abuses you."

"The future has a right to abuse us," said Massarotti. He took his limp left hand with his right hand and let it slide into his coat pocket. "I take it, Signora, that I have not succeeded in interesting you in my project."

A few weeks earlier she could not have resisted the temptation.

With the money Massarotti had offered her she could have paid for the most urgently needed repairs and induced Luigi Primavesi to give further help. Patchwork! Two more sessions, as Mozetti called his counterfeit work, or three at most, and the palazzo would be saved! Once you had opted for the grand fraud, you could defend your principles against such minor corruption.

"That's right, you have not," she said. "What decays will decay, but let nobody say that even decay is for sale. A lot of gaiety is being sold these days, sadness should not be for sale."

Massarotti bowed gracefully in a way the Signora liked.

"Please don't think," she said, "that I am against making the Palazzo Santarato available for a film. I would even have gone to see it. I do not want to help you because anyone who does not at least try garlic is making things easy for death."

She accompanied Massarotti through the dark corridor. He kissed her hand.

"The adversaries part unreconciled," he said. "But it was a good contest."

"You see," said the Signora. "Even Carlo Massarotti would have been proud of it."

29

Dario was sitting at the Signora's bedside.

She had never before received him in her bedroom. He knew every nook and corner of her house, but when he inspected the bedroom, she had left him alone. In former years this might have been modesty—or coyness. To this day he had only seen her as a woman about to receive guests or ready to go out. Once she had told him that throughout her marriage she had never appeared at breakfast in her dressing gown— "not because Vincente wanted it that way, but because intimacy should stop at breakfast." Another time she had mentioned the great Duse: *She* said: "In old age you do not dress, you cover yourself." That too had been merely coyness, for she would never have forgiven him if he had not at once noticed even a new blouse. Now for the first time the remedies had been ineffective, and the doctor had confined her to bed for a few days. "I still had to ask you to come and see me, Dario."

She did not show any sign of the illness. The windows were open, the curtains waving; the summer noises from the Canal Grande did not seem to bother the Signora. She lay propped up in her pillows. A sunbeam touched the stylized gondola: the Napoleonic parvenu Empire offended Dario's eye. But at the same time he was reminded of the blissful age of the rococo: the bed of a *grande cocotte,* lace and frills, the cover as if wafted on, the pink silk pillows. The Signora was wearing a pink bed jacket; Dario was amazed at the youthfulness of her skin, the neckline of a thirty-year-old. Age had dealt mercifully with the small body.

The Signora did not admit that it was the conversation with Remus which had thrown her into bed; like all old people she accepted illnesses more readily than their psychological causes. Yet she spoke of Remus immediately.

In her conversation with Remus, she said, she had realized after a few minutes that her grandson had an ultimatum to deliver to her. He had done it with the indifference of a postman dropping a tax demand into the letter box. That had hurt her, more than his mission as such.

Dario was not surprised. In Remus's childhood, particularly before Romolo was born, the Signora had devoted herself to her grandson with a love she had never bestowed on her children. She had found a hundred explanations for the fact that her love had remained unrequited, she blamed only herself for it, and it was not till after Romolo's birth that she calmed down. Later she said to Dario: "How can the two be so different? The same parents, the same surroundings, I have loved them equally–do children really fall ready-made from God's hand?"

She had referred to an ultimatum; when Dario wanted to know more, she used the word blackmail. "He said he was meant to break it to me gently, but that he had no use for Paolo's hypocrisy–he always calls his father Paolo. 'If you don't come to your senses, they are going to declare you incapable of managing your own affairs, and then we'll have a fine mess.' A fine mess he calls it. 'This is a rotten trick,' he also said, 'but it happens to be one of the rules of the game in a rotten society. Honor your father and your mother, and blood is thicker than water, but they don't mind stepping over corpses.' They think they've found a psychiatrist already. Teresa is getting the best lawyer–doctors and lawyers are the hired hands of the rich, he said. What do you think?"

In order to avoid answering, Dario went to the window and adjusted the curtain which had been caught in the frame. Was she afraid? Was her fear justified? Could she stand up to the painful proceedings? Red spots were showing on her face. This despondency before a challenge was not like her at all. Dario began to think she was keeping something from him.

"Is that all?" he said.

"Isn't it enough?"

She wanted to get Dario's advice and yet did not tell him the whole truth. Since her youth it had been like that. Whenever she went to the doctor, she boasted of how well she felt, and sometimes inquired after the doctor's health. "How is anyone to make a diagnosis with you," Dr. Einaudi used to say, "when you conceal the symptoms?" Remus had been snooping around the house. The room where Mozetti worked was bolted, and she had succeeded in keeping secret the forger's visits, but Remus had repeatedly scrutinized the Titian, and Romolo, as if he guessed something, had said: "Be careful, Remus could do anything!"

To her relief, Dario did not probe further. He said: "What does Romolo know about the blackmail?"

"He came into the room at the end of the conversation. The two quarreled so loudly that you could hear it down on the canal. 'If Father does that, he's not going to see me ever again,' Romolo said. 'He'll get over it,' said Remus."

She noticed that Dario was still regarding her distrustfully. Did he guess that Remus had said more than that? "You can be glad someone is going to be put in charge of Grandmama, at least she won't go to jail." She expected a diagnosis and concealed the symptoms.

"I felt paralyzed," she quickly went on. "I couldn't stop their quarrel, I couldn't even forbid them to revile their parents. You know, Dario, at that moment I was not sure if the palazzo was worth defending. Sometimes I feel that all the words which have ever been spoken in a house are enclosed in its walls. With Remus, more refuse has been washed into the house than you and Romolo and good old Carlo could sweep out again. It is easier with the flood."

The business of a petition to the court of protection, said Dario, wasn't nearly as easy as Paolo and Teresa imagined. Even the most primitive judge would see through the purpose of blackmail, and no court psychiatrist would lend himself to such macabre comedy. "But it doesn't have to come to that. Paolo will not jeopardize the name of Santarato, it would ruin him socially."

"Then you feel I should say no?"

"That would upset you as much as saying yes. First you have to get well. I'll come back tomorrow. Think it all over. Perhaps you have forgotten something."

He had come on foot and left the palazzo through the garden. After closing the gate, he took off his tie and set out on his way home.

The sky was that shade of blue known only to the seamen who have escaped the poisoned shores. In the Campo Santa Maria Zobenigo, and in the Calle Larga XXII Marzo, the summer invasion had already started; but the presence of the foreigners did not annoy Dario. He saw the city with their eyes, its imperious and morbid and defiant and wheedling beauty. Dario was grateful to the foreigners, as an actor is grateful to an audience, or like a man who is reminded by other men's infatuations of what he possesses without noticing it.

On the bridge which slopes down to the Campo San Moisè Dario remembered that he had met Naville here yesterday. Naville had greeted him cordially, but acted as if he had never asked him to intervene with the Signora. Perhaps the Signora had already sold him the Titian. Perhaps she hoped that her children, once the deed had been done, would not take action against her, and now, after her talk with Remus, she knew she could not count on their forbearance. What would he do in her place? An idle thought, since nobody could take anyone else's place. He could advise her to resist, but if she took his advice she would have to carry the burden herself; yet if he advised her to surrender, wouldn't he too have given way to revulsion?

Again the Talmud came to his rescue. The Jews had sent a man by the name of Nahum from the city of Gamzo to the emperor with a sackful of precious stones so that he might make the monarch favorably disposed toward them. In the inn where Nahum rested on the way, the jewels were stolen; the thieves filled his sack with sand. Unsuspecting,

Nahum presented the gift to the imperial lord, who flew into a rage at the insult and sentenced Nahum to death. But it was no accident that had made the Jews entrust Nahum of Gamzo with the hazardous mission. They did so because, no matter what happened to him, he would always say: "You must believe." And still believing he prepared to mount the scaffold. But before he could be executed, war broke out, and the emperor recalled the legend that every grain of dust scattered to the wind by the patriarch Abraham would turn into a sword. Therefore, the Jews had sent him swords, more precious than all jewels. He had the sand scattered to the wind, and the grains of dust turned into swords; thus he vanquished his enemies. He pardoned Nahum of Gamzo, indeed overwhelmed him with honors, but he also wanted to know from him how grains of sand could have turned into swords. "You must believe!" said Nahum, and he returned to Gamzo.

"I've thought it over carefully," said Dario to Francesca, after telling her of his visit to his "daughter." "I'll advise her to say no."

30

Paolo lodged at the Hotel Danieli. The two guest rooms at the palazzo were taken, so it was a good opportunity to spend a few days with his mistress.

Eleanora had long been insisting on such a trip. She was an ideal girlfriend, young, pretty and independent, three attributes he appreciated, for the less young, pretty and independent a woman was the more difficult it was to break up. But since Eleanora's husband, a friend of Paolo's, had died, Eleanora had more time at her disposal than he could devote to her; he hoped the excursion to Venice would placate her. It was not her fault that his hopes for an undisturbed holiday proved illusory.

He had prepared himself for a quarrel with his mother, but the Signora, fully recovered, received him with great warmth. She did not mention a word of the conversation with Remus. Did she not take the ultimatum seriously, or was she so cunning that she was trying to disarm him by her confidence? Since she would not do it, he was obliged himself to bring up the sale of the palazzo. Teresa had directed him to present the big deal with "Dick" Wilcox as his own most fervent desire, the chance of a lifetime. Since he left Teresa out of it, and withheld the fact that he was himself the receiver of an ultimatum, he could not make the Signora responsible for a conjugal crisis. The Signora easily managed to represent Teresa, for whom she had nothing but kind words, as in a way her ally: Why did he want to risk such a happy marriage for a business adventure? Would Teresa forgive him if the adventure failed? Adventure, that was the word she used. With it she brushed aside the great business deal, the unique opportunity. For the time being he had to accept a refusal that was unconditional and seemed almost unconsidered. He reported it to Teresa in cryptic allusions and asked for more time.

What had happened since his last visit to Venice? The Signora's behavior puzzled him. When he mentioned the desolate condition of the palazzo, she quoted his own words: the palazzo had defied time for four hundred years, it would surely survive her. Whereas in the past she had asked for his support, at times rather shamelessly, she did not even mention the word money this time; and when he mentioned her annuity, she said with a chuckle: "You know, my son, it is the same as with physical strength—as it dwindles, so do our needs." Had she tapped secret sources? The gondoliere who had fetched him, old Carlo, had told him of repairwork in the palazzo undertaken by Primavesi, but when he tried to play the detective by telephoning Primavesi, the architect declared that he had done only what was essential and that he was perfectly willing to wait for his fees.

Paolo was not used to completing a mission successfully, but he was resolved to do a thorough job this time. He jotted down in his diary the names of all the people who could help him—Remus, Romolo, Dario, Claudia; and he would also try to see the lawyer and the psychiatrist.

Remus appeared unannounced in the bar of the Danieli on the first evening. This was most embarrassing, as Paolo did not dare suggest to Eleanora that she might prefer to stay hidden, but at the same time he was constantly wondering what he would do if she suddenly appeared in the hall.

In the small bar with the red easy chairs, smelling of leather and literature, he sat with his face toward the hall. His ability as a dissembler was evidently rather poor, for Remus asked several times if he was expecting someone. His eyes were on the hall; but there might be a dagger in his back! At the bar behind him three figures had taken seats. They were the characters Remus called his associates, though he did not offer to introduce them. They didn't stand out particularly. Paolo had observed that the old exclusiveness had completely lapsed these days, even at the Danieli. The hall of the old Palazzo Dandalo, though the style was preserved in its Moorish tinsel, now offered a complete assortment of dignified couples, girls with unwashed hair, Americans with Pan Am travel bags, salesmen of art and oil, young men of good families doing their best to conceal their upbringing. Even so, the "associates" seemed sinister to Paolo; in Milan Teresa had managed to keep them away from the house.

Help from Remus? That young man kept talking about his film, about an advance on the money Teresa had promised him. "You'd better get the cash ready. We'll have it one way or another, and the old boy"–he meant Andreoli–"might regret his stinginess."

Paolo enjoyed playing the part of a tough dealer. What, he asked, had Remus to offer, what did he expect payment for?

"Something's being painted in the palazzo," said Remus.

"You mean whitewashed."

"If I say 'painted,' I mean 'painted.' Without too much trouble I could produce evidence against the old girl, the mental incapacity business should be dead easy. But you must bear in mind that I won't do anything really mean–unless I get paid for it."

Hard bargaining on both sides. "I'm not buying a pig in a poke," said Paolo.

"Well," said Remus, "it's the Titian. The paint brushes in the kitchen. And every day the Titian's in a different place. Only a few inches different, but you can tell from the marks of the easel on the carpet. Yesterday I met a bald guy, I seem to know his face. She's probably having a copy made and selling it for genuine. She's so crazy I find her positively funny."

Should he set his son to spy on his mother? He was disgusted with himself, but he was also disgusted with the image of weakness others had formed of him. He went to the telephone booth to call Teresa in Milan. Eleanora, in the room adjoining his upstairs, would make a scene if she heard him telephoning his wife. Teresa praised his detective abilities, and he decided to reward Remus's efforts.

For the following morning he had planned his visit to Dario. It was a sunny morning. Eleanora insisted on accompanying him part of the way. Like many of her compatriots, she knew Paris and London and New York City better than Venice. He caught himself speaking of the salvation of Venice with the same words his mother had used. "Every hair-spray bottle in the lagoon hurts you," said Eleanora. Perhaps. He didn't as a rule bother about his feelings, nothing would be more uncomfortable. After all, it was not St. Mark's Church he was going to sell to an oil magnate, only the Palazzo Santarato. But with the Palazzo Santarato wasn't he also selling the *Serenissima?* He felt he would rather have gone through Venice blindfolded.

The antique shop was closed. He rang at the door of the apartment. Francesca showed him into the living room. Nothing had changed here since his last visit ten or twelve years ago; oh yes, there were more netsukes.

"Dario Ortelli is the real enemy," Teresa had told him. Francesca's chilly reception proved his wife right; women are bad dissemblers. All the better, a brave man will venture into the lion's den.

"I've not come to get you to change your mind," he began. "It's anxiety about my mother that has made me call. I certainly find her in excellent health, but she has never been on very good terms with reality, and now she's positively fighting it. I suspect she would be ready to use any means to stop the palazzo being sold."

Dario replied in a friendly tone that it had not been exactly clever to send Mr. Wilcox to the Signora. "She's certainly not going to smooth your way into the oil business."

"The oil business!" Paolo said. "It's an obsession."

"The whole of Venice is an obsession," said Dario. "You should understand that, you're a Venetian."

As a diplomat he had failed; as a detective, at least, Paolo did not want to fall down. "I can understand that she does not want to sell the palazzo, but she seems to feel that she doesn't have to. Where does the money for the repairs come from?" He noted an uneasiness in Dario's eyes, but Dario merely said: "I often think of the sonnet in which Wordsworth laments the end of Venice:

Yet shall some tribute of regret be paid
When her long life hath reach'd its final day:
Men are we and must grieve when even the Shade
Of that which once was great is pass'd away.

Wordworth was speaking of Venice's last day—and that was exactly a hundred and seventy years ago. We know the reasons for destruction; salvation is always a miracle."

When Paolo was leaving, Dario stopped at one of his showcases. With a loving hand he took one of the tiny ivory figures from its case; it represented a horse, with an old man mounted on it. "This is Ivagenki, one of the Taoist wise men. Magic powers were ascribed to his horse. As long as Ivagenki holds the reins, he will enjoy eternal youth. If he lets the reins go, he will drop dead from his horse. Your mother, Paolo, cannot dismount from her horse."

Dario was an eccentric with his netsukes and his Talmud. Such odd fellows could be dangerous, they didn't get involved in the social game and were incorruptible. At least he had not given away anything to Dario which the latter would at once report to the Signora.

Paolo's diary gave him orders to visit the lawyer Flavio Bellomo and the psychiatrist Attilo della Torre. He telephoned them both to ask if they could see him, but not until the next day. While doing so he realized that he wanted to postpone the leap from intention into execution. The diary, however, was adamant. The following morning he went to the lawyer's office, near the Rialto bridge.

Bellomo, he thought, might have come straight out of some nineteenth-century English novel: a small, deformed man with a cheap pair of spectacles on a pointed red nose, an unconscionable narrator of anecdotes, with a self-importance it was hard to endure. He spoke in a low voice, smiling, without ever gesticulating, like someone serene in his dishonesty. He also resembled a vain magician who is not satisfied with performing his sleight-of-hand, but wants to show his sheepish audience how he has fooled them. He seemed to enjoy his ill repute as if it were his reputation: "I do not win every lawsuit, but I never lose one either." The petition to put the Signora under a court order would be an impossibility, he implied, except for a magician like himself. He enumerated a series of evidential factors which would have to be brought in, in particular recommending evidence of pathologically ruinous extravagance. Paolo objected that his mother was living modestly, even in poverty, but Bellomo did not admit the validity of this. "It is a symptom of pathological extravagance that it is accompanied by pathological meanness. What else would you call it but feebleminded, if somebody grudges herself every morsel in order to renovate some piles which will turn to Gorgonzola in the next flood?" He presented several documents to Paolo, but Paolo signed only the power of attorney.

Now that Paolo could cross off in his diary the appointment with the lawyer, Teresa would have nothing to reproach him with, but he was glad he had made things more difficult for Bellomo. He had not disclosed his suspicion that his mother might be obtaining the money to save the palazzo by criminal means; that would have made a better case than pathological extravagance. Nor would he tell the psychiatrist; he was a messenger, not a hangman.

The psychiatrist received him in his private consulting room where the windows opened on to Teatro La Fenice. Paolo was surprised at the friendly feelings he felt at once for Professor della Torre, for the man in the severely cut, somewhat old-fashioned suit—fiftyish, with gray hair, light-blue eyes and whiskers reaching almost to the corners of his mouth—proved extremely obstinate. "What you have told me about your mother does not convince me at all. I would be prepared, if the court should order it, to examine the old lady's mental condition, but nothing would convince me except my own findings. Statistics prove, Signor Santarato, that out of every ten people who are put under a court order for mental incapacity nine are as capable as you or I. There are no statistics on those who are never in danger of being put under restraint, but I would presume that at least half of them are acting 'completely irresponsibly.'" When Paolo raised the question of a fee, the professor was neither impressed nor insulted. "I get paid by the court, and so poorly, it's true, that my objectivity is not impaired."

Paolo would have been glad to take a rest; he felt more and more like a postman calling at one house after another. But if he was going to have to report to Teresa that his Venetian mission had failed, he was determined this should not be due to him—a good tool for a bad job.

Claudia had told him on the telephone that she was busy with her preparations for the Biennial, but perhaps they could meet in the evening at Harry's Bar; when he declined because evenings belonged to

Eleanora, they agreed on the Café Paradiso outside the gates of the exhibition premises.

She kept him waiting a long time. From the terrace in the Giardini Pubblici he looked across Venice, and while he was looking he realized why he was pleased with his visit to Professor della Torre. He did not want to strike a deal or seize an opportunity, and what Teresa called a career was indeed nothing but a senseless *avventura*. He was of an age when you still make the gestures of youth—and burn up powers which do not renew themselves. Eleanora had come to his bed once more at two in the morning, but he had satisfied her without getting excited himself, a first defeat for his virility which heralded a bigger reverse, possibly a definitive one. Teresa might not care if he fell into bed dead tired in the evening; she had talked to her father of a financial genius, not of a lover. Work was the enemy of potency, and it might well be that Teresa knew that also. But now that he had reluctantly started to think about himself, he perhaps hoped his mission would fail because he did not want to betray his mother.

It was he, not Teresa, who would have to sign the fatal petition, and someday the pleadings, horrible word, would be handed over to his mother, and she would put the spectacles on her small nose—in his childhood they used to laugh because her spectacles always slid off her nose—and she would shake her head, and then she would take up the gauntlet. She was strong, and Teresa was strong, and he was under crossfire from both.

Or was it something entirely different? From the terrace of the café, beyond the Canale di San Marco, you could see the cupolas of the Salute in the afternoon sun, and if you leaned forward, you could make out the building of the Zecca at the edge of the Piazzetta, and the Campanile. One day it had tumbled down, but only the foreigners believed that. In fact it gently lay down to rest, nobody was hurt, and the Venetians had built it up again; nothing tumbled down here, people lay down to rest, and when you were rested, you got up again. The air was as clear as if there had never been any Marghera or Mestre; the island of San Giorgio Maggiore moved closer. In Milan, even yesterday, he had maintained that the palazzo and Venice had nothing to do with each other, the palazzo was a house like any other house. But now he felt as if everything were joining up: his mother and the palazzo and Venice. All this was home—the school on the canal, the birdcages over the balconies of the houses in the Rio del Santissimo, the nocturnal cry of amorous cats, the wrong notes of the orchestras on the market square, the stench of the lagoons in the heat, the pathetic majesty of the palazzi, the haggling of the women in the *mercato,* the weary light of the chandeliers in the Palazzo Santarato, the "gondola-gondola" call of the oarsmen, addressed to the tourists, not to him.

The proud feeling of having to resist evaporated when he saw Claudia. For several minutes he was preoccupied with his shock: she had become skinny, the green flowered dress seemed to hang loosely around a skeleton, her eyes were sunken, her speech agitated—he understood her as little as he did her paintings.

He did not reproach her for having agreed to the sale of the Titian. She said: "Did I agree? I can't remember." Did she agree to the sale of the palazzo? "Of course," she said, but she might forget this too by tomorrow. She scarcely listened when he described his conversation with the Signora, and when he tried to convince her that the only course left for him, Laura and herself was to put the Signora under a court order of restraint, "in her own interest," she said: "You might lend me a hundred thousand lire, I haven't sold anything for months." He wrote out a check for two hundred thousand lire, for which she did not thank him. She did not ask if she would see him again, and when he said he would send her a document she would simply have to sign, she said: "Send it to Mamma, I'll fetch it." She did not let him take her into town, she said she had to return to the premises. He watched her go. The green shape disappeared in the shadows of the trees, as if a thin tree had stepped out of the forest and was now rejoining its fellows.

Romolo had avoided having to talk to him, but Paolo did not want to go back to Milan without being able to tell Teresa what Romolo was thinking.

Black linen trousers, an open black linen shirt, his face suntanned, his hair in well-groomed soft curls: Paolo felt he could recognize himself in Romolo. But he knew that nobody resembled him less than Romolo. They sat on the terrace of the Quadri, Romolo spooning up hazelnut ice cream and answering his father's questions. No, he was not sorry he had spent his vacation in Venice again, the Lido was a bit dirty, but still great, he knew lots of young people, he had made friends with an English family: "My English is fantastic." Girls, perhaps someone in particular? Romolo muttered an indistinct yes. Then, with his nose still in the ice cup, he said: "You want to sell the palazzo?"

"There's no other choice," said Paolo.

"It's not true what Remus says, is it?"

"When somebody is as old as Nonna," said Paolo, "others have to think for her."

"Then you won't see me again, ever," said Romolo. "I don't care whether I finish school. I'll stay with Nonna."

Paolo had intended to ask his son about the bald man, but now he only said: "Oh, you don't understand," and was ashamed of his cowardice.

On their last evening he took the motorboat to the Lido with Eleanora, and stood beside her while she was losing some hundred thousand lire at roulette. He went to the telephone booth, spoke to Teresa and told her that he had not achieved anything definite, but had taken several steps in the right direction. He sat at the bar and drank more than he wanted. Eleanora reproached him for calling his wife behind her back, and he denied it, but was glad they were quarreling, for he hoped she would bolt the door of her room. She was one of those women, however, who will open the door after a quarrel. In the morning he sat at the breakfast table as tired as the aging men who need a lot of luck to get any enjoyment.

The sky was gray as lead when he said goodbye to the Signora. The wind slammed the balcony door. It was sweltering and dark in the drawing room. He noted all the tracks the easel had marked in the carpet. The Signora pretended she didn't notice. She said she had received a letter from Laura, Laura was planning to spend some weeks in Venice.

"I am worried about Claudia," he said.

"I am worried about Remus," she said. "It is not easy to have children."

"Romolo loves you, neither of them loves me."

It was not until he rose that she said: "I am sorry you came to Venice in vain."

He said: "It was good to see you."

She looked out and said: "It is starting to rain. Do you have an umbrella?"

*   *   *

31

This time Romolo had not lied. Barbara's parents actually *had* invited him to dinner.

From the beginning he had felt a liking for Mr. Donovan, whose English sense of humor appealed to him. Mr. Donovan, known as Clean-with-Donovan in England—he owned a chain of dry cleaners— was a giant of a man, two heads taller than Romolo; he sported a red moustache which was usually wet with Scotch; he drank almost unbelievable quantities, without showing the slightest sign of it. He was amazed that Romolo should ask for an orange juice: "You must learn how to hold your liquor, my boy." He talked all the time in clichés, yet he did not give the impression of being uneducated or stupid; he was simply a man who did not bother to do his own phrase-making. In particular Romolo was pleased by the keen interest Mr. Donovan showed in Venice. It was a disgrace that the most beautiful city of the world—"I've been here at least twenty times"—was going to the dogs. There was no necessity for it; with an international loan Venice could easily be saved.

Romolo was less fond of Mrs. Donovan, although Barbara was the spitting image of her mother: a beautiful woman in her early forties, who spoke stilted English and was always referring to the fashionable finishing school where she had acquired her education. She spoke of people whose names Romolo did not know, but who must have been as fashionable as the school. The invitation came from her, he presumed—after inquiries she had made as to the Santaratos's social status.

The attention bestowed on him by Barbara's parents embarrassed Romolo. He did not want to appear in Barbara's eyes as a good little boy from a good family. Once in a while he noticed a searching glance in the eyes of his hosts, though these glances were not directed at him but at Barbara, as if they feared their daughter might do or say something improper. This anxiety, ill concealed by Mrs. Donovan and drowned in loud pleasantries by Mr. Donovan, made him uneasy. There was much more to it than the desire that Barbara might show her best side to the son of a Venetian aristocrat.

From the restaurant, which unlike the grill room breathed middle-class comfort, they went over to the Excelsior nightclub. Here an unobtrusive band was playing in the open, and the colorful lights brushed elderly couples who combined memories of their dancing-school days with the exuberance of today's swingers.

Barbara yawned. "We're going for a little walk," she said, and Romolo was surprised that her parents accepted it without objection. "See you later."

"Let's drive to Malamocco," said Barbara, and went to the porter's lodge to ask if one of the small electro-jeeps was available—"put it on my father's bill."

She took the wheel. The perfectly straight road led past villas and parks which were soon lost in scattered vegetable gardens and scanty grass. But a few miles away from the Excelsior, there were only a few shabby fishermen's huts to be seen. The sea was shining through the sparse trees. "Have you been to Malamocco before?" Romolo asked. "Once, with the group," she said. "We bathed in the dunes, naked." He tried to hide his discomfiture and said: "Lord Byron wanted to be buried here." She said: "I'd like to live with you in one of those fishermen's huts."

She turned off Via Malamocco and drove the car into the dunes. The sand creaked under the wheels. "We'll drive until we get stuck," she said, but then stopped. "Come on!" she said, and took off her shoes. He also took off his shoes and turned up his trousers.

They reached the sea. In the distance you could see the flickering lights of Venice. It was warm, and the water smelled like hay after the rain. Unconcerned about her dress, she lay down in the sand and reached out her hand for him.

His ears burned with excitement as he lay down beside her.

She groped in the pocket of her long dress.

"Let's smoke," she said.

"You know I don't smoke!"

"Marijuana," she said.

He took the cigarette from her hand.

"You shouldn't smoke this stuff," he said.

"Why not?"

"It's harmful. You get used to it."

"I have got used to it. If I can't get hash."

"Do you take hash?"

"Of course."

"Why of course?"

"Everything is shit."

"What is everything?"

"Everything."

He broke the cigarette between his fingers. He was afraid she might be angry, but she crossed her arms behind her neck and turned her face toward the moon.

"Are you cross with me?" he said.

"No, I didn't want to smoke anyway."

He turned on to his belly, propped his head on his elbow with one arm, while with the other he held her around the hips.

"Do your parents know?" he said.

"I don't care. And don't you go thinking you can cure me. I'm not ill."

"You said that everything is shit."

"So what! I take pot because it's fun."

It was quiet. They were silent.

"It's beautiful here," he said at last.

"Yes," she said. "Why don't you touch my breasts?"

He put his hands on her breasts.

"Not through the dress," she said.

He let his hands slide into the décolletage of her dress.

"You shouldn't think," she said. "I can see the wheels in your head. They're turning like mad."

He really had been thinking. Marijuana, and did love begin like that, and why did she contradict herself, and pot, and how many had she loved before, and why was everything different from his solitary imaginings, and why did the touch of her small cool breasts not excite him, and did she expect him to tear her dress off? All that was going through his head.

With a slight movement, almost without stirring, she let the shoulder straps down. Then she crossed her arms once more under her neck.

"We could go for a swim," she said.

Now he was no longer thinking, he kissed her breasts, her throat and her mouth, but excitement did not well up in him until he opened his eyes and saw hers were closed.

"Say that you love me," she said.

"I love you."

"No, in Italian."

"*Ti voglio bene.*"

"That's better. Do you really want me well?"

"*Ti voglio bene.*"

She searched for the hem of her dress, pulled it up slowly. "Take off my briefs," she said.

Her dress was nothing but a belt around her body.

It was all a matter of course. But since he had read about it often in books, he asked: "Do I have to be careful?" She shook her head.

On the way back they stopped several times and kissed. She did not speak, so he thought *he* ought to speak; she put her hand on his mouth.

He accompanied her into the hall of the hotel and was disappointed because the only person there was an old man sleeping in one of the wicker chairs. His feelings were all mixed up, happy at what he had experienced, and glad the experience was over, a victor and jealous of her experiences, satisfied curiosity, and curiosity about the day to come, proud of his possession and uncertain whether he possessed what he loved.

"I shall be on the Lido early tomorrow," he said.

"I shall sleep late," she said.

32

Venice, Saturday, July 15, Afternoon

Egidio Albertini, fifty-one, looks after two rooms at the Art Biennial. It is the thirty-sixth Biennial. Albertini is a veteran among keepers. He is with it for the seventh time.

To guard objects of art is not his main occupation. He is a printer, a machine operator. Working with lead has affected his lungs. When the paper moved to Mestre, Albertini quit. He now has a lease on a paper stall in the Campo San Bartolomeo, right beside the funny monument to the writer of comedies Goldoni. Business is not very brilliant, but it has to do with printer's ink. During the Biennial his wife minds the newsstand.

Albertini feels like the most superfluous man in the world. No painting has ever been stolen at the Biennial. Nobody has ever tried to damage a painting. Demonstrations are not his responsibility.

Although the Biennial is not yet open, he has to wear a uniform. The uniform consists of khaki overalls. In it he feels like a gas pump attendant. Since he is of a quarrelsome disposition, which shows, by the way—there is a green lemon protruding from his scraggy neck—he tried to organize a strike against the overalls. But only two of the keepers wanted to go along, not enough for a strike.

In his khaki overalls Albertini is sitting on one of the steps leading to his pavilion.

He is reading a Mickey Mouse comic strip. Mickey Mouse comics are very popular among keepers. None of them considers Mickey Mouse a part of higher education. But if you have to make the rounds in two or three rooms for months, Mickey Mouse takes on the appearance of reality. Walt Disney is also in great demand in jails. Albertini basks in boredom.

He longs for his newsstand. The foreigners who buy papers are the same ones who will soon flood the Biennial. But the buyers of papers do not ask silly questions. They know what wars, plane hijackings, peace conferences, famines, train crashes, earthquakes and royal weddings mean. In the exhibition they ask: "What does it mean?" What are paintings and sculptures supposed to mean? Nothing at all, Albertini would like to say, but one of his colleagues was fired for such a remark.

Albertini deliberates whether to give notice or not. All summer he will stare at a picture which consists of sixty-four squares. *Otto serie sistematiche di colore in ordine verticale.* Someday the painter will sell the picture. Even though of a quarrelsome disposition, Albertini is not an envious man. But he would like to advise the buyer against buying. For he knows what it means to live with sixty-four squares.

Possibly he could ask for a transfer to another pavilion. He has thought of the pavilion *Venezia: Ieri, oggi, domani. Ieri* and *oggi* would pass, but *domani* is a bleak business. One painter has painted Soviet flags behind the photograph of the U.S. pavilion. *Ancora io credo che sia possibile.* Albertini does not mind communist posters, he merely doesn't understand why he should guard them. The young people admire them, and the old American ladies nod. People nod at anything they don't understand. And if a hand reaches through the canvas and slaps you, you look it up in the catalogue. His friend Federico, Federico Boschetti, works in a pavilion where the images move. Only if the electricity is functioning, of course. You have to be an electrician to keep all the fuses in order. When there is a short circuit, the works of art are out. For his main occupation Federico is a clown, just as Albertini is a machine operator. Neither of them knows anything about art or electricity.

Albertini goes into the pavilion, he has to dust. Most of his colleagues don't often do it. That's his hard luck.

In the middle of one of the two rooms he is responsible for, there is a work of art consisting of mirrors. They are oblong mirrors, as tall as a man, hanging from a clothes rack. They're not ordinary mirrors, they're distorting ones. Looking into such a mirror, you bloat like a balloon, especially around the belly. Head and legs recede; you look like a pregnant dwarf. In another mirror you shrink like towels hanging from clothes lines. But since you are not a towel, it looks as if the angels were pulling you heavenward, the devils hellward, a miracle you are still in one piece.

Albertini takes a cloth and polishes the mirrors. The closer he gets, the more terrible he finds his own face. His mouth turns into a monster's jaws. He remembers that he ought to see his dentist. But a monster cannot be helped, even by a dentist. In another mirror he sees himself in the coffin, shortly before decomposition. He thinks of his six children, aged eleven to twenty-five. The younger ones still need their father. He would have done better to stay in the printing shop, you don't die as easily of lead as you do of mirrors.

He should give notice. He makes a last try. Can you escape this work of art? He tries all four corners of the room. From all four corners he sees himself in the mirrors. The images intersect, he is half brute, half corpse. He runs crisscross through the room. He throws himself on his belly, crouches, bounds off like a runner, moves along the walls, carefully putting one leg in front of the other. But from the walls the squares are staring at him, yawning holes, a picture with a hundred and fourteen question marks, he has counted them.

Albertini thinks of the future. Of the immediate future. That is more difficult than thinking of the distant future; with the distant future you have illusions to help you. For months he faces squares and holes and question marks. And the mirrors. And frightened people who ask "What is this?" and who admire what they cannot understand and who leave you behind, pitying you. Albertini thinks tenderly of the wars and plane hijackings and train crashes. He stops in front of the clothes rack with the mirrors. He slips off his overalls. Then he sticks out his tongue. It is partly thick like a cake, partly thin as spaghetti. But he has reached a decision, he no longer cares.

He stuffs the folded overalls under his arm and goes to the office at the entrance gate. He says he is feeling ill, he won't be coming in tomorrow, there will be time to find another keeper. Then he goes outside to the Giardini Pubblici. A mother is sitting on a bench, moving a pram to and fro. A pair of lovers seek the shade. An old man is reading his paper. From the boat station you can see Venice in the afternoon sun.

Karl-Heinz Petermann, sixty, of Petermann & Petermann, Hamburg, is one of the tourists who often honor Venice with their visits. Such tourists are welcome. But they had better keep away from business deals in Venice. At least that's what the Venetians say. They watch

what is going on in Marghera. Because they believe it will not really
end well, for the foreigners.

Karl-Heinz Petermann wants to do business in Venice. He has
studied Venetian history. A good businessman ought to be a good
history man. In the years 1505 to 1508, German merchants had gained
a foothold in Venice. To their mighty merchandise and trading house
they gave the name Fondaco dei Tedeschi. That is where the main post
office is now.

Karl-Heinz Petermann does not attach any importance to the
building. The administrative building of the German free port is to be
erected in Marghera. Of the forty-five acres of the north quay, over half
have already been acquired by a German group. The ground area can be
enlarged by drainage. In the plan worked out by the firm of Petermann
& Petermann it says: "There would be ample room for helicopter
landing sites, for building hotels, swimming pools, shops, banks,
exhibition halls, convention and congress. centers." Karl-Heinz Petermann wants nothing but the best for Venice. Of course there are still a
few difficulties to overcome. A group wishing to build helicopter
landing sites will first have to do something for historic Venice. Karl-
Heinz Petermann knows what to do. He has not only studied history.
He also knows a good deal about the arts.

On February 13, 1883 Giuseppe Verdi decided to visit his beloved
rival Richard Wagner. In the morning, the maestro had admired
Venice from the Campanile. When he had himself rowed to the
Palazzo Vendramin-Calergi in the afternoon, the ten double windows
of Wagner's palace showed no sign of life. After some hesitation Verdi
pulled the bell rope. A footman opened the door. His collar was open,
his hair wild, and there was a wild look in his eyes. "Herr Wagner?
Herr Wagner died an hour ago."

Eighty-nine years later, Karl-Heinz Petermann, of Petermann &
Petermann, Hamburg, remembers the occurrence; yet no memorial
plaque recalls this example of German-Italian friendship. Verdi the
Italian and Wagner the German, both in Venice. Something has to be
done for historic Venice. Before steps are taken to drain a part of the
lagoon.

Karl-Heinz Petermann has founded a memorial plaque committee. It
is only fair that he should be its chairman.

Karl-Heinz Petermann, single, millionaire, a former captain in the

Wehrmacht, socially ambitious, has combined the pleasant with the useful. He is of humble origin, something forgiven in Hamburg only to those who have a great name. As chairman of the memorial plaque committee he has met the aristocrats, practically the whole of the Venetian nobility. That will be talked about in Hamburg.

This afternoon, everything is ready for the unveiling.

The grandiose Lombardesque balconies of the Palazzo Vendramin are crammed. On the center balcony the city council, in black. In black, with bright purple, the clerical hierachy. *Principesse* and *contesse* in gauzy flowered dresses. Children neat and tidy in their best clothes, as if out of the neat and tidy nineteenth century. Opposite, on the other side of the canal, the populace, tightly packed, gondolieri, market women, workmen, passers-by, foreigners. Only Karl-Heinz Petermann is missing, the official speaker. He will speak in Italian—he has taken lessons.

Karl-Heinz Petermann, however, is already on his way. He is approaching the Palazzo Vendramin from the opposite south side of the Canal Grande. He is dressed in black, with a silver-gray tie. He wears a wig with fair hair, which is carefully combed. He could, of course, afford a gondola. Or a motorboat. Come to that, he could buy them. But from his past, which he does not like to mention, he knows the phrase "solidarity with the people." He has had a splendid idea. Right opposite the Wagner house there is one of the ferry stations, the *traghetti.* The gondolas crossing the canal from that spot are the cheapest in Venice. He will cross over in one of these forms of public transport. For a long time to come it will be the talk of Venice that Karl-Heinz Petermann, the industrialist, memorial plaque chairman, *spiritus rector* of Wagner-Verdi veneration, official speaker, used the people's means of transport.

He goes through the Calle de Megio. When he arrives at the Canal Grande, however, he finds that there are rather too many of the people he is solid with. Crying *Pope!* the Venetians have called the gondola. The first departs without Karl-Heinz Petermann.

On the second gondola, in the end, he wins his fight for a seat. He is not sure he can be seen from the balconies. Unless they see his blond wig. The gondola does not leave yet. A teacher has arrived with his pupils. Now a small boy makes a dive into the gondola.

It is Karl-Heinz Petermann's undoing.

The gondola capsizes. The people on the narrow side of the gondola tumble into the water. Among them, Karl-Heinz Petermann.

At such a moment you don't think of Wagner and Verdi. Not even of banks, shops and convention halls. You might if anything think of the swimming pools. Karl-Heinz Petermann thinks of nothing but his wig. He is a good swimmer. With two or three powerful strokes he could reach the shore. But he is swimming like an Olympic champion. For he wants to reach his wig which has come off his head and is floating on the water like a hairy buoy.

It sinks before he can get hold of it. Only then does he swim to the shore.

All the others are safe.

Karl-Heinz Petermann cleans the green slime off his face. Green slime clings to his silvery tie. Oil is running over his white shirt. The speech in his coat pocket is a glutinous pulp. He dries his bald head.

The unveiling festivities are out of the question. The people of rank and the priests and the children and the *principesse* have fled. Only a few gesticulating men are still standing on the balconies. The ruby-colored velvet tapestry with gold letters announcing the event is hanging sadly in the afternoon sun. The siren of the fireboat is heard. All around there is great cheerfulness. Perhaps because the children were saved. Perhaps because of the blond wig. Perhaps because the Venetians believe that in the direst need there will always be a gondola to capsize.

In the morning Severino Martinelli, thirty-six, said mass at the Church of San Polo. He could count the faithful, there were eleven of them. Old women, one young man. And a young couple, probably foreigners; the young man had whispered something to the woman, probably pointing out the Tiepolo on the wall of the choir. The church is always sparsely attended. Now the word must have got around that its priest is getting married.

Carmine, his bride, thirty-five, lives near the town hall. The priest, in a dark business suit with a white carnation in his buttonhole, started out early.

When he said mass that morning, Severino was saying goodbye to his church. Now he is saying goodbye to Venice. He has found a position with an Italian foreign workers' school in Switzerland, as a teacher. They cannot stay in Venice.

Severino's parents and Carmine's have been living in the same house, at the eastern tip of Venice. The district of Sant' Elena is a large village, not cut by any waterway. There are lawns with grass that is late growing and withers early. The trees are thin, and if you shake them they rattle with dust. On the stone benches of the Parco della Rimembranza sit people turned to stone. From the soccer field the children's balls sometimes fall into the water.

It happened on the fifteenth of July, exactly twenty years ago. The boy was sixteen, the girl fifteen. The night was hot, the playground deserted. The boy had kissed the girl, not for the first time. For the first time he had taken her breasts into his hands. Then they lay down, on the dried-up grass. They made love, as this is called, as if they had not loved each other before. When they opened their eyes, they felt as if they were lying in the moon shadow of a gallows. In fact they had been lying under the soccer goal.

Six years have passed since the priest returned from Sicily. The model student has kept the vow of chastity like a boy doing his math homework. He had no talent for the priesthood, not even for believing. Carmine had no talent for infidelity. She had not married. Because during the years of his absence they had relived the two years of their childhood over and over again, they had loved each other again, like that time under the goal gallows. It all seemed intended like that by God. And he had no guilty conscience.

Carmine has advised him not to call for her. She is a secretary and lives with her widowed mother. The whole family hates Severino.

Severino has been fond of his church as you would be fond of a familiar place of work. Leaving Venice is harder for him.

He is not a rebel. When he confessed to his bishop that he had broken the commandment of celibacy, he had not yet thought of marriage. The bishop could have guided him back on to the right road. But all the bishop minded about was that the conduct of his sheep might become known. All he had thought of was the salvation of the church.

Severino steps on a bridge. He remembers the bishop's words: "You want to enjoy the respect paid to our position. But you are not willing to make the sacrifice." What is he going to say when they ask him at the office what his profession is? Priest? No longer. Teacher? Not yet. Couldn't they have stayed in Venice? It was Carmine's wish that they should go to Switzerland. The churches of Venice are empty. Faith is decaying, like Venice. Only the faithfulness of the priests must not decay.

He goes up the steps to his bride's apartment. The house is noisy with quarreling voices.

The sitting room is crowded. More crowded than the Church of San Polo. Carmine is wearing a white dress with a small white hat. She has white shoes, and in her hand she holds a white bag which is much too small, a child's bag. Severino does not know the dress. It looks faded. For the first time he realizes that Carmine's face looks faded too.

Men and women, young and old. Two small boys, one girl. They fall silent when Severino enters the room. Nobody greets him, nobody speaks to him. Only the little girl says to him: "You look funny . . ."

"We're not going with you," says Carmine's mother. She is like Carmine, with an old woman's face.

Everybody nods.

"Let's go," says Severino.

Nobody moves. Only Carmine's mother suddenly clings to her daughter. Her care-worn face is flushed, she sobs with anger.

"What a misfortune, what ruin . . . you're plunging us all into misfortune . . . I won't let you be ruined . . . he's plunging you into ruin . . ."—*sventura, disgrazia,* Severino hears nothing else. The mother clasps her daughter's legs.

Carmine tears herself away. Severino gives her his hand. At the gate they still hear the mother's curses.

The man in black and the girl in white walk in silence through the calli. Just as Severino felt uncomfortable at first in his priestly garb, he now feels uncomfortable in the unfamiliar suit. He feels as if the walls of the houses were drawing away from him, as if he were crossing empty squares, Venice is drawing away from him.

Outside the town hall there are people standing around. Severino does not notice at once that some are carrying cameras. He feels Carmine's nails in the palm of his hand.

Then long-haired figures hurl themselves at him and Carmine. "You are getting married, Father?" The click of the cameras. "Have you seceded from the church?" He does not answer. "Has the church excommunicated you?" He quickens his steps, Carmine stumbles over her long dress. The *paparazzi* pursue the couple right into the registrar's anteroom.

They are called up first.

When the registrar asks Severino's profession, Severino says: "Priest."

The registrar hesitates. Severino does not know what the man is writing in the big book.

Severino gives a tip to the municipal attendant, who shows them to the rear entrance.

Tears are rolling down Carmine's face.

"Don't mind about anything," says Severino.

They pass a church.

"Let's sit down inside," says Severino.

"It is hot."

Tortorella means turtledove.

The man whose name is Tortorella has a narrow head as bald as a billiard ball. He has a moustache as black as the clothes he is known in to the foreigners.

Tortorella is the receptionist of a luxury hotel on the Canal Grande. As a matter of fact, a famous French poet who wrote of him decided that Tortorella was merely in disguise—"on the model of Greek gods who did not scorn appearing in a lesser shape. This man, then, a master of Scapinism and of Goldonism holds all the threads of intrigue in his hand."

This afternoon, like every other afternoon, Tortorella is spinning his intrigues through the telephone.

Nobody knows how many telephone lines converge under his desk. At any rate Tortorella must have more than two hands. Tickets for the sold-out concert at the Teatro Fenice? Why not? A bellboy will accompany the gentleman to the theater and show him to his seat. All the cabins on the Excelsior beach taken? One moment! Cabin eight, first row. You are going to the Salzburg festival? No hotel room? The connection with Salzburg takes somewhat longer; in the meantime Tortorella is on the phone to various other hotel guests, in Italian, German, English, French, Spanish, Dutch. Salzburg on the line. Do you prefer a room or a suite? The plane to Munich cannot take another passenger? Well, it's not essential for the pilot to be on the plane, is it? Tortorella's visiting card will take you through all barriers. The jeweler from St. Mark's Square. Is the gentleman good for a check of ten thousand Swiss francs? Of course. Tortorella's word is enough, Tortorella has lent money to the Prince of Wales. The weather tomorrow? Excellent. The weather is always excellent. And suppose it rains? Have sun in your heart! Tortorella hums a little tune to himself.

It is his own. The gondolieri sing the songs Tortorella composes. His songs are played at serenades, on the lute or the mandolin. The songs of the gondolieri are Neapolitan. Except those by Tortorella. Are you glorifying Venice? Venice, my dear sir, does not have to be glorified, Venice is glorious.

"Can your records be bought?" a hotel guest asks.

"If you like them," says Tortorella.

Three small record players under the table-cum-desk. Tortorella snaps his fingers at one of the white-clad bellboys: "The record player to room three hundred and twelve!"

"Is there a boat to San Michele?" asks the Dutchman.

"You are not going to visit the cemetery, are you?"

Tortorella's hand goes to his heart, but he does it as if he wanted to remove a speck of dust.

The Frenchman with the small white bread puts down a bunch of flowers in front of Tortorella.

"As usual," says Tortorella.

The Frenchman is an admirer of a Venetian woman. The flowers have to be conveyed anonymously, the florist is not reliable.

"Is it really dangerous to bathe at the Lido?" asks the American girl.

"A complete myth," says Tortorella. "The water is as crystal clear as if it came from a mountain spring."

The hotel doctor has arrived. The lady in a hundred and three believes she has caught a cold at the serenade. Nonsense, nobody ever catches a cold at a serenade. "A couple of aspirins, tomorrow she will be all right."

"Do you think so?" says the doctor.

"Have sun in your heart," says Tortorella.

"And you?" says the doctor.

"I'm all right again," says Tortorella.

"The cardiogram . . . ," says the doctor.

"What does the cardiogram know?" says Tortorella.

He looks at his watch. It is half past six. He should have left at six. The doctor's orders were not more than two hours in the morning and two in the afternoon. If Tortorella is sick, Venice must be sick too. Venice must not be sick. Tortorella changes. Since he always wears the black uniform with the golden keys when on duty, he always wears a white suit in his private life. The street painter outside the hotel entrance looks after him. The thin white figure disappears in the motley crowd. Is Tortorella unsteady on his feet? Is he sick? The painter shakes his head.

33

Although Dr. Einaudi, the old family doctor, did his best to spare the Signora, she understood at once that something terrible had happened.

"Don't be frightened!"—these were the frightening words Dr. Einaudi used on the telephone when she picked up the receiver. Something "had happened," but Claudia was out of danger now, an overdose of sleeping pills; no, no, why should she have tried to take her life? Really out of danger? He could vouch for it, otherwise he would have informed the Signora earlier. Earlier—when? The old charwoman had been unable to wake Claudia and had called the doctor. Certainly a substantial dose, but he had been able to pump out her stomach at home—"that should reassure you." He had been there a second time, in the Giudecca, Claudia would sleep for twenty-four hours at least, the good woman had offered to stay with her—"Please don't get upset, I could have kept it from you, everything is all right." When he advised the Signora against riding to the Giudecca, she was no longer listening.

The paralysis lasted only a few minutes. Then she got dressed, faster than she had done in years. It was five past three. She had not seen Remus that day and Romolo was on the Lido. She ordered a motorboat.

It did not matter whether Dr. Einaudi really believed in an unfortunate accident. It was no accident, she knew, and if it was, it was a fortunate one. What Claudia planned had failed. The Signora felt she ought somehow to have intervened much earlier, there were so many reasons why Claudia should have taken that decision. Against one kind of sorrow or another, this despair or that. When somebody very dear is murdered, the first thing you ask yourself is what he must have suffered before he died. What had Claudia suffered? And was she somebody very dear? The Signora thought about giving love to one's children. Love meant a lot of different things: sternness and gentleness, anxiety and relaxation, curiosity and silence, possession and giving up possession, action and passivity. What should you give if you wanted to give love? She had spoiled Paolo and been strict with Laura, and allowed Claudia to go her own way. She was ashamed to be thinking of herself. Anybody who accuses himself is already half acquitting himself. She wanted to think only of Claudia, who had had her life returned to her as a wife who has run away is returned to her unloved husband. Dr. Einaudi had believed her capable of staying at the palazzo and waiting for reassuring news!

Life on the Canal Grande was like in midsummer. In the Canale della Giudecca the Signora's motorboat was caught in the wake of a tanker; she had to cling to her seat. Like the tourists, she had not believed until now that Venice was living like other cities: with joy and sorrow, with good intentions and bad marks, with lottery winnings and poverty, with convalescence and lost lawsuits. Reality disappeared in the eternity of the backdrop. The Signora began to doubt. Even in Venice one could be longing for death.

She paid the skipper who had helped her to the bank over the wet stones, and started to look for Claudia's house. For twenty years her daughter had been living here, and she had never visited her. She told herself in vain that Claudia had never invited her. She had avoided seeing what she was bound to disapprove of. People talked about doing the right thing by your children, which was unfair, since it implied that you knew what the right thing was. If you let your children go, you were evading your obligations; if you smoothed the way for them, you tied them down; if you walked alongside, you were indifferent. The minute a child was born to you, you were doomed to act wrongly. Still, she found the palazzo without asking for the way even once, and that brought the Signora some relief.

The gate stood open. Climbing the steep steps to the second floor, she looked through the tarnished windows into the garden, which was like a thick copse, with hopelessly entangled branches, weeds and thistles. Mortar from the wet walls lay on the grand marble steps. A cat ran away.

The Signora did not feel her heart. She remembered only for a moment that she had forgotten her nitroglycerine capsules. If she stopped it was because an idea worse than Dr. Einaudi's implication had occurred to her: Would Claudia want to see her? For years she had been talking about the palazzo to her daughter when she should have talked about her, Claudia. "Now you come?" Claudia would ask. "Now you want to know what I was up to. You should have asked what I have been through."

The door of the apartment was ajar. The Signora called: "Claudia!" but nobody answered. Had the charwoman left, was Claudia alone?

The shutters were lowered, the room was in half-darkness. Paintings on the floor, a crate torn open, a nailed lath, an umbrella, stacks of books, newspapers, a useless frying pan. The Signora had merely guessed how her daughter was living, and her heart sank, because external disorder had always seemed to her a sign of the internal sort.

Claudia was sleeping deeply, breathing evenly. Only now did the Signora admit to herself that she had not believed the doctor. For a while she stood at the bed. The pillowcases were freshly changed, but the silk cover, which the Signora vaguely remembered, was crumpled and full of stains. She searched for her daughter's pulse. A cross sound came from Claudia's mouth, but she did not open her eyes.

The Signora cleared a chair of sundry junk, pulled it up to the bed and sat down. She contemplated her daughter. Claudia's face seemed many years younger than she remembered it. The nights at the child's sickbed. At least you could watch over sick children. Why was this beautiful creature alone, at the mercy of a charwoman who had irresponsibly gone off? Was it a man who had left her, or had she grown tired of many men?

An irrepressible urge to do something, to make up for something, overcame the Signora. She looked around. Claudia could not speak, the room would have to tell her.

Although she was sure she would not wake Claudia, she went to work quietly. She put the paintings, some of them so heavy she could scarcely move them, neatly against the wall. She saw that several of them had deep gashes. Had vandals done this? Long ago she had stopped liking Claudia's paintings, and some of them had filled her with anxious revulsion. Perhaps there were people who could not bear what they didn't understand and destroyed what they disliked.

After arranging the paintings, she rolled up the umbrella. She looked in vain for an umbrella stand and put it on the chest of drawers. As best she could, she arranged loose papers in squares; squares give an impression of order. She found a cloth and wiped the dust from some furniture, thinking of the charwoman in expressions unworthy of a Signora Santarato. Oh yes, the frying pan! For a while she had avoided it. Where was the kitchen?

She went back to Claudia's bed. She stroked her daughter's thin arm. Was it age that had crept up on Claudia unawares? Didn't everybody, at one time or another, think of returning to the Creator what He had given, unsolicited? The Signora had never considered making use of the questionable right to your own life. "No return of goods purchased," it used to say on the boards in the stores. She had never felt superfluous, not even now that she was old—in the days of superfluousness. Had Claudia believed that she was superfluous? As far as the Signora knew, the charwoman came only once a week. Had Claudia counted on the charwoman finding her? Should one smile over those who would set only half a foot over the threshold of death! Wasn't the half-despair of others enough, did it have to be the full load?

The Signora was still holding the frying pan. There was no kitchen, just a cooking corner in the bathroom. At the door she stopped, appalled. The dressing table had so many bottles, make-up jars and powder compacts that it would have been fit for an actress's dressing room; but right next to the dresser was the gas range, and on it dirty saucepans and greasy frying pans. In the sink, four or five plates with the remains of food, knives and forks; on the tiled rim of the bath three half-empty wine bottles next to a graceful container with bath salts, then a crushed yogurt carton; the bath with a black rim and full of rotting rose leaves. Had Claudia entertained—given a party, as they put it nowadays—were these the roses somebody had apparently brought along, who were the guests, when had they left, had Claudia said goodbye to them and then grabbed the pills?

The Signora heard a sound. She hoped the charwoman had returned, but it was only a cat which had sneaked through the door. The Signora chased it away. The air in the room was stuffy; a sunbeam fell on Claudia's mouth. The Signora opened a window and dried the sleeper's forehead.

She went back to the bathroom. She never cleaned up at random, she always started in one corner, whether it was the untidiest or not. She let hot water run into the sink and started to wash the plates. After drying them, she scraped the pots and pans free of their ugly caked deposits. Empty bottles, wine, brandy, whisky. Claudia had been drinking a lot–it must have been more than the Signora had suspected. She put the bottles into one corner, cleaning liquids and detergents which had been standing on the dresser into another; she arranged the cosmetics in a semicircle. With clean plates you could have a new start.

She folded the bath towel that had been tossed onto a stool and threw the used tissues into a basket. On the medicine chest, crammed to bursting point, she found a spoon. Illness? Dr. Einaudi would have known. Poverty? Claudia could have turned to Paolo. For the first time the Signora remembered the Titian. She would open an account for Claudia. Profit from a fake? Claudia did not have to know.

For a moment she stood in front of the bath, but she did not feel tired, and her heart was beating regularly, more so than it had done for ages. Since she was small and supple, she had no problem in removing the rose petals and scrubbing the bath. The steam rising from the water made her slightly fuddled for a moment, but that was soon over. Only the white cuffs of her dress had become wet.

When she stood again at the bedside, a little color had returned to Claudia's face. Dr. Einaudi had not been lying. What would Claudia do with the life that had been given to her unsolicited a second time?

It was almost six o'clock, and no sign of the charwoman. Anger welled up in the Signora, fury at the indifferent woman, the calm doctor, the absent friends, her own absence until this day. She looked for the telephone; it could not have disappeared. Again she proceeded methodically and discovered the instrument under a pile of newspapers. She dialed Dr. Einaudi's number, found him at home and let herself go in bitter reproaches.

"Where are you?" the doctor interrupted her.

"Where on earth do you expect me to be? At Claudia's, of course! You must get me a nurse."

"How am I to do that now?"

"I don't care how you do it, but it has to be at once. I'll wait until she comes."

"That will cost a lot of money ..."

"Be so good as to leave that to me. By half past seven at the latest ..."

Meanwhile Claudia had opened her eyes. She seemed to know where she was and asked: "What are you doing here, Mamma?"

"I tidied up," said the Signora.

Claudia looked up at the blue Madonna on the ceiling.

"I didn't want to go on," she said.

The Signora sat down on the edge of the bed. "We'll talk about that later," she said. "When you feel like it."

"I'd like to sleep."

"And so you can."

"I believe Dr. Einaudi was here."

"Of course. He'll come again."

Claudia inclined her head to one side and fell asleep. The Signora stroked her cheeks lightly, careful not to disturb her.

Six o'clock. Romolo had probably returned from the Lido; she had to get his supper ready. She had forgotten to leave a note for him.

She waited. A thought occurred to her: one ought to start a new life. Strange: her daughter had just escaped death, and she wanted to start a new life! This was nothing unusual, though, she had often gone to bed with that thought; in the light of morning the new life had invariably dissolved. When you were nearly seventy-five, it was improbable you would start a new life, but perhaps you could prop up the old piles. On the way here she had reproached herself for having thought exclusively of the palazzo during the past years. But perhaps the palazzo was merely the order Claudia had left behind?

At seven-thirty on the dot Dr. Einaudi appeared with the nurse. To the Signora's relief it was an elderly nun who did not look as if she would leave even for a few minutes. Dr. Einaudi went to the bathroom to wash his hands, and when he returned he scrutinized the Signora.

"Did you do that?" he said.

"What?" asked the Signora. To the nun she said: "Stay until eight in the morning. I'll relieve you after eight."

34

It had not rained for a fortnight, and although the Venetian blinds were lowered from morning till night, the Signora suffered from the heat. She wondered if she had not been mistaken when she thought of the palazzo as an island where no boat from the mainland will moor.

She did not know how to banish her doubts. She caught herself roaming aimlessly through the house; with new eyes she saw the cracks in the walls, the crumbling stuccowork, the wrinkles in the paintings. Decay had seemed something unnatural to her, therefore she could fight it, but perhaps it was all quite natural, and because it was natural she could see no sense in rebeling. Were the wrinkles in the face of the palazzo at all different from her own? If people said she had remained young because she had not defied age, then was it right to defy the frailty of the walls? She had not numbered her years, but numbered they were; she had been thinking of what she would leave behind. Did it matter what you were leaving, or rather, was it not more important who you were going to leave it to? There were children who did not want to inherit. She had thought of Venice and the tourists, not of her own children; she had believed Dario, who sometimes spoke of the world's heritage. But what *was* the world? And it was uncertain whether the world would accept its heritage. The world was made up of people's children.

Sometimes the Signora shivered in the heat. She looked toward the windows, as if a cold wind were blowing through them. In the hours of anxiety over Claudia she had asked herself whether it was admissible to commit suicide, but surely the real question was whether it was admissible to save suicides. There was scarcely one poet of Venice who had not compared the gliding gondolas to coffins. But the gondolas were not coffins, they carried coffins.

She fought against this new weakness. Whenever she saw the palazzo as if through one of those thick dirty ice blocks the iceman used to bring to your house in the old days, she tried to tell herself that she had seen right the day before, that she had only been feverish since that day when she entered the haunted castle in the Giudecca and took for reality what was just a nightmare.

Claudia had recovered quickly and visited her mother almost every day. She did not say a word about the Signora's visit, nor did she thank her. The Signora realized that Claudia's visits were her thanks.

The Signora learned no more about the causes of Claudia's dire decision than on the afternoon she had watched the sleeping woman. Once Claudia used the words "weary of life"—not speaking of herself—but that meant little to the Signora. Like most elderly people, she clung to events. Weariness, discomfort as well, revulsion, bitterness, boredom—had to be caused by a motive you could touch and grasp. Claudia was no longer young, but she belonged to another generation. Perhaps that generation painted, sculpted, and wrote in the abstract because they thought and felt in the abstract. They needed no reason to do something or not do it, so the Signora wondered if she was being unfair to them and to herself when she blamed herself for lack of understanding: where there are no motives, they cannot be recognized. Maturity means motivation. The things which the mature and the immature do or leave undone are similar, but the mature know why they do one thing and leave another undone. Perhaps, however, there was a generation with a climate like the climate of polar regions, where nothing matures, and the autumn is as unfruitful as any of the other seasons. Again, this did not mean that such a generation was more unhappy than the one before; it did not aspire to maturity and was happy like Peter Pan, the boy who never grew up. Claudia was in her middle forties, and it was only now she said she was looking for her self, or that she had lost and refound it, that she was now an adult, or that she would never be one, that she was beginning to understand herself, or that she would never do so.

One day Claudia declared that she wanted to leave the Giudecca and rent a new apartment; the Signora felt this at least was reassuring. She consulted with Dario, called Primavesi, cut out advertisements, but when Claudia made no contact for twenty-four hours, she found a pretext to phone her daughter. Somebody who had been weary of life yesterday could be weary again today. At the same time she doubted whether Claudia would find her way in a new life. Claudia was now aware that the bedspread she had taken from the Palazzo Santarato twenty years ago was full of stains, and that she would feel ashamed in the morning if there was no knowing what the man she had gone to bed with had looked like, and that a black canvas meant nothing more than a black canvas. But wasn't the disorder that had been Claudia's lot for twenty years too big? Would she have the courage to tidy up, whichever corner she started in? Because too many men had not had faces, wouldn't those who had them lose the clear line of their features? Wasn't she too tired to paint anything but black surfaces? Only a better knowledge of Claudia's life could have appeased the Signora's fears, but her restlessness increased, for it just might be possible that everything was understandable—Paolo's behavior and the ruin of Venice, Claudia's weariness and the indifference of the citizens, Remus's perfidy and the greed of Marghera—and that she had merely taken for protective walls what had been dead walls all along.

Claudia could have explained to her mother how close the Signora was to the truth. A man. This one word would have answered the Signora's mute questions. An aristocratic son of Venice, who had emigrated to America over thirty years ago, a professor of geology at Princeton University, almost twenty years Claudia's senior, married, with grown-up children, on a visit to his hometown. In a few weeks he had brought order to Claudia's life; that is, disorder. Suddenly it was no longer good to sleep with twenty-year-olds, no good to go without food, often right till the evening, no good to fasten the bra with a safety pin, no good to infer oppression from poverty, no good to express moods in colors. No promises, no lies, no drama, farewell at Marco Polo airport. A man whose life had been thrown into disorder would return to order; a woman whose life had been put in order would return to disorder. Which of them had the easier lot? Claudia did not ask, she went home, threw everything into disorder, wanted to sleep, and when she woke up she found it ridiculous that people spoke of suicides because somebody had wanted to sleep long and deep and not wake up ever again.

The Signora was glad Claudia came to see her. Sometimes her daughter would stay two or three hours, sometimes just a few minutes. But when she left the Signora always felt disappointment. Superfluousness, something she had never known, was prowling around her now. Claudia did not ask her advice. Was she unable to give any? She accompanied her daughter to the garden gate and looked after her. It was a narrow, dirty *calle* which led to the palazzo. The backs of almost all the palazzi faced such streets. The houses to the left and right had long been unoccupied, but further down toward the city drying washing hung between the houses, noisy children threw their balls against the dead walls, cats flitted past in the shadows. Life goes on, the saying has it, when something menacing occurs, but the Signora wondered if one should not stop sometimes to get one's breath, look back, reflect, remain in front of the mirror and shed a tear. She knew this street where Claudia's shape was getting smaller, just like her own garden, but to her the palazzo had been only on the Canal Grande; and she was no longer sure if she was trying to preserve the palazzo or in the end merely a facade.

Claudia's attempted suicide was not the only cause of her doubts. Remus showed no signs of wanting to leave Venice, and as long as he lived at the palazzo every boat seemed to put in. The Signora had grown used to his snooping around everywhere, asking awkward questions, about the locked room for instance, to his taking furtive looks at the Titian. Once, out of the blue, he even started talking about picture faking. He said that the lower story, deserted for many years, made an excellent "fun room"; he brought friends into the house; and though they did not go up to the hen roost or enter the apartment the Signora often heard down below, in the middle of the night, speeches on one note, cries, stamping of feet on the stone floor, records playing and the radio bawling far into the early hours.

Was it worth defending a fortress which opened itself to the attacker so unresistingly? Remus had not asked for her permission a single time; that did not surprise her; it frightened her, however, that she was lying in her bed awake without taking action. But for her decision to save the palazzo at all costs, but for the fake Titian in the locked room, the first noisy night she would have appeared in her nightgown at the top of the stairs and put an end to the din. If she refrained from selling the Titian, and it was not too late yet, then she could repel the invasion, and would lose the palazzo in the process; if she proceeded with her plan, she would keep the palazzo, but could not drive the invaders away. Was her courage forcing her into cowardice?

Through Paolo and Romolo she had heard a lot of disturbing things about Remus, but when she stood on her balcony and saw that on this

side of the Fondamenta Santa Lucïa the sky drew a line between the
dark clouds of smoke and the expanse of light blue–this was a
remarkable sight, and often unnoticed just because it repeated itself
regularly–she believed in the miracle of Venice. If the sky put up a
barrier, then men could do it too. What Remus did in Milan happened
beyond the gray curtain. Indeed, she could have banished the nightly
row, could have banished Remus too. But from the moment onward
she would have seen before her eyes that prematurely worn face, these
weak and defiant. features, these insolent and helpless grimaces. The
curtain had a hole, but no blue showed through.

Should she ask Romolo's advice, an old woman asking advice of a
boy? She had long since seen through his lies. Almost every evening he
found a pretext to leave the palazzo. She was not afraid of *him*; she did
not have the heart to forbid him something so important to him that
it made him lie. He often looked haggard for want of sleep, and even
though nothing had changed in his tender care for her, even though he
asked about her wishes and fulfilled them at once, the Signora observed
more and more often that his voice was irritable and his movements
agitated, that he seemed pressed for time. She discarded the idea of
speaking to Paolo about him, but she feared he might be keeping bad
company and brooded on how she might find out more about his
double life, or whether she ought to ask him straight out, as had been
customary between them.

Bad company, double life. There could only be bad company if there
was good company, and the walls of the Palazzo Santarato were no
longer so impenetrable that the Signora could fail to notice how the
good company cringed toward peace with the bad. When she read in
the papers that drug addiction had not spared her own circles, when
she heard that it was the spoiled sons of the middle class who marched
under the banners of rebellion, then she laughed at herself for having
stopped Romolo bathing on the popular beach. If Remus, a Santarato,
had kept bad company, you could have rescued him from that
company, but bad company had intruded into the Palazzo Santarato
with Remus. Who was to distinguish the seducer from the seduced?
Remus did not lead a double life, and she began to fear that Romolo's
life was also a simple matter. To lead a double life had always been a
genuflection before your own society; you went to a prostitute, but you
did not bring her into your house. It was quite possible that Romolo

was simply considerate of her outdated opinions and was lying in order to spare her for one summer; that his company was barely different from Remus's; that he took for granted things she couldn't understand at all. If that was true, then her children were right: it was indeed feebleminded to support piles, to restore frescoes and to whitewash walls. Then she had no heir.

35

If Romolo had not tried to understand Barbara, this summer would have been the happiest of his young life.

Night excursions to Malamocco, walks in Venice, bars in the Rialto and near the Frari church, games on the beach; once they had taken a gondola and revisited the same canals as the first time. Already they knew the word "Remember ...?" and that evening, his heart thumping in his throat, she had smuggled him into her hotel room. Reality surpassed his fondest dreams, and apparently he did not have to fear comparison—marvelous and wonderful and heavenly. Those were no mere words of passion, they sounded like *his* virility.

And yet he did not understand her. He desired her, but was not sure whether he was happier when their naked bodies touched, or when she went one pace ahead of him on the jetty to the sun platform. He felt that she had no other thought but to take and to be taken. While he devised a thousand roundabout approaches, she would slip her hand into his trousers in the middle of a matter-of-fact conversation, making him fear the gondoliere would notice the outrageous gesture. But then she said, "When my parents go home, you will hide me in the palazzo"—an absurd plan she embellished with romantic arabesques until he felt like a medieval knight. How was he to explain the fact that on the following day she asked him not to speak of love, it was just stupid, something for elderly crooners.

She was his first love, and he did not realize that he had already admitted the enemy of love into his soul: he wanted to change what he loved. He was sure she had not given up her marijuana cigarettes, and was hurt by this, since he took love for a panacea. If you loved, you could not be ill; if the illness persisted, you did not love. Her weakness, the anxiety she caused him, the doubt she sowed incessantly, the passion which drowned her tenderness—she was all of that. But he did not ask himself whether he would still love her if and when he had succeeded in shaping her after his dreams. He slept worse and worse, his reactions grew more and more feverish, he thought increasingly often of giving her an ultimatum. But then he felt miserable, for he did not know what to demand, and even more miserable when, lying close to her, he could not remember anymore why he had wanted to change something that made him so happy.

He would have understood it all more easily if she had given him cause for jealousy. Practically every day they met Remus and his friends on the Lido, and they seemed to enjoy courting Barbara with obscenities. She simply snuggled closer to him. It was difficult to get away from the group, of course, but after the law of a younger generation which accepts fidelity while making fun of it, the group accepted that Barbara and Romolo belonged together. One day when it was raining and Romolo found no pretext to go to the Lido, she said, "I am staying in my room, I don't want to see anyone. We can telephone for hours. Your voice is enough for me."

One night the illness that had lain dormant inside him erupted.

He had spent the morning on the Lido. The Signora had asked him to run some errands for her in the afternoon, something he used to enjoy very much. He thought it wise to stay at home in the evening too, so that Nonna would be more inclined to believe his excuses the following day. About half past ten he went up to his room, but soon afterward sneaked downstairs again to phone Barbara. He was informed that there was no answer from Miss Donovan's room.

Not long after eleven the ground floor became alive. Although the second floor separated the bedrooms from the ground floor, there was no end to the bawling of the record player, the thud of steps, the jumble of voices from below. Couldn't Remus and his friends find some other night billet? Admittedly there was only one discotheque in the whole of Venice, but at least Remus might have asked the Signora's permission. He was a guest in the palazzo after all. "The old girl had better keep her cool," Remus replied once again to Romolo's remonstrances. "If she's lucky, she'll be put into an old people's home; if she's unlucky, she'll go to a bin or to jail." Romolo had not said anything to the Signora about those abominable words, although that very evening they had been discussing the siege of the palazzo. "You know," she said, "I sometimes feel that Remus is doing it on purpose. Perhaps he wants to defy these old walls. I am not going to give him the satisfaction of being upset. The noise will die away, but the walls will stand."

Toward midnight Romolo decided to go downstairs. Was it his curiosity to see what Remus meant by a jam session? Was it the musical term for an orgy? What was an orgy? Three or four boys couldn't set up such a racket, they must have brought along some girls. In Milan Remus had spoken of group sex.

On tiptoe he closed the door to the Signora's bedroom. He had noticed for some time that she always secretly opened her door a crack. After lighting his bedside lamp he hesitated. Should he go down in his pajamas? It was a disadvantage to face a gang in pajamas. Did he want to have the odds on his side? Now he knew that it was not curiosity pushing him. He was somebody Remus could not threaten with an old people's home, or a bin, or jail; he would chase the gang out of the house. During the past weeks he had grown markedly more self-assured. He was a man. Merely going to bed with a girl did not make you a man. Remus had never made him feel the difference in age too much, and for that very reason Remus could not know that he was suddenly facing a man. He, Romolo, was by himself, and down there, who knows, there might be five or six men. The Signora's rest at night—and the walls—were worth a beating to him. He dressed in haste.

He did not light a lamp. The door from the corridor into the drawing room was open. Through the curtains in front of the balcony, moonlight fell into the drawing room. The flower basket of the Titian was shining. Romolo had been too busy with Barbara during the past days to wonder what Remus had meant, but there had to be a connection between his brother's threats and the Titian. Possibly he was not doing a favor to the Signora by challenging Remus. On the other hand, he might be merely afraid. He was not in the mood to do something or leave it undone out of fear.

The music had stopped, but the voices could be heard all the louder from below, male voices, female voices. Then he heard Remus alone, apparently delivering a speech.

Romolo opened the door at the top of the steps, which gave a full view of the large room. On the stone floor there were some candles—Romolo had discovered traces of wax during the past few days. The light was scanty, and because there was smoke coming from the cigarettes, he could see only the black shadows of the columns and the black shadows of the people, each appearing to have several heads. There was the sweet smell of marijuana.

Remus, standing upright on a stone pried loose from the wall, was finishing his speech. He alone was facing the stairs; the others, about a dozen boys and girls, were listening to the speaker, sitting, crouching, lying around in a semicircle. Now they cheered. The clapping of hands still reverberated from the naked walls when the applause had subsided.

Remus saw Romolo and called, "Hey, junior, come down. You aren't disturbing us, you might learn something."

Romolo was at the bottom of the steps now. He would not have recognized Barbara immediately, but she was wearing the bright yellow blouse he had admiringly helped her choose at the Pucci store. She lay propped on her elbow against a column. Nobody was near her. She scarcely lifted her eyes when Romolo stopped in front of her, almost like that time on the jetty.

He forgot what he had come for and said: "What are you doing here?"

"Nothing."

"Why did you come here?"

"I wanted to see the palazzo."

"Did Remus invite you?"

"I invited myself."

"This is not the palazzo."

"You didn't show it to me, did you?"

"I thought . . ."

"You think too much."

She was smoking marijuana.

"Did Remus give you that stuff?" he said.

"I don't have to anwer questions."

Nobody bothered about the two of them. Remus had sat down on his stone and was conversing with Masina and Gaillard. Cesarini sat against a column; he had a marijuana cigarette in his mouth and was reading a paper. The pince-nez dangled on his naked chest. Two young men Romolo did not know held a girl between them. One had his hand in the low-cut bosom of her dress, the other had his hand under her skirt. All three were lying on their backs, as if they were sunbathing. No one seemed to be paying any attention to the others. At the far end of the room, near the gate on the Canal Grande, a young man was lying on a girl. Romolo could not see their faces. Their shadows on the ceiling moved like those of two mating giants.

Romolo sat down next to Barbara and pulled up his legs. After a while he said: "Didn't it occur to you that I might be here?"

"I didn't think you kept such bad company."

"Would you have told me tomorrow?"

"No, why should I have?"

Some minutes earlier he had been afraid the boys would thrash him. No one had touched him, yet he felt as if he had been beaten senseless. In vain he told himself: What is there to it? She wanted to have the stuff, she came along. But why to the palazzo? Why did it matter so much that it was the palazzo? He felt as if an iron curtain had clanked down before his eyes. Everything that had happened during the weeks since the Signora had met him at the Santa Lucia railway station lay behind this curtain. By the light of the moon they had looked down from the Rialto bridge to the dark canal. Had that been Barbara? At the same time he felt the urge to kiss the girl surge hotly to his head. He did not understand this either.

Barbara smiled, as if she were still surprised at his dismay.

"Why did you come down?" she said.

"I wanted to chase the gang away."

"I find them boring."

The boy who had been amusing himself with the girl in the shadow of the gate–Romolo thought he recognized him as one of the Excelsior bellboys–moved toward the center of the room. A long shadow moved with him, its refracted outline followed him on the wall. He was going to put on the record player.

Romolo rose. "No more records," he said.

"Why not?" asked the boy.

"Because my grandmother can't get to sleep."

Remus had overheard, and said: "Cool it, junior."

Romolo lifted the record player and positioned himself with his back against a column.

"If anyone comes near me, he'll get this thing on his head," he said.

At school he always avoided fights, but he was muscular, he could finish off the bellboy with one blow. The others? He'd have liked nothing better than a good brawl.

The bellboy turned and looked at Remus, but Remus was still sitting on his stone.

Cesarini looked up from his paper.

"We don't dance," he said. "We discuss."

The girl at the gate rose. The shadows on the ceiling melted into a dark semicircle. Only Barbara remained motionless. She got up and said: "I'm going home."

Romolo took her to the door that led to the garden. At the steps she said: "Don't you want to show me the palazzo?"

"Not now," he said.

In the garden he put the record player down on the fountain.

"There are no more boats," he said.

"I'll take a motorboat," she said.

A thousand questions raced through his head, but she would interpret any question as a sign that she still meant something to him. Why should she apologize? She had been lying against the column alone. What would a man do in his place? A man would be strong, he would not take her into his arms. He waited for her to say something.

St. Mark's Square was deserted. Some long-haired shapes rested under the arcades. There was a couple with a baby sleeping next to them in a wooden box. On the tables in front of the Café Florian the chairs had stuck their legs into the air. The pigeons were spending the night on the cornices of the palaces. The church bells began to peal.

There still was a motorboat at the pier but it took Romolo a while to find the driver. What would happen tomorrow? Should he cross to the Lido? He wished it would rain tomorrow, but there was not a cloud in the sky. Remus and his friends and the bellboy. Should he pretend that what he had seen on the ground floor of the palazzo was a matter of course? The thought had never occurred to him that something could be beyond repair. Nothing beyond repair had happened, and yet it was beyond repair; this was driving him insane.

She jumped into the boat and the driver untied the ropes.

36

The Signora was not expecting visitors and was surprised to find Naville at her door. He was perspiring and panting. It was not only the ascent of the steep stairs that had exhaused him, it must have been the weight of the suitcase he held in his hand—although it was not a leather case but one of those light aluminum affairs which are preferred for air travel.

"The weaker the currency, the more of it you need," said Naville, pointing to his case. He put it on the carpet in front of the easel. This was the amount agreed upon, he continued, all in ten-thousand-lire notes, she could check, but that would take the whole afternoon. He hoped she trusted him, he continued jovially, for he was also trusting her. Here was the money he had received, although the buyer was not yet in possession of the picture. Tomorrow, or at latest the day after tomorrow, the goods would have to be deliverd. "Delivered," he called it.

The Signora adjusted her easy chair so as not to see the case under the painting. It seemed as if the girl with the flower basket were reaching for it and wanted to leave.

Her aversion to Naville was so strong that it always diminished a little in his presence. This often happens with people who cannot possibly be as repulsive as the principle they symbolize. His crudeness was less than she attributed to him in her thoughts, nor was he as slippery as she always pictured a con man. He showed his vulgarity without hypocrisy, and she would not have noticed it had he not been dealing in art. It was not an insult to her, but to Titian. At the same time she saw him as one of those people you want to hurt in order to find out if they are capable of feeling anything.

His surprise attack was against their agreement, she said. There had to be four accounts, one in her name, three for her children.

Did Naville know that she had no right to sell the Titian? He didn't seem to care that she had pretended to own it. Or did he really not know, and was it therefore doubly reprehensible to do what she was doing?

"Nonsense," he said, "that business with the accounts really was utter nonsense." He put the purchase agreement on the table in front of the Signora. "Get a porter and take the money to the bank." His client was buying the painting from its owner, he didn't care whether she wanted to give her children half, three quarters or nothing at all. "I know you, he does not. You might say in the end that you received only twenty-five per cent of the sum. My principal pays cash or not at all. Didn't Ortelli tell you that?"

"Did you speak to Dario about the sale?"

"Only indirectly."

"I did not authorize you to do that."

"How do you hope to keep it from him?"

His distrust was aroused, though, for he went to the easel regardless of the insulting nature of his gesture. He bent low, close to the Titian, scrutinized it, and–apparently satisfied–returned to his seat.

"You have struck oil, Signora," he said. "You get the money under the counter, the tax collector is left out in the cold. Cash in hand is worth twice as much as a check, even in lire. Cash is guaranteed, something you can't say of all checks."

Tomorrow, at latest the day after tomorrow! It is not the evil intent but only the deed that distinguishes the criminal from the good citizen. Thieves who don't steal are the basis of society. And she? She was a thief who did steal. In the large stores there were now those dreadful escalators which seem to devour themselves, while they devour those who step on them. They lead upward, but also downward. Once you put a foot on the hungry grating, there is no escape, you cannot leave until they disgorge you. The copy was ready, the original could be delivered, tomorrow or the day after tomorrow. Naville was right— what difference did it make whether he opened four accounts or she divided the money herself? To strike oil! Dario had always filled in her tax return, an easy matter, for there was little to return. If she admitted what had come to her now, she would have to initiate Dario into her secret; if she kept it to herself, she was guilty of a crime for which she could not expect her children's indulgence.

She watched Naville fumbling in his inner coat pocket; an arsenal of fountain pens and pencils appeared, but suddenly she saw a record player.

A few days ago, when she had accompanied Claudia through the garden, she had noticed a record player on the edge of the fountain. Since she did not want to speak to Remus about it, she had asked Romolo. At first he had avoided answering. It was only when she said that the noise in the entrance hall had stopped, and this must no doubt have some connection with the strange find, that he hesitantly told her he had been "fed up" with the nightly goings-on below, that he went down and put an end to it.

"How did you dare do it?"

"I know this kind of gang; they're only brave as long as you don't show them your fist."

"Why did you do it?"

"I couldn't sleep."

"You mean to say that *I* couldn't sleep."

"That too."

And what there had been to it besides the disturbed sleep he did not tell her. But everything, all the doubts and fears that had haunted the Signora since Dr. Einaudi's telephone call, all the self-accusations and the confusion, fell off her now. Romolo would never be "fed up" with anything that happened in another house. But he had defended the palazzo, and since he had not disappointed her, she could not disappoint him. The gang was only brave as long as you didn't show them your fist.

"Black, blue, green or red?" said Naville in an attempt to be affable, while he fiddled with one of his fountain pens.

Did she feel some moral scruples, or was she hesitating only because she didn't know how to get a big suitcase to the bank or how to smuggle a painting out of the house? The drowning man who sinks because he dislikes his rescuer's appearance is an absurd figure. If she did not sign now, she was defenseless against dispossession and decay. "Do you have to sell the palazzo?" Romolo had asked on the first day. "I don't have to do anything," she had answered. If she was unable to foresee the consequences of her deeds, then she was a feebleminded old woman, just as Paolo and Teresa maintained. When she went to see Mozetti, she had decided to save the palazzo—by straight means, if possible, by crooked means if she had to.

"When shall I send for the picture?" she heard Naville's voice saying.

"Black," she said. "I shall send the painting to you at the Bauer-Grünwald. The day after tomorrow."

Naville nodded.

She said: "Please carry the case upstairs. It is too heavy for me."

37

Venice keeps a jealous watch over its Titians, for their number is small; they are scattered to the four winds.

No city in Italy, no city in the whole world, can boast of having been cradle and home to so many immortal painters as Venice. Giovanni Bellini was born here, and Giovanni Antonio Canal, called Canaletto; Francesco Guardi and Jacopo Robusti, called Tintoretto; Giambattista Tiepolo and Vittorio Carpaccio; Lorenzo Lotto and Marco Basaiti; Carlo Crivelli and Jacopo Palma, called Palma Vecchio. El Greco and Albrecht Dürer lived or taught here. But none was as typical a Venetian as the painter from the dark fir forests of the southern Tyrol, Tiziano Vecellio of Pieve di Cadore, who called himself Titian.

In Titian the virtues of my city are typified, as well as her weaknesses and peculiarities.

Titian's rise was meteoric. Eight years at most after succeeding Bellini, he was the official painter of Venice. When Charles V held the Diet in Augsburg, Titian held court. In the Palazzo of the Via dei Bixi, across from Murano, he received Henry III. He expressed his gracious thanks when he was graciously raised to an earldom. Laura Dirento, subsequently the Duchess of Ferrara, was his mistress. He was the richest painter of his time, not one of those unappreciated geniuses whose tombs are fondly crowned by posterity. In his first self-portrait he wears the Order of the Golden Fleece.

Venice loves gold. We make use of those who come to us from the jungle, and it does not weigh heavily on our conscience. Around us we see the cement jungle, the motorway desert, satanic factories, prefabricated ruins. The world gives us its gold, and we lend Venice to the world.

In the language of our times Titian was a superstar. It is easy to speak of compromise and time serving and opportunism. But Titian did not bow to convention; convention bowed to Titian. He allowed others to flatter him, but he painted Charles V with almost Goyaesque realism as a thoughtful citizen, Pope Paul III as a dotard with vacant stare, the extortioner Pietro Aretino as a prince. The Inquisition could do no harm to Titian—in Venice it had to strike its black sails. There is no Inquisition without martyrs, nor are there any martyrs without an Inquisition; Venice has no martyrs. Its triumph is the opportunism it forces on its enemy.

Without Giorgione, Titian would never have become Titian. If it is true that he pretended to be older than he was, he did so in part to prove that Giorgione had learned from him, not he from Giorgione. But he put the velvet cloak of conservatism around Giorgione's revolutionary shoulders. Titian did not invent the dissolution of contours. Venice did not stand godmother to baroque, it married baroque. The greatness of an epoch begins at the altar. Venice is order following chaos. It is the result which follows an experiment.

When Titian emerges from the shadow of his master Bellini with his first independent work, *The Triumph of Faith*, there is nothing immature about the series of woodcuts. The hatred my city encounters—hatred, I say, because it is an impious myth that Venice inspires nothing but love—the inexhaustible hatred of intellectuals against Venice is their hatred of perfection. The seeker always hates the one who has reached his goal. Since the intellectual thinks he can fathom everything, he is out of his depth in face of the unfathomable. The boundless beauty of Venice confines him to his own limits. He is convinced that he can distinguish kitsch from art. The harmony of Venice silences criticizing, the intellectual's favorite pastime. On the lagoons contradictions die.

I shall not settle the dispute as to how long Titian lived. Most of us believe that he died at the age of one hundred and three, distrusting immortality. Yet it is true, no doubt, that Titian enjoyed playing the part of the old man. He never painted spring; autumn was his season, the afternoon his time of day. His Madonnas are surrounded by full fruit baskets, his daughter Lavinia carries a bowl full of shining fruit; *L'amor profano* is as ripe as *L'amor sacro*. His flowers are of a rich ocher and a deep purple, and when he depicted Adam and Eve, he did not forget that the weather must have been autumnal in Paradise; otherwise Eve could not have picked the fruit of the tree of knowledge. When the plague ravaged Venice, the centenarian locked himself up within his walls and subsisted on piled-up stores. When he died, an almost completed painting stood on his easel.

Venice was born mature. My city excites people's envy, but has left envy behind. She is as grand as a beggar whose last garment is a dinner jacket. She rouses not sentiment but passion. She is not lecherous but amorous. She does not fight but lets others fight for her. She is not arrogant but proud. She is not clever but wise. In times of plague she subsists on her reserves. She does not want to die. And should she die, she will leave behind the memory of perfection.

38

The only person the Signora could trust was Anselmo Mozetti.

Now that she had decided to run the risk, she could again smile at herself. At one time she had enjoyed reading detective stories, in particular certain English ones about a very crafty old lady who constantly exposes herself to danger and always prevails. That heroine, though, was a clever amateur detective standing on the side of the law: crime doesn't pay. The Signora was playing the reverse part—but that was no reason to play it less expertly.

Nine o'clock in the evening was a good time. Romolo had asked her the day before if he could attend a concert at the Teatro Fenice. Possibly he was really going; she had looked it up in the paper. It was true that the noise in the entrance hall had stopped, but there was no certainty that Remus and his friends had been chased away for good. At any rate they never occupied the "fun room" before eleven at night. She also considered it a good omen that the sky had become overcast in the afternoon. Night fell early. Dark deeds in a dark night, she told herself.

On the stroke of nine Mozetti arrived. She did not recognize him immediately, for he was no longer wearing a beard, only a thin moustache. A slight fuzz framed his long chin. Which famous painter was he now?

He had brought a large flat crate, nails and a hammer. He put the crate on the floor, collected the cotton wadding that had fallen from it, and went to fetch the copy of the Titian upstairs.

"Have you ordered a gondola?" asked the Signora.

"As agreed, at ten sharp."

After putting his own Titian on the easel, he sat down in an easy chair and examined the two paintings.

No idiot of an expert, he laughed, would be able to distinguish the two pictures, but it was advisable not to have the Mozetti looked at too closely. The paints were still a bit soft; this could be checked with a fine needle. "Nothing you can do about it."

"You are in a good mood," said the Signora.

"This is because I have become Degas. What a holiday – after Titian! Actually, I am the most enviable person under the sun. When I am tired of being an Italian, I turn into a Frenchman, and when I don't want to be old, I become young." Degas had painted his last self-portrait, he continued, at the age of twenty-six. At that time he had still been completely under the influence of the old masters; it could be a Velázquez. And yet he had nearly reached Titian's age, eighty-three.

Disregarding the Signora's impatience he began to talk of age. When Degas was about sixty-seven, Jacques-Emile Blanche had painted him. It was the end of their friendship, for Degas forbade him to exhibit the painting. Blanche deceived him and published the portrait in an art periodical. Degas was a man who did not want to face himself in a mirror. Titian was only a monument. It was a strange thing with mirrors, Mozetti continued, you couldn't rely on them. You couldn't even be sure that they deceived you. "For years they keep the contract, they hide wrinkles and little veins and paleness and weariness and sorrow, and then, some morning, they tell you the truth. But scarcely have you resigned yourself to it, when the mirror starts lying once more. The early self-portraits of painters are not quite as insincere as those of their later years; the mirror doesn't yet lie so blatantly to a young man, so a young man who sees himself in it does not lie either. Did the aging Degas refuse to see the truth? This was the extent of his honesty, the ability to admit defeat. It is not heroism but deceit to continue a lost battle."

He frowned. "Alas, when I am not Degas, I am Mozetti. In fact, I ought to be in a terrible mood, for you are embroiling me in a most embarrassing affair. Up to now I could have said, Signora Santarato ordered a copy from me, period. But now I am smuggling the Titian out of your house, which makes me a party to your fraud. Your children will forgive you, and I shall be the crook they put in jail."

"There's more than that," said the Signora. "I would like you to go to the bank with me tomorrow and deposit a case full of money."

He rose, and went to work with a sigh. "In the clink I had plenty of time to study the natural history of crime," he said. Whenever he recalled that time, he fell into the jargon of the gray buildings. While he was carefully removing the Titian from the easel, he told her about a burglar with whom he had shared his prison cell, a youngster from a good family who had visited other people's residences because he wanted to buy jewels for his mistress, a lady of luxurious habits. That woman had later sat in the courtroom, shedding crocodile tears. It was true that she had not known about the burglaries, but she wanted to keep the "sparklers" anyway. "With the exception of a few perpetrators of sex crimes, all criminals do their deeds to please someone, and it is that someone who should be locked up, whether he instigated the criminal act or not. Everything wrong in the world happens because somebody is unable to say no, but nobody asks who made him say yes. I didn't say no to you, Mousie, and therefore I shall sit in the dock while you shed crocodile tears."

"All this is very true," said the Signora, glancing at her watch, "but you must hurry now."

"The gondoliere will wait. He is a friend of mine."

"Remus may be back any moment. He has inquired twice already about a 'bald-headed guy.'"

"When I was arrested and my photos appeared in all the papers, I was bald-headed, but I did not wear a beard. I was Tiepolo then." Very carefully he laid the Titian into the crate. "I have also changed in many

other respects, especially since I met you. You are a danger, like all
people with a fixed aim. What the jewels were to that spoiled mistress,
the palazzo is to you. And what your palazzo is to you, my ghetto
suddenly is to me. I want to save it. Nothing is more catching than
fanaticism."

"The entrance hall is still empty," she said. Fear had gripped her;
within a few minutes she had looked at her watch twice.

"I take comfort," Mozetti said, "in thinking that the whole of
humanity ought really to be locked up. I don't say no to you, and you
don't say no to your grandson. Everybody is somebody's yes-man.
Sentimentality as well as fanaticism is the enemy of humanity. You
should never have told me the truth; that was my undoing. Sometimes
I think that we Italians alone are human, that is, both sentimentalists
and fanatics. But can you say anything worse of a man than that he's
human?" He picked up the hammer. "Now you have reduced me to a
carpenter, and that's the one thing I didn't want to be, if only because
my father was one." He reached for the lid, which he had rested against
the easel. "I don't care. And now say a nice goodbye to your flower
girl."

The Signora bent over the Titian, which he had wrapped in cotton
wadding. It was impossible to distinguish the painting from Mozetti's
work. Was it really that easy for her to part with the picture she had
known ever since Vincente Santarato had shown her his palace for the
first time when she was a girl? He had inherited it from his father, who
had inherited from *his* father. Was not the Titian also a part of Venice?
The pawnshops were full of family paintings and family china and
family jewelry to which the owners of the palazzi had said farewell, not
au revoir, pawned to save some naked walls from decay. The Signora
understood them. Venice was a vessel which contained many things—a
past that belonged to the world, and memories that belonged solely to
the individual. What the vessel contained could be loaned and
mortgaged, given away or thrown away, but if there was to be any
hope, the vessel had to be saved. *Girl with Flower Basket*, a genuine
Mozetti, would adorn her drawing room quite as well as the genuine
Titian. And should she ever view it wistfully as proud women look at
the copies of their necklaces whose originals are worn by other women,
unbeknownst to society, then she would tell herself that the fake Titian
was standing in a house that was proof against the elements.

"At least this is not a sentimental parting," said Mozetti.

She nodded with a smile which she had prepared like a veil, then she excused herself and went upstairs to her bedroom. She took a bundle of ten-thousand-lire notes from the case and put them in an envelope.

"This is a trifle you are not going to refuse," she said to Mozetti, who was about to nail up the crate. "I am a rich woman."

"Once again, I can't say no," said Mozetti. "I do it to please *you*. You know this makes you an accomplice."

She sat down, exhausted, and watched him put his painting on the easel. He was working too slowly, it seemed to her. She thought she heard the creaking of a door.

"A bit more to the right," she said, "otherwise it will be obvious that the easel has been moved."

"The perfect crime," said Mozetti. "Now all we need is for you to keep a lookout. If you don't come back within five minutes, I'll know that the coast is clear."

She obeyed. On the way down to the entrance hall, on the narrow stairs, she felt great tenderness for the counterfeiter. He used expressions such as clink and crook and keep a lookout, but those were new colors in his soul. A fine needle was enough to discover the fake. In reality he was Titian and Degas and Tiepolo and El Greco. Once he had finished his Degas, she would ask him to help her with the restoration of the palazzo. She was going to miss his visits.

She opened the door to the side canal. She admitted to herself that she was scared.

A gondola was tied to the white and violet post. The canal was dark, but the lights of the Canal Grande fell on the dark waters as if they were shining through hundreds of keyholes. In the reflected light of a passing vaporetto she saw the young gondoliere.

"Signor Mozetti is just coming," she said. Her model from the English detective stories would never have done that. Perhaps Mozetti had given his name to his friend as Titian or Degas.

Five more minutes, then she could say that the die was cast. Her accomplice was taking the painting with him, he was "delivering" it, as Naville would say.

If only she had let Dario into the secret! Conscience is a curious thing, it sleeps most peacefully when surrounded by enemies.

To distrust those who are unworthy of trust, to hide from the talkative what they would divulge, to dupe the sly, even to deceive the deceitful—all that does not disturb the conscience in its guilty sleep. But why had she closed her doors on her friend? In a few minutes she would go upstairs to the drawing room, check that her accomplice had not left any traces, and then, until Romolo and Remus returned, only the dim light in the corridor would be lit. People talked of being alone with your conscience, and by that they meant that you were in bad company. She had included a price in her deed, but it had not occurred to her that loneliness could be that price.

She heard steps behind her and turned, alarmed. Mozetti was carrying the heavy crate on his back and made no move to put it down when she reached out to shake hands with him. She stood on the tips of her toes and kissed him on his cheek.

The gondoliere had left his boat and helped the painter to stow the crate.

Then the gondola glided past the palazzo toward the Canal Grande. Mozetti waved to her. "Go indoors!" he called. "You'll catch cold. It's starting to rain."

39

In her feverish activity the Signora was unconcerned with the inevitability of discovery. She was sure not even Dario's expert eye would recognize the fake, but everybody, Dario and Primavesi, Romolo and Remus, would ask her where the money for the repairs had suddenly come from. She could not think of an answer, but found relief in the thought that well-prepared lies are worn thin even before you utter them, whereas spontaneous excuses dazzle by their freshness.

For years she had kept a careful account of everything needed for the salvation of the palazzo. As she took up her papers, she smiled because she had applied the Mayor's principle in her classifications: urgent, more urgent, most urgent. Even during the years when her list had been nothing more than the record of a dream, she had always thought first of the essential things. The rotten piles had to be supported. But no dead body will come back to life because crutches are forced under its arms. The Venetians spoke of stone cancer, but they were thinking of the marble cancer above all. Whether the marble they had used came from Istria, from Carrara, Verona or Brescia, it was all calcium carbonate, and no other raw material is as vulnerable to the murderous mix of oil vapors and humidity. That famous ancestor of Vincente Santarato who had built the palazzo had been a lover of marble. The weakened marble construction would have to be renovated simultaneously with the wooden piles. After that the plaster of the facade had to be renewed; the posts in front of the gates, the cracks in the walls and on the ceilings, the glass in the lanterns needed mending; there was the restoration of pictures, statues, paneling; miscellaneous painting and decorating jobs. Her share of the sale would barely be sufficient for the most indispensable repairs, but again it was the same on a small scale as with Venice on a large: hope meant doing what was indispensable. The Titian, at least, did not require restoration; it was as good as new.

She pressed Luigi Primavesi to submit an estimate of costs. He seemed to question her sanity. She spoke of a benefactor, an American millionaire, who had fallen in love with Venice, with the palazzo. "All he wants is a memorial tablet, and he can have that." When Primavesi left, she was convinced that he would not pass up this business. As long as there was a bourgeois world for Luigi to fight, work and profit were inseparable.

A few days later he returned with an estimate. "Prices for a friend," he said, although they turned out to be higher than she had anticipated. However, he continued, it was not possible to begin the work right away. For her, exceptionally, he did have a group of skilled workers available, but they were at the moment on strike: "*Scioppero*, you know, Italy's daily bread."

"The work is urgent, Luigi," she said.

"To you, Zia Anna-Maria, but for the workers that is one more reason not to do it. If the hospital orderlies—who are on strike for a change—did not know that the patients need them, their strike would be a lost cause."

"And you approve of this?"

"It doesn't matter whether I approve or not. It doesn't even matter whether the workers approve."

"What does matter?"

"The labor unions."

"Aren't they composed of workers?"

"Yes, but the union bosses make the decisions."

Was this the same Luigi Primavesi who had praised the world of the workers just a few weeks ago? Perhaps he still approved of the hospital orderlies' strike. His mother, she remembered, enjoyed remarkably good health. It was only the building workers' strike he did not seem to accept quite so enthusiastically. The marble was sick, and Luigi was running a clinic for sick marble.

"The concept of the strike," he said, "dates back to a time when the employers didn't yet know how far they had to give way to avoid revolution and still make a profit. In 1894, in a strike of two million seven hundred thousand workers, England lost a hundred and sixty-two million working days—what an age! The employers became ruthless and the workers revolutionary. Now strikes are harmless duels, after which each of the survivors—both survive!—believes that his honor has been vindicated. These are contests between gentlemen. The unions distribute the pistols and see to it that their adversaries shoot into the air. The worker doesn't really want to go on strike, either because he is stupid enough to be satisfied with his wages and his working conditions, or else because he is wise enough not to jeopardize the final success by false results."

Luigi had not changed, after all. Although she did not want to become involved in a political discussion, she felt she had more to gain by showing understanding for Luigi's aversion to the strike. She said: "Would you prefer to lose two million working days?"

"When the workers take over the factories, I shall march with them. But they do not march, because the unions prevent it. They offer satisfaction to the worker with the capitalist's money; the satisfied worker is lost for the revolution. You are going to say: 'Don't you want to see the workers satisfied?' I don't want to see any moderate workers. Just as satisfaction is the enemy of the revolution, moderation is the enemy of power. Hegel and Marx ... " He stopped short.

"Go on," she said. "One is never too old to learn."

What she really knew was that one is never too old to listen. Young women were said to know how to revive tired men, but men never grew tired if you listened to them.

"Marx spoke of alienation," Primavesi said. "The worker is alienated from his product. That's to say he doesn't reap the benefits of his product. In Marx's time the miner who hauled coal was freezing. Now that he has central heating, he no longer understands that alienation is evil in itself."

"I see," said the Signora, although she did not understand. She did not always understand Dario either, and for twenty years he had not realized it.

Primavesi, used to talking to people who did not understand him, seemed concerned only with developing his theory.

"As long as higher wages or better working conditions were the objective of the labor movement," he said, "striking was meaningful. The fact that the worker continues to produce something he does not really own is incidental, since he is alienated from the power; it is withheld from him by the employer, just like the coal in former days, and with the assistance of the unions at that. This is the alienation of today. Listen, five or six of my best workers came to see me yesterday and asked me to raise their salaries a little bit, because they wanted to get back on the job. What a state of affairs, I thought; what was I to tell them? If I let them work, they consider me a very fine employer, something most embarrassing to me, since I know that I exploit them. Furthermore the union will pounce on me, because it wants to be the sole peacemaker between the exploiter and the exploitee. If I refuse the workers' request, they will not believe for an instant that I am acting in their own interest; they will appeal to the union, which I am thereby supporting, even though I know it is alienating the power from the workers. If I give in to the unions, I increase their power, which prevents the assumption of power by the workers. If I oppose them, I become an enemy of the labor movement. If I give the Fuerede Primavesi firm to the workers, I am a benevolent employer creating the impression that there might possibly be some other charitable employers. If I don't give it to them, I am condemned to continue exploiting them." He cleaned his clean spectacles.

All this sounded quite logical—from the point of view of a man who believes that a better world could only come into being after a great flood, but who takes an umbrella so long as it is merely raining. Since

at present it was merely raining, the Signora was wondering how she
might get him to take his umbrella. She had noticed a certain lack of
assurance in his voice, and she thought also that he might have left her
long before had he not himself been seeking a solution.

"I'll admit," she said, "that two years ago, when the doctors were on
strike, Dr. Einaudi still came to give me an injection."

"That was probably an emergency."

"Is the palazzo not an emergency?"

"The strike will come to an end someday. The workers will get
higher wages. I've included that in the price, by the way."

"You see, Luigi, it is a matter of difference in age. I don't know who
invented the idea that youth is impatient. They have all the time in the
world, and they know it. We old people are impatient. My patron may
change his mind any time, and I want to see the palazzo restored
during my lifetime. I am lucky. I don't have any principles. When Dr.
Einaudi came that time I told him: 'I know you are working illicitly,
but I do feel better.' "

She had uttered the lie quickly, but Primavesi did not seem to notice
her furtiveness; he had taken off his spectacles and was leafing through
the cost estimate.

"Of course there will always be strikebreakers," he said.

"If the five or six men who came to see you . . . you could give them
some work; they would certainly consider you an exploiter anyway, and
five or six revolutionaries more or less cannot make all the difference."

"The unions are watchful," Primavesi said. "Nothing remains
hidden on the Canal Grande. If divers started work tomorrow, half of
Venice would be gaping."

"You could start inside."

"True; the kitchen is really unfit for use. The cracks in the walls . . .
This is an emergency."

"Precisely. But so are the stones which have to be replaced in the
basement . . . How does it help you or the workers if I have to call the
fire department . . . ?"

"I condemn strikebreaking," he said. "It undermines proletarian
solidarity. But since the union has broken its solidarity with the
workers and is merely an intermediary who on the one hand raises
production prices and on the other forces up consumer prices, I don't
see why the workers should show solidarity with the union."

"I see your point, although you have done me too great an honor with your explanations. At any rate I pay cash."

"Of course. You will have to pay every day, direct to the workers. It must not go via the firm."

After Primavesi had left, the Signora put on her spectacles and checked her list. Urgent, more urgent, most urgent. Everything was urgent.

40

Bruno Cesarini had prepared everything most carefully. Pietro Masina, the sound engineer, had pleaded for a dramatic kidnapping. Remus was to take a gondola at night. The others—Masina, Cesarini and Gaillard— would approach the gondola in a motorboat, overpower Remus, who would pretend to resist, and, should it prove necessary, the gondoliere as well. Then they would drag Remus into the motorboat and make a quick getaway. Cesarini, Gaillard and Remus himself had voted Masina down. It would have been difficult, if not downright impossible, to find an accomplice among the motorboat skippers. Even in a deserted canal the kidnapping would have caused a stir and the involvement of the police, and if all that *could* be carried out, the elaborate "timetable"– one of Cesarini's favorite expressions—would have to adapt to un- foreseeable events. Uncertainty, Cesarini believed, was part of the psychological warfare. Remus should remain missing for a few days before the blackmailers contacted the family with their demands—they had agreed on half a million dollars. If the question should later arise how the kidnappers had seized Remus, they could say that young Santarato had been held up while walking in a secluded street and had then been bound and taken to a secure place.

Remus had dinner with Romolo and the Signora at the palazzo. After ten he said he was going for a walk and would be back rather early. "I have no plans," he said. He went to St. Mark's Square, walked

past the Danieli, along the Riva degli Schiavoni; he was to meet
Gaetano Balmelli; the gondoliere involved in the plot, at the mouth of
the Rio Ca' di Dio. The clothes on his back were all he had.

Although it was nearly eleven and the meeting was set for a quarter
past eleven, Remus took his time. To spend five to six days, perhaps
even a week—as Cesarini's timetable provided—in the rooms of a
gondoliere in Murano was not a tempting proposition. But it was not
the discomfort or the consequences that worried Remus so much as the
question why he had agreed to play this risky game. His desire to shoot
a film which would contribute to the collapse of the establishment and
make him one of the most famous directors in Italy, if not in the
whole world, had solidified into an obsession, and as prospects looked
increasingly unhopeful, it had grown more and more compulsive. The
specter of dilettantism rose before him very clearly: they had been
talking for far too long, now it was time to act. The arguments of the
cameraman and ideologist, Gaillard, that basically the money would
have to be acquired by violence, even if there were other ways and
means, convinced Remus. Legal financing represented a compromise
with the establishment, with venality and corruption—like Stalin, who
had started his career robbing trains.

But as Remus walked through the misty evening, past the equestrian
statue of King Victor Emmanuel II and the moored tugboats, he felt
his own will dwindle. He felt like an object, at best like a robot which
staggers along, putting one foot in front of the other. In the days Paolo
had spent in Venice, Remus's contempt for his father had increased to
infinite proportions, less on account of Paolo's plans, but because those
plans were not Paolo's own. Remus knew, of course, that his father was
a puppet in the hands of his despicable society. The rag doll rose, it
clapped its hands, it wielded the broom, only when the wire puller
chose. But as long as this society existed, didn't the wire pullers belong
to it, as well as all the puppets, Punch and Judy, the Fairy Godmother
and the Demon King? His father put up no resistance to his mother,
but then he, Remus, was letting Cesarini banish him into a gondoliere's cottage. Wasn't he just like his father whom he despised?
Even on the bridge over the Rio della Pietà he thought of turning
back. But the fears that had assailed him were so manifold that he
didn't know which fear it was most cowardly to run away from and
which it was bravest to resist.

There was only one gondola where the Rio Ca' di Dio flows into the Canale di San Marco, but he greeted the gondoliere with the password impressed upon him by Cesarini, "*Fedelta.*" The gondoliere replied "*Fedelta,*" and the boat moved off.

The moon was hidden behind a cloud and Remus could barely see his rowing jailer. Gaetano Balmelli was not much older than himself, in his late twenties, a strong man with a particularly small head. It looked all the smaller because his chin receded to the throat in an almost geometrically straight line. Cesarini had told him that Balmelli was a member of the communist union to which many gondolieri belonged—"contact with the exploiters gets the lumpenproletariat roused"—but he was not so prominent in it that the authorities would hit on him in search for Remus. An unselfish man, too, since the quite considerable sum for which he had agreed to take part in the risky adventure was to go to the party after deduction of Balmelli's actual expenses.

Remus was talking a lot, too much, he felt. He wanted to make friends with his kidnapper, perhaps because he did not trust his partners implicitly and might have to rely on the honesty of his host. Balmelli, however, was evidently not inclined to converse. His brief replies sounded surly, like those of a man who feels that conversation is not a part of his role or his fee.

The gondoliere had to row past the cemetery island of San Michele, which had made Remus shudder from his childhood on. This was less because of the ghosts which—so it was whispered—would rise from their graves here at the midnight hour and celebrate a skeleton's carnival. His shudders were caused by the sinister sliding planes leading everywhere from the elevated bank to the water. The coffins in their funerary gondolas adorned with wreaths were taken to the white marble gate with much pomp and song and incense, but some years later they slid down the slanting boards, like barrels from the breweries, into anonymous barges for burial far away or, as some people alleged, to be dumped into the sea. The moon, now that the clouds had glided past, shone down on the white tombstones towering above the walls, and on the runways for superfluous coffins.

"Let's hope you'll get used to it," said the gondoliere at last. "I don't live in a palazzo."

Remus had not bothered his head too much about his lodgings, but the area where Balmelli moored was decidedly unpromising. It was the jetty of a decayed glassblowing plant. All you could see was the rear wall of an ugly brick building. They had to climb over rubbish and ashes, rubble and discarded tins. Balmelli said: "I could have moored in front of my house, but Bruno didn't think I should."

Remus did not know much more about the island than the foreigners who come to Murano to admire the glassblowers at their glowing work, to buy glass gondolas, glass horses, glass clowns and in the dusty museum to remember the glassblowers of the past. In their time they enjoyed aristocratic privileges and had to atone with their lives if they dared to export their art abroad. And yet he soon realized that through the dark, narrow alleys they were approaching the Canale Grande di Murano. There was a smell of fish and fire. Remus asked if there was any risk of meeting people who might give them away later on, but Balmelli answered with a shrug—there was nobody to be seen anywhere. Murano, the malign "M," just as in Mestre and Marghera and Malamocco, had menaced Venice once upon a time, but most of the factories were abandoned, their chimneys burned out, the windows of the workshops boarded up, the workers' dwellings deserted.

Under the street sign VIA GARIBALDI Balmelli stopped and made a sign for Remus to wait. This at last was a residential district, houses with at most one upper story, with brightly colored walls like African houses. Only an occasional light filtered through a window to the street.

Balmelli returned after a few minutes: "My house is the third one on the right. Keep close to the wall."

On the ground floor of the house there was a shabby stationer's shop. Remus wondered how the fact that a stranger was living on the second floor could be kept from the stationer and his customers.

The door at the top of the wooden stairs stood open.

Remus had expected to meet Bruno, André and Pietro, but there was only a young woman waiting. "My sister," said Balmelli. Remus could not detect any family likeness, for the girl, in her middle twenties, was at least a head taller than her brother, with dark hair, fleshy lines and a whipped-cream complexion—so that she looked like the cream puffs with chocolate icing in pastry shop windows. She did not deign to smile at the stranger; the cream had curdled. Remus's friends had not mentioned that anyone else had been told about the kidnapping, but come to think of it he realized there had to be someone to look after the prisoner. Still, he was disappointed, for if the accomplice was going to be a girl, she might at least have been more attractive. Also, Remus had not pictured a "reliable comrade"–as Balmelli called her–in the shape of an overweight matron.

"I will sleep next door with Maria," said Balmelli. "You will sleep here on the couch." Remus was not to go near the window nor, of course, to move out of the house. He should move as quietly as possible, especially during the day. The comrades had got him all the underclothes he would need. Maria would cook for him. "You'll eat what *we* have." There were some books if he wanted them. No visitors, naturally, except that Bruno would come tomorrow, with the tape recorder. "He will tell you what to say."

Remus wiped the perspiration from his forehead. Balmelli opened the window. He said: "You may open the window at night."

Maria brought a bottle of wine and three glasses. When she saw that her brother was pouring a glass only for himself, she filled Remus's glass.

"Couldn't you be a bit more friendly?" Remus said to Balmelli.

"I don't see why," Balmelli said. "I am friendly all day. With people like you."

"You don't know me."

"To me you are a pampered rich boy wanting to make a film. When everything's over, you'll denounce me. Unless you understand that you'd be in for something if you did. I hope Bruno told you that."

"Bruno trusts me."

"At any rate, you'd better remember it. And remember too that you can't change your mind. If you try to run away, Maria will shoot you."

"I volunteered for this."

He looked at Maria, who was arranging the cracked oilcloth on the table with her soft, fat fingers. She did not utter a word, but she was eying Remus with a mixture of scorn and sensuality, as if to say that she wouldn't mind having a little fun with him, with the gun always at her fingertips, of course.

Balmelli took the bottle and put it in the cupboard.

"You can wash over there," he said. "We don't have a bathroom."

After the two had withdrawn, Remus flung himself on the couch, fully dressed. This was obviously a misunderstanding. He was here of his own free will, and he was free to leave again, without a cream-puff amazon stopping him. But if Balmelli was serious about his threat, then he was a better gondoliere than a kidnapper. The prisoner slept alone in the room with the window toward the street. He could simply open the window and call for help. His comrades probably wanted to put him to the test. But wasn't it humiliating to be put to the test? The taciturn gondoliere who couldn't care less for his film, who would pocket the promised money and afterward continue to row pampered rich boys from the Danieli to the Madonna restaurant, was sickening. His fat sister with her lecherous eyes who would certainly place her pistol next to the pots and pans, was also sickening. Suddenly he felt as if Cesarini, who never finished the script, wrote lousy poems and gesticulated with his pince-nez, had always seemed sickening to him. What about himself? Wasn't a person who found everybody sickening just as sickening?

He looked at his watch. Early tomorrow the Signora would find his bed empty. She would consult with Romolo. He would answer: Remus has disappeared in Milan before, don't you worry! But in the evening she would inform his father anyway. His father wouldn't do anything about it because he was not the type to do anything. Therefore nothing was going to happen until they asked for the ransom. And suppose old Andreoli didn't shell out? It was anybody's guess how long he would then have to stay put in this damned hole, and in the end he might even sleep with this comrade whose elbows were like shapeless knees. He should have thought about all this earlier. He had imagined it differently. A charming gondoliere, perhaps with a charming mamma cooking spaghetti. Script conferenes with Bruno and André and Pietro while they were waiting for the money. Bruno would bring a tape recorder, would he? There had never been any mention of a tape recording.

The silence was interrupted by occasional snoring sounds from the room next door, and it was not exactly funny to rack one's brains as to whether it was Balmelli snoring or the girl, whether it was possible to distinguish a male snore from a female one. Neither Romolo, who slept in the adjoining room in Milan, nor the Signora ever snored. Perhaps only the "proles" snored. But for once this newly discovered class distinction, probably as unjustified as all class distinctions, did not rouse Remus's revolutionary consciousness. He caught himself thinking of the Signora with a certain tenderness. Unlike his parents, she was a respectable adversary who did not squander her possessions but defended them, and if it were true that she had sold a fake Titian, then she was a small-scale train robber, even though for a bad cause.

He went to the window. Some lighters with a freight of glass— *Fragile!*—were tied to the bank of the dark canal. Wasn't he a freight of glass himself? The slumbering, single-floor houses on the other side seemed to stare at him malevolently; they were guarding him just like the fat girl.

Well, he would have a serious word with Bruno. He was the hero of this adventure, for he alone had something to lose, and furthermore he would have to spend a whole week with this horrible fellow whose chin reminded him of the slides of San Michele, and this new La Pasionaria who had eaten too much spaghetti, while Bruno, André and Pietro were amusing themselves on the Lido. Perhaps the plan was not his own, but he was certainly not a mere tool.

He began to undress and switched off the light. The voluntary prisoner contemplated ways of escape.

41

The morning after the night in the palazzo, Barbara had been waiting for Romolo at the jetty. She had not said a word about the incident, nor did she broach the subject in the next few days. But they had not kissed again.

He could not understand her silence. Was it all unimportant to her? Then she would have pretended that nothing had happened. But she wasn't doing that, she simply remained silent. He had to make her realize what was important to him and what wasn't. "Your face is different," she once said, but she did not ask why it was different. He began to suspect that those who know how to keep silent will always win the argument in the end, but he did not yet suspect that stronger nerves generally go with a weaker character. Should he take her as she was? What was she? He only wanted to talk to her. Quarrel, parting or reconciliation—the conversation would decide that. Could he give her up? He would have had to know if *she* could give *him* up. He could have started to speak of the evening in the palazzo, but he had picked up the gauntlet of silence; he did not want to surrender now. Perhaps she was only waiting for a word from him, just as he was waiting for a word from her. Was it sensible to give in because only children don't give in, and anyway it might be all a misunderstanding. He was afraid that nothing could repair what had been done, but he was even more afraid that it would be irreparable because of a misunderstanding. Time passed. The Donovans would soon be leaving.

One evening, in the midst of the confusion, which was accentuated by the disappearance of Remus and the work in the palazzo, Barbara's parents invited him to dinner again.

They sat on the terrace of the Excelsior. It was a sweltering evening; the sandy beach at their feet and the sea were shrouded in haze. The lights of the lighthouse were lost in the fog like fishhooks in murky water.

He couldn't tell how the conversation had come around to the Signora. Mrs. Donovan remarked rather tactlessly that Venetians were said to be very reserved and that they very rarely and reluctantly invited foreigners into their houses. That did not apply to Romolo, Barbara said, but Mr. and Mrs. Donovan ignored her remark as if Barbara would certainly not have accepted the invitation. Not at all, said Romolo, it was not his grandmother's way to shut her house to foreigners, she simply had a lot on her hands, the palazzo was being repaired, and she was supervising the work in every detail. He talked himself into a passion. He only dimly remembered that at his primary school he had at first often talked of his home; insecure among his schoolmates, he had looked for something to hold on to. Now he exaggerated. Once the palazzo was restored, the city would have to restore all other palaces—this would no doubt interest Mr. Donovan, since he had hinted something in that line. Mr. Donovan did not react; he had probably long forgotten what he had said about the salvation of Venice. Romolo was unperturbed, and he even made an almost aggressive remark about his grandfather: that he would rather fly to Hong Kong than visit Venice. He boasted that his grandmother's taste was unequaled: for weeks she had been looking for an old lantern to replace a broken one. "Everybody knows my grandmother, she is simply called the Signora." But he always called her Nonna, as little boys do. He thought he registered an ironic glance in Barbara's eyes, but he didn't care. Nonna this and Nonna that, she had made a speech at a meeting of citizens, by the way, there were at least two thousand people present, a triumph.

"We'll go for a little walk," said Barbara, when her parents decided to spend the next few hours at the bar.

"Look after Barbara," said Mrs. Donovan. "I'm afraid there's going to be a thunderstorm."

The other hotel guests seemed to be afraid of that, too, for the electric jeeps were standing in front of the entrance in a long row.

"Do you want to drive?" said Barbara.

"I haven't got a driving license."

"Nor have I. You don't need one for these toy cars."

"Where to?" he said, as he took the wheel.

"To Malamocco, of course."

Of course. They were going to drive to Malamocco, of course, they would lie down in the grass, of course, she would tell him to pull off her briefs, and that he didn't have to be careful, that she had taken the pill. And all that, she believed, was a matter of course, without their having discussed the evening in the palazzo. He kept his neck stiff, looking straight ahead of him. She was wrong.

The silver leaves of the trees were tinkling. Any minute now the wind would grow violent. In the light of the headlights they saw a woman and a man hastily covering a fishing boat with a tarpaulin. Romolo drove slowly, the windshield was clouded, and also speckled with the bloodstains of foolish insects.

"You were almost beautiful when you spoke of your grandmother," said Barbara.

"I thought it worried you."

"But you wouldn't have minded?"

"No."

"You love your Nonna very much, don't you?"

"Yes, I do."

"I envy you," she said. "I have never loved anyone very much."

"No one?"

"Not very much."

There were flashes of lightning over the golf course, at the eastern end of the island.

"Do you want us to go back?" he said.

"You, a little bit," she said.

Soon they would reach the spot where the road branched off to the dunes. He would drive on, around the golf course.

"Was I your first woman?" she asked.

"No. Why?"

"Because you're so disappointed."

"I'm not disappointed," he said, but he was sorry immediately, for that was no way to start a conversation.

She put her hand on his hand on the wheel and said: "I should like to be friends again."

Had she said: Let's be friends, or: Be friends again, he could have accepted or refused. But what she said sounded so helpless that he forgot all the conversations he had carried on with her in his mind. A man does not start a conversation when a woman tells him: "I should like to be friends again." He took one hand off the wheel and put it around her shoulder.

At the fork in the road he did not slow down, but she said, "Right fork!" and as he went onto the narrow path she said: "When you spoke of your grandmother, I loved you more than just a little. We'll talk about everything, later."

He stopped the car.

"Leave the lights on," she said.

The intervals between lightning and thunder were growing shorter, and it started to rain.

"Hurry!" she said.

She ran ahead of him, toward the sparse trees. She threw her dress over her head. She was wearing nothing underneath.

Among the trees he caught up with her.

42

Every summer Dario would invite the Signora to eat a *cassata* with him at the Café Florian. This summer she had declined twice already. That hadn't surprised him, but it disturbed him that she accepted at once this time.

He hesitated to talk to Francesca about his hunch that the Signora's acceptance might have something to do with the Titian, and when he did, because he was unable to keep secrets from her, he felt he had to defend his friend.

Francesca had never uttered a derogatory remark about the Signora; the idea that she might be jealous of the old lady seemed absurd to her. Dario saw it differently. In more than twenty years, since he first met the Signora, the two women had met four or five times at most. The Signora had never set foot in the house in the Piscina di Frezzeria, she had never asked Francesca to visit her. Francesca, who was given to temperamental outbursts, would have rebelled against such treatment, but she sensed that Dario's life too, like hers, was excluded from the Signora's existence. Once in a while she would remark on Dario's "one-sided love" and Dario would not protest, although he felt the term was inappropriate female terminology. The Signora, who trusted him, made little demand on his trust—probably less because she didn't care about his private life, than because she did not want to care about Francesca. Though he did not admit it, he felt flattered by the Signora's jealousy.

And now, as Francesca was once more criticizing him for his "one-sided love," what grieved him was that the Signora was apparently locking him out of one compartment of her life, for the very first time. But how heavily the secret must be weighing on her mind, if she did not disclose it even to him, and how terribly she must be suffering from her disingenuousness! Their conversations, for which there never used to be enough time, had on occasions been very sticky lately, because disingenuousness is like those modern keys which lock all doors by locking one.

Now that he expected her to break her silence, he was afraid. Perhaps the partition in the confessional was there to safeguard the sinner's anonymity, but in fact it might also protect the confessor if he could not bear to see the sinner's expressions. He had to stop her from humiliating herself before him.

He was there half an hour before their appointment. Although in the afternoon, when the sun is blazing down on the Café Quadri, Venetians and foreigners alike choose the shady side of St. Mark's Square, the Café Florian, there were people only on the terrace, and the interior of the café was empty. Nothing had changed here since Dario's childhood: there were the same low plush chairs, the same oriental glass paintings in the grandiose style of the turn of the century, showing black servants, Arabian potentates, beautiful golden-haired mistresses, shepherds with a Biblical radiance. The smell of coffee had impregnated the walls. Dario chose a table in one corner, a ceremonial arrangement he had never made before.

Then he paced up and down under the arcades, keeping his eye on the western side of the piazza. At last the figure of the Signora appeared. Her step was less firm than usual, but then Dario had for some time seen her only inside the palazzo. Everyone walks differently inside his own house than between any other walls—and yet even now he admired her graceful dignity as she moved through the crowd.

As he was listening to her, he smiled at his fear that she might humiliate herself. The waiter had barely brought the ice cream when she said that she owed him a confession, but that word "confession" always seemed to imply regret, and she did not regret anything, except that she had not let him in on the secret from the beginning. If she had never been alone after Vincente's death, she owed it to him; she had found this out the minute she started to lie to him. Regret? Morals were a strange matter, a sort of chemical process; one person would find your reaction moral, another immoral. "I am capable of an immoral act. The only thing that pained me during all these weeks was the secrecy toward you." She loosened her corset—he had never seen her without one—without uncovering herself, but he could still see into her bosom. He fought his corruptibility; he had better watch out.

"Do you too consider me feebleminded?" she said.

"Feebleminded and out of your mind are not the same thing," he said.

"Out of my mind, then?"

"At any rate we shall have to clear up the mess you have produced."

Naville was lying, Dario thought, when he told me that the painting was destined for a Venetian collector. There isn't a single Titian collector in Venice, least of all one who could afford such a sum. Naville will have to return the picture, the Signora the money. If I, Dario Ortelli, tell the Frenchman to his face that he is intending to smuggle the Titian out of the country, then I might succeed in forcing him to return it. I've never followed the practices of other antique dealers. I've never said that this work or that is "attributed" to one old master or another. I've never deliberately presented old rubbish as an antique. When naming the century I've never used the word "approximately." To lots of astonished customers I've said: "If there were as many antiques as are on offer, then they'd have had to produce Madonnas on the assembly line during the Gothic period." And now I'm prepared to cheat someone, even to blackmail him. But do I, who consider it absurd that the Signora should be put under restraint, have the right to act on her behalf? And was it unreasonable to sell the Titian? Perhaps it was the only reasonable thing to do if the palazzo was to be saved.

The waiter offered pastries. Dario marveled at the care with which the Signora made her choice from them.

"I know what you are thinking, Dario," she said. "It is good to seek a friend's advice, but it may also be a sign of friendship not to ask for any advice. I do not need help or absolution. At seven in the morning I am wakened by the hammering of the good strikebreakers. I go through the house and breathe the smell of paint."

"You have offered Paolo and Teresa on a plate the grounds for incapacity proceedings. What you did is fraud, and Paolo will even appear as the good son by declaring that you are not responsible for your actions."

"Who says the fraud will be discovered?"

"That's just what *I* have to discover. If Naville sends the painting abroad, it cannot be kept a secret."

Dario had never wanted to be rich. Now he wished he were rich to buy back the Titian and have the palazzo restored. He was not rich, but he was corruptible: instead of demanding that she exchange the fake Titian for the genuine one, he merely tried to protect her against the consequences of her venture.

"You don't know how relieved I feel," said the Signora. "I don't even feel the heat. All the same, I'll order another ice cream, if I may."

Soon afterward he offered to take her home, but she declined. She had planned to do a bit of shopping.

He took his leave of her at the druggist's in the Calle Larga XXII Marzo, turned around and went to the Bauer-Grünwald. The gray-haired street painter was making his charcoal drawings outside the hotel, surrounded by a curious crowd. Why here, seeing that they were of the Ducal Palace, the Rialto bridge, canals with gondolas? He recognized Dario and asked him for the hundredth time if he would take his pictures for sale. "We'll talk about it next time," said Dario.

The moment he entered the icy foyer, he knew that something unpleasant was in store for him. He wasn't really surprised when the receptionist told him that Monsieur Naville had left. Had Monsieur Naville left a forwarding address? No, they knew only his Paris address. And they had got him an airline ticket to Athens.

43

Remus put on the tape recorder, for the fourth or fifth time this evening. He heard his own voice. The tape that reproduced it was not the same one Bruno, André and Pietro had approved. He had spoiled three recordings. In one he had spoken too fluently, like somebody reading a text—he *had* been reading, from Cesarini's script; in a second recording he got entangled several times; on the third his voice had sounded too unconcerned, no mortal terror. The syndicate had taken along the definitive version, but the three had forgotten to destroy the discarded recordings. Remus considered this amateurish.

Now, finally, the recording would be sent to Grandfather Andreoli. They had decided to skip Paolo. A heart-rending appeal from the kidnapped grandson. With corresponding instructions for his ransom. Half a million dollars, in a funerary gondola at anchor outside the repair shop of one Sandro Carnielutti, in a flat briefcase, pushed under the posterior of the angel of death. The idea of the angel of death was Gaillard's; he was proud of it.

Maria entered the room. She was wearing a short nightie, of the kind called "baby doll" some years ago when it was still in fashion.

"Switch off that silly gadget," she said. "It might be heard downstairs."

"There's nobody downstairs. I've closed the window."

"But I can't sleep."

"Isn't Gaetano coming home?"

"He's driving tonight. For a friend."

"Sit down, comrade," said Remus. "I can't sleep either."

"I've told you a hundred times that I am not your comrade. You are a pampered rich boy." But she sat down on the made-up bed.

"Where's your gun?" said Remus.

"That's none of your business."

He switched off the tape recorder.

He had seen all the films of the old masters and he remembered Chaplin's *Gold Rush*. Snowed-up mountain hut in Alaska, the storm raging all around, Chaplin alone with his companion, bitterly hungry. In the gold digger's feverish fantasy of hunger, the bearlike companion turns into a chicken. Remus had now been in the gondoliere's flat for a week; for ten days he had not slept with a girl. He had read, eaten, read, thought, but mainly he had been bored. With every day that passed the cream-puff amazon seemed more appetizing. The bosom swelling forth from the nightie was enormous but surprisingly firm. The smooth thighs were so large that the short garment slipped even higher when she sat down; it barely covered her private parts.

"Now you'll soon be rid of me," said Remus.

"You have behaved quite well considering everything," said the girl.

"Then why can't Gaetano stand me?"

"Because you're an intellectual."

"Marx was an intellectual too," said Remus, and he sat down next to the girl.

"But he didn't make films."

"Yes, he did. Detective films." He didn't know why he had said that; perhaps he wanted to find out if the comrade knew her Marx. When she did not reply, he said: "What is Gaetano going to do with his share?"

"He'll give it to the party. What did you expect?"

"You could have a better life ..."

"Gaetano does not want a better life."

"You smell of lavender," said Remus.

The girl blushed.

"If I felt like it, I could run away now," said Remus.

"You just try! I am stronger than you. I have worked all my life."

"Work weakens you," said Remus.

"I can shoot you."

"Without a gun? Or have you got it hidden?"

He put his hand on her thighs, and since she did not resist, he let his hand slide under her nightdress.

"I'll shoot you anyway," she said, but a moment later she was groaning so loud that he put his free hand over her mouth.

He was always thrilled when a woman screamed in her ecstasy of love, but this one screamed louder than he approved of. Once in a while she whispered: "Pampered rich boy," then she screamed again.

"We'll have the whole street here," he said, and groped for the tape recorder. He heard his own voice: "My kidnappers are serious ... in one-hundred-dollar notes ... they will shoot me ... under the angel of death ... should you call the police ..." but the girl was moaning so heavily that he could understand only half of it.

It was not until he was lying beside her that she said: "If Gaetano finds out, he'll kill me. But I was randy from the first moment I saw you."

"So was I," he said politely, and stroked her breasts. "Gaetano certainly isn't going to find out from me."

"He'd shoot you."

"I don't know why there always has to be violence."

"Because your lot don't understand anything else," she said, and caressed him to indicate that her appetite was far from satiated. "Your grandfather could have peeled out the money just like that."

"Then I wouldn't have met *you*," he said.

"Men are always doing the stupidest things," she said. "We're all going to land in jail."

"Is that what your brother says?"

"He doesn't care."

"We've got to get up," he said. "He may be here any moment."

"Not before two," she said.

It was just after midnight, and he realized that he would have to share his bed with the girl for another two hours. It was wiser to undress. While he was taking off his trousers, he was gripped by fear. The tape was probably on its way to Milan. His friends had gone about it all in a most amateurish manner; it could not possibly succeed. It made no difference to the old man whether his grandson was murdered or not. The family had not even reported him as missing, just as nobody bothers to go to the lost property office for a worthless object. I shan't be murdered, he thought, but the film will never be made. Paolo will take his restored son into his arms, for the photographers, his first success. I should have told Bruno and André and Pietro that their plans were completely unmarxist; there's no world revolution by installments. World revolution by installments ends in the bed of a fat girl who's poured lavender water all over herself. To get this cream-puff amazon screaming is something even Paolo could have achieved. All I've inherited from my father is the ability to sleep with any girl.

"Come on," said the girl.

He heard: "... they will shoot me ... funerary gondola ... unmarked notes ..." then he switched off the light.

"You mustn't scream," he said. "They can hear you in St. Mark's Square."

44

Venice, Friday, August 4, Afternoon

Professor Achille Santi, forty-six, head of the Venice Health Department, is sitting on the roof of the Procuratie Vecchie. A small wooden shed has been built for him there, and boards have been laid on the roofs. What acrobats and building workers can do isn't going to scare Professor Santi.

He eats a sandwich, the last of his provisions. He has spent seventy-

two hours on the roofs of St. Mark's Square. He looks down on the
piazza and contemplates the end of a daring enterprise. It was called
Operation Pigeon.

Below, thousands of travelers, many in typical knee-bending positions, are photographing women and children as they feed the pigeons.
Little stalls, folding chairs alongside, where corn is sold in bags, for the
pigeons. There are a hundred and eighty thousand pigeons in Venice,
about twice as many as there are people. It seems to Professor Santi as
if they were all assembled in St. Mark's Square today, a gigantic
demonstration, against him, Professor Santi. He, their enemy? Achille
Santi, a Venetian, grew up among pigeons. He fed them from the
balcony, he gave them names, he felt he knew each and every one of
them. Now he is called the Genghis Khan of the pigeons. His three
children look askance at him. His wife reproaches him sadly.

At least sixty thousand pigeons are ill. They die during the night; in
the morning they are cleared away. Many of them are unaware that it is
night; they are blind. Overfed. Disease carriers, a danger for the people.
And for the works of art. Their excrement bites into the statues,
particularly those on the roofs which are spared by the flood. The
ground can be cleaned, but not the angels.

On the roofs of St. Mark's Square, Professor Santi has been looking
for pigeon's eggs. In seventy-two hours he has only found one.

That was the last resort.

He has proceeded very humanely. He thinks the contraceptive pill,
now modestly called the pill, is a humane thing. It cannot be mixed
into the food for the Indians, because the Indians have nothing to eat.
The pigeons have too much to eat. They got the pill. It was a fruitless
effort, the pigeons remained fertile. The anti-pigeon preparation from
France! It causes aversion to pigeon feed. Similar preparations have
been tried on men to stop them smoking. Because the man who
smokes less dies later. The pigeons would have died earlier, without
pain. But they had no appetite for the appetite spoiler. Then there was
the Society for the Prevention of Cruelty to Animals, and deportation.
The deportation of pigeons cannot be compared to the deportation of
people. Nobody wants to take the deported people. New York City and
Tokyo and Berlin applied to take the pigeons. Genuine Venetian
pigeons for Times Square, the Ginza, the Kurfürstendamm. But the
stupid pedestrians couldn't distinguish the Venetian pigeons from the
others. Now nobody wants to have the exiled pigeons anymore, like

the exiled people. Besides, pigeons do not thrive any better in foreign squares than people on foreign soil. Japan Air Lines doesn't fly them anymore.

The city council had traps set up; five thousand pigeons were trapped and poisoned. Against the Professor's will, although his wife doesn't believe him. And although nobody knows what the pigeons would do to sick people if they had the power.

Professor Santi wanted to spare the lives of fifty thousand pigeons. Fifty thousand were to stay in Venice, in the ghetto. Just like the Jews in former times. Professor Santi had special bins made. Far away from works of árt and the tourist racket, the pigeons were to be given their feed and water. But pigeons, unlike Jews, can fly. Next day they were sitting on the roofs of the Ducal Palace.

The Professor on the roof smiles bitterly, like a defeated commander at his command post. He has not found a single egg today.

A swarm of pigeons flies up, toward the Professor's wooden shed. The pigeon squadron is like a gray-blue magic carpet. Below, two children run from the Café Quadri toward the corn seller's stall. Pigeons sit on a woman's bare arms like sparrows on a telegraph wire. In Lyons and Málaga and Rotterdam and Frankfurt, the family albums ill be taken out in winter—here's Mother feeding the pigeons, on our honeymoon. Like any other defeated commander, Professor Santi broods over the reasons for his defeat. A hundred and eighty thousand stupid pigeons are cleverer than a learned professor. Pigeons are doves—you can't win a war against the symbols of peace. All God's creatures—and a crime against nature bears its own nemesis. Wise old saws.

Who in hell appointed him the Genghis Khan of the pigeons? The city council has led him onto slippery ground. Venice employs enough statisticians. No one, so far, has worked out how much damage the pigeons actually cause. Probably less than a single chimney in Marghera. Does the petty dirt get cleared away all over the world, so that nobody need mention the big mess? Few benefit from the oil storage tanks in Marghera. Millions enjoy seeing the pigeons. Perhaps his wife is right. He should have thought about this earlier. And perhaps he would never have thought about it if he had found more than one pigeon's egg. Failure makes one wiser. Sometimes even more humane.

Two workers climb up the ladder to fetch the Professor.

Pigeons have settled at Achille Santi's feet. They have discovered the crumbs—from his last sandwich. The victors always feed on the vanquished. The Professor hopes they'll enjoy their meal.

In a rather worse humor than usual, Judge Umberto Colognesi, sixty-four, enters the courtroom. He registers that the parties are present—the Mayor as plaintiff, journalist Plinio Foschini as defendant.

Commendatore Colognesi takes his seat in the black leather chair under the crucifix. He notes that the room—unchanged for a century—is half empty. Really he could have settled the whole matter in his office. It is hot. The windows are open. The courthouse is near the *mercato,* the voices of the market women can be heard.

As a rule Judge Colognesi presides at trials where human lives are at stake. True, the defendant claims that the fate of Venice is at stake, but that, of course, is journalistic hyperbole.

Il presidente hates libel suits. Two people have impugned each other's honor. He knows nothing else about them, but he is supposed to decide about their honor. He is supposed to say whether they lied or told the truth. Sometimes both lie. And there are even times when both are telling the truth.

Commendatore Colognesi is particularly irritated by libel suits between prominent citizens. Every gondoliere will occasionally tell another gondoliere what he thinks of him. Prominent citizens have a special honor, a public honor. Honor with an adjective, what nonsense! Besides, prominent citizens usually withdraw their mutual reproaches when they face each other in court. That at least a gondoliere will not do.

The Mayor has appeared with a considerable retinue and with a young barrister whom the judge does not know, but who is said to be fond of long pleadings. Today is one of the judge's grandchildren's birthday, and his wife has baked a cake. He does not intend to miss the birthday party.

The defendant, Foschini, is known to Commendatore Colognesi by his articles only. They have caused an enormous furor. At least once a month Foschini appeals for the salvation of Venice, although he is himself a Milanese. The judge cannot stand journalists, but the slim gentleman with the head of a medieval monk does not look like a mere sensation monger. Antipathies do not impair a judge's objectivity, but one had better beware of sympathies. The Mayor's counsel present his accusations with a passion Commendatore Colognesi does not like. The judge is familiar with them from the writ.

"The defendant called my client a thief!" says the counsel.

That is an exaggeration. The judge turns over the pages of his dossier. Foschini did not speak of theft. He asked questions.

Where did the millions go which UNESCO had put at the city's disposal? Seventy-five million dollars, as claimed in New York, two hundred and fifty million dollars, as they say in Rome? What happened to the thirty thousand million lire which Rome did in fact mobilize? To what end have the five hundred million dollars of the British loan been applied? Why have private financiers who donated two million dollars for restoration work been refused an exemption from taxation?

"Did you allege," the judge asks Foschini, "that the Honorable Mayor embezzled these funds or part thereof?"

"I wish the Honorable Mayor had indeed embezzled a part of these funds and spent the rest for Venice," says Foschini. "I asked a question. Thirty thousand million lire have flowed into Venice. Have twenty thousand million disappeared without a trace, or are they going to waste in banks? Or have they been invested in industry?"

"Typical journalistic demagoguery!" shouts the Mayor's counsel. "By his questions the defendant has created the impression among the uninformed readers, that is, the majority, that the money has disappeared. Or that the Honorable Mayor has been bribed by industry."

"Did you intend to create that impression, Signor Foschini?" asks the judge.

"My client is not concerned at all with the Honorable Mayor," answers the defendant's counsel, an elderly gentleman with a gray goatee. "The one and only thing he is concerned with is the preservation of historic Venice. His questions have not been answered."

"That is not the subject of this suit," says Commendatore Colognesi.

He himself would like an answer to the questions asked by Foschini. No doubt they are questions which may be answered someday, decades later—or not at all. Too much time has been spent on idle talk, and little Umberto, named after his grandfather, is having his birthday. Not only Foschini, but hundreds of journalists all over the world ask similar questions, the informed and the ignorant, Venetians and foreigners.

If the court acquits the defendant, then the Mayor is a thief. If it condemns the defendant, then nobody will dare to ask questions again. A verdict against the Mayor will bring in the majority parties, all the way to Rome. A verdict against Foschini will bring in the world press, all the way to New York City.

Commendatore Colognesi is a Venetian; he has the fate of his city at heart. But the fate of Venice will not be decided in the courtroom. At any rate, it is not he who has to decide it. He will be sixty-five next year, he will retire. It is best to stick to the subject of the suit. He says: "I ask you once more Signor Foschini, did you intend to insult the Honorable Mayor?"

Foschini remains silent. His counsel answers: "My client did not intend anything of the sort."

"There you are," says the judge.

He pretends to be deep in his dossier; looking up behind his spectacles, he observes the Mayor smiling equivocally. But the judge knows that smile. It is a pre-settlement smile. Foschini would not like to be acquitted on purely technical grounds, and the Mayor would not like to answer questions.

The haggling of the market women penetrates into the courtroom louder and louder. The judge wonders whether to have the windows closed.

"Gentlemen," he says, "I believe that this sorry affair can be settled with some mutual goodwill." This sentence has worked wonders many a time. "If Signor Foschini declares that he had no intention of insulting the Honorable Mayor, I assume that the Honorable Mayor will not insist on pursuing the matter further."

"Who will pay costs?" asks the Mayor's counsel.

"The costs will be shared," says the judge. "If the parties agree in principle to clear away the misunderstandings, then the court is prepared to draw up the statements." He looks at his watch. "I adjourn the case for fifteen minutes."

They all rise. Commendatore Colognesi withdraws to his office. On the way through the corridor he stops at the window. UNESCO millions, millions from Rome, millions from London, millions from private financiers. With sums like that it is best to operate with the honor concept; honor cannot be expressed in figures. The Mayor is not a thief, nor the journalist a libeler. *Italia farà da sè* was the tenet of the Italian war of independence in 1849. Venice too will manage by itself. One simply has to stick to the subject.

Although he is a good sleeper, Gino Targa, thirty-seven, gondoliere, has slept very badly for two nights. During Monday night Gaetano Zardinoni died at the age of seventy. He was president of the gondolieri, and one of the oldest. His funeral is scheduled for today. Gino had only a slight acquaintance with Zardinoni, whose gondola used to wait for the tourists in front of the Ducal Palace, while Gino's gondola is right at the entrance of the Hotel Bauer-Grünwald.

The two men never quarreled, but neither did they understand each other. The younger man used to call the elder a radical. By that, Gino was not referring to Zardinoni's political convictions. Gino, the eldest son of a gondoliere, single, has always felt that life is a matter of working things out. *Arrangiarsi!* is his philosophy. Zardinoni had chosen progress as his motto, but he fought motorboats to the hilt. Progress and tradition cannot be brought to a common denominator.

It is not Zardinoni's death which keeps Gino awake. It is the funeral.

This afternoon not a single gondola will cross the lagoon, not a single one will turn noiselessly around the corners; not a single time will the calls *Sià de longo!, Sià premi!, Sià stali!* be heard. For at two o'clock all the gondolas in Venice will assemble at the Rialto bridge. They will pay the last honors to Gaetano Zardinoni, through the Canal Grande, along the Riva degli Schiavoni and past the gardens of the Quartiere Santa Elena, to the island of San Michele, where the dead lie at rest. And Gino Targa does not know if he will be there.

Since early morning he has been quarreling with his colleagues who loaf about the bridge over the Rio San Moisè.

It started on the third of July, with his new gondola. Oh, if only it *were* a new gondola! But it is the same old gondola, only the engine is new. It is at the stern, a small motor, scarcely audible, and it does not emit any poisonous gas. It is right behind the double seat for the passengers, at Gino's feet, and it cannot be seen from outside. But that is just why the motor has started all the trouble.

Gino has worked something out. After all, who really has enough time to be rowed to the Lido, or to Murano or Burano? People peep shamefacedly from the gondolas, as if they were some strange kind of cab. Nobody argues with the motorboat drivers who ask five thousand lire for a ride from the railway station. Five thousand lire for a few minutes! And five thousand lire for one hour in a gondola is something only one in ten tourists can afford. Gino could have bought a motorboat. But gondolas are a part of Venice, after all. One has to work things out.

"You're just a lousy taxi driver," says Mazzo Fattore, thirty-six, one of the gondolieri. Gino went to school with him.

"But taxi drivers at least have the decency not to pretend they're gondolieri," says Vittorio Marchi, twenty-two, who inherited his gondola just a few months ago. "The fare gets aboard because he thinks he's dealing with a gondoliere. And then you pull that filthy string and–puff, puff–you go stinking into the lagoon."

"A gondola is a gondola," says Gino.

Diego Roxas, thirty, well known for his good humor, spits over the parapet into Gino's gondola. "Why don't you wear a white shirt," he says, "like those bloody motorboat skippers who want to look like the captains of transatlantic steamers?"

Gino is about to seize Diego by his singlet, but a fight wouldn't work anything out. He turns to Gerardo Lojacono, sitting silent on one of the steps. Lojacono is over sixty; he was one of the dead man's best friends. Gino says: "You don't think, surely, that I would use the motor in the funeral procession? I shall row like everyone else." And since there is no sign of emotion on Lojacono's deeply furrowed face, he says: "You know that I was in hospital for four months last year."

Everybody looks at Lojacono.

Lojacono does not raise his eyes. He says: "You are not a gondoliere. You are not coming."

The others shout: "Bravo!"

Gino goes down into his gondola. With a defiant gesture he starts his engine, or he would have if the motor had worked for him. But it is not until he pulls the string for the third time that the motor utters a sound of assent. His colleagues laugh.

The area around the Rialto is black with gondolas. In rows of four they wait for the departure. The gondolieri stand at their oars, heads bowed, motionless. The silver and gold of the funerary gondola shine in the afternoon sun. At the prow is the angel of death, a torch in its hand. It looks like a weary cupid. The gondola is overflowing with flowers and wreaths, as it normally is with the tourists' suitcases. Eight gondolas with flowers and wreaths. Each of the gondolieri is wearing a striped shirt and a straw hat. Their gay attire contrasts with the blackness of the gondolas.

The people on the bridge and on both sides of the canal stand tightly packed. Not a sound is heard.

Then the gondolieri start to row. Who gave them the signal? Two gondolas to the right, two to the left of the gondola bearing Gaetano Zardinoni's coffin. A velvet carpet covers the coffin. The coffin is raised on a platform, but it does not move, as if the two gondolieri had never rowed anything else but this dead weight.

The bright array of summer flowers floats past Gino. The eyes of the gondolieri are looking straight ahead, nobody pays any attention to him. Gino feels a pang at every gondola that passes. Four hundred gondolas take a long time. Why didn't he go home? That would have settled the difficulty. Three gondolas alongside, then two, then a single one at the end wind up the procession. Where the Riva del Ferro merges into the Fondamenta del Carbon, the gondolas disappear. The end of the procession is like the tail of a black bird floating away.

The people at the pier realize that one gondola has remained behind. A fat couple approach Gino. *"Un ora ... quanto costa?"* asks the man.

"Five thousand," says Gino.

The couple deliberate.

"O.K.," says the man, and starts to get in.

"No gondolas today," says Gino.

The art critic Felix Burger, fifty-five, has traveled for twenty years from his home town, Zürich, to the opening of every Biennial in Venice. This time he has brought his wife Cristina, a Ticinese, thirty-five, a cellist.

They agree about music, a subject on which Burger is no expert. Cristina thinks she knows something about the visual arts. This leads to arguments. Burger, to be sure, is not a radical apostle of the avant-garde; he is a Swiss citizen and averse to radicalism. But you have to see both sides. He is very well able to distinguish modern art from humbug. His young wife is intolerant, probably because of her Italian blood. She can just about tolerate Picasso and Braque and Dali. After the surrealists, she says, imposture begins.

The room dedicated to a new artistic school—*Opera o comportamento,* work or behavior—will be opened only on the second day, exclusively for critics and press and television reporters. Burger has managed to secure a ticket for his wife.

It is a large hall which has been left to the manager, Gino de Dominici. There is no display of paintings. Up high, almost at the ceiling, two chairs are suspended with ropes, as for children or revue stars. Two assistants to the manager are seated on these, staring down either into the depth of the hall or into the abyss of human existence. In one corner, a sad couple all in black are dancing. In the center a young man sits at a plain table, reading something aloud. Burger thinks he cannot understand it because his Italian is inadequate. Cristina tells him that it has nothing to do with his Italian. Continuous laughter comes from a tape recorder; it sounds half ironical, half desperate—and anyhow loud.

Burger says they should stay near the door. But Cristina has already stumbled over a skeleton. It is lying on the floor, with glittering silver roller skates on its feet.

Burger recognizes a Swiss cameraman with his camera shouldered.

"Aren't you shooting?" he asks.

"The real thing's just coming up," says the cameraman.

Burger watches his wife, whose eyes scan the walls suspiciously. There is a giant swastika. Below it an inscription: "Survival of the race." A little further, hammer and sickle: "Survival of the species." This must be a mistake; the manager was probably not given enough time. Above a cross hangs a sign: "Survival of the soul." That must be an ironical statement, or else the sign belongs to the skeleton. But the skeleton does not have a sign, it merely has roller skates.

"What does all this mean?" asks Cristina, as if she really wanted to know.

"Let's listen," whispers Burger.

In their immediate vicinity there happens to be a group of assistants, young men, some of them skinny, some like soldiers. Presumably they drew lots to decide who would be allowed to sit on the suspended chairs. The five in the group are merely allowed to discuss. One of them notices Cristina. She is pretty. He says that Man is not a reflective animal. "That depends," says she. The young man says that everyone simply wants to survive. "You may be right," says she. "To enjoy physical well-being," says the assistant. But he cannot explain it to her fully, since he has to relieve the black dancer, who looks very tired.

Burger would like to move away from the group. Cristina's intolerance has maneuvered him into many difficult situations before. The wives express their opinions freely, and the husbands get the whipping. But meanwhile, a second assistant has taken over. He says: "Art has to break through the barriers of social relevance, to expose the bowels of existential fear which determine human behavior, which is self-oppressive, because the whole system of social achievement violates the soul, which in turn submits to violation for fear of behaving inadequately, since man is after all only a thing, so that he is never actually alive, he is born with roller skates, that is original sin, but it has been stolen by the church and passed on to Hitler and Stalin."

One of the two men up at the ceiling is feeling sick. At any moment now he will vomit onto the floor or onto existence. The assistants hurry to get him down.

"That wasn't easy to understand," says Burger. "This endless laughter . . ."

"I understood every word," says Cristina.

Burger wonders if she is making fun of him, or if he didn't understand simply because he is too old.

All the cameras are facing the entrance door.

The main attraction is approaching.

The main attraction is a boy or young man. It is impossible to say how old he is, perhaps fourteen, perhaps twice as old. He is pushed in in a wheelchair and set on a platform. A sign hangs around his neck: "Second solution for immortality—an immobile universe." But although evidently half blind, this universe is not immobile. It is a mongoloid idiot. His red face is bloated, nose, mouth and chin close together, as if coarsely painted in reduced scale on a balloon. The second solution for immortality sprawls on the easy chair and laughs. It is a babbling laugh, different from the tape recorder's half-mocking, half-desperate laughter. The idiot is not only blind; he is also deaf and dumb.

The critics and the reporters gather around the second immortality solution. A journalist says to Burger: "He is one of the harmless mongoloids. He gets mad only when they stop him taking part in processions."

The Swiss cameraman prowls around the exhibited object. "He lives quite close," he says, "in the slum district. De Gindice has bought him from his father, for five thousand lire. Only for an hour, though, and for television. I must hurry."

When the cameraman kneels, the idiot claps his hands. He has the fingers of an eight-year-old.

The assistant who felt sick before, up on that chair, says: "Man has to be maltreated before he can know that man is being maltreated."

The young man at the table reads his text. The tape recorder is now set at full volume. The sad couple are dancing.

Saliva is running from the idiot's mouth, saliva drips over his tight suit. During a break in the laughter, arguing voices are heard from outside. A critic comes in and says: "His father. He's bellowing. He didn't know the idiot would be displayed."

"He'd probably have asked ten times as much," says a journalist.

The assistant lowers his eyes and says: *"Opera o comportamento."*

The idiot is about to tumble forward. An assistant holds him by his shoulders. The two assistants above start to swing, as on a garden swing, like children or revue stars.

The idiot is chewing the string by which the sign is fastened around his neck. An assistant tries to take it away from him. The idiot starts to cry.

Cristina clutches at her husband's sleeve. He has gone pale. He says: "How do you say swinishness in Italian?"

"Porcheria," says Cristina.

Suddenly she hears her husband's voice, so loud that it can be heard above the laughter. He shouts: *"Porcheria! Porcheria!"*

Pandemonium follows. The cry *"Porcheria!"* can be heard on all sides. "Diabolical!" and "Brutality!" and "Sadistic swine!" and "Rotten trick!" and "Stop it!"

The idiot is no longer crying. He just gapes. The swings come to a halt. The couple breaks up. Somebody kicks the tape recorder; one more laugh, then silence. Two assistants, hard pressed, lift the idiot from the platform, seat him in his wheelchair, make a dash for the exit. The cameramen run ahead of the wheelchair, a close-up *en face.*

Nobody feels like arguing. Silently they walk to the door.

"I'm proud of you," says Cristina to her husband.

In the empty room there is only the young man sitting reading his text. Now he can be clearly heard.

*   *   *

45

The Signora was having lunch alone. There was work going on in the kitchen, but that was not why she was eating in the dining room. She always set the table for herself very carefully.

When the bell rang, she looked at her watch; it was too early for the workmen to be back.

Claudia was standing outside the door; she was wearing a shiny green dress, and shiny green shoes, and she was made up as if ready to go out for the evening. She held a huge bunch of flowers in her hand, white carnations.

"Have I disturbed your lunch?" she said.

"I had just finished."

"I wasn't going to tell you, but I've changed my mind. I've got married."

"When?" said the Signora, although she knew that was irrelevant.

"An hour ago," said Claudia. She smelled of alcohol She had wanted to bring her husband along, she went on, but the Signora would scarcely consider him presentable. An abstract verse poet, two volumes published by the author, poor as a church mouse, long hair, blue jeans, what people call a leftist. "Also, he's fifteen years younger than I."

The Signora kept a grip on herself. She said: "Are you happy?"

Claudia had expected the question. That was all that mattered to old people—whether you were happy. They spent their whole lives asking themselves searchingly whether they and others were happy, particularly others. Happiness was a virtue, and anyone who avoided it was without virtue. But at the same time they expected you to be happy only under very definite conditions. If you felt happy in different circumstances, you were suspected of being secretly unhappy, or depraved. When somebody got married, they were even more inquisitive than usual. At a wedding, the happiness thermometer had to shoot up to a temperature of at least 106 degrees, almost off the scale. If it was only

100 degrees, say, something must be wrong and the worst was to be anticipated. Should she oblige her mother and say that she was happy? That she had achieved what no other woman had done before—lo, she approaches, the angelic one; wedding march from *Lohengrin?* Or should she say that she had no aspirations to being happy, that she was neither sixteen nor sixty years old, that in between it was enough not to be unhappy. Presently her mother was going to ask her where and when she had met her husband, for that was also very important, where and when.

"You've never said anything about him," said the Signora.

"I've only known him for quite a short time," said Claudia.

That should do for her mother. She had met Fabio Storni at a happening; a painter from Siena had introduced them. Afterward they had gone to the Giudecca. She had not slept with any man since the day the professor had flown back to Princeton, to his geology and his wife and his children. Storni had stayed with her; for three days they did not move out of the house, scarcely out of bed. In bed she was happy with him, under the wrong conditions, but her mother would not have understood this. He treated her like a prostitute and was as compliant as a lapdog. He told her she was a filthy whore; he called every part of her body by name, also everything they did. If she asked him to, he told her about other women and the games he had played with them, and when she was tired he cooked their meals, fed the cats and carried the garbage downstairs. He ate huge quantities of spaghetti, listened indifferently when she spoke of the professor and said that they ought to publish a joint book, with his verse and her illustrations, a subscription book, since no publisher of course would be bright enough to accept it. When she asked him if he didn't feel she was too old for him, he said that he hadn't noticed, and second that he had a mother complex.

Now the Signora would say that there was no need to get married— so much for bourgeois morals, no need to get married—when a man was penniless and was fifteen years your junior. She had never thought of getting married, except in the case of the professor, but he was already married, to his wife and Princeton University. The sudden fancy to marry Fabio had occurred to her when he said he would have to go home because he was completely broke and his mother, a country woman living near Siena, always had enough to eat and drink, with chianti from their own vineyard. "I can still afford spaghetti," she said. "We could do that book together," he said. They had gone on drinking red wine continuously from midnight on. "I'll find two witnesses and we'll get married," he said. She answered: "Why not? I have no prejudices, not even against marriage." They had gone through the formalities faster than Claudia would have thought possible. This morning, on the way to the registrar's office, she had bought the white carnations.

The Signora tried not to betray her feelings. In old age you had to act understandingly; there was nothing left but understanding, a consolation to no one but yourself. The older you got, the less you understood. You showed understanding for something you did not understand. If you learned anything at all, it was not to give advice.

"You aren't shocked?" said Claudia.

"I don't know your husband," said the Signora. "I'm sure you know what you are doing."

She surprised herself by the conviction with which she had said it. Perhaps Claudia did know what she was doing. She remembered that in her childhood they had had a lady's maid called Rosita who was said to be the most beautiful girl in Venice. Whatever the daughter of the house learned, Rosita learned twice as fast; on her day off she looked like a contessa, there was scarcely a visitor who did not cast an eye on her. Then she married a gondoliere; he was a head shorter than she, and looked a bit like a monkey. Later she used to visit the family, with their three or four children. She no longer looked like a contessa; she was merely happy. Claudia had probably not taken long to restore disorder in her apartment. But perhaps the poet with the long hair could bring order into Claudia's life, at least for a while—an order which had nothing to do with clean dishes. The Signora still didn't know why Claudia had been longing for death. Loneliness is so dangerous because the lonely do not discriminate and lower their defenses. At any rate she was not going to condemn Claudia. She had won her daughter back, and did not want to lose her again. Since that afternoon in the Giudecca, there had been hardly an hour in which she had not felt anxiety for Claudia. Remus had not come back, and Romolo had a secret; Laura didn't answer letters, and Paolo would someday discover that the Titian in her drawing room was a fake. She had demanded too much of her sick heart. It was not strong enough to carry Claudia's burden as well. For something to say, she asked: "Will you live at your place?"

"Oh no," said Claudia. "We're buying a small apartment where we can work. Fabio doesn't care for my palazzo. He's tremendously gifted. He's a country boy; he needs order."

The Signora pricked up her ears. Just after she had gone to the bank with Mozetti, she told Claudia that she had opened an account for her. Claudia had been so occupied with herself she had not inquired about the source of the money, or the amount. She had been satisfied with the Signora's remark that she had sold "some things" and that "you children inherit everything anyway." Claudia had seen the Titian in its place almost every day. Now, while Claudia spoke of Fabio, the Signora was wondering when her daughter would ask about the money. It would be money thrown away, but that did not bother the Signora. The money Paolo would spend on his mistresses, and Laura on a trip around the world, was equally thrown away. The whole amount, of course, all four parts of it, would have been enough to save the palazzo, not just to give it some paltry protection against trials to come. But she had known, after all, that she could not depend on her children. She had to prevent them from positively setting fire to the ark.

"You're not listening," said Claudia.

"Oh yes, I am," said the Signora. "I should like to meet my son-in-law. It is possible to make friends with blue jeans."

"I am working again," said Claudia. "In the meantime I need money, for the apartment and for the book."

"You have more money than you think. You only have to go to the bank. I told you about the account." She rose. "I'll get you the confirmation."

When she returned, Claudia said: "Where did you get that money?"

"I sold my pearls." She touched her string of pearls. "This is an imitation."

"So much money?" said Claudia.

"I also sold some other things."

"The Titian?"

"You can see that it is here. But everything else was just as illegal, of course—according to the will." She smiled. "You see, Claudia, I am still able to adapt myself. I don't mean this as a reproach, but the three of you, you and Laura and Paolo, do not abide by the unwritten laws.

Therefore I told myself one day that I did not have to abide by the written ones. I am much more modern than you all believe. I am having the palazzo restored, you are buying an apartment and publishing your book. By the way, you can do me a favor. Don't mention anything to Paolo! Someday he'll be pleased with the money, but he would be upset to think I spend my money on something as absurd as these old walls."

"You're great," said Claudia. "I told Fabio that." She got up. "How do you like my dress?"

"I find the dress charming, but I'd rather try it with black shoes. It is no longer the fashion to wear everything matching."

Claudia gave her mother a kiss.

"Put the carnations in water," she said. "Fabio is right, I look idiotic with a bridal bouquet."

46

The exposure of the Andreoli Grandson Affair, as the press called it—the name Santarato played a dominant role only in the Venetian local press—took slightly less than forty hours.

When Lodovico Andreoli was telephoned at his villa in Milan by one of the kidnappers and heard his grandson's voice, he reacted exactly as Remus had foreseen. One need not be surprised that Remus failed to proceed according to his knowledge of human nature. The greatest mischief in the world is caused by the fact that most people think like pessimists and act like optimists.

Andreoli immediately summoned Paolo and Teresa to his house. He declared that he did not intend to invest—he used the word "invest"—a single lira, much less a dollar, to save his grandson. The kidnappers had said they would inform the press at the same time. Either they were a bunch of idiots, since it was obvious they had a better chance of getting their money if they attempted to settle the matter privately, or else they were speculating on his dashing off to deposit a briefcase with half a million dollars under the backside of the angel of death, simply for fear of being considered a heartless grandfather. The latter would indicate an incredible lack of psychological judgment. For one thing, he did not care whether he was considered heartless or not, since the consumers were interested in the beer's alcoholic content, not the brewer's emotional make-up; and for another, the public did not know about Paolo's financial circumstances and would expect the son to be freed by the father.

After Andreoli's reflections had developed this far, a storm raged over his son-in-law's head. Only a complete idiot would have brought up his son in a way that was bound to lead him into the company of kidnappers. "I have already spoken to Signora Santarato," said Andreoli. "She has admitted that she did not inform you of Remus's disappearance, but her explanation was completely plausible, to wit that Remus had already disappeared from his own home. She said the only thing she was afraid of was that he might burn the furniture after his return. Whereas you two were very thankful that he was back, and damn the furnishings."

Paolo had not been able to get a word in edgeways. Now he ventured to ask what there was to indicate any connection between Remus and the kidnappers.

"You should use your common sense," Andreoli said, "assuming you possess even a trace of such a commodity. Any criminal worth the name, as I said before, would have contacted the father, at least to start with. The son's complete disregard for his father, quite justified too, was obvious from the phone call to me, his grandfather. If this was not a put-up job, Remus would have been kidnapped in Milan, where things happen practically every day. In the lagoon city it's pretty well hopeless trying to kidnap anyone, particularly a strong young man who could, after all, defend himself. Further evidence for the kidnappers being idiots, by the way, was the bit with the angel of death. If a decision had already been taken to kidnap Remus in Venice, he would have been packed into a car instantly and driven out of the city, which could be barred off like a mousetrap. No, the blackmailer's name is Remus Santarato, and if I attach any importance to family relationships, one thing it does mean is that members of the family are the last people I'll let myself be blackmailed by."

Teresa protested amid tears. She said she would sell her last jewel to save Remus, and she would tell the press that of course it was Paolo who had provided the ransom.

Paolo did not argue, nor did he support his father-in-law. He was quite sure old Andreoli was right. He remembered Remus's remark in the bar of the Danieli that Grandfather was going to be sorry he had not shelled out the money for the film in time. But Paolo did not say anything of this, because he did not want to mention Teresa's promises and because he feared Andreoli's wrath. He was embarrassed by the melodramatic way Teresa spoke constantly of "my poor Remus" and even called him "my child" all of a sudden. If Paolo had learned anything from his mother, it was that you had to control yourself in any situation. Teresa wanted to save her son, but above all she wanted to defend him, Paolo. Till now, at least when the three of them were together, old Andreoli had avoided expressing his opinion of his son-in-law so candidly. Paolo could not tell Teresa that he didn't care what her father thought of him. He merely objected briefly when she blamed the "feebleminded old woman" in the palazzo. He asked Andreoli what he proposed to do.

"I don't propose to do anything I have not already done," said Andreoli. "I certainly wasn't waiting for any advice. Contrary to the kidnappers' instructions I immediately contacted the police. Police officers are now in the house and in the brewery offices. At the next phone call, which I have requested"–he looked at his watch–"the blackmailer's voice will be recorded, and so will Remus's if he speaks again. You are not going to sell a single ring, my dear Teresa, it's too late for that anyhow, you wouldn't be able to obtain the dollar notes they've demanded. I've given Remus's picture to the press–I happened to have it on the piano. If these boys think they can alert the press before I do, they're even bigger fools than I take them for. Just now it's the Andreoli Breweries which are advertising, not any moronic kidnappers. Signora Santarato–I must say humanity goes downhill with every generation, Paolo; one could talk sensibly to your mother–gave me some important information on the people Remus associated with in Venice, and she was about to get hold of Romolo on the Lido, he'd probably know some of them by name. I'm going to stall the kidnappers, with the full agreement of the police, by the way. The only thing that makes me doubt the idea that Remus thought up the whole charade is his respect for me. He can't have mistaken me for Paolo."

In the car Teresa no longer wept; as soon as they were alone, she accused her husband and the Signora. When she and Paolo got home, they found their house surrounded by the police and besieged by reporters. The evening papers would present the news accordingly. While an energetic young police inspector questioned them, Paolo was amazed at Teresa's behavior. Although not even she could exclude the possibility that Remus's friends were involved in the matter, she only reluctantly agreed to let Remus's room be searched. The father-son relationship, she said, had always been most cordial, and it was completely incomprehensible that the kidnappers had not contacted Paolo. Why had Signora Santarato in Venice not reported her grandson's absence? "Well, you see—my husband's mother is not quite herself." Paolo waited for an opportunity to see the inspector alone. It occurred when he was checking Remus's papers with his officers. Now Paolo confided to the inspector his conversation with Remus in Venice. He asked him not to mention it to Teresa.

The police proved every bit as zealous as old Andreoli had expected. Even before the inspector in Milan had finished his questioning and *Il Gazzettino,* a morning paper, could report on the event, the Venetian police officers appeared at the palazzo.

The Signora could not recall that she had ever come into contact with the police; at any rate no police officer had ever set foot in the palazzo. Remus was hand-in-glove with the kidnappers. On that point she agreed with Andreoli, whom she had last seen at Paolo's wedding. At the same time she felt a certain solidarity with Paolo, either because the family was moving closer together, or because she had welcomed his phone call. He spoke like someone secretly holding his hand over the mouthpiece. "Don't keep anything back," he said. "We both have to help find Remus. Teresa would use it against you if you impeded the investigation." And he said: "The Santaratos have never before been in the papers." Would Paolo be surprised if he read the name Santarato in the paper? Remus had opened the door a crack; now it was fully open. Did that mean it could never be closed again?

Even before the police arrived, the Signora had taken control. She had informed Dario; he was on his way to the palazzo. She had spoken to Claudia, who was now phoning her every ten minutes. She had reached Romolo at the Excelsior. He would take the next motorboat, but in the meantime she could take down the names of Remus's friends. He remembered now that they had disappeared at the same time as Remus: Cesarini, Masina, Gaillard. She wanted to know their Christian names, and she noted these too. You could not deal with disorder by closing your eyes. Her tidying up at Claudia's had not helped much, but who could tell what would have happened if she had left it undone?

On the following morning the entrance hall was like a film studio. Since the Signora had locked the door of her living quarters–no *paparazzo* was going to take a shot of her–the crowd of reporters, photographers and cameramen spilled into the empty ground floor. Dario and Romolo answered their questions–Dario sulkily, Romolo not without a sense of his own importance.

At half past nine in the evening the police superintendent at Milan informed old Andreoli that his grandson had been found safe and sound. He had just been eating spaghetti with the gondoliere Gaetano Balmelli in Murano.

Cesarini, Masina and Gaillard had drawn lots to decide who would remain in Venice to fetch the money during one of Balmelli's casual visits to Carnielutti's repair shop. The lot fell on Gaillard. Cesarini and Masina went to Milan. Gaillard left his hotel and rented a room under a false name with a retired gentleman in the Campo Grappa in the Quartiere Sant' Elena. The morning papers had published only the names of Remus's friends–photographs could not be found at such short notice–but they had given detailed descriptions of them and mentioned that one of them spoke with a French accent. The police had offered a reward–not all that high but substantial enough–for "relevant information" which could lead to the arrest of the delinquents. The retired gentleman, encouraged by that prospect, had voiced his suspicion at the nearest police station, namely that his tenant, who was anyhow of questionable appearance–he did not explain what he meant by that–might be identical with the Gaillard they were looking for. Gaillard, in whose possession the tape recording was found, had given up lying after the first few minutes. He maintained that the kidnapping had been a mere hoax, that the capitalist daddy's boy had planned it all. He pretended not to know where his accomplices, Cesarini and Masina, were to be found.

"Gaillard, Balmelli and his sister are under arrest," the police superintendent told Andreoli. "We might free your grandson on certain conditions."

"If you don't ask for bail, I won't mind," said Andreoli.

47

Laura's departure from New York was delayed by her own fault.

Should she fly or should she sail on the *Leonardo da Vinci?* Although she discussed this problem with the other girls *ad nauseam*, she could not make up her mind. Speed and the low price were in favor of the plane trip. Points for the *Leonardo* were the beauty of an Atlantic crossing and the possibility of carrying more luggage. Furthermore, Geraldine only wanted to come in on an ocean voyage, which in turn raised the question of whether Laura herself wanted to travel alone or with company. There was no better place for relaxation than a luxury liner, said Geraldine. A more convincing argument was in the phrase "making new friends." Many a middle-aged woman had boarded a steamer with a heavy suitcase and disembarked with an invisible bridal veil.

Laura was not sure how much she was concerned with making the right decision, like some games players who only play to win; perhaps she was more like those who play for the game's sake. Indecision was not a characteristic of hers, it was a diversion to pass the time. Anybody who decided things at once, who acted on impulse, was conjuring up the spare time he dreaded most. The game of decision-making would have been a well-tried means of amusement, but for the player's fear of losing. Laura was afraid that in the end, after lengthy consideration, she might still do the wrong thing or miss the right one. She did not want to forego a single concert, meeting, sale, or discussion. Once you chose an alternative, the other one, the one you discarded, seemed to be the prize-winning chance. It was little help to remind oneself that in most cases the decisions concerned minor matters; for the more trivial one's life had been in the past, the more important was what the future would bring.

Yet Laura would have decided more quickly between the air trip and the ocean voyage had she been sure she really wanted to visit her mother. Either nothing happened, or everything happened at the same time. If somebody gave her a ticket to a special first night, you could be sure there would be the long-awaited program on TV; when she was invited to a promising party, a friend would call on his way through New York. But this time it was a more serious matter.

Over a year ago, at the opening of an exhibition, she had met a man, Geoffrey L. Tunney, who had asked for her telephone number and always called her on the phone whenever he came to New York on a business trip from Philadelphia. Some weeks ago she had invited him for a drink, and around the third or fourth martini he had made the confession of love not uncommon among married men: he complained about the wretchedness of his marriage. He was an attractive man, in his early sixties, a tennis player with many trophies, extremely well informed in matters of art, and blessed with a patience Laura missed in most Americans. He had obviously come hoping to take his clothes off, and yet he departed without a trace of hurt feelings even though he had not loosened his tie. After every visit Laura was sure Geoffrey would not call her again, but before long he had come three times to the house on 70th Street. When she mentioned her trip to Venice, he did not hide his disappointment. However, she was convinced that in the autumn he would no longer ask for her "unique martinis." It was a missed opportunity if she gave up the Venetian trip, a missed opportunity if she left New York City now, of all times.

It is mainly the lonely who study the horoscopes in the newspapers, and it is they more than others who believe in an erratic fate. Laura deemed it a stroke of fate that Geoffrey invited her for dinner on the very day she had to choose between Pan Am and the *Leonardo*.

By the afternoon she had already started her preparations. The low-cut dress would flatter her neckline, but also betray only too clearly her intention to please him. The plainer dress would hide her most attractive feature, but it happened to be the product of a French boutique and the girls envied it. She was sorry she couldn't wear both dresses—the one she did not choose was sure to be the right one—but when she examined herself in the mirror, in the dress which more generously revealed her swelling bosom, she was rather pleased with her decision.

In the restaurant Caravelle, which appeared all the more American to Laura for trying to look European, she still wanted to please Geoffrey, but her resolve to go to bed with him—the girls had recommended it most emphatically—was beginning to waver. This disturbed her.

Bachelors loved their own comforts, but apparently a female bachelor was not exempt from similar temptations. Once a woman reached a certain age, she either met tired old men who had lost their wives, their potency or both, or she met married men. Those were not themselves tired, but tired of their wives, and they were inflamed less by the fire of their love than by the pilot light of their own boredom. Those among them who did not turn to "kidlings"–one of Geraldine's favorite expressions–found themselves a vacation island where they had fun. But after a while things were no better than at home and the holiday-maker soon returned to the mainland. The inhibitions Laura discovered in herself were not concerned with the lady in Philadelphia–Ed's mistresses had had no regard for her–but with her fear of personal involvement. Unlike Geoffrey, she was in danger of mistaking the holiday paradise for the real garden of Eden.

When she asked Geoffrey to buy her the *Daily News* as they were leaving the restaurant, Geoffrey should have known that the night would not take the course he wished it to. But his sensitivity did not go that far. He asked Laura if she would invite him to her apartment for a brandy. She agreed to this because she did not want to make a fool of herself or because she did not want to obstruct her fate–Kismet, she called it.

Geoffrey, flushed by the drinks, immediately took her into his arms. She did not resist, but his kisses barely aroused her. She went to the bar.

"Do you really want to go to Venice?" he said.

"Yes, I think so."

"Too bad . . ."

"I won't stay more than four weeks. I have to see my mother."

"A remarkable old girl, according to what you tell me. You were going to show me the palazzo, remember?"

"Oh yes . . ."

She brought some photographs from her bedroom; she had taken them on her last visit. Sitting next to Geoffrey, she observed how much the American was impressed by the pictures. Paolo wanted to sell the palazzo. It was one thing to say "this was my palazzo" and a different thing to say "this is my palazzo."

"When I see these pictures, I understand you better," said Geoffrey, and put his arm around Laura.

Now he was going to explain her to herself, as men always do when they want to sleep with a woman. But in his words she found only the American inferiority complex. Why should it be such an eccentric thing to have been born in a Venetian palazzo? She suddenly felt the desire to challenge him. She said: "Come along with me. I'm taking the *Leonardo*."

"You know I can't do that."

"Tell your wife you have business in Europe."

"You don't travel by luxury liner for that."

"You could follow by plane."

"That's an idea . . ."

She knew he didn't think it a good idea at all. He would consider it a good idea if she let herself be undressed by him—his hand had moved closer to her bosom—but in a week or so she would receive a cable from him: DUE UNEXPECTED COMMITMENTS IMPOSSIBLE LEAVE PHILADELPHIA ALL MY THOUGHTS WITH YOU LOVE GEOFFREY.

She stroked his temples. "We'll see," she said, "when I get back from Venice."

"Nothing will change," he said, and brushed the narrow strap from her shoulder.

He must have realized before that she did not wear a bra. He kissed her breasts, but she thought of the procedure that would follow—groping for the electric switch, romantic lighting, it's hot, let me take you into my arms; open the buttons, go to the bedroom in a tight embrace, fold back the bedspread, fumble with shoelaces. Besides, it was not hot. The air-conditioning was humming—the small brown boxes on the walls of the old houses in Manhattan always reminded her of Venice's birdcages. She looked down on the head with the carefully concealed bald spot, a stranger's head. When his hands slipped up her thighs, she slowly rose, arranged her dress and said: "I'll be back in four weeks . . ."

She liked the way he resigned himself at once, but perhaps he was quite happy to have proved his success without having to prove his virility.

They chatted for a while—about their first meeting at the opening of the exhibition, about Geraldine, about Philadelphia, about Venice, and finally about his children. They were at the university. Emily was going through her pot period, whereas Geoffrey Tunney III, thank God, was through with his pot period. When Geoffrey II left, they kissed, a last, hopeless attempt. "Let me know when you get back, I'll meet you."

She had never grown used to the sound of the air-conditioning; it got on her nerves. She opened the windows. Seventieth Street by night was covered by such a thick haze, the penetrating humidity of Manhattan—humidity one hundred—that she couldn't see the street from her apartment on the eighteenth floor. She remembered the sultry summer nights of Venice and thought she got a whiff of the rotting smell of the lagoons.

When she saw her body in the bathroom mirror, she felt an excitement she had not felt all evening. How silly to start thinking; she should not have let Geoffrey leave! Naked, she crossed the living room to close the windows. Her glance caught the *Daily News* on the table. She didn't feel like going to bed. It was too late to call one of the girls, she didn't know what the television program had offered that evening, and the last thing she wanted to do was admit to those women who had practically pressed their ears to her bedroom door that she had not slept with Geoffrey. She sat down on the couch and started to browse through the paper. She skimmed the headlines and turned to Ed Sullivan's column. In the center of the column she read in bold type:

PARTY. At an intimate dinner party in the house of the well-known collector and philanthropist, Nelson E. Anderson—only Mr. and Mrs. Jerome F. Paddington, Professor Frances E. Konecki of Yale University, Mr. and Mrs. Anthony Breevort from Westchester, the Baron and Baroness de Malfleur from Paris and yours truly were present—Mr. Anderson proudly showed his latest acquisition, a Titian, *Girl with Flower Basket,* which had just arrived.

What was she to do? Paolo? Paolo was the only man in the family. Keep quiet about it, see for herself in Venice? Call up her mother? Who would not tell her the truth. Anderson? The Andersons would be fast asleep long ago, and anyhow the well-known collector and philanthropist was bound to have an unlisted number. Then Paolo after all.

While she waited for the connection, she was figuring out what the time would be in Milan. It must be eight or nine in the morning, depending on whether it was daylight saving time.

Teresa answered.

"I *must* speak to Paolo, right away," said Laura; and she put a cushion on her belly because she suddenly found it grotesque to sit at the telephone in the nude.

"Are you calling about Remus?" said Paolo.

"No. What's the matter with Remus?"

"Don't you read the newspapers?"

"Newspapers? For Christ's sake!"

"He was kidnapped. But he's back now, everything is all right."

"There's nothing in the *Daily News* yet. But it's because of the *Daily News* I'm calling you."

She told him what she had read. There was so long a silence at the other end that she asked if Paolo was still there.

"Yes, yes," he said. "Don't you worry. It must be pure nonsense, or else it's a fake."

He sounded doubtful, or perhaps he did not want to speak in front of Teresa.

"You must do something," she said.

"Yes, of course. Weren't you planning to go to Venice?"

"Right away, the minute I get a reservation. Tell me about Remus."

She was only half listening. Fate had taken the decision out of her hands. Well, she preferred to travel without Geraldine anyway.

48

When Remus failed to show up at the palazzo, Romolo decided to ask for him at the Danieli. Barbara had heard him say on television that he intended to stay there.

The afternoon was even hotter than usual for the time of year. And yet the mass of humanity was flowing over the Ponte della Paglia to admire the Bridge of Sighs.

Romolo was curious. What was it like to be kidnapped, voluntarily or involuntarily? What had Remus experienced at the gondoliere's? His relationship with Remus was off-balance, his regret weighed heavier than his admiration. He himself would never have had the courage to stage such a performance, but he was not sure Remus had really staged it. Nor was he sure if courage was always worthy of admiration; perhaps it all depended what you were courageous for. He did not intend to preach to Remus; they had always agreed about closing their ears to sermons on morality. But even an adventure had to make sense. The adventures he imagined did not end in blackmail. It would be fun to see your own picture in the papers: Barbara said Remus looked simply fabulous on TV. But it was relatively simple to get into the papers—the murderers and burglars probably didn't enjoy that very much. In Venice you made it in the papers at your funeral at least. The death notices usually carried a photograph from younger days. If Remus was going to have himself kidnapped, he might have planned it more intelligently. Remus despised their father, Romolo knew, and *he* wouldn't have gone about it with any more skill, but probably with no less skill either.

At the boat station opposite the hotel Romolo stopped. He had not told the Signora that he was planning to visit his brother. Remus had now become the black sheep of the family; perhaps he needed help. Romolo was impressed by the fact that Remus had not returned home as a penitent sinner—nor would I have done, Romolo thought. To stay at the Danieli without money is pretty cool. The family certainly won't pay for him there, and he must need money. I might give him my savings book, that should be enough for a night or two at the Danieli. At any rate it'll stop him feeling completely on his own.

The moment he stepped into the hall, Romolo realized that something unusual was going on. At this time of the afternoon the hall was usually empty; now Romolo had to force his way through the crowd. A flock of reporters were thronging toward the small lounge on the right, its doors were open, and it was bathed in the blue light of the spotlights. It had "full lighting," as Remus and his friends would call it.

Romolo asked for Signor Santarato. It felt rather odd to be speaking of Remus as Signor Santarato. "The press conference starts at four o'clock," said the receptionist. "Where is Signor Santarato?" "Still in his room." Not until Romolo, with a certain pride, said that he was Signor Santarato's brother did the receptionist deign to put him through.

"Well, junior, it's great to see you here," said Remus. "I wanted to invite you, but I just didn't have time. Well, you can see for yourself ..."

Remus, clad in blue jeans with a flowered shirt which was open almost to his navel, was in splendid form. The old man, his grandfather, had not come through with the bread, naturally, but "between you and me" that had not been the purpose of it all. The one thing that mattered was the publicity. "The hall is full, how did I do that?" "Weren't you afraid?" "Why should I be? I was among my friends after all." "But it could all have turned out rotten if the police had not let you go." "Sure, even more publicity." Pacing to and fro in the spacious room, Remus said that he had been completely broke when he moved in the day before. Now he could buy the entire hotel. Cinecittà had flown in two men, no less, put a secretary at his disposal, and drummed up the press. "They think they can get me cheap." All the film companies were bidding for the film. "I'll upstage old shits like Fellini anytime." The Americans too wanted to come in; cables from France and Germany—he pointed to the table—advances for the asking; in the evening he was going to move to a suite. "I've got to receive those people in the right setting—now, how did I do that?" The telephone rang, and Remus took the receiver standing up. "Just let them wait a little, it improves the image." Would he be able to make the film without Gaillard and Cesarini and Masina? "They were real smart guys, but they're cheaper by the dozen." Then he sat down. "What happened at home? Tell me!"

Romolo, impressed and slightly dazed by the surprising reception, reported in minute detail. But the longer he spoke, the more he felt his rediscovered admiration for his brother wane, and the more his regret gained ground. It seemed to him that Remus wanted to know too much, about his parents and the Signora, whether they had been worried and why he had not been reported missing, whether they were pleased in Milan and in the palazzo that the plot had failed.

Romolo thought: so it failed, did it?

And even though Remus said it served high society right that the noble names of Andreoli and Santarato were now being dragged through the newspaper columns, he gazed at Romolo with a solemn expression on his face, seemed affected by the family's indifference, and it sounded bitter when he said: "You can have my room, including hifi system; you're welcome to them." But immediately afterward he spoke of the film: "If those shits the financial backers think they can bribe me, they couldn't be more off-course. I've got that shitty establishment taped—with their own money. You must admit I've done a great job."

"If you say so," said Romolo.

In the elevator Remus put his arm around his brother. "Do you want me to introduce you to those people? You're a great guy yourself, you just don't know it."

"Thanks all the same," said Romolo. "I'd rather creep into a corner."

The lounge was crammed full. The cameras followed Remus to a long table which was placed where the hero of the day could be seen from every angle. In the background the secretary arranged some papers.

Remus elegantly expressed appreciation of "your presence in such numbers" and said he would be pleased to answer the press's questions, he was only sorry his comrades could not be there. "As you all know, my friend Gaillard has been caught in the clutches of class justice, and there is a search on for Cesarini and Masina, hopefully in vain."

"Then you admit that you were involved in this affair from the very beginning?" said a reporter in the first row.

"Yes, of course. There is always money available for any soap opera, but if you want to make an artistic film with social criticism in it, you have to come up with ideas."

"Who thought the plan up?" said a journalist with an English accent who was standing next to Romolo.

"It was exclusively my idea."

"That guy has guts," whispered a pretty young woman.

Remus answered the questions as if press conferences were part of his daily round. "How did you get on at Balmelli's? "His sister cooks the best spaghetti in all Venice." Laughter. "Why did your grandmother not report you missing?" "She probably hadn't noticed my absence." "Why did you choose Venice?" "My film is set in Venice." An approving murmur. "Don't you feel the thing was handled rather amateurishly?" "The Palestinians would have done a better job. After all, I'm a film director, not a kidnapper." "Tell us about your previous films." A brief hesitation. "I expected you to ask something of the sort. If I wanted to work with the old hacks, I didn't need to have myself kidnapped." "Will you make it up with your family?" "I don't think they're terribly interested." The girl sitting in front of Romolo thought that a charming reply. "Are you a member of the Communist Party?" "Artists ought to remain independent." The cameraman on the other side of the lounge had been filming all the time and was inserting a new film. "Will you change anything in the script after this experience?" "I haven't learned anything about the establishment that I didn't know already." "Are you going to miss your collaborators?" "I wrote the script myself." "Weren't you putting in danger people who don't have such a generous grandfather?" "He wasn't so generous at pay time." More laughter. "My comrades know why they are being hunted." "Would you accept money for your film from Andreoli?" "The financing of the film is assured."

He did not want to reveal too much of the film's contents, Remus continued, but it was about the unfortunate little lace makers of Burano, the most exploited people of all. "You and I know what is hidden behind the sham facade of this city, but who else does? If you criticize me for not making a tourist film, then I tell you: no, that's not my intention. I was fortunate enough to have the chance to look into the palazzi. They're not decayed from the outside, but from within. The American tourists will discover a Venice that looks different from what they thought up to now." He still had to decide whether the film would be made in an American-Italian co-production; the Germans wanted to come in, but he would prefer to do an exclusively Italian picture. At any rate he was not using the excuse of the unemployed Hollywood film hacks, that they were "between pictures." He would start shooting in September, or October at the latest, and three hundred thousand dollars would be enough. "I'm not making a spectacular for the rotten Biennial. Half of the net profits would go to the unfortunate young lace makers of Burano." "Bravo!" said the woman reporter who had found Remus charming before. "Any more questions?" said Remus.

A man up at the front raised his hand. Romolo, who was standing against the wall, could not see his face, but it was evidently an elderly man, with a rim of gray hair around his bald head.

"I don't quite understand," he said, "why you wanted to get the money from Andreoli when the financing is already assured."

Romolo wondered if Remus would be caught in the trap. His

feelings were ambivalent. He had disapproved of Remus more and more every minute, but still this was his brother sitting under the floodlights, and Romolo felt sorry for him.

"I don't know what you mean," said Remus, which evidently did not make a good impression.

"I just wanted to know," said the bald man, a Venetian to judge by his pronunciation, "whether the manna only started dropping from heaven now that the world press is suddenly full of your affair. I take into account the fact that you had to get kidnapped to make the capitalists line up outside the Danieli."

"Yes, indeed," said Remus. "Any more questions?"

Nobody asked any more questions, but the reporters still surrounded Remus. Romolo was glad he could clear out without being noticed. Heated discussions were going on in the hall. Opinions were divided; there was approval, disapproval, criticism. Romolo felt he would not learn anything new by going on listening.

The Riva degli Schiavoni was tinged by the yellowish blue of the early August evening. The press conference had lasted over two hours, and Remus was famous now. He, Romolo Santarato, was currently the brother of a famous director, and Barbara was going to see his brother on the television screen that very night. What was the matter with him, that at the beginning of the summer, he had longed to see the Wilcox yacht from the inside, and now he was not even tempted by the prospect of being present during the shooting of a film his own brother was directing? Perhaps he was not quite such a great guy as Remus imagined. Basically, Remus and he had always got along well. Why should he no longer get along with his brother; why did he think of him as a stranger, almost like someone dead as pictured in the newspapers—"*ricordano con profonda tristezza ...*" Did he envy his famous brother? No, that was certainly not the case. Did he despise him? No, not really. Remus had always lied, and he had not lied more than usual this time. He was probably very happy in his hotel suite, with the reporters and journalists of both sexes, with the script that did not exist, and with the prospect of outdoing Fellini and making the young lace makers happy. Of all the questions asked and all the quick-witted replies, Romolo remembered only the last, unanswered question. "Yes, indeed," Remus had said, nothing but "Yes, indeed." Was it really necessary to be kidnapped in order to make a dream come true?

Who were those people who queued up because Remus had fooled them? He, Romolo, would soon be fifteen; everything he had thought in his fifteen years of life couldn't just be wrong, could it?

He stopped outside the Quadri, where the musicians had started to play. He had promised Barbara to ring her immediately after his visit to Remus. But he did not know what to say to her. He would tell Nonna, after all, that he had gone to see Remus and ask her what she thought of the whole thing.

49

"You sold a fake, and you will have to take the consequences," Paolo had said on the telephone. And now he was on his way to Venice.

The Signora had swallowed a nitroglycerine capsule. She sat motionless in her easy chair. The pain had started during the brief conversation. She was seized with mortal terror. She knew the feeling, but this time it was not the dull, diffuse fear of dying, it was the panic fear of being torn away from her work, of not being able to accomplish what she had planned. She had to be ready for the encounter with her son, she could not afford to show any weakness. Paolo would exploit it or else interpret it as an appeal to his sympathy.

She contemplated the fake Titian as one might stand helplessly before a house that has burned down. She had taken the crooked way, but secretly she had felt a certain pride. It had been an idea even Dario had to admire despite his disapproval. She had believed herself proof against all suspicion: wasn't her Titian here! And now it had happened, so soon. Lying would be no use; Teresa and Paolo could prove her guilt in the shortest possible time, and all they would need to say then was that she was a stubborn old woman persisting in her lie. Should she beg for their belated understanding? Claudia had used some of the money, Laura would be amenable to reason. But Paolo and Teresa would allege that they could not consent without becoming accessory to a crime. And even though this American collector, Anderson, of whom Paolo had spoken, could be forced to return the painting—the damage could not be undone. Did she want to undo anything? After her conversation with Paolo she had dismissed the workers for the day. They had told her the strike was over. Luigi Primavesi had orders to start immediately with the most important tasks. She considered plans and possibilities, but it did not occur to her to stop the work for good.

She was glad Dario arrived before Paolo. The pain had subsided. She did not mention that she had had an attack, and when he remarked that she looked under the weather, she merely smiled and said: "Is it any wonder?"

While Dario was speaking, she remembered an accident she had witnessed in her childhood, somewhere in Rome. A man had been caught under the wheels of a tram. The strongest impression made on her was not the blood in the street, not the confused crowd, nor even the seriously hurt man lying on the cobblestones, groaning. No, it was the man—she could have drawn his face this very minute—who cared for the bleeding victim, chased away the curious bystanders and gave instructions to fetch help.

Dario did not complain, he did not blame her. He seemed to review the situation quite calmly, just like that unknown man in the Roman street.

"You made a mistake when you didn't get Naville to confirm his promise that he would sell the painting in Italy. Still, you sold the Titian in Italy; what Naville did with it afterward is not your business. Once the Italian consulate in New York reports—it's not certain but probable this will happen—that a Titian has appeared in America, it will be established that the said painting is the property of Signora Santarato. All important works of art are registered at the Ministry of Culture in Rome and with the customs authorities. Anderson will say that he bought the painting in good faith from a French art dealer. That will probably not settle the matter. They'll search for Naville, with or without success. Anderson will have to surrender the painting, and it will be attached in America for months or years. I know a similar case. The claims of the Italian state will be investigated thoroughly. Anderson should undoubtedly have satisfied himself that the painting left Italy in a legal manner. Naville probably took it to Athens first, or somewhere else. Such practice is not unknown either.

Anderson will probably have to bear the loss. It's his own negligence, and that too is quite common among passionate collectors—he can afford the loss. All this looks better than it is, because really the family holds the key. Suppose Naville is caught; he can't offer any excuse for the smuggling; but he'll try to get his money. Had the Titian been solely yours, we'd have nothing to fear. But if Paolo and Teresa expose you, then Naville can say that he was deceived, that he bought the painting on false premises. Then you would have to return the purchase price at once, not to mention a possible fine."

In the middle of these reflections, the Signora heard the slam of the side entrance. Paolo had arrived.

Parents become old only when they feel their children are old. The Signora had never been aware of her son's age. He passed the old Venetian mirror hanging next to the door, one of those mirrors where the gay pink and blue glass frames contrast with the brittle tarnish of the plateglass. The Signora observed her son and at the same time she registered his reflection in the mirror. She could barely distinguish the image from the true man: the same proud bearing as before, his exterior the frame, his face tarnished and brittle.

"You need reinforcements, I see," said Paolo, glancing at Dario. "Did you know about this fraud, Dario?"

The Signora had expected it to be bad. Now she knew that it was going to be worse.

"Fraud? What are you talking about?" asked Dario.

"Come on, now! My mother sold a fake!"

"I don't blame you for not knowing anything about paintings," said Dario, "but you should not doubt your mother's honesty or her sanity. This one here is a copy. Your mother sold the original, of course."

"In other words, she wanted to deceive us, only us, her children?"

"Your share, like Claudia's and Laura's, is deposited at the bank. Your father's will was well conceived on the whole but foolish in detail. He wanted to preserve the palazzo for the family, but gave no consideration to how it could be done."

"My mother"—Paolo spoke of the Signora as if she were not present—"has no right to interpret my father's will. Does Claudia know about this swindle?"

"She has accepted her share," answered Dario.

"That's just like her. Who painted this trash?"

"It is an excellent copy," said the Signora. "The painter's name has nothing to do with it."

She was grateful to Dario, but she did not want to leave the discussion to the men. For twenty years she had felt tender sympathy for Paolo, because he walked on crutches. Teresa had been one of the crutches, herself the other. Now that he relied on only one crutch, he believed he was walking without them. He was old enough, he had to try.

She remembered every conversation she had had with Paolo about the palazzo, every begging supplicatory letter she had written in connection with the Titian. After the disastrous flood in November six years ago she had wanted to sell a mirror, some plates and china. She had written, begged him, implored him, and every time the answer had been no. She had been ill for a long time then; Paolo had come to see her for a day, but Teresa not even once. Had Paolo ever asked if she could manage on her annuity? One piece of jewelry after another had disappeared into the pawnshop. She had sent Emilia, the charwoman, here as her confidante, out of respect for the name of Santarato. Over and over again the answer was no! It was not good form to dispose of trinkets, to sell a mirror, a plate, a tea service. That kind of thing was simply not done by a Santarato, by a son-in-law of Andreoli. But it was not beneath his dignity to arrange a complete clearance sale, you could even have a catalogue printed. The Andreolis did not sell anything, they only auctioned off, wholesale. They did not try to repair anything shabby and brittle from the past. They threw it indiscriminately on the scrapheap. No repair, just destruction!

The Signora brought all this out with a vehemence which left Dario speechless and put Paolo right off his stroke.

He had expected his mother to make a contrite confession. It was not the purchaser she had deceived, but him; and on top of that the accused was acting as accuser.

"You and Claudia are going to give back everything you pocketed," he said. "We shall recover the painting at once."

"Don't you smell anything?" said the Signora.

"What am I supposed to smell?"

"Paint," said the Signora. "The palazzo is being fixed up. They've started inside, illicitly because of the strike, but tomorrow they will start work on the oak piles. You and your wife and your father-in-law, you don't ask whether everything is really doomed. All you wonder is how soon it's going to happen. The Flood doesn't worry you, as long as you're sitting pretty–but do you think anyone can sit pretty in a flood? How stupid!"

Before Paolo could retort, Dario said: "Andreoli did the right thing when he refused to pay the ransom for Remus. He would be doing the right thing if he paid the ransom for the palazzo. It's the same thing, you know, whether you understand that or not."

Paolo did not bother his head over Andreoli; this concerned *him*. The age, or society, whatever you cared to call it, did not even let you fail comfortably. Andreoli considered him an idiot, and Remus refused to see him. He was blamed for his son's having gone astray, and now he would be held responsible for his mother's offense. Did she think he would spare her? Did she also consider him a driveling idiot? He had played this part long enough, it was merely a part. Only Teresa believed in him, and Teresa alone was right. She wasn't only wanting to prove to her father who he was; he had been mistaken there. She knew him, understood him, loved him. Now it was up to him not to disappoint Teresa.

"As you wish," he said, apparently fully in control of himself. "What you have done is a crime, whether the law says so or not. Teresa saw through you from the first moment. You can thank me for now initiating the proceedings to put you under restraint. If what you did is not criminal, at the very least it shows you are mentally incapable. The palazzo will not be touched; no architect can be paid with smuggler's money. The entire junkheap will be sold. You'll be put in an old people's home, your share will pay for that. You can no longer stop me from realizing my dream and becoming independent. The umbilical cord is cut."

Indeed he felt as if after fifty-five years he had been cut free of the umbilical cord. For a moment he thought of Eleanora: he would break with her. There was only Teresa in his life from now on.

Dario took a step toward the Signora because he thought he would have to support her. It was only now that he saw the small box with the capsules next to her on the table. But she did not reach out for the box. She was pale, but otherwise nothing betrayed her emotions.

"I blame you, too," Paolo said to Dario. "At the very least I would have expected you to leave me alone with my mother. And like my mother, you're in a very exposed position."

Dario stood silently behind the Signora's easy chair. An exposed position? Perhaps resistance did not start sometime in the future, it started now. And not somewhere, but here, on the Canal Grande. He was not surprised when the Signora turned to Paolo.

"Your visit was superfluous. You can now go."

50

I said: in A.D. 2000 Venice will no longer exist. I catch myself thinking that I don't believe it. We Venetians don't believe it, nor does the world. There is nothing you get used to more quickly than hopelessness. "A miracle is faith's dearest child," the saying goes. But faith is the dearest child of hopelessness. Once you put yourself completely in God's hand, you may merely wait for a miracle. And if you are merely waiting for a miracle, you stop looking at the compass.

What am I to answer when asked: can Venice still be saved?

Only a miracle saved Venice on November 4, 1966. A freak storm swept across nothern Italy at sixty miles an hour. The rivers overflowed their banks and hurled immense masses of water into the sea. After midnight, the flooding waters, lashed by the hurricane, were two and a half feet above the level of a normal day. At four in the afternoon the level rose to nearly four feet. Venice is not on the sea, it is in the sea. When most of the houses were built, the water level was four inches lower than today. On that fourth of November there was not a single house on the lagoon where the gate could be opened or closed. Houses, churches and palaces were like stranded submarines. For twelve hours, from six in the morning until six in the evening, *finis Venetiae* seemed to have arrived. How did Venice escape death? A great drought had preceded the storm, the water level was lower than usual; the powers of destruction had mounted their attack from unfavorable positions. Had the situation been different, or had the storm raged another six hours, Venice would have been destroyed on November 4, 1966. Miracles do not repeat themselves.

Foolish blindness is the enemy of my city. The blind see only its beauty. Anybody who walks through Venice on a glorious summer day cannot imagine its distress. Children feed the pigeons in St. Mark's Square. The waiters on the terraces of the hotels on the Canal Grande move as if they were floating on the water. Motorboats hurry to the Lido, their white flags of foam flying behind them. But even Venice's *morbidezza* has irresistible charm. Only a fleeting thought is spent on the horror of her dying, everyone marvels instead at so majestic a demise, Pompeii in evening dress, lively death throes.

It does not occur to anyone to think of Venice's symbolic status. A Canal Grande with the city dying behind it is shoddy elegance, serene self-delusion, careless despair, indolent admiration, hopeless faith. We were taught freedom from fear, but only fear can lead us out of the darkness. The blessings of the world we live in are not sheer unreality; the only unreality is that they can survive without action. So much freely given beauty, so much laboriously achieved, so much rightly conceived, cannot be destroyed! Anyone who hopes in his heart that the flood will someday withdraw must work on the ark. But work he must! It would be mad to believe that the world is already saved; to refuse to believe that it can be saved is sacrilegious. Belief in miracles is superstition, and yet Noah was not superstitious. It is not logical that God, who said of men: "I will wipe them out from the face of the earth," should instruct a man how to build an ark. It is not logical, it is divine. Anyone who builds an ark must know that the Flood is coming.

When you think of saving a city, you think of money. Venice is a sick child, shivering with fever in a cradle set with precious stones. It is surrounded by a solicitous family, the most learned doctors have been summoned. Save Venice! Senators hurry over from America, special stamps are issued, imperial and royal purses are opened, the proceeds from concerts are donated, loans are offered for subscription and are oversubscribed. Everybody wants to win favor with the earth's favorite child. But Venice is not Tennessee, which could be rescued from the waves by just one presidential signature. Tennessee was saved because it yields fruit. Venice does not yield fruit. Venice is not the pharaonic temple of Abu Simbel, just one temple. Somebody who cannot decide how his gifts should be best spent is a spendthrift. He tosses his alms into the street, not into the beggar's cap.

Man's eternal question as to Satan's identity, whether he is a second deity and why God suffers him, is answered in the Talmud. Although the words "test" and "temptation" mean two different things, they are closely related. When the Devil tempts man, he puts him to the test, on higher orders. When Satan induced Aaron to present the golden calf to the people of Israel he did what he was commissioned to do: it was both temptation and test. This is how my city is being tested. When the flood withdrew in 1966, the government made some first aid available; as usual with first aid, it may have been last aid. The golden calf around which the Jews danced was made from their own gold, but in Venice foreign gold is torn from the calf's clay body, golden rings from the loot. The proceeds are used for expansion of the canals, synthetic fertilizer is bought for the fields which once were lagoons. In addition to the oil refineries there are twelve canning factories in Marghera, thirty-two haulage firms, thirty-nine machine workshops, sports grounds and swimming pools for the young who are leaving Venice, loans to businessmen in Lombardy, Tuscany and abroad, relief for striking unions. Gold enough and to spare—and a total of forty-five buildings, including monuments, have been saved! Sixty-nine churches, monasteries and abbeys are on the brink of ruin, so are four schools and likewise thirteen historic palazzi, among them masterpieces such as the Palazzo Soranzo-van Axel, the Palazzo Gradenigo, the Palazzo Zorzi. Two hundred of the four hundred and fifty palazzi are in disrepair, and over a hundred of the two hundred churches. The frescoes of San Sebastiano and San Nicolò dei Mendicoli are broken, the marble of Miracoli is split and the paintings on canvas of San Martino, San Pietro di Castello and San Pantaleone are wormeaten. Bellini's *Madonna* in the Church of San Francesco della Vigna has been sacrificed, the statues of *Moderation* and *Charity* on the Porta della Carta of the Ducal Palace have fallen from their niches, and Tiepolo's *The Triumph of Faith* is full of holes.

Some time ago I stood in the court of the Palazzo Ca' Foscari, a citizen among citizens. The Mayor was about to speak. The Mayor probably doesn't care to think of the doge Francesco Foscari, unless he likes his long term in office: Francesco Foscari ruled for a longer period than any of the other doges, 1423–57, thirty-four years. Francesco Foscari achieved one victory after another: he brought Ravenna and Padua, Verona and Vicenza, Brescia and Bergamo under the rule of Venice; but he also brought the beginning of misfortune. Macchiavelli wrote: "The period of decline began when the Venetians tried to fight a land war like the other peoples of Italy." Our Mayor spoke from a balcony of the Palazzo Ca' Foscari and asked for proof that Venice was in danger. Nothing of the sort was true, he said; the enemies of Venice were at work with false statistics, they alone were obstructing development and progress. There we stood, looking at the decorated balcony, and we did not reply, for the blind are joined by the mute. I did not say anything either; I sneaked away and remembered that the doges did not have death sentences proclaimed from the balconies of the Ducal Palace. They proclaimed them from a balcony of the Palazzo Ca' Foscari.

Can Venice be saved? The number of plans is legion. There is talk of an immense dike which could isolate the lagoon from the sea. But what use would it be, since access to Marghera would be even easier? The construction of sewage farms is planned, but how are they to operate without further and further borings for fresh water? The fresh water supplies cannot possibly suffice; a single industrial installation uses up 12,000 cubic meters of water per hour, and it has already had to be rationed. The vibrations of the motorboats, and there are far more motorboats than gondolas, could be stopped, but the damage they cause to the monuments is negligible. The adventurous spirit of the rescuers is unlimited. A tire firm would like to cordon off the high water with a flexible dike system; tubelike pipes made of nylon fibers could be anchored along the tanker waterways of Malamocco. But progress cannot keep up with progress, for the bigger the tanker, the cheaper the shipping, so oil tankers of half a million tons are under construction. Giant ships need giant ports. Hydraulic sluices would keep the industrial installations—and Venice—alive. Cost estimates speak of three hundred million lire, but since they would be a hindrance for the tankers of the future, the plans lie rotting like Titian's paintings.

Have the friends of my city seen the full-page advertisements published in the local press by IBM, the powerful American corporation? It is a very beautiful advertisement, with a picture of the Canal Grande, the Salute in the foreground, three gondolas and no motorboats. Above the picture you read the words: "Every year, a little more of her beauty is lost." IBM has much more to tell us than that. "For centuries Venice seemed to be safe on the sea. Now the sea has become its enemy." But the liberation troops are coming: "Italy's National Research Institute has now set up a special laboratory in Venice where experts from all over the world endeavor to study the geophysical conditions on the spot." Only wait, and soon the sea will be calm, for it ends well in bold type: "Computers help people help–IBM." There is indeed an IBM computer, 360–40, in one of our palazzi, spitting out its wisdom. But computers don't give any answers unless they are asked questions. And a Devil who asked the computer questions about Venice would be leading himself into temptation.

For he would have to ask: Can Venice be saved if the refineries of Marghera are not abandoned, if they are not rebuilt in some other part of the country; if there is not a halt to the continual building of more channels; and if heavy shipping is not forbidden in the existing ones? Can Venice be saved without letting Mestre's sea of stone go to waste and the chimneys on the lagoon shore fall into ruins, and without forbidding further drillings?

These would be the questions. And since the computer in the palazzo is an honest computer, honest and well made and as humane as those who operate it, it would reply: No, without the sacrifice of Mestre and Marghera Venice cannot be saved.

And if it were asked whether Venice could be saved if Mestre and Marghera were sacrificed, then it would answer: Yes, then Venice can be saved, even now.

But if it were asked: Will Mestre and Marghera be sacrificed? then it could not answer.

For computers take no cognizance of miracles.

51

Laura had herself taken from the airport to the Hotel Monaco e Grand Canal.

The Signora had cabled her that she was welcome at the palazzo, that Remus's room was free. Remus's room—it had been her and Claudia's room. Among all sentimental misconceptions the memory of a happy childhood is the most untruthful. Laura's psychoanalyst dug for her hidden misery like a gold digger in reverse, but she could have saved herself his fee. The grounds were obvious. All his life her father had been what Americans with some relish call "a failure," but since he was unable to face the storms from outside, he ruled like a potentate within his own house. Paolo's personality had not been crushed, but he was a man, and that was crushing enough for Laura. The room she had shared with Claudia had in reality been Claudia's room. Claudia sparkled in a thousand colors. Her own or Claudia's opinions were not asked, but Claudia stated hers unasked. From the earliest years of her youth Laura had been proud of being a Santarato. To herself she called the big drawing room the baronial hall, the small dining room was the refectory, and she used to imagine that she had been Titian's model for the *Girl with Flower Basket*. But when Claudia started to rebel, she felt ashamed for not rebelling herself. When Claudia went out, she tidied up the bedroom. She could take the whole day over it, and Claudia would have everything in disorder again within a few minutes. Disorder was stronger than order. She suffered most from the dominance of her mother, who tried not to dominate at all. In the shops she was asked if this item or that which she had chosen would appeal to the Signora. If she wanted to buy a dress, she was told that she could take it home, perhaps it would not be to her mother's taste. Although the Signora was the shortest member of the family, all eyes went to her in church, and the young men who came to the house hardly talked to anybody but the Signora. At Laura's wedding, Ed had gazed at the Signora. No, she would rather stay at the hotel on the Canal Grande.

From Paolo she knew that her mother had indeed dared to sell the Titian. While reading the *New York Times* on the plane, she had come across a short paragraph to the effect that the Italian government had lodged a complaint in Washington regarding the illegal importation of a Titian which had been bought by an American collector. There was no mention of the name; Nelson E. Anderson was a man of influence. So that's what her vacation looked like being; once again she had chosen the wrong alternative at the wrong moment.

After unpacking her clothes, her lingerie and her beauty case and carefully arranging all her toilet articles on the dresser, just as she had done for many years in every hotel room on her search for a home, Laura set out for the palazzo.

If her sister-in-law hoped to have found a reliable ally in her, Teresa mistook her for Paolo. But her mother should not suppose that she would sink sentimentally into her arms. There had always been a lot of fuss in the Palazzo Santarato about moral behavior, and now the old lady had blotted her copybook. Why had her mother entreated her to consent to the sale of the Titian if she had decided to go ahead even without her agreement? Or was Paolo right, and her mother was feebleminded after all? It was sad to think that old age should have destroyed the most sensible person in the family. Still, if Laura had learned anything in America, it was that you made provisions for the infirm, but you did not stay with them.

She walked more slowly. Every house reminded her of something. As a girl she had stood yearningly outside the shoe shop; she was not yet allowed to wear high heels. In front of the bank to the left she had had her first date. She no longer remembered the boy's name; he probably had a wife and children and had never left Venice. In the café on the right Claudia used to meet young painters, and Laura had to say that they had spent the afternoon together at a museum. There was the narrow alley leading to the canal, where the Major had been billeted. He had wanted to take her up to his room, but she had refused.

Laura met no one she knew, as on Madison Avenue, but she seemed to know the strangers. If she spoke to one of them, he would surely say: "Where do you come from?" The tourists were the same ones who used to ask her for directions to find a certain street or a church. She could have showed them the way even now. She had been told that there had been no rain for a long time; she did not need telling, the smell of the lagoons was enough. On hot evenings on the Hudson she had sometimes said: "This is the smell of Venice." Her friends had laughed and said: "Hopefully the stink here isn't quite as bad." They had not understood her.

The garden of the palazzo was not as untended as she had expected it to be. On the doorstep she met some workmen. In the entrance hall there was a ladder, tools lay around, a drilling machine stood in a corner, some floor stones had been removed, others were already replaced.

Her mother embraced her, kissed her on both cheeks. Even in Laura's childhood the Signora had been sparing with her kisses. The Signora had always seemed old to Laura; old she was, but apparently she had not aged. The limpid eyes, the flagpole back, the flowing hair, the dragoonlike step, which the family used to laugh at and mimic, were all unchanged. Did living in a fortress keep you from growing old?

The Signora's delight at seeing her daughter seemed real. The tea table was set, the fresh pastries had clearly been brought from Quadri's, among them Laura's favorite cream pie. The Signora unstintingly admired Laura's appearance. "You don't look a day older—your print dress is simply lovely. Oh, well, you can only find such things in America." On the other hand, she did not stint her reproaches either. She had cabled Laura expressly about the room. "It is yours, after all, and what good is this big house if you go and stay in a hotel? Please think it over again; also it's not much further to the Lido from the palazzo than from your hotel. . . . How have you been doing in New York lately? Letters can't convey what one really wants to know. Isn't there someone who has fallen for you, don't Americans have eyes in their heads?" Laura was hard put to it to answer all the Signora's questions. Her resolution to resist her mother's charm began to waver. She had had time enough to think about herself. Loneliness had made her receptive to love, whether true or pretended, and that too was a part of the loneliness. Although disappointed time and again, you would accept further disappointments for a little bit of love.

While Laura was still wondering how she could turn the conversation to the subject that was occupying her mind, the Signora directed their talk almost imperceptibly, at any rate without inhibitions, toward her own misdemeanor. When Laura involuntarily apologized and said that she needed "a real vacation," that she would spend three or four weeks on the Lido, at the Quattro Fontane, a nice but modest hotel, the Signora said that if Laura did not want to live at the palazzo she might at least treat herself to the Excelsior. "Your share of the sale of the Titian is deposited at the bank. It doesn't make sense just to watch the value of money going down."

The sudden transition took Laura's breath away. Was her mother trying to bribe her, and where did she get the nerve to talk about the fruits of her fraud as if they were a bonanza?

"I hear," said the Signora, "that the Italian authorities are trying to get hold of the Titian. But that doesn't make any difference, seeing that I didn't know anything about the smuggling. Paolo wants to file a petition for my mental incapacity. The fact that I have touched the money will probably be a point in his favor: that's my extravagance. Admittedly, obstinacy can degenerate into feeblemindedness, but for the moment I'm still at the obstinate stage. This may be a sign of old age, but in my case it's difficult to prove, because I was as obstinate at eighteen as others are at eighty.... Look at the ceiling." The cracks there were deep, and in one spot the bare stone was visible. Part of the stuccowork was hanging from the wall like dog-ears in a well-thumbed book. "Sheer extravagance, as you can see."

Laura tried to remember what she had proposed to say or do in New York, on the flight, and before she reached the palazzo. It was easy to carry on a conversation when you were alone. She pulled herself together and said: "Yes, of course, but the palazzo is not everything. You cannot sacrifice your children to it."

The Signora, who had not touched her tea or the pastries, sat down by Laura on the sofa. "Listen to me," she said, and put her slightly reddened hand on her daughter's beautifully manicured, but strong, almost masculine hand. "You can't know," she said, "how close Claudia and I have come during the past few weeks." She did not mention Claudia's suicide attempt, but spoke with tolerant serenity of her impulsive marriage. "I was here when Claudia needed me, and I was able to help her a little, but without the palazzo I could not have done it. This is a bit difficult to understand, I'll explain it to you later.... I admit I have lost Paolo because of this tiresome business, or

rather, he has withdrawn from me even further. But the change in him
is more than a weak man's brutality. He secretly knows, of course, that
he can always come back to me. And as for you ... I have followed
your life from afar, more than you might think. That life has not been
as happy as it may look to those who do not know you, and as you
have tried to make out whenever you wrote. But you have not gone
under, when it would have been so easy to go under, and so hard to
maintain any dignity. I imagine that sometimes when you saw no way
out, you would think of the Palazzo Santarato."

Laura was about to say, "The palazzo doesn't mean anything to me,"
but since she had entered the drawing room, since she had stirred her
tea with the old silver spoon, since her glance had taken in the Canal
Grande through the balcony door—since then she suddenly felt more
resentment against Teresa than during the years of hostile indifference.
An Andreoli could easily give up the palazzo—after all, it wasn't a
brewery. For herself, she had realized during the first few hours that she
could no longer have lived in Venice. She found the city provincial, for
all its beauty. The unchanged city seemed a pool of stagnant water. In
New York, whatever the standard of life, at least people lived it. Here,
life was not lived; it was in mothballs, sterilized and embalmed, a
walking mummy. But how would everything have felt—her hectic
existence in New York, her television friendships, those casual love
affairs, the floating on the surface and the swimming against the tide—
had there been no Venice?

"I want to see the house," she said.

The Signora took her to the dining room, which looked even
sadder and shabbier in the afternoon sun, its patched wallpaper more
dreadful than the gaping holes. She led the way up the stairs to the
bedrooms. In Romolo's room, the least affected, where strangely
enough there was no musty smell, the Signora said, "Sometimes I am
grateful to Teresa, she gave me Romolo. It doesn't matter that she
didn't mean to give me anything." The humidity had been more cruel
to the walls of the room Laura and Claudia used to share. It had
stained them a grayish black; the old furniture seemed to be standing
in a warehouse. Laura quickly turned away before the Signora could
notice how glad she was she had decided to stay at the hotel. "My
room is passable," said the Signora. It really *was* passable, so Laura
could not understand why a sudden emotion should seize her here and

make her grasp her mother's hand. She recognized all the objects which in former years had stood or lain in some other room, in the "baronial hall" or in the "refectory." As from a burning ship, the Signora had hastily rescued one thing after another. The sight of the curtains, of the lace and frills, moved Laura deeply. So did the dresser with its innumerable small bottles, many still unopened, as if the Signora were saving up these treasures for a time she was not going to see anyway.

"And now," said the Signora, "nothing but pleasant surprises."

She had left the kitchen to the last. It smelled of fresh paint, the walls were shining, only a few patches showed the scars of healing wounds. "My men have really done wonders here," she said. Laura did not have the heart to tell her mother that she had already seen the entrance hall. Not heeding the steep stairs, the Signora led her downstairs. There she stood, in the middle of the cold stone hall, a tiny figure who seemed to fill the space. Like a builder proud of his new building, she explained to Laura what had already been done, and the plans for what was still to do. "One can't make much of this white elephant, of course, but the hall happens to be most exposed to the high water. There'd be no sense in repairing the stuccowork upstairs when we can't be sure the foundation walls will stand up to the next catastrophe."

It was not until they were back in the drawing room—dusk was falling, the lights of the ships floated by—that Laura remembered she had not asked her mother properly about her health.

"Thank you for reminding me," said the Signora. "I have to take one of these silly capsules. It really doesn't happen often, but the heart is rather foolish, it reacts in exactly the same manner to a happy excitement as to an unpleasant one."

Although Laura tried to avoid looking at the fake Titian she could not stop her eyes going to it.

"Sit here with me," said the Signora. "I want to tell you a strange story. You mustn't tell anyone, but this copy was painted by a young professional counterfeiter. I declare I fell in love with him. And I cannot complain, for my love is reciprocated. That's why he packed up the original, to please me. We had formed a conspiracy. It all went very fast and more or less painlessly. To be honest, I was pretty apprehensive when he left; we had grown so used to each other, the Titian and I. It wasn't till the painting lay in its crate that I wondered whether everything would have gone off so smoothly and without tears if the Titian had been framed. You remember, your father never wanted that. And a few days later it occurred to me that probably one can only sell or throw away things that are unframed. I've often had the feeling before that paintings without a frame were looking at me reproachfully, as if they were begging for a frame. Can you understand that?"

Laura was astonished that she did understand. She wondered if she would have understood without the tour of the palazzo. The Signora didn't even have a television set; yet a riddle Laura could not understand, though she listened to the news until two o'clock in the morning, was solved by the Signora with a single parable: the longing for a frame, the decay without one. The Titian was only a painting, the walls were its frame. Her mother had been living with her in spirit all these years. She knew the dangers that had threatened her and why she had been able to resist.

"I'll try to make Paolo see sense, Mamma," said Laura. "If I don't succeed, you and I will stick together."

The Signora made a gesture as if she were about to embrace her daughter, but she had stood out too long against big gestures. She withdrew her half-raised arms and dropped them into her lap. Laura pretended she did not see the tears in her mother's eyes.

52

One day the sky was overcast. Not black and rainy, just rather autumnal, as if the sun were wondering whether to shine or not. What happened that day surprised Romolo. He had felt like a man, and made all sorts of plans. He and Barbara would write to each other, he would persuade his father to send him to an English school, or else he would simply run away, like Remus. Or he would sometimes flatter himself that he could forget Barbara; it was the sort of summer romance grown-ups have. The disillusionment surprised him, he did not know what it meant. The end of an illusion, not a surprise.

The Signora was in the kitchen getting breakfast ready. She heard the ring of the telephone, answered it, and called Romolo. A Mr. Donovan wanted to speak to him.

"My humble apologies, Romolo," said Mr. Donovan, "but I'd like to ask you a great favor. I know I invited you to the opening of the film festival tomorrow, but a friend of the family has unexpectedly turned up from London; he's my lawyer too, and the festival's completely sold out. I wonder if you'd mind very much giving up your ticket."

"Of course not," Romolo said. He had known that Barbara would be leaving with her parents the day after the opening, but at least he would be sitting next to her that last evening, and now it would be this lawyer instead. He didn't dare ask who the lawyer was, but it could only be Bob, the fellow Barbara had talked about so much at the beginning.

He was on the Lido just before ten. Even when it was fine the beach did not start filling up until eleven or so, and today the uncertain weather had scared off many regulars. There were mainly photographers, already on the lookout for a celebrity; on the jetty heavily made-up models sprawled for fashion photographs. In front of one *cabina*, canvases full of glittering foil were set up, and on the terrace a lot of young people were assembled to discuss the demonstration that was being planned against the film festival.

Romolo thought time might pass faster if he turned away from the electric clock. But then he began staring at it again, as if he had the power to speed it up. Sometimes he looked toward the bar from where Barbara usually came to the beach. Sometimes he would walk away; she would appear only when he wasn't expecting her. He wanted to call her up on the house telephone, but she would think he was pushing himself too much, and yet if he didn't, she would say: why didn't you simply call up? Nothing had happened, really. Mr. Donovan had asked him a favor, the lawyer could be some quite old man. While his imagination ran away with him, he felt ashamed of imagining so much. But at the same time he couldn't imagine enough. Did she know he was waiting for her? What would she say to him? Was she as disappointed as he was? Had she told Bob about him, it must be Bob, what had she told him, what and why and why not? He rehearsed all sorts of indifferent poses, but when she walked toward him he was sure he had already given away everything he felt.

Bob, in his late twenties or early thirties, was just as handsome as Romolo had pictured him. It was cold comfort to see that he had bad front teeth sticking out over his lip.

"I am the creature who robbed you of your ticket," said Bob, "but the receptionist is working on it, he might be able to get a fifth one. So sorry!"

"I see too many films as it is," said Romolo.

The three of them went swimming, dried themselves on the jetty under a tired sun, cleaned the tar from their feet, ran across the prickly carpet of seashells, made fun of the dumb starlets and the dumb photographers, and sat at the bar. Bob talked to Romolo like a grown-up. If he knew anything, he probably didn't care. Bob and Barbara mentioned names Romolo didn't know—"Ruth won't be pleased," "John is crazy," "just like Gladys." He did his best to smile. Then Bob said that the photographs should be ready, he would go and see. When they were on their own, Barbara said that Bob would be staying until the day after tomorrow. That his trip to Venice had been quite a sudden idea of his; it suited her mother pretty well, Bob could carry the suitcases. "How do you like him?" she said. "Very much," he said. Bob returned with the pictures the hotel photographer had taken the evening before, in the bar. Barbara and Bob and the Donovans; at least Mr. and Mrs. Donovan had been with them. The lunch bell rang. Bob asked if Romolo wanted to join them. He said he would just have a sandwich. "See you later," said Barbara.

He sat in the sand, a long way from the grill, and swallowed his sandwich. He felt like a beggar who had had some crumbs thrown to him. A grown-up man would have gone to the dining room and ordered the whole menu, from the hors d'oeuvre to the dessert. Would Barbara try to see him alone, would she tell him the two of them must drive out to Malamocco in the evening? Tomorrow it would be too late. Tomorrow was the opening of the festival, and perhaps Barbara thought he would stand outside like a sightseer. Eventually he formed his plan and carried it out. A few minutes after Barbara and Bob had returned, he said he had something important to do in Venice. "See you tomorrow, then," said Barbara. "We'll be down here early. Let's hope it doesn't rain."

There were only two old ladies taking the motorboat. Romolo stood next to the driver. Some sad fishermen were sitting on the ugly sandbank which sticks out of the water halfway between the Lido and Venice, and there was a child playing with a battered refrigerator, perhaps transforming it into an ocean liner. Venice's skyline of dark silver drew closer—the Ducal Palace, the Campanile, the Piazzetta—and the closer it drew, the angrier Romolo felt. The whole year he had longed for Venice, and now Venice had hurt him; it must be Venice's fault. He wished Venice would drown, and his whole ridiculous childhood would drown with it. The best thing would be if he could leave Venice that very day.

But when he had left the boat at the Danieli, he started to run. It seemed as if the waves had in fact swallowed the Lido, the sandy beach and the *cabine,* the barman, the old ladies, the photographers and the film starlets, even Bob and Barbara, the whole hotel; only the green domes still floated on the water like forlorn buoys. He raced toward the palazzo as if pursued by the waves.

He did not want to say anything to the Signora. Nobody should learn of his suffering, a man keeps a stiff upper lip. He would not talk of it at all, perhaps he would never talk of it again. He had not expected the Signora to notice anything. Because she knew at once that something out of the ordinary had happened to him, and because she asked without pressing him, and because it didn't make any difference whether he talked or remained silent, he began to talk. He talked and talked as if he could not get his heart to stop the flow. The palazzo had always been his home. Now he had nothing left but the palazzo and the Signora.

It was almost as dark as evening. Their conversation was interrupted now and then by distant thunder or by hammering on the ground floor. He told her everything he had earlier withheld. He expatiated on minor details, like how he had tuned Barbara's transistor, how on their first ride in a gondola he had been afraid they would meet old Carlo, and how he had seen that film in Milan already. But he also talked about Barbara's marijuana cigarette, which he had taken away from her, about her life in London, which he could not picture at all, and about the night in the palazzo; also about Bob. One thing he did not mention was Malamocco.

He only half listened when the Signora began talking. A man solves his problems all by himself, and you certainly couldn't expect an old lady to help solve them.

"I'm not going to tell you Barbara was unworthy of you," she said. "Because that doesn't really matter, or anyhow it has never been a consolation to anyone. First, because nobody believes it, and second, because the human species would have become extinct long ago if the only people who got loved were those who were worthy of it. Even if that wretched Bob hadn't come, Barbara would still be leaving tomorrow or the day after, and she couldn't have behaved any differently. She would have said 'goodbye' or 'see you later' or whatever people do say when a summer ends."

Romolo pricked up his ears. "How do you know that?" he asked.

"Because two people never love each other in the same way," she said. "They only believe they do. That's not saying anything against Barbara. And even if they do love each other just as much, that doesn't mean their love will leave equally deep marks. Love changes many things, but it can't change a person's character, that's something he keeps as his own—again I'm not saying anything against Barbara. You probably feel hurt now in your manly pride, but that's doing her an injustice. Her 'goodbye' and 'see you later' just show she's treating you like a man. From all you've told me, Barbara is a grown woman. Grown women find it easy to say 'goodbye' and 'see you later,' and they expect grown men to do the same. What else but 'goodbye' could she say, with or without Bob? And what else but 'goodbye' can you say, today, tomorrow, or the day after tomorrow?"

Now he was listening, though with part of his mind he was wondering whether to go out to the Lido again tomorrow. After all, his grandmother could be wrong. Perhaps if he had stayed there this afternoon, Barbara would still have said something about Malamocco. He saw her face on the face of the girl with the flower basket, and on the faded wallpaper, and in the threatening sky.

"To show you I don't consider you a small boy," the Signora continued, "I want to tell you something else. At my age every experience makes one poorer, it merely confirms what one already knows, which isn't very pleasant. It's like pouring milk into a full bottle. It spills over, and all you experience is spilt milk. But when one is young, every experience enriches you, even disappointments; they help to fill your bottle. 'It's easy for her,' you're thinking now. I know how you feel, but when you look at it, you'll see that even if you had a touching farewell, things would be much the same afterward. She'll go back to London, you'll go back to Milan. There'll be letters, but hers certainly, and perhaps yours too, will be at longer and longer intervals and less and less on the same wave length. By the way, I wanted to ask you if you could stay a little longer in Venice. You can get ready for school here. You see, I need you."

"Shall I go to the Lido tomorrow?" he said.

"It's going to rain tomorrow," she said. "A good excuse if you find it too hard to see her, but still an excuse. I could have saved myself a lot of unpleasantness lately, that's what I was talking about just now. But I believe that between two actions the brave one is always the right thing to do. And I think you're like me in that."

Romolo had felt this likeness for a long time. He said he was going to the Lido tomorrow, even if it rained. Defiance had replaced the pain, not completely or without a trace, but with only a little room left for pain, and none at all for self-pity.

A cold rain had started to fall during the night and continued on the following morning. A burning pain came back when he remembered how for weeks he had looked at the sky every morning, fearing the clouds.

He did not take off his raincoat in the foyer of the Excelsior. On the phone he said that he had come to say goodbye; he had to return on the next boat.

The foyer was packed with refugees from the rain. Only two wicker chairs in the center of the room were still free. They moved the chairs closer because an old man was sitting at the table with a young woman.

"It was nice of you to come," she said, "a shame we can't see each other this evening."

"What time is your plane?" he said.

"Quite early, nine o'clock," she said.

"I hope the weather gets better," he said.

"The weather in London is fine today," she said.

"They say there'll be demonstrations this evening," he said.

She said, "Will you write to me sometimes? You've got my address, haven't you?"

"Of course," he said.

"Perhaps I'll come to Milan someday," she said.

"I shan't be in Milan," he said.

"Why not?" she said.

He said, "I'm staying in Venice. My grandmother needs me."

"I envy you."

"You said that before." Then he got up and said, "All the best to your parents, many thanks for everything. A shame I couldn't see them."

"Mum's packing," she said. "They wish *you* all the best, too." She kissed him on the cheek.

53

The demonstrators were lucky. The rain stopped an hour before the opening of the film festival.

Laura had invited Claudia to go with her to the festival film at the Lido Cinema Palace; she also wanted to meet Claudia's husband. "I'm afraid he can't come," Claudia said. "The festival is a fascist scandal, and Fabio has to take part in the *Controfestival* they're holding in town, at a cinema which is at present named after St. Margherita, but they'll soon change the name, you can't have a saint as patron. I'll be very glad to accept, though, and then I can report on it to Fabio; and after the film we'll have a chance to talk. Perhaps Fabio will join us later on."

Although in New York Laura had grown accustomed to not asking the reasons for demonstrations, she inquired why the Biennial had evoked such protest.

"They used to award prizes," said Claudia, "but these have now been done away with, thanks to the protests. But there's still the same old competitive spirit, our rat-race cancer, everyone still wanting to outdo everyone else, big business as you call it in your country. The Biennial constitution has been in force for twenty-seven years, it dates back to the Mussolini era; nineteen new draft constitutions in thirteen years have all been thrown out. This time there are ninety-six films from thirty countries, but the young actors and the unions weren't asked.

That's censorship. The festival still means truckling to dull audience taste, everyone still impressed by big names, and the stars on parade again, as you saw at the hotel. On the opening night there'll be dinner jackets and evening dresses, that's the only thing that matters to the audience, for Venice is just a facade and deceit, playing at being civilized. And if anyone wants to demoth Venice, they'll first have to chase away the moths dancing around the light."

Laura had asked her question simply to please Claudia. She had not been expecting such a tirade, and anyhow in New York she had already seen *Cabaret,* the anti-fascist musical which was to open the thirty-third festival. Still, she listened carefully. She had known Claudia's sympathies were always with the rebels, but it had surely been more of an artistic rebellion. Claudia had always prided herself on her independence, long before American women declared their independence from men. And now, thought Laura, for her to go to bed with a rebel, even to a marriage bed, was enough to make her follow him from bed to barricades. Laura was reassured, however, when they met at the Hotel Excelsior to go to the festival cinema, because Claudia was wearing a long evening dress with a low neckline, shiny green, and black silk pumps.

By New York standards the demonstration proved quite mild. Perhaps the *Controfestival* had split the protesting forces, and moreover, the communist union had issued an order that, in view of the threat of unemployment, the festival should once again be allowed to proceed. At any rate there were only a hundred or a hundred and fifty rebels behind the barrier thrown around the picture palace. Lined up directly behind the ropes were the forty-two employees of the Biennial who had refused to co-operate in a fascist concern. Two of them carried a placard to distinguish them, whereas other placards, almost as numerous as the demonstrators, protested either against the Mussolini criminals or against Italy's liberators from Mussolini, the American imperialists. One placard said Venice must be returned to the Venetians. Laura felt this applied to her even less than did the slogan about the American tyrants.

And yet, as she gathered up the hem of her white evening dress and hurried past the barrier, she felt a certain uneasiness. All the other ladies and gentlemen flocking to the cinema seemed to be walking with eyes lowered like herself, not exactly fearfully, but as if troubled by a bad conscience, as if they had been caught wearing black shirts under their white and midnight-blue dinner jackets, or the daggers of Mussolini's Fascist Youth under their low-cut dresses. Her uneasiness increased when Claudia suddenly stopped, went up to the taut rope, reached out and shook hands with Remus, who had stepped forward from the crowd. Laura gave an embarrassed nod to her nephew, who greeted her in return with an embarrassed smile. When she got inside the cinema foyer, she felt like a thief who has been chased through the streets and has finally found shelter in a dark doorway.

A hundred or a hundred and fifty demonstrators outside the gates, and in here a few thousand people had gathered to see a film showing the cruelty of the frenzied masses in the early days of the Third Reich. But there was no sort of festival atmosphere. The speakers presented their laudatory addresses like apologies; the flowers in crackling cellophane were placed in the actresses' arms like wreaths on a grave.

People in open-necked shirts, looking somehow defiant, were not refused admittance, though their neighbors eyed them suspiciously. In spite of the heat many women kept their coats on to hide their naked flesh or their jewels. The police in their formal uniforms tried in vain to appear unobtrusive. Friends recognized each other with a glance that seemed to say "how brave!" or as if they were surprised to see familiar faces in the lifeboat. At last the lights went out, to be greeted by a general sigh of relief.

The streets were empty when Laura and Claudia left the cinema; some workmen were removing the ropes of the barrier.

The bar of the hotel was crammed; the two women could only sit down on the floor, where some leather cushions had been placed.

Laura had noticed in the cinema that Claudia was not quite sober. She had taken a double vodka in the hotel foyer before meeting Laura, and it was obviously not the first that evening. Now, as Claudia was again ordering a double vodka, Laura wondered whether she had chosen the right moment for a serious conversation.

At their first meeting after Laura's arrival, which was in the palazzo, the two sisters could not speak of the Signora and what might be in store for her. Now they found out that Paolo had telephoned them both asking them to support him in his petition to put her under restraint. He had specified an enormous sum which an American, Mr. Wilcox, would be willing to pay for the palazzo, as soon as the Signora could no longer oppose the sale. He had promised to pay Claudia her whole share, without deducting the money she might have spent in advance. To Laura he had said that he would make her a partner in his future business, a unique investment—after all, she had often asked his advice on good investments. He had assured both his sisters that he wouldn't dream of putting Mamma in an old people's home, as Teresa proposed. Instead, he would set her up in a nice two-room apartment; she could bring along from the palazzo a few trifles she was specially fond of. As for the rest, he was asking them as their brother, friend and adviser. His lawyer had assured him that he could manage very well without their consent, and that the forensic psychiatrist's verdict had been reached; he was to present his formal report within the next few days.

Claudia said she would neither consent nor stop Paolo from going ahead with his plan. "Mamma told you the truth, we have grown closer lately. I tried to kill myself, you know, an affair with a man who was quite wrong for me, eleventh-hour panic, Mamma really did her stuff." She spoke of her attempted suicide as if it were an everyday occurrence, and seemed to have lost the thread. Her glass was empty; she waved for the waiter like somebody drowning. "Oh yes," she continued, "Mamma! Old age, Fabio says, is nothing but the intensification of existing characteristics. The stingy become meaner still, the generous more lavish, the brave braver and the nervous more apprehensive; in old age character is more or less set rigid. Mamma has always had quite perverse ideas about property, Paolo says, and now her property mania is expressing itself in this senile, childish glorification of the palazzo, an old ruin on oak piles that are sheer illusions themselves. And to justify herself, he says, she's identifying that ruin with Venice, and seriously thinks of herself as almost the figurehead of a sinking ship. Anyhow, Mamma lied to me, she didn't tell me where the money came from."

The second vodka was served, and Claudia drank thirstily. It seemed to Laura that her younger sister looked older than herself. Strange that before the film showing she should have admired Claudia's youthful appearance; now the beautiful face seemed ravaged, it had dark rings, almost bags, under the eyes.

"What Paolo is planning for Mamma," said Claudia, when she had reassembled her thoughts, "is not only sensible, it's the kindest thing as well in the long run. The reason I don't want any part in it is because of Paolo's plans for the future, because after all they're just a chase after rotten old property too. He wants to put Mamma under restraint for the wrong reasons. Extravagance—that's a term in the vocabulary of this society which has made an idol of property, an idol that must not be touched. Just the opposite, Mamma ought to be put under restraint for her property mania, only of course there's no legal provision for this, or the whole of society would have to be put under restraint. Not a bad idea at that, but to start with one old woman is absurd."

Laura couldn't understand her sister mentioning her suicide attempt as if it were something quite trivial. She would like to have heard more about it, but did not dare to ask. Which is the more unstable, she thought, who is less aware of her goal and more unsure of how to reach it, an old woman defending her property—maybe a figurehead, but wasn't Noah too a figurehead?—or Claudia with her eleventh-hour panic—don't I know the feeling!—in which she was ready to throw her life overboard? This is the woman who has married a young man and drunk herself old; who knows so well how society can be cured—Which society? Her own or other people's?—but cannot heal herself. The palazzo isn't a symbol for her, and yet it somehow is, because she hasn't decided *against* Mamma, although she hasn't decided *for* her either. In her green evening dress she can shake hands across the barrier, but she's out of her element both among the demonstrators and in the festival audience. She climbs out of bed and onto the barricades, but on the barricades she's probably thinking of bed. I admit I would have agreed with Claudia only a few days ago, Laura thought. I'm like a proselyte passionately embracing her new faith. Still, why despise proselytes? They're acting out of conviction, and who knows, they may have believed all along and simply not been aware of it. A new feeling of security swept over her. She had always envied her sister, now she envied her no longer.

Claudia had turned away and was watching the people at the bar. Soon a man came toward them from the crowd there, and Claudia introduced him: Fabio.

At first Laura believed it was the mere sight of her brother-in-law (brother-in-law, a strange idea) which had irritated her. But in his worn linen trousers and open shirt Fabio was not at all conspicuous. Among the festival audience in their evening dresses there were enough men here who resembled him. Laura wondered if she was stirred by jealousy.

For a moment she saw the two of them in bed, the sturdy country boy and the delicate high-class lady. Easy enough to resist temptation, Laura told herself, if it never comes your way—and no Fabio has ever approached me. Is it pity? Doesn't Claudia realize she's acting in eleventh-hour panic, the very thing she wanted to run away from? Doesn't she see that she's deluding herself, that for this half-naked giant their liaison must be merely an escape into the unfamiliar? That she'll end up in the loneliness of the palazzo in the Giudecca. No, Laura decided, it's neither envy nor pity, it's my pride that's hurt. It's anger at the casual way he treats me as a member of the family, anger too at his mocking disapproval as he looked me over, and at society, *my* society, which is afraid of the Fabios, which drives a Santarato into a Fabio Storni's arms, which is submissive for fear of being supercilious.

Fabio spoke over her head, literally and metaphorically, about the anti-festival, which had not been the success its organizers had expected. "Sixteen-millimeter products for TV, half-empty theaters, the people it was really about not there, too little film, too much chatter, the Russians did send one of their three-hour spectaculars, but that was about war and glorified their heroic warriors, who make you throw up."

Claudia, who also ignored Laura, remarked that *Cabaret* was an anti-fascist film, "and really wasn't too bad artistically either—of course the fascists in the audience clapped like mad."

This made Fabio furious. "Can't you understand this is just a rotten bait? The establishment taking a swipe at fascism, indirectly even then and only over the past. That's the sort of thing they always show at the openings, but by tomorrow we'll see the nice bourgeois horrors. With competition like that the *Controfestival* can't keep going. The younger generation will never get a hearing till the Biennial is stopped for good."

Claudia defended herself. "I didn't fail to understand anything, and I don't need *you* to tell me anything." She was on to her third double vodka, and used language very much in her husband's style.

Laura interrupted their conversation as if she had not registered it at all. "We were talking about my mother," she said. It was her only remark addressed to Fabio. She had the impression that Claudia was not listening to her—her sister had put a hand on Fabio's arm with a tender-apologetic gesture—but all the same Laura said what she had meant to say from the beginning. Only she said it more harshly and incisively than she had intended. "I shall oppose the mental incapacity petition. I don't know whether that's legally possible or not, but I shall do my best to be heard as a witness and shall vouch for my mother being in full possession of her mental faculties. I don't care if Mamma sees herself as a figurehead. At any rate we Santaratos have been in Venice for four hundred years, and the Palazzo Santarato is not going to be bartered away to some oil magnate nor to anyone else, by the way. We are not going to be dislodged from our palazzo any more than the festival will be dislodged from Venice. I shall save up so that I can come and applaud again next year."

She would have been happier if Fabio or Claudia had replied, but Fabio only looked at her, half-ironically, half-blankly. He did not seem to know anything about the Signora and her troubles. Claudia leaned on her husband and babbled something to the effect of "do as you please ... you're right ... the film was really quite good ... they're all idiots ... I want to go now ..." Laura paid the bill.

Outside the hotel gate Fabio asked politely where Laura was staying and if they could take her home. She said she would take a taxi, she was staying at the Albergo Quattro Fontane. She had told Paolo in the morning that she did not intend to touch her share of the Titian sale.

54

Dario had predicted to Francesca what would happen, but he had not believed it. He was one of those optimists who talk pessimistically so as to avert the worst disasters.

Romolo telephoned in the morning, telling him that after receiving her mail the Signora had had a heart attack; the nitroglycerine capsules hadn't helped this time, and he had called Dr. Einaudi, who was on his way to the palazzo.

Dario feared the worst. He had always been afraid that his friend's weak heart would not stand up to all the agitations. The less attention she paid to her heart, the more attention it would demand. He was therefore almost relieved when Dr. Einaudi, who had examined the Signora and given her an injection, told him that the attack differed only in its intensity from previous alarm signals of a similar kind. "She's not giving in. A few days in bed, and she'll be quite all right again."

What was in the mail? It was not one letter; there were two which had hit the Signora hard. She had instructed Romolo to show Dario both letters.

The first letter said that her son, Paolo Santarato, had filed a petition for mental incapacity. The court had ordered a psychiatric examination, and would she kindly contact Professor della Torre at a time convenient to her, but within a week? The Signora had not doubted that this would happen, but like Dario she had foreseen the evil without believing it. Now it was there in black and white, a petition for mental incapacity and psychiatric examination. Dario could have told the Signora that the authorities had no alternative, that the psychiatric examination corresponded to a preliminary inquiry, no more; and that if the result was negative and the forensic psychiatrist confirmed that the person examined was in full possession of her mental faculties, then that was the end of the matter. Professor della Torre? He had the reputation of being opinionated, erratic and grumpy, but also incorruptible, the author of famous publications, an authority of international standing, somebody the Venetians were proud of.

It was really the second letter, Romolo said, which had knocked his grandmother out. In connection with the legal proceedings the court had ordered "indefinite cessation" of all work on the palazzo, with the terse explanation that expenses in excess of daily requirements were inadmissible while the court's judgment was pending. Since the doctor had said the Signora must have twenty-four hours of absolute rest, Dario could not tell her the conclusion he drew from this court order: that Paolo had evidently cited extravagance in support of his petition.

Dario was not surprised. For Paolo, the palazzo was at stake. He had little hope of ever installing the Titian again. But a restored palazzo was difficult to sell; Paolo would have a long and probably fruitless search for an "admirer"; whereas with a ruin there were enough firms anxious to· establish offices on the Canal Grande. People talk of development and tear down existing structures; they fear the traces of the past, so even the present must disappear without trace. Nor was Dario surprised at Paolo's reckless behavior, for the proverbial noblesse which obliges had ceased to exist ages ago. It had always been a doubtful rule anyway, as if someone acts nobly only because it is expected of him. And now a Santarato could bring evidence that no noblesse was to be expected of a Santarato. Dario reproached himself for not having said all this before.

Meanwhile, the Signora was indulging in similar reflections, as she lay in her bed gazing up at the ceiling. They brought her no comfort. She had come into conflict with the law, and it was probably only the American collector's confirmation that he had not bought the painting from her which had protected her from the worst. Any jeweler in St. Mark's Square, Dario's lawyer told her, who sold a necklace to a tourist who took it abroad, was as guilty or innocent before the law as herself. But once you had taken such a risk, you couldn't afford any further provocation. She had therefore sent away the workmen immediately after receiving the letter.

All was quiet. In the drawing room Dario and Romolo spoke softly; she could not hear them. Through the half-open window she could hear the familiar noises of the Canal Grande, but this was not the happy hubbub which had been the background to her days. It was no longer raining, but soon the autumn storms would come, every day was costly. A ladder and drills and concrete rammers and hod troughs and trowels and screening frames were lying about—she had not allowed them to be removed. She saw them in her mind's eye, but if no hand touched them they too were only instruments of decay. The palazzo needed her. Her heart had let her down, she had let the palazzo down. Now that she was free of pain she fought the sedation. She would have liked nothing better than to get up and dash off to Professor della Torre's. If she did have to put up with an examination, it had better be soon. She didn't think she would need more than twenty-four hours to be on her feet again.

It took three days; difficult days, but also happy ones. Something inexplicable had happened. The Signora had never devoted herself to the palazzo as she had this summer. By rights she should have become more alone in her obstinacy, more forlorn in her adventure; but the opposite had happened, as if the walls of the palazzo had reflected her love onto others, and that light were now falling back on her. Romolo could not be induced even to go for a walk, let alone to the Lido. Since Emilia could not come before noon, he got her breakfast ready and brought it to her bed with all sorts of courtly obeisances. Emilia came every day and spoke of "a lump sum"; she did not want to add up her hours of work. Dario called several times a day, appeared punctually after closing time, and once brought flowers. The Signora would not have believed that Francesca sent them, had they not been accompanied by a very warm note. Laura came toward evening and stayed at her mother's bedside. Claudia called only once but the Signora smilingly excused this as to do with her honeymoon.

Her rancor against Paolo increased however. A brief thunderstorm got her into a panic, which was quite alien to her. On this day, the third of her illness, the first scaffolding was to be put up on the palazzo. All her life she had mistrusted the people who complained that they didn't have time. Time was not impatient, but men were; time was there, always ready to be taken—those who had none did not take it. And now she had no time.

On the second afternoon she called Professor della Torre's number. A maid answered and gave her information which almost set the Signora back into the state for her initial shock. Professor della Torre could be reached at the mental hospital on the island of San Servolo. There was nothing terrible about that, the Signora finally told herself; after all, he was the hospital's medical superintendent. Romolo got her put through to San Servolo. The secretary said that the professor had been expecting her call. The examination was fixed for 3:30 P.M on Thursday, in the professor's private apartment.

55

Venice, Wednesday, August 23, morning until night

At eight forty-five the scheduled Alitalia flight from Rome lands at

Venice airport. The plane arrives according to schedule, and yet it is an uncommon aircraft. The cockpit bears the papal crest.

Monsignore Giovanni Meccoli, thirty-six, is the only Venetian in the Pope's entourage. He is aware that the honor of accompanying the Holy Father is due to his place of origin. Monsignore Meccoli had hoped for bad weather; it had rained in Rome. The Monsignore, son of a small Venetian bookseller, would like to show the Holy Father a sinking Venice. Paul VI is the first pope in over a century to visit Venice during his tenure. Except for John XXIII, the former patriarch of Venice, all the popes had picture-postcard ideas of the *Serenissima*. They were infallible, but ill-informed.

A few minutes before landing the wind changes. It blows the blue of the sea toward Venice.

Chaos and confusion reign in Venice. The Canal Grande has been barred to all traffic since eight forty-five. About a hundred thousand visitors arrived the day before, wanting to see the Pope. Some fifteen thousand went to St. Mark's Square on time. The others flock to the Canal Grande from all directions. Most of them don't know their way. The police are helpless.

The motorboats carrying the Pope and his retinue moor in front of Santa Maria della Salute. The Pope bows to the Madonna who heard the prayers of the Venetians and drove away the plague. The state launches are waiting, the *Bucintoro*, the *Bissone*, and the *Bissoncelle*. The golden *Bucintoro* is rowed by the winners of the historic regatta. They have insisted on taking the Pope to the Ducal Palace. Two of them are members of the communist union. Dozens of gondolas with the city's dignitaries and the celebrities follow the state gondolas. Monsignore Meccoli, in the second grand gondola, thinks that a forbidden vessel is taking him across the canal. After the plague in the sixteenth century all the gondolas were ordered to wear mourning.

White boats are gathered in a semicircle, their sirens wailing. All the church bells ring. Water spouts from the fireboat hoses.

The gondolas have reached the Ducal Palace. The Pope turns toward the island of San Giorgio Maggiore. A hundred and seventy-two years ago another successor of St. Peter, Pius VII, was crowned Pope here. The Napoleonic Wars had prevented the conclave in Rome. Four years later, however, Pius VII decided to crown the conqueror in the church of Notre-Dame. A Christian, the Pope had said, could still be a democrat. Napoleon banished him to Savona, and only released him after the defeat at Leipzig. On his way to Elba, Napoleon said: "The Pope still believes in Jesus."

Mass in the basilica of San Marco, prayers at the Tomb of the Evangelist, and then the Pope speaks to the people in St. Mark's Square.

His throne has been erected in front of the portal, its rear toward the Quadriga, the proud horses above the gate. Only three of the horses with their greenish-brown patina lift their hooves. One of the horses, of Greek or Roman origin—two thousand or two thousand four hundred years old, nobody can be precise—is surrounded by laths; only its head protrudes over the wooden casing, as if from the upper part of a stable door. Bronze cancer was the verdict, one of many wrong diagnoses. The proud horses are not made of bronze at all; it is gold over copper. And the sickness is not bronze cancer; their bodies have been corroded by the gases of Marghera, twenty thousand tons of poison a year. One idea was for fans to be installed behind the horses, a foolish proposal. Then they were to be removed, for restoration and rescue work. But the superstition of the Venetians would not permit that. Napoleon had carried them off; in the First and Second World Wars they had left their Square. Every time they trotted away a catastrophe was certain.

What does the Holy Father know about it? Monsignore Meccoli wonders. The Pope has heard something about Marghera and the infection spreading over Venice. He carries the cross and the ring of Pope John XXIII in a casket; he will bequeath them to the city. And he will hand over to the Mayor thirty million lire from the purse of St. Peter, and thirty million from his own. For charity. The poor of Venice will welcome the gift. What sense of poor Venice does the Holy Father have?

With folded hands the Monsignore listens to the Pope's words.

His voice is high-pitched and brittle, it breaks from his lips in tortured sounds. "Venice must live, not just survive the corrosion of the sea!" says the Pope. The crowd cheers. The Monsignore has read a copy of the speech. Good words, he thought at the time, elevating words, some of them useful too. "Difficult is your task, and great your responsibility before the world and before history." Why have such phrases impressed the Monsignore when they concerned cities and countries and peoples he did not know? Why do they sound trivial and empty now? The Pope raises his arms in entreaty. "May you find courage in the example of your forebears who built such massive works for the defense and protection of the city and of her marvelous lagoon." Marvelous lagoon! The Monsignore is tempted to stop up his ears. Is it right to crown those who banish you? How hypocritical is a good action when you know that it does no one any good? Isn't it discouraging to preach hope where there is none? Is it admissible to speak of protection and defense without saying who and what is to be protected, who and what you need defense against? The example of your forebears? Those forebears moved out to defy the sea. But the sea is an enemy no more. Will the Holy Father name the enemy? The Monsignore has read the speech.

The acclamation is so rousing, the crowd applauds so passionately that the pigeons flutter off in fright. The people of rank nod approvingly, the Mayor smiles gratefully, the ladies are much moved and lower their eyes.

A few hours later the Holy Father leaves the city on the lagoons aboard the scheduled Alitalia flight. The sky is a pale blue. Tomorrow Monsignore Giovanni Meccoli will take the script of the papal address to the Vatican printing shop.

Bareni is the term Venetians apply to the sandbanks which stick out of the lagoons here and there, all around the city. In earlier times they were covered by the flood and uncovered at low tide. Now the sea, with its water removed, releases them by the hundreds. Whether they expose a seventh or a tenth of their power, like the icebergs, is known only to the geologists—if to them.

There are *bareni* which please the honorable muncipal council. For *bareni* tend to turn into solid land, *terra firma*. And on solid land construction is possible. But there are also *bareni* which displease the lords of Venice, because they catch the tourists' eyes. Some of them are along the waterway between the city and the Lido. But no municipal council can calculate the whims of the lagoon.

For several years the fisherman Vittorio Vettorato, sixty, has been driving almost daily to the *barene* between the city and the Lido.

His children, six of them, let him go, although Vittorio usually returns with only a modest catch, sometimes without a single fish. Two of his sons were fishermen, but they took jobs in Marghera long ago. The fish are poisoned; fishing is no longer a profession in Venice. They let the "old man" have his way, but not out of sheer filial love. For Vettorato always takes two or three of his nineteen grandchildren along on his fishing trip. His favorite is Fortunato, eleven years old, a most intelligent boy. He invented Robinson Crusoe. That is, Crusoe was invented by Daniel Defoe, of course, but the Venetian Crusoe is Fortunato's invention. He read the juvenile edition of the book about the Scottish sailor Selkirk. He himself is Crusoe, and the *barene* is his island.

Fortunato's imagination surpasses Daniel Defoe's. It is easy to imagine a lonely island in the archipelago of Juan Fernandez. To imagine that a *barene* between Venice and the Lido, where tourist motorboats pass and Italian, Yugoslav, British and Russian ships can be seen, as well as tugboats and yachts and tankers—to imagine that this is a lonely island, you must be more than poet, you must be a child.

Today it is Fortunato's turn, and that of his brothers, Armando, nine, and Turrido, seven. To have his brothers present on the island causes some difficulties, of course. To play Crusoe by yourself is no problem, and it works if necessary with two people because of the docile savage, Man Friday. Turrido is used to playing the subordinate role of Friday. Armando would like to be Crusoe, but he has to be content with being Crusoe's younger brother. After all, there's no need to keep strictly to Defoe.

For two hours Vittorio Vettorato has been sitting in his boat a few yards away from the *barene,* on the city side. He has not yet netted a single fish.

In the meantime Fortunato has lit a campfire. The *barene* is full of discarded driftwood. It is a rich island altogether. There is a rail which Fortunato erected in the sand one day with the help of his elder brothers and nominated it a date palm. The lunch which Fortunato brought along is not eaten from the basket; it is carried to the rail tree and the bread is picked from the date palm. Fortunato has built a fortress from beer bottles, against the snakes. Bits of coal mark the path into the jungle. Some, however, are in a crate, salvaged treasure. And the rusty refrigerator is the boat they use to row out on the sea for fishing.

Fortunato is secretly pleased that Armando does not join in the game today; he says it bores him. Fortunato watches his grandfather.

But Turrido is all the more enthusiastic. Fortunato treats his Friday patiently and condescendingly, as befits Crusoe. He allows him to crawl through the jungle on all fours, and to kill snakes with a wooden plank. Or to bring bread from the date tree. Only the blood of the fishermen in Turrido's veins is a cause of concern to Fortunato. What Turrido likes best is to sit in the refrigerator, paddling with his hands, or throwing out the lunch basket to catch fish in the sand. At such moments he cannot be bothered with anything else.

"Be careful or the door will slam shut," Fortunato has shouted to his brother several times.

But that is impossible. The battered refrigerator is much too small for Turrido, his head and the upper part of his body stick out.

"Come back at once and fetch dates, Friday!" shouts Fortunato.

"I've just got a giant fish on my hook," answers Turrido.

"All right," says Robinson. "But just this last fish."

He crosses the *barene* to encourage his grandfather. On the way he collects some empty cans for his fortress.

In the meantime Turrido has made a great effort and pushed the refrigerator closer to the water in order to throw the basket into real water. The basket is tied to a string. Now he returns to his boat; the giant fish will swallow the bait any moment now. Two motorboats, one on the way to the Lido, the other on the way to Venice, cross near the *barene*. The waves surge.

The bottom of the sandbar is soggy with rain.

A wave washes the refrigerator into the lagoon. Armando is the first to hear his brother's screams.

Fortunato jumps up, runs to the other shore.

"Turrido is drowning!" Armando shouts to his grandfather. Vettorato knows he will be too late if he rows around the island; he runs across the island.

Fortunato has plunged into the waves. But he sees neither his brother nor his boat.

A motorboat fishes the swimming Fortunato out of the water.

Man Friday is not found.

On August 18, a Friday, the ladies Marcella Moschini, fifty-five, born in Venice, Lidia Rizzo, fifty-three, also born there, and Carla Capoferri, fifty-one, born in Turin, all of them prostitutes by profession, appear at police headquarters. They make the following statement:

An alleged colleague, Margharete Müller, called Mizzi, allegedly married to one Comazzi, about twenty-three, allegedly born in Graz, Austria, is strongly suspected of spying against Italy and/or NATO. The ladies Moschini, Rizzo and Capoferri consider it their patriotic duty to bring these facts to the authorities' attention. The above-named is believed to be working for Eastern intelligence, and/or the Soviet Union, or she is acting as a "letter box" for the same.

Upon questioning for further details, the ladies Moschini, Rizzo and Capoferri declare that the suspect is going to receive a Russian sailor on Wednesday, the 23rd of August, to hand over to him secret documents deposited with her. The authorities, thus alerted, check the statements and discover that a Soviet freighter is due to call at the port of Venice on the morning of the 23rd of August.

They are not particularly struck by the age of the ladies Moschini, Rizzo and Capoferri. Prostitution in Venice is in a sorry state.

In the sixteenth century there were two thousand five hundred nuns in Venice, but twelve thousand harlots. The disproportion is particularly disquieting because the nuns include many former whores, for instance, the poetess Veronica Franco, who had some amiable lines dedicated to her by Montaigne. At least two hundred of the twelve thousand whores deserved the honorable designation of courtesan, and their names, addresses and prices used to be presented to the foreigners in a catalogue, *Principali e più honorate cortigiane di Venezia.* Although they were not allowed to wear conspicuous clothes, they were easy to find even without a catalogue. They were enjoined to sport yellow handkerchiefs, not white ones, and to place a red light in the bow of their gondolas. So they probably had their own gondolas.

Today, a Venetian whore can scarcely pay the price of a gondola ride. In the days of the gallant knight Casanova, the foreigners came to Venice in search of adventures. Today they come to rest here from their adventurous existence, mostly with their families. So an unkind joke has it that the tiny number of whores in Venice are too old for street walking, they can only manage street standing. One of them, age seventy-three, has express permission to ply her trade at home.

In the city, the beat is concentrated round the Frezzeria, mainly at the corner of the Calle Selvadego. The word Frezzeria probably comes from the German *Fresserei,* meaning gluttony, and dates back to the time when Venice was Austrian. Today there are no more food stores in the Frezzeria than in any other street; there are only more whores. The ladies Moschini, Rizzo and Capoferri have very few customers, and most of them are very stingy, but the Dutch naval officer Adrian van der Harst, fifty-nine, is a shining exception. He is also, indeed, the central figure in the events of the 23rd of August.

Twice a year the tanker on which Adrian van der Harst is a second officer calls at the port of Venice. This has been going on for the past thirteen years. When leaving port in Rotterdam in March, Il Capitano sends a postcard addressed to Marcella Moschini, and in August a similar card to Lidia Rizzo. Carla Capoferri has no business with him; she accompanied her colleagues to police headquarters because she also has grounds for resentment against Margharete Müller, called Mizzi.

Adrian van der Harst is a man of extreme generosity, and with appetites on the same scale. He expects the two girlfriends—it is only out of politeness that he writes to them alternately—to escort him to their apartment. There the captain drinks their whole stock of chianti and reports on his adventures. Then he undresses and has himself tied to the bedpost, with his face toward the wall. This is Lidia's task; he is very particular. After that Marcella has to flog him. Meanwhile Lidia must beg for mercy for the sailor. Neither of the ladies must undress, not even when Marcella has untied Il Capitano. But under their dresses they must be naked, so that no time will be lost.

Adrian van der Harst has no connection with Italy or NATO. And yet the statement at police headquarters refers exclusively to him.

Twenty-three-year-old Margharete Müller, called Mizzi, who three months ago swept through the Frezzeria like the foehn in winter, is considered a foreign worker, although she is allegedly married to an Italian. She maintains that she is on her way to Munich where a modeling job is waiting for her. Her demeanor is correspondingly arrogant. In addition, she has been boasting for weeks that Adrian van der Harst, the golden pheasant of the Frezzeria, will be unable to resist her. She has brought her clothesline and the dog whip from Graz, she says, and she wouldn't dream of sharing Il Capitano with any of her colleagues.

The idea of the spying charge is Lidia's. She is an avid newspaper reader and in particular she studies the daily broadsheet *Navi in arrivo.* She read the term "letter box" in a novel.

However, the suspicion reported against Margharete Müller, called Mizzi, is not completely beside the point, seeing that this foreign worker has been informed for days about the Dutchman's imminent arrival. She has placed bets for a total of twenty-five thousand lire–that she will bag the golden pheasant within a few minutes.

At 5 P.M. on the dot, at the beginning of the whores' regular working day, their extremely busy rival disappears with a suitor into her apartment in the Calle Selvadego. Five minutes later Marcella rings up the inspector known to her by name and informs him that the Russian spy has come to the Frezzeria.

At ten past six Margharete Müller, called Mizzi, is marched off by two gentlemen in dark suits. All her colleagues, aged forty-five to sixty, have assembled inconspicuously in the Frezzeria, unless professionally detained. There is also a young man marching between the policemen, looking dazed. When he was dragged out of bed with the foreign worker, he gave his name as Federico Orsatti, a student from Modena. His Italian is unaccented, but that is to be expected of spies. At half past six the massive figure of the captain comes around the corner.

Shortly after eight o'clock Marcella and Lidia return with the captain. He seems completely satisfied, for he promises to write again next March, this time to Marcella.

Eugenio Airoldi, sixty, a bachelor, still not unfavorably disposed toward his own sex, a gray-haired man of attractive appearance, comes from a long line of waiters. His grandfather served in the smartest hotels in Venice, Paris and St. Moritz, and so did his father. He himself has for decades been one of the mainstays of the Venetian Gritti Palace. The Airoldis have considerable means. Eugenio therefore retired from business last year. He accepts only occasional assignments, at his own choice. His address is well known in high society.

The arrangement of the dinner party to be held at the Sala del Gran Consiglio in the Ducal Palace has been entrusted to the Hotel Gritti. Naturally, the hotel management has turned to Eugenio.

The sponsor of the party (admission a hundred dollars) is the Save Venice Association. The invitations have been issued by its president, Mrs. Mary Macintosh from Dallas, Texas. She is the widow of the oil magnate Joe Macintosh, the founder of Progress Oil. It is her idea to organize fund-raising dinners all over the world; she pays all expenses and the proceeds go to Venice. The first is held in Venice. Although more than five hundred people have gathered, practically all of them foreigners, this hall, 180 feet long and 80 feet wide, is not exactly the most fortunate choice. Most guests, however, are unaware of its symbolic significance. This is the place where, on May 12, 1797, the hundred and twentieth doge of Venice, Ludovico Manin, said goodbye forever to the sovereignty of the *Serenissima*.

Eugenio, who is responsible for the cocktails, recognizes many of his former patrons, and they in turn greet him with the warmth customary between aristocrats and aristocratic waiters. Eugenio duly rebuts a young waiter's remark—"I smell oil"—but he cannot deny the presence of the familiar presidents, vice-presidents, chairmen of the boards of directors and of the supervisory boards of all the oil companies at Marghera. His trained eye also recognizes the magnates' ladies, although they are wearing silk masks in accordance with the tradition of the Venetian *Carnevale—Carne vale*, meat, goodbye!—and in compliance with Mrs. Macintosh's wish.

During the cocktail hour and during dinner Eugenio is too busy to devote any time to his own thoughts; besides, he has cast an eye on a young waiter from Bergamo. Like many of his Venetian colleagues he is a man of refinement and registers a certain incongruity between the painting of *Paradise* by Tintoretto, Christ crowning Mary Queen of Heaven (the largest painting in the world), and the paradise of the feasting and drinking rescuers of Venice. But his attention is focused on the martinis, manhattans and champagne flips.

Not until the band strikes up for the dancing does Eugenio remember the often-quoted saying of Rosalba Carriera, a famous portrait painter of the *settecento*: "Pleasure and entertainment are the best remedies for our illnesses." He does not like to hear the waiter standing next to him at the door still talking drivel about the smell of oil. But it does occur to Eugenio that the people who spread illnesses are perhaps not the most qualified to cure them. Anyhow Rosalba Carriera meant something quite different by her remark.

Although half the hall is occupied by the restaurant tables, the dancing couples look lost in space. The band plays the latest dances. Not all of the guests take part. The elderly, in the majority, watch the younger ones writhing to the rock sound. It is only when older melodies are played (Mrs. Macintosh has slipped a reminder to the band leader) that the couples waltz past the glorifications of Venice:

Victorious Venezia by Veronese; *The Doges Rendering Homage to Venezia* by Tintoretto, and *Venice Accepting the Submission of the Cities* by Palma di Giovane.

Midnight is still far off, but the ladies have taken off their masks. The film stars who have come over from the Biennial are all Italians, but the others are mainly German and American ladies, most of them of mature age. Their bulging flesh—How can anybody say women are beautiful? thinks Eugenio—reminds the *maître* of the cushions at jewelers' shops, which have no other purpose but to bring out the shine of the jewelry more brilliantly.

"If they donated some of their bracelets," says the heretical waiter next to Eugenio, "they could save Venice all right."

"He's very pleased," says Eugenio, pointing to the Mayor who is dancing past them.

"They're just out for amusement," says the waiter.

Eugenio would rather chat with the boy from Bergamo, but he is nowhere to be seen. He thinks: a hundred dollars per plate, a total of fifty thousand dollars, not bad at all. Mrs. Macintosh on her partner's arm stops in front of Eugenio.

"Did you see the Pope today?" she says.

"I was in St. Mark's Square," says Eugenio.

"Wasn't it edifying!" says Mrs. Macintosh.

As they go on, the waiter says, "The fat chap she's dancing with is in Shell."

The band labors in vain; more and more guests are leaving. There is a rumor that there is a party on at one of the palazzi. Eugenio helps some of the rescuers into their coats. He looks for the boy from Bergamo, but he has already left.

Soon after midnight Eugenio leaves too. The night is chilly, he is shivering in his evening dress. He looks up to the windows of the Ducal Palace. In the hall of the Great Council, where counsel failed for centuries, only a few lights are burning.

On the vaporetto, Eugenio looks back to the Canal Grande; Marghera seems to be ablaze behind it. By day Venice is bright and Marghera is dark, by night Marghera is bright and Venice is dark. Fifty thousand dollars for the city's salvation. He is rather pleased with the tips he received. "Pleasure and entertainment are the best remedies for our illness."

56

It was Professor della Torre's custom to write out his psychiatric reports in longhand and dictate them the following day into the dictaphone. Although he usually left out half his draft when dictating, or even two thirds, his reports still caused much head shaking. They contained details and reflections that were legally quite irrelevant, they digressed from their subject matter, and they would conclude with a judgment which sometimes had to be translated into legal parlance before it could be presented to the court.

This time the Professor had reserved the evening for composing his report, but it wouldn't bother him if he had to spend the whole night on it. Since his wife's death he no longer had to show consideration for anyone else, and he had got out of the habit of showing it to himself. He would drink cup after cup of coffee, which he made in an espresso machine, and smoke one pipe after another.

After grumpily disposing of the indispensable formalities–Psychiatric Report on Anna-Maria Santarato, reference number, date, age, status and address of subject examined–he wrote:

Signora Anna-Maria Santarato, who arrived punctually at half past three in the afternoon as I had requested, did not object to my examining her, though she revealed the most unusual ideas about a psychiatric examination. She probably thought I would have on hand certain appliances, measuring apparatus and the like, and she seemed relieved when I told her that my sole intention, and indeed the sole possibility open to me as well, was to have a talk with her. During our talk I was several times disconcerted by remarks expressing what seemed genuine curiosity. This happened first when she asked me whether with all my experience I believed I could assess a person's mental capacity in a conversation lasting an hour, or even a whole afternoon; for her part she had known a number of people for many years and still could not really pass judgment on their mental capacity.

I told her it was not at all my function to decide on her mental capacity; that this was not being questioned by anyone, at least not at the moment; but that the matter at issue was her capacity for judgment, her ability to act reasonably. In the document known to her she was alleged to have shown extraordinary irresponsibility over a certain transaction, namely the sale of the Titian painting *Girl with Flower Basket;* and she was showing the same irresponsibility, to a pathological degree, it was asserted, in using the proceeds of the sale. I said that a petition to put someone under care, which is after all what this case is about, is often, though not always, granted for the legal protection of a person who consistently acts without due reflection and who may be expected to indulge in further irresponsible behavior.

These explanatory remarks did not seem to make any impression at all on Signora Santarato. She declared, in fact, that she considered my remarks about responsibility and irresponsibility to be quite beside the point, since there were surely different kinds of responsibility and somebody who did not feel responsible in any way for her grown-up children—all her children were over forty—could act most responsibly in other respects. For instance, she said, she did not assume any responsibility for her son, of whose mental capacity she had been convinced, at least until now, but she did feel responsible for Venice in general and her palazzo in particular.

Professor della Torre put down his pen, poured himself some hot coffee and thought about how to go on. His respect for the honorable gentlemen of Venice's civil court, who were to receive his report, was extremely low. For some time he had, in fact, been on the wrong track. He had felt that the Signora showed certain signs of fanaticism such as his colleagues Kujath, Sterzt, Horstmann and others had analyzed in terms of paranoid delusion. If he mentioned that, the judges would remember only the word "track" for they welcomed any track, right or wrong. They had not read his own book, *Fanaticism and Paranoia;* fortunately, since they would not have understood it. In it he had explained that justice and humanity are absolute terms, and everyone knows what is meant by them; but that they get misinterpreted when someone starts asking what they really are. Such questions sound deep, but they are often asked in order to judge the issue. The individual who does not sacrifice humanity to justice or justice to humanity is by no means paranoid, even though his actions may show traces of fanaticism.

Instead of letting the court in on his suspicion, which had meanwhile been invalidated anyway, the Professor merely mentioned that he had asked Signora Santarato a series of test questions which had nothing to do with the subject of the examination. At the risk of having almost certainly to eliminate this passage later on, the Professor continued:

> The questions were partly general, even political and philosophical, partly of a private nature, and I purposely changed the subjects in rapid succession. I questioned her on current phenomena such as murders, airplane hijackings, acts of terrorism of every kind, on her attitude to pornographic films and publications, on the society she had grown up in and on the society that had grown up around her.
>
> In between I confronted her with a hypothesis which I had planned to present to her from the beginning. Seeing that she already had a considerable sum in her possession at the time her grandson Remus Santarato was kidnapped, I asked her whether she would have contributed to the young man's rescue.
>
> Without hesitating she replied that she would never have decided on such a course because she was quite out of sympathy with continual surrenders, attempts to curry favor with implacable enemies, and bowing and scraping in general. She also approved of the family's behavior (she added this unasked) in not bothering about Remus after his portentous press conference, which had been sufficient proof of his incorrigible vanity. If, however, he should fail in his undertakings, which, knowing him, she confidently expected, then Remus would indeed be welcome in her house. "Though that cannot be of any interest to you," she observed, a remark I was bound to confirm.

At this point Professor della Torre began a tour of the room, which was extremely hot, because he had forgotten to open a window.

He felt it would be useless to explain to the court the meaning of

his experiment—because that was what it had been. He had long
realized that the term "mental capacity," the substantive factor in this
case, was closely related to the term "predictable." A person is
predictable who adapts to the norms of convention: norm and normal,
again related terms. If on the one hand it is predictable that someone
who disagrees with something or other will set an airplane on fire, then
it is predictable on the other hand that a second airplane will be put at
his disposal for a free getaway. It is predictable that weapons are
supplied to our enemies for them to kill us with, and that this will be
deemed humanitarian action. It is predictable, too, that after sexual
intercourse between man and woman has been shown in public, acts of
sodomy will get a public showing as well. It is also predictable that this
will be praised as progressive, in which case anyone who does not
regard all that as normal has to be regarded as abnormal.

Since in this sense Signora Santarato did have to be regarded as
abnormal, the Professor preferred to restrict himself to putting down
concrete facts which the judges could understand.

My interrogation of Signora Santarato after this [he wrote]
centered basically on two main issues, the so-called Titian case and
the use of the sum obtained through the sale of the painting.

By selling the Titian without her children's consent, I told her,
she had committed an offense, at least in civil law. As far as I knew,
this was something new in her life. Had she failed to weigh the
consequences? And if she had recognized them, would she not have
shrunk from such action?

"It is conceivable," Signora Santarato replied, with obvious irony,
"that in earlier years, when in full command of my physical powers,
I should have looked for more legal means to save the palazzo. For
instance, I might have tried to blackmail my son's father-in-law,
Andreoli, by referring to disagreeable publicity. But in my present
circumstances I had no alternative to the possibility of selling part
of my property. I did not have any moral scruples over this because
lesser considerations had to yield to the overriding objective of
saving the palazzo. As to the consequences, however, I did not in
fact think my son would be capable of a denunciation such as has
brought me to you now."

After I had interrupted her with some inquiries regarding her means of existence, Signora Santarato grew impatient, although only for a moment. "I have already answered your question," she said, "regarding the use of the proceeds of the sale. If it is extravagance to use money for a particular purpose when you have obtained it precisely for that purpose, then every investment is pure extravagance, and one had better take all the industrialists, company directors and shareholders to San Servolo and concede sound judgment only to those who keep their savings in their stockings. Except that *they* aren't exactly handling their money sensibly either, since sooner or later they will no doubt be robbed of their stockings—though I admit hardly anyone objects to that nowadays."

Now the Professor began to draft a paragraph he was sure he would have to cross out, since he would otherwise be charged with partiality. But he could not resist the temptation and wrote:

Signora Santarato's action was obviously feebleminded. She gets a palazzo repaired which may be doomed anyhow. In an era which is ashamed of property, she holds onto her property. She wants to save one house in a thousand and even believes that thousands will follow her lead. Instead of relapsing into skepticism she hopes against hope. And then she goes and does her adversaries the favor of being ready to stoop to their own underhand methods.

After jotting down "Not for dictation!" in the margin, the Professor started again:

Without commenting on the matter of investments I put it to Signora Santarato that she set up to be the keeper, defender and protectress of existing property, but that she had evidently disposed without much fuss of a work of art that was also highly important for her beloved native city. How, I asked, could she resolve this contradiction?

The Signora smiled; I had noticed this smile before. I fully agree with Sullivan who is convinced of the physical manifestation of mental disorders; the Signora's outward behavior is inconsistent with any such diagnosis. With a smile, then, Signora Santarato asked me whether I regarded it as "crazy" to make a distinction between the replaceable and the irreplaceable. The Titian was replaceable; according to her latest information it would very soon be returning to Venice and adorning a public collection, although she was not going to "shell out" a single centesimo for that. Still smiling, she said that she would have been crowned with laurels if she had made over the Titian to the Accademia. Her son could not have protested against that, which was sheer hypocrisy, since it was apparently acceptable to make extravagant donations, but not to sell at a profit. The Accademia would have received the painting, and this was going to happen anyway, but the palazzo would have gone down. "I have been extremely thrifty," she said, "and anyone who called that extravagance should be sitting in this chair now."

Professor della Torre finally realized that the unbearable heat was due to the closed windows, and he got up to open at least one of them.

It was past midnight now, and the square in front of the Teatro La Fenice was deserted, except for some waiters in their shirt sleeves upturning the chairs on the terrace of the Ristorante Antico Martini. The doors of the theater were closed, not because it was late; they had not been opened for days. Above the porch hung a Bordeaux red tapestry such as is used for announcing opera performances and concerts in golden letters. Now the golden letters said: IL TEATRO È OCCUPATO. The striking employees had demonstrated all day, the marble walls of the theater were pasted with slogans, hammers and sickles; bills were posted on the small fountain in the middle of the square. TO SAVE VENICE FULL PRODUCTIVE ACTIVITY MUST BE MAIN-TAINED! The entrance was blocked with placards, the pavement strewn with handbills: BISOGNA LOTTARE, you've got to fight.

The Professor had stood at the window with the Signora. They had remained silent for a while, and then talked about Venice. But that was none of the honorable court's business. BISOGNA LOTTARE. You had indeed to fight, particularly if you objected to letting the inmates of San Servolo be declared normal, and everyone else feebleminded.

Vexed because he had to substantiate his judgment, the Professor returned to his work.

I by no means omitted tests designed to show whether one could detect in Signora Santarato the characteristics of psychopathic fanaticism, such as are associated by some of my eminent colleagues (including Koch, Rudin and Kraepolin) with the concept of "the righteous man acting as the whole world's conscience" or "attributing ... public importance to private affairs." Signora Santarato no doubt tends to overestimate her palazzo's importance and to identify it with the fate of Venice. In this respect, however, although seventy-four years old, she is a child of our age, which has been foisted with an outlook of universal ideological significance, so that it is becoming increasingly difficult to go to the lavatory without thinking of the social implications of defecation. But if we acknowledge the social relevance of anything and everything, this cannot go exclusively to justifying revolutionary ideas and actions. We have to admit that the defenders of the existing order may also think in terms of social relevance.

It is not for the composer of this report to decide whether the salvation of Venice, as envisaged by the Signora Santarato, is indeed as important as she maintains, but this writer, whose ancestors must have come to Venice at latest by 1499, since one of them lost an arm and a leg in the somewhat inglorious battle of Zonchio against the Turks–this writer cannot refrain from remarking that the honorable members of the government of Venice had better squander a little more of the available funds on Venice. As far as this writer is concerned, they may rest assured that they will not be charged with extravagance or with any irresponsible action.

The examination of Signora Anna-Maria Santarato was concluded at 4:40 P.M.

The writer does not recall having ever yet met a wiser citizen of Venice.

The undersigned requests the honorable court to dismiss the petition for mental incapacity submitted by Paolo Santarato, born 1917 in Venice, businessman, domiciled in Milan, as unfounded on all counts.

Professor della Torre read through the manuscript and decided to dictate only a small part the following day. The conclusions, however, would be transmitted verbatim to the civil court.

57

The disappointment lingered on, but the feeling of hatred toward Paolo, which the Signora had vainly tried to fight during the past few days, began to fade almost at once when she received the news that his petition had been dismissed. At the same time the injunction against further building had been revoked. The workmen prepared to erect the scaffolding in front of the facade.

But the Signora was granted no peace and quiet in her mind.

The beginning of the school year was imminent, and Romolo should have returned to Milan a week ago. He refused. He had asked the Signora to let him stay with her, and had indeed developed a hectic manner possibly connected with his frame of mind and with his decision not to live with his parents anymore. He had investigated all the possibilities of going to a Venetian secondary school and by his own efforts had eliminated every difficulty.

The Signora had condoned his intentions rather than backing them up. To have Romolo with her for the remainder of her life would, she felt, be the crowning glory of her existence. But how long was that remainder going to last? Might she not be offering him an illusory security? What would happen if she died and his way home was barred? Could she let her selfish interests prevail? Paolo and Teresa had lost their eldest son. Well, he would soon have left the nest anyway, it was their own fault. But wasn't it too much of a punishment to lose Romolo as well? And finally, wasn't she overestimating her powers once again? Would she be able to stand up to the next onslaught which Teresa, if not Paolo, would certainly launch? On the other hand, she was not strong enough to resist her more fervent desire. She did not say no to Romolo; she waited.

The telephone rang constantly, and by tacit agreement Romolo answered it. One day it was Paolo on the line, then Teresa. More and more pressingly they demanded their son's return home. They begged and threatened, acted as if his return were a matter of course or produced deadline dates. They made accusations against him or said they would set the authorities on the Signora. When nothing produced any results, Teresa informed her son that his father would be arriving in Venice the following day. He would expect Romolo at the Hotel Danieli (Remus had left for Rome long ago). Romolo was to present himself there, with packed bags.

It was September 3, a Sunday. Autumn had come early and suddenly. It had rained for two days, rain which the Signora knew and feared. When the Venetian rain is accompanied by a drop in temperature, it bodes ill; the rain feels at home in the cold. And it was a soft rain, despite the cold. The drops trickled down the windowpanes, a bad sign. The rain in Venice is treacherous, like a caressing hand which all of a sudden is clenched to strike.

Romolo had not packed. An hour before he was to present himself at the Danieli, he was sitting at the Signora's bedside. She was feeling weak and had stayed in her bedroom. "I'll talk to my father," Romolo said, "but I shan't give in."

"They can force you," said the Signora.

"Let them try."

"I'm afraid they'll be successful."

Romolo's mouth went so hard that the Signora, although she recognized herself in him, found him almost a stranger.

"Papa won't want to see his name in the papers again," he said.

"But nor shall we," said the Signora.

"I'll try to do it without a declaration of war," Romolo continued. "I needn't tell them it's for good. I might just as well study in Venice for a year. Perhaps they would even have sent me to London," he said bitterly. "They often talked about a boarding school. Papa can't claim that I'll be worse off at my grandmother's than at a barracks. They always wanted to get rid of me. It's their fault you've been so upset this summer. You said you needed me. You're not backing out of that, are you? Work on the palazzo will be going on all autumn, you can't keep an eye on it all by yourself. I shall have plenty of time; compared to Milan the school here is dead easy."

"I shouldn't mention the palazzo," said the Signora. With this remark she had betrayed how ardently she hoped he would succeed in convincing Paolo. She passed over it quickly. "Yes, I do need you, and I'm not backing out of that at all, only I meant it differently. I'll have to tell you something. You never wanted me to talk about death, I can understand that. But after all, I'm going to die before you, that doesn't take much working out."

"What has this got to do with my return?" he asked sulkily.

"It has to do with the palazzo," she said. "I've never made a will, perhaps because your grandfather's caused me so much trouble. Yesterday the lawyer was here, as you know. He informed me that I cannot disinherit Paolo, or at least they could contest the will if I did. But I can settle a nominal share on him, and then have entire disposal of the rest, except for the lawful shares due to Laura and Claudia. I've done that, and named you, Romolo, as my residuary legatee."

He put his hand up defensively; the Signora felt he was trying to hide his emotion.

"All you are inheriting is a big No," she said. "Claudia is a broken reed. But Laura will be on your side when you refuse to sell the palazzo. Your No alone would be enough; together with Laura you can prevent the sale at any time. This is called a blocking minority, the lawyer told me. Naturally, your parents will try every trick to tear down the palazzo or sell it all the same. But even if your father's guardianship were not in some question"—she laughed—"with his petition against me he really did land in the soup; he can't in any case oppose the testamentary disposition. The guardian may act as a trustee for his ward's inherited property—you see what a lot of expert knowledge I've picked up!—until his coming of age, but he can't spend it. What is true for money also applies to the palazzo. The guardian is not entitled to override the will and the ward by converting property into money, even if he claims it will be profitable. By the way, I have appointed Dario as my executor, you can rely on him. Well, what do you think of all that?"

"You're great, Nonna," said Romolo. "But you will live to be a hundred and the school year . . ."

"If you don't succeed in convincing your father, I shall insist on your coming to Venice several times a year. We must certainly be together over Christmas. You will then be able to check on the progress made. In the meantime Dario and I will hold the fort. You must go now."

He sat on the edge of the bed and hugged her so tight that she had gently to free herself.

She heard his steps on the stairs. Her heart was heavy, but she was overcome by a peace she had not known for a long time. Since yesterday she had been feeling better. She would live for quite a few years yet, but living was easier when you had made your last will. The last will was like a hand reaching out from beyond the grave to give just a little guidance to those who think they know better but don't. It was continuity, that was all she wanted to maintain. For many years she had not thought of Vincente quite so intensively. Memory was a deceptive sunshine, but was it really so deceptive? Perhaps it merely distributed light and shadow more evenly. Vincente's unfortunate coldness, his jealous lack of understanding for his young wife, his domineering impatience, lay all in the shade, and his last will was in the sun. Now she had taken refuge in the same goodbye that had made her suffer all her life.

Meanwhile Romolo had reached the Piazzetta. He had turned up the collar of his raincoat; the cold seemed to go right through him. The steps which lead from the lagoon to the square had disappeared; the gondolas tied to their posts were rocking at the same level as the stone floor; water was dripping from the café's empty chairs; people ran looking for refuge under the arcades of the Ducal Palace; San Giorgio Maggiore disappeared in the fog.

When Romolo asked for his father, the porter gave him two room numbers: so Paolo had come with Teresa.

It didn't take him long to suspect that his parents were playing prearranged parts, and also that they had exchanged roles. Neither had ever treated him with severity, but his mother had always found it easier than his father to say no, and if ever he did want to turn to one of them with his problems, he had always chosen his father. Now his father descended on him harshly with the question "Where are your bags?" whereas Teresa embraced him, inquired about his health, and acted as if she did not mean to press him on something he was obviously going to do anyhow. The question of his return couldn't be shelved, of course, and Romolo began to explain why, far from packing his bags, he wanted to spend next term and the year in Venice.

He was proud of his restraint and of carrying out his plan. He repeatedly thought of his grandmother; she also kept her cool. "I've always been extremely fond of Venice, that's nothing new to you," he told his parents. "This time I've been happier than ever here," he lied. "I've made friends. In Milan I don't have any friends, as you know, and now Remus has gone too. The grammar school here has a very high standard, and they don't make so much of stupid old math, they go more for languages. Anyhow," he said rather reproachfully, "you were planning to send me to a boarding school."

Teresa did her best with persuasion, sentiment, even bribery. "Now of all times a change of school would be quite the wrong thing. You've been spoiled more than you realize. Instead of having servants, you'd have to look after yourself in Venice." She wouldn't utter the word "palazzo." "That's why comparing it to a boarding school isn't really fair. How am I to do without you? The house is so empty now, I miss Remus in spite of everything, it's just because of him you simply *must* come home. We've been thinking of giving you his room, it's nicer, and you can have friends in there undisturbed. After all, you're no longer a child," she said, a hint he was sure to register.

"You're coming with us, and that's it," Paolo interrupted his wife.

For a moment Romolo was speechless; he was quite unprepared for his father's new tone. As long as he could remember, he never got anywhere in discussions between the three of them, not because there were two against one, so to speak, but because his father wanted to show who was master in the house. But afterward his father had generally fallen in with his wishes, sometimes with a wink or a confidential "between you and me." And now, he realized, there was not a chance Paolo would behave like that.

Still, Romolo would probably have tried once more with appeals and well-rehearsed arguments, if Paolo, pacing angrily up and down the room, had not let himself go in remarking to Teresa: "Obviously Mamma has talked him into this—the old witch wants to get her own back on us."

Romolo's face flushed. Not a word that his grandmother was ill, that she needed him, that he wanted to help her, that *he* needed understanding, too! He said: "I asked you at Quadri's whether you were planning to do anything against Nonna; you dodged the question. I told you you wouldn't see me again if you tried such a filthy trick . . ."

"And you took that from him?" Teresa asked Paolo.

"Anyhow you did try that filthy trick," Romolo said, "and you fell flat on your face. It's not Nonna getting her own back on you, you're trying to get it on her, and you're going to fall flat on your face again.

No squad of police will drag me from the palazzo, it's my home, and the scaffolding is up already, in case you'd like to know. You can't sell that palazzo, and you can't buy me, I'm not Remus. Perhaps you can buy him back tomorrow, he can have my room."

To his surprise Paolo stared at him mutely, exchanging only a glance with Teresa, as if he wanted to apologize for not having put her in the picture earlier, or as if asking for advice. And she said:

"You're talking like a three-year-old. Papa shouldn't have said that, and you are not to behave like a street urchin. Nobody wants to drag you from the palazzo with the police; you will simply do what is right. You always have. It is all the palazzo's fault; the palazzo is a giant toy for you, but soon you'll be grown-up and leading your own life. We're going to have a long talk together directly you're back in Milan, and you'll understand. Next summer you may go to Venice, of course, I promise you that. You know that I always keep my promises."

"He's coming with us," said Paolo.

Teresa touched her eye lightly with her handkerchief, but smiled as she said: "I have two silly boys, but I love them both equally. Romolo will not be coming with us, he has to say goodbye to his Nonna, her life is hard enough as it is. A week from today you will take the train. I have a surprise for you, by the way. And now shake hands, you two. Let's forget this horrid scene."

She embraced Romolo. Paolo was standing with his face toward the window. Romolo did not go near him.

The rain had grown more violent and pelted across the Riva degli Schiavoni. The bare irons of the gondola prows stuck fast on the marble. In a tightly packed mass the passengers were waiting under the protective roof of the vaporetto station. As he had done some days before, when he had come from the Lido, Romolo began to run. He had gained time, no more but no less. He ran toward the palazzo, but this time he was not driven by his imagination: the flood was after him.

58

For two days, rising from the deep, streaming from the sky, the waters had prepared the attack. Now they launched their assault.

The storms settled around Venice. They withdrew for an hour or two and came back with redoubled strength.

No ship left the Canale della Giudecca; fleeing ships made for the port. The huge stone buoys in front of the mouth of the Canale della Giudecca and the Canal Grande were rocking on the water.

The Canal Grande was no longer a waterway, it was the sea bordered by terrorized houses. The water permeated the doors. Wooden planks which had protected the windows for years offered only token resistance; the water seeped through their cracks and finally tore them from their gratings. Posts bent like trees in a storm, but they were not trees, they were man-made. The water vomited into the ground floors of the palazzi.

The sirens wailed at regular intervals; sometimes they were drowned in the thunder. The church bells remained silent.

The Signora had sensed what was to come and yet was surprised by it.

The entrance hall was flooded. An overturned ladder was floating on the water, then it sank. A shovel drifted to and fro. Formwork sections and cement mixer were half submerged. The mouth of the mixing drum was like a spouting fountain. The wet death battled with the stones.

The Signora feared most for the scaffolding in front of the facade. It shook. The planks moved like a child's swing. The rope pulley knocked against the wall. A hod trough fell crashing on the steps below the porch. The chains and cable joints rattled like the fetters of prisoners trying to get free. A newly erected straw wall was nothing but soggy paper.

Although the storm abated a little during the night, sleep was out of the question. The telephone was not working. Romolo rolled up the carpets in the drawing room and dragged them into the corridor. He tried to stop up the lower joint of the balcony door with newspapers, but an hour later the paper was soaked. Rags he had collected from all over the house resisted longer, but already puddles were forming on the marble floor.

"I must get the furniture to safety," he said.

"You can't do that," said the Signora.

He did it, though. He took chairs, stools and tables into the corridors. As he carried Mozetti's *Girl with Flower Basket* to the kitchen, he laughed. "At least it's not a Titian." He took off his shoes. "Go into the dining room. The balcony is the cause of it all."

The electric light went out. Romolo looked out on the Canal Grande. The canal lay in the darkness, but lightning lit up the palaces on the other bank. "Thank heavens!" said Romolo, "it's not only us. They'll need repairs too."

He took the Signora by the hand and led her gropingly to the dining room. They sat down at the table.

"Lucky I didn't leave," he said.

"Very lucky," said the Signora.

"Tomorrow it will be over," said Romolo.

"Another twenty-four hours at least," said the Signora. "Like that time in November."

"Not half as bad," said Romolo.

"It was all in vain," said the Signora.

"That's just where you're wrong," said Romolo. "If those men had not reinforced the pilework, we would be sitting in the water."

The Signora knew he was right. The rotten piles on the north side could not have stood up to the weather. Now they creaked in their concrete casing but did not give way. Still, she was right too. Everything she had so far repaired was doomed. What she had done had not been a mistake, she had simply thought of it too late. She had done the urgent things, now she would be able to do only the most urgent.

They sat in the dark.

"You're very quiet," said Romolo.

"I'm working something out," said the Signora.

"When it's over, we'll take the most important things upstairs," said Romolo. "I'm still here, aren't I! It won't cost a great deal."

The lights came on again. The water stood almost an inch high in the drawing room. Romolo brought a broom and pails.

A sheeting board fell from the scaffolding. The Signora winced.

"At least it can't fall on anybody's head now," said Romolo. "I'll have a look downstairs."

"Oh, no you won't!" said the Signora.

"It seems quieter now," said Romolo.

They listened. The flood was rolling through the Canal Grande, the waves dashed against the walls.

"Those stupid sirens," said Romolo. "As if we didn't know what was going on."

"Rest a bit," said the Signora. "What about a snack?"

She went to the kitchen. The wetness was seeping through the walls and attacking the fresh paint like creeping leprosy. Plates and cups clattered.

Romolo was reaching for his sandwich when the lights went out again.

"Never mind," he said, "I can find my mouth in the dark."

"Perhaps your father is right and I'm feebleminded after all," said the Signora.

"But look, the scaffolding's still standing," said Romolo.

A moment later the light came back once more, and he began carefully placing some vases on the sofa.

"You ought to lie down," he said. "I don't need you. Where are your pills?"

"I feel perfectly all right," said the Signora.

She knew the weather as well as she knew Venice. The storm raged until the following evening. Before that they had taken turns watching, and had a few hours' sleep each.

They were both standing in the kitchen getting dinner ready when the telephone rang. It trilled clearly through the whole house, for the storm had passed, the rumbling from the Canal Grande was no longer deafening, the all-clear siren had sounded.

"So you see, it's working again," said Romolo.

It was Luigi Primavesi asking about the damage.

"I can only tell you tomorrow, my boy," said the Signora. "I don't know, but I fancy we shall have to begin all over again."

59

The storm has subsided, and now this story too, which began three and a half months ago when I went to see the Signora on a delicate mission, has come to an end. But who could declare that this is really the end? In Noah's story it says: "And the Ark rested in the seventh month, on the seventeenth day of the month, upon the mountains of Ararat." Ararat was not an end, it was a beginning.

Noah was six hundred and one years old when the "waters were dried up from off the earth." Let nobody say that life expectancies are higher today! Frail, ailing and old, the Signora is on most friendly terms with survival.

Strange things happen with an ark; it attracts all those who want to survive. When I went up the hen roost on that afternoon in June to warn the Signora against the shady deal, I flattered myself I was her only friend. Laura is back in New York, but she too is aboard the ark. She has promised me she will come to Venice again next year, and someday, who knows, she may help me to administer the estate, this inheritance of a No which the Signora mentioned to Romolo and with which the flood must be fought. Practically everybody believes in the flood nowadays, only a few believe in the ark. Yet I should be surprised if we three, Romolo and Laura and I, could not carry out the Signora's last will, for we, the ark guests, are fairly inured to the Flood and convinced of the freshly plucked olive leaf.

But there is also Mozetti. The Signora did not give away his name when the inquisitive authorities pressed her for it. He often comes to see her and has promised to give her his latest Goya, as soon as he transforms himself again. There is Luigi Primavesi, the revolutionary on the rocking horse who, as it were, has one foot in the ark: he admires the lady of the house and cheats with his prices, downward, mind you, not upward, for he is beginning to believe in a new heaven, even if it should be Marx on the throne of glory. Charwomen are represented in the ark by a single specimen; I now see Emilia in the palazzo at unusual hours. And if I were jealous, then Francesca's pointed remarks could well excite my jealousy, because the Signora has had other meetings with Professor della Torre since that first one. It was only the other day I caught him on a visit to the house on the Canal Grande. Loneliness is a trait in a person's character; the Signora does not possess this trait.

How could she, when she has Romolo? He returned to Milan, to his parents, one of many orphans living with their parents. By the way, he never moved to Remus's room, it wouldn't have suited him. The wounds his first love inflicted on him are, I think, beginning to heal, but it is not certain that they will never break out again. The soul's wounds are unlike those of the body: the younger one is, the longer they take to heal.

But being the chronicler of the ark, as I introduced myself at the beginning, I must, of course, report on the flood.

When the damages inflicted on the palazzo by the early autumn storm were examined and assessed, we were obliged to begin all over again, as the Signora had suspected. And when her means were examined and assessed, we both recognized there was nothing left of the hope of salvation except just hope, or to be more precise, only enough for the most urgent repairs. Yet what is hope but an oar of a boat? Those who would speed into the future under full sail wait in vain for the wind. "And . . . the waters prevailed, and increased greatly upon the earth; and the ark went upon the face of the waters." It is an ark, not a sailing·boat, that is the symbol of the future. The palazzo would have perished in those three days of violence. But the Signora had started to repair, and when it was over the piles still stood. We are not strong enough to set up new pilework, but we can reinforce the existing piles, we can make various improvements, replace the brittle and rotten parts, and in the next storm we may be stronger, and even stronger in the one after. In the end the storm will not harm us. And in the end all those who were in the ark will still be there when it comes to rest upon the mountains of Ararat. For as a chronicler I can confirm it; of those whom Noah took aboard, not one died.

All this sounds like sanguine prophecy, but I still see what I have seen for so long: the deadly danger threatening the palazzo and my city and my world.

Marghera was not damaged this time either. For a few days the fires of destruction were extinguished, now they are burning once more. The assassins took a rest; now they are approaching anew. They have all the weapons we neither can nor want to use: the greed of rulers and the envy of their accomplice-subjects; the power of gluttony and the power of hunger; the industry of destruction and the indolence of the heart; the craze for novelty and the obstinacy of the old; brute force and hypocrisy; the lie that all men are alike, and the fraud against all alike. But even though they may have all these weapons, the assassins are not as irresistible as we tend to assume trapped in the mystique of decline. They can inflict mortal wounds only on the sleeping man, they triumph only when our wounds have stopped bleeding because we have died before they approached our bed. Everything depends on waiting alive for the assassins.

With hope, but without illusions! Who else but man in his boundless corruption has unleashed the elements which threaten my city. Ebb and flow are the same as hundreds of years ago. And the air is also the same. Even the things made by men, the beauty of their handwriting on nature's blackboard, are still there, although the characters are now unintelligible. Not everything we have destroyed can be rebuilt, but we can cease to destroy.

That first morning, when the waters began to recede and the sun started to absorb the ugly spots like a piece of blotting paper, I drove to the palazzo in my rickety old boat. I met many boats: cheerful foreigners sat in them, cheerfully the gondolieri rowed, and cheerfully the lighters putt-putted to market. I should have liked to shout to the people in those boats what I had read in the Talmud: "Oblivion leads into exile, and memory is the secret of salvation." Every time my city finds itself alive once more, it rejoices as if it were safe. It has only been placed on probation, and it will have to prove itself if it wants to be saved.

I should have liked to take those cheerful people to the palazzo. The high drawing room, in which much of my story is set, was half empty, and since the first workers were already on the spot, they, Romolo and I carried many other things to the third floor, where the bedroom and the guest rooms are. We took particular care of anything fragile. The room where Remus lived, where Claudia used to make a mess and Laura tidied up, we are going to furnish as a boudoir for the Signora, a small private sitting room, not so grand or spacious as the drawing room on the second floor, but comfortable and with its own charm. Anyone who wants to preserve the walls has to be easily contented within those walls.

No, we did not have to convince the Signora of this move; she had been thinking along similar lines. With the cheerfulness that had seized her this morning the same as it had seized all of us, and the quick-wittedness typical of her, she immediately found a name for the new room. She calls it the waiting room. What does my new rival, Professor della Torre, say? *"Bisogna lottare."* Wait and fight.

It was noon when my work was done and I returned home from the palazzo. The September sun seemed to be burning the Piscine di Frezzeria. The baskets outside the Ristorante alla Colomba were full of red lobsters. On the balconies the women were pouring the rainwater from their geranium pots.

When I entered the apartment, the steaming fettucine were already on the table. Francesca eyed me with a suspicious smile. I looked at her inquiringly.

"You're wearing your tie," she said.

I had forgotten to take it off.